ONE
HALF
TRUTH

ONE
HALF
TRUTH

EVA DOLAN

R A V E N BOOKS

LONDON • OXFORD • NEW YORK • NEW DELHI • SYDNEY

RAVEN BOOKS

Bloomsbury Publishing Plc
50 Bedford Square, London, WC1B 3DP, UK
29 Earlsfort Terrace, Dublin 2, Ireland

BLOOMSBURY, RAVEN BOOKS and the Raven Books logo
are trademarks of Bloomsbury Publishing Plc

First published in Great Britain 2021

ISBN: HB: 978-1-4088-8655-7; TPB: 978-1-4088-8666-3;
ePUB: 978-1-4088-8654-0

2 4 6 8 10 9 7 5 3 1

Typeset by Integra Software Services Pvt. Ltd.
Printed and bound in Great Britain by CPI Group (UK) Ltd, Croydon CR0 4YY

To find out more about our authors and books visit www.bloomsbury.com
and sign up for our newsletters

Nights like this it was easy to believe nothing had changed.

Time was, they'd start coming into the Club from five o'clock. Shift ended, work gear still on, sweaty and covered in dust. Grab a beer, talk through the day, decompress so they didn't take it all home to their wives and kids. Thirty or forty men most evenings, sixty or seventy on a Friday, and on Saturday nights they'd have a band on or a quiz, and the families would come along. The blokes clean and tidy now, the women all done up, kids left to their own devices. Everyone flush and happy. A community coming together.

The good old days, Bruce Humble thought, as he moved behind the small bar in the corner to pull a couple more pints.

Usually it was bottles only but the crowd was heavier for big Monday night games and it was worth hooking up a barrel. Once a month they put on live music and he did the same then. They had a local band coming in the weekend after next. Eighties covers. A prize for the best vintage outfit. It would be wall to wall *Miami Vice* and shell suits for the men, batwing sleeves and fingerless lace gloves for women; multiple Madonnas, judging by last time. His wife had dressed up like Sonia and he'd told her she'd won but he couldn't give her the prize because it wouldn't look right. He doubted she'd be coming this time though. Too much work, she'd say. But he knew she didn't have as much invested in the place as him.

She had only worked at the Greenaway Engineering factory for a year while she was finishing her degree. Left as soon as there was something better paid on offer, even though they'd tried everything to keep her. Promised her the management track was ahead of her once she graduated. Company car in two years, a fancy title, bonuses.

Humble told her she was crazy not to take it. They'd argued but she'd stuck to her guns. Like she always did.

She'd never said, I told you so.

He was grateful for that.

But he wished she'd get more involved with the Club. The other women asked after her and he was tired of making excuses that he knew they didn't really buy. There would be talk about their marriage, he'd bet. Snide little comments. Thinks she's too good for us. Always was up herself.

Not entirely untrue. But not fair either. She didn't fit in here any more. Hadn't for a long time. Or maybe she never had.

They looked tired, he thought, as he leaned on the bar, eyes running around the large, low-ceilinged room. The bright white strip light was unforgiving as it fell across the men's faces. Everyone older and greyer than he wanted them to be. Just like when he looked in the bathroom mirror and found the face staring back at him didn't match how he felt. Still forty in his head but somehow another twenty-five years had passed.

Even now, drunk and relaxed, shouting at the football and each other, there was strain visible on every man's face. Lines deeper cut, mouths more pinched, the hunch of shoulders weighed down under too much pressure; bad backs and dodgy hips and sciatica stabbing up their legs. A lifetime of hard work stamped all over them and nothing to show for it but the last remaining bonds they'd brought with them from Greenaway's factory gates.

Humble took down a glass and drew a shot of whiskey from the optic. Told himself not to start thinking like that. Busy nights were always worse. The nostalgia turning bitter and poisonous if he didn't watch himself.

Luckier than most, he mumbled into the glass before he sank the shot.

Steve Gurney came over to the bar, pulling a face of mock suffering. 'Dick's doing my bloody nut in.'

'He's not talking about –'

'Nah,' Steve said, eyes going hard for a second. 'Not a peep about that.'

'What about Jordan?'

'Nothing.'

Humble watched the lad drain the last of his Coke.

Didn't drink, didn't smoke, vegan but he managed not to go on about it after he'd told them the first time. Anyone walking in off the street would wonder what the hell he was doing there, sat between two rare-looking lads like Caxton and Ridgeon, this twenty-year-old kid with his skinny jeans and his geeky glasses and the scrubbed-clean look of a boy who had not only never done a hard day's work in his life but likely would never have to.

Dick Caxton was bending his ear and Jordan seemed to be listening, occasionally looking away to the big screen, alerted by the swell of crowd noise when something almost happened.

'Told you it was sorted.'

'Not the first time you've said that.' Steve leaned on the bar, shoulders rounding. 'Suppose you can't blame him for being interested.'

'No.'

Humble didn't want to talk about it. Not here. Not ever again, if he could help it.

'Jordan's not a bad kid,' Steve said, flashing him a shallow grin. 'He's stopping the rest of us from having to listen to Dick.'

'What's he going on about now?' Humble asked, taking a couple of bottles of Stella from the fridge.

'How his phone's secretly talking to all the other phones in the room so they can make a map of where we're all standing and then sell the data to McDonald's. I'm telling you, he's off his fucking rocker.'

Humble snorted. 'I might have to cut him off after this round.'

He grabbed a beer and a Coke for Jordan, told Steve to keep his wallet in his pocket, getting a look of vague irritation for the gesture. But Steve didn't insist and by the time they were both settled at the table with the rest of them, he was smiling again, listening as Caxton continued to hold court.

3

'These smart beds, right? They monitor your pulse and body temperature and your movement patterns while you sleep, yeah?' Caxton checked they were all paying attention, eyes wide under his sparse blond brows. 'So they know when you're asleep but they also know when you're having sex.'

'Wouldn't be owt for 'em to report if you bought one,' Ridgeon said, reaching for his beer.

'Can it tell when you're stroking one out?' Steve asked.

Jordan nodded, face entirely serious. 'They can. And they know who you're having sex with because they automatically connect to *their* phone when they come into the bedroom.'

Humble listened bemused as Jordan went on, not sure if he was winding Caxton up, egging him on or supporting him because he felt sorry for him. It was difficult to tell with the kid, because he wore such an earnest expression at all times.

Jordan started talking about smart toilets that could monitor every bowel movement and then send the information back to your doctor so they could tell if you had any emerging conditions. Steve was cracking up at the idea, slapping his thigh.

'Hold on, does the toilet talk to the bed?' he asked, Humble already knowing where he was going.

'It's all connected,' Caxton insisted. 'Everything, in one big network.'

Steve grinned at him. 'So if I shit the bed it'll tell the toilet about it?'

Ridgeon laughed, one quick bark, and even Jordan shook his head in reluctant amusement.

Just like old times.

Humble had first come in here as a teenager, starting the job at Greenaway his dad got him, being inducted into the fellowship of tough, mouthy men who would rib you hard to see if you could take it. And you had to, because they'd never stop if you rose to the bait. Take it and then give it back so they knew you weren't a pushover.

Jordan hadn't quite got the drop of that part yet.

But then he wasn't one of them, Humble thought.

And they'd all do well to remember that.

DAY ONE

TUESDAY

CHAPTER ONE

It was barely light when the call came but Zigic was already up, trainers on, standing in the kitchen, stretching his hamstrings, seeing the frost sparkling across the gravelled driveway and the thin remnants of a freezing fog rolling slowly along the lane, drifting over from the lakes on Ferry Meadows.

He slipped his phone out of the holder strapped to his bicep, Ferreira's name on the screen, driving away the momentary flicker of relief he'd felt at having a good excuse to avoid this morning's hard slog around the village.

He'd been back at it for two weeks and it still wasn't getting any easier. His runner's high seeming to have deserted him, while all the old twinges and aches remained, hardened by neglect. The days when he'd do a swift 10k before work felt like a lifetime ago.

'What's up, Mel?' he asked, already kicking off his trainers.

'Murder,' she said, a caffeinated clip to her voice. 'Back end of Fletton, Phorpres Way. Young guy. All I know right now. Cordon's up. Forensics are on site.'

'Alright, I'm on my way.'

He dressed quickly and quietly in the hallway outside the bedroom, wanting to let Anna sleep; pulled on jeans and a T-shirt and a heavy woollen jumper against the November morning. He saw the light on in Milan's bedroom and knew he would be curled in the armchair in the corner, reading before school, his homework done and filed away in his bag, his uniform laid out at the foot of his bed ready. He'd taken to making his own packed lunch the evening before. It was a far cry from eighteen months ago, when every morning was a guilt-stricken fight to get him up and dressed and breakfasted, while he complained of stomach aches and headaches, the manifestation of his unhappiness at his old school. He was like a different boy now. Or, rather, he was back to being the boy he was before the bullying started.

Zigic poked his head around the bedroom door to say good morning.

'Are you going to work already?' Milan asked.

'Yep. Can you tell your mum when she wakes up?'

'Sure,' Milan said, eyes dropping back down to his book, not wanting to talk about it any further.

Zigic nodded. 'Have a good day at school, buddy.'

'I will.'

In the car, pulling out onto the narrow lane between the house and the allotments opposite, Zigic wondered if it was time to have a talk with Milan about his job. He'd been avoiding it. Was dreading it more than the birds and bees conversation they'd managed to get through with the minimum of embarrassment or awkward questions. Death should be easier, he thought. He guessed most parents would have taken the death talk over the sex one if they had an option.

But it wasn't just about the fact of lives ending, which Milan already understood. This was about death that wasn't innocent or peaceful, or the painful but inevitable end point of disease. He would have to explain to his kind-hearted, sensitive boy that some deaths were the result of rage or jealousy or contempt.

And, on some level, he was sure Milan knew this already. He read too many books not to understand. But it felt like Zigic needed to contextualise his own part in the aftermaths of these deaths. Explain that somebody needed to find the guilty and give those left behind justice and closure.

It was *that* he was dreading, he realised, as he turned onto the dual carriageway that ringed Peterborough city centre, where the earliest starters were already heading into work. He was dreading being asked what happened when you didn't find the guilty person. He wanted Milan to have a few more years believing in the justness of the world and his father's ability to make the bad things go away.

He drove fast through the sparse traffic on the parkway, cutting between the sheer, blank faces of sprawling superstores and warehouses and delivery hubs, their buildings brutal in scale despite the softening intentions of the landscaping. Everything was greener than it should have been at this time of year, nature unaware that it was winter. Across the roundabout and past the garden centre onto Phorpres Way where, between car dealerships and low-rise retail spaces, yards were beginning to fill as the workers arrived.

This was an area of the city that had been wasteland a few years ago but was now packed tight with businesses, all huddled in the lee of the parkway that ran high along their backs.

As he turned onto London Road, he saw the crime scene.

One lane of traffic had already been blocked off. Council workers with stop/go signs were controlling the cars while two of their mates got the traffic lights up and running and a generator was rolled out of a van, a uniformed officer watching them. Zigic caught a glimpse of the white plastic forensics tent erected behind them and he strained to see more as he waited for the sign to spin.

He parked at the end of a line of familiar vehicles in front of the first in a row of red-brick houses that had been built for brickyard workers at the clay pits that used to dominate this part of the city. Now they sat slightly adrift from the rest of the homes further along London Road.

Potential witnesses, he thought, eyeing the distance between the houses' gable end windows and the crime scene tent as he got out of the car. The new estate a hundred yards north on the opposite side of the road might yield some too.

A place this open, with so many comings and goings, someone would have surely seen something.

The tent was set close to the flyover's ridged concrete wall, sitting unevenly where the land climbed to meet the road at a steep angle, the grass long and tussocky, a thicket overgrowing it. High and dense enough to conceal an attacker, he thought. He looked back along the road towards the town centre, imagining someone walking home along here, where the street lights got sparse and the rumble from the parkway overhead would mask the sound of quick footsteps rushing up behind you.

Judging by the area cordoned off at the centre of the footpath, there had been a scuffle. Serious enough to leave blood on the pavement. The victim dragged out of sight of the main road, into the undergrowth. Longer before they were found but more potential trace evidence.

He'd noticed Kate Jenkins's car, but there was no sign of the chief scene of crime officer, so he guessed she was already inside the tent. Two of her assistants were examining the ground around it, one of them halfway into the undergrowth.

DS Ferreira came over to him as he approached the cordon, black beanie pulled down to her brows and her hands punched into the pockets of a grey wool coat.

'You been in yet?' he asked.

'I was waiting for you.'

They suited up, Ferreira grumbling about having to take her hat and coat off to pull on the forensics suit.

'What have we got?' he asked.

'Victim's a Jordan Radley. His wallet was still on him, cards and everything still intact.' She drew her hair into a ponytail and tucked it away. 'Twenty-one. Lives on Hampton, so it looks like he was on his way home. There's a footpath around the corner that would have taken him under the parkway and straight to his front door.'

'Phone?' He zipped up his suit, swearing as his jumper snagged in the teeth.

'Gone,' she said. 'No sign of any house keys either.'

'Anything else on him?'

'Nothing.'

Zigic took a deep breath, steeling himself for the sight that awaited them, and stepped into the tent.

CHAPTER TWO

Jordan Radley was laid out on his front, head turned away from them, in skinny jeans and a green parka with a fishtail hem, bulky but not enough to hide how slightly he was built. Zigic doubted he was more than ten stone, the kind of young man who would likely avoid trouble at all costs, knowing his chances of coming out of it on the wrong side. A pair of heavy-framed black glasses lay next to him at the wrong angle to have come off as he fell. They looked like they'd been thrown down there, lenses crazed, one arm cracked.

Clearly visible, just below Radley's shoulder blades, was a bullet hole torn through the heavy cotton of his parka, a puff of white wadding stained red. But it was the second shot that would have killed him before he had chance to bleed too heavily. A small hole bored into the curved hollow at the base of his skull.

Zigic frowned.

'Execution style,' Kate Jenkins said, voice slightly muffled behind her mask, eyes hard above it. 'One in the back out there on the pavement. Then his killer dragged him over here and put one in the back of his head. He wouldn't have seen it coming.'

Overhead the traffic noise was a near deafening roar, vibrations running down the concrete flyover wall, shaking the ground under his feet, sending tremors up his legs and into his gut. It was like standing in the belly of a beast.

This felt wrong.

A kid just walking home, shot in the back out of nowhere. They didn't deal with many shootings in Peterborough and Zigic struggled to remember the last one he'd worked on. Usually they were linked to organised crime or drugs. Targeted assassinations in the homes or businesses of people already known to the police. That or acts of domestic violence carried out by individuals with licensed firearms they never should have been allowed access to.

'Does he have a record?' Zigic asked.

Ferreira shook her head. 'Totally clean.'

'He could be a courier,' Jenkins suggested.

'He doesn't look like one.'

'The best ones don't.'

He eyed Radley's checkerboard skater shoes and his digital watch.

'Who found him?'

'Bloke who lives along the road,' Ferreira said. 'Out walking his dog before he went to work. Saw him lying here, called 999.'

'What time was this?'

'Just after seven. He's at home, in a bit of a state. I've got Parr round there, taking a statement.'

'How long do you think he's been dead?' Zigic asked Jenkins.

Her eyes scrunched up. 'Preliminary, but less than twelve hours, more than four.'

'So last night,' Ferreira said.

Zigic nodded. Thinking of all the vehicles that would have driven past while Jordan Radley lay dead. Visible from the road if anyone was looking. Definitely visible from the path less than six metres away. But nobody had reported it. Kept walking, likely telling themselves he was a drunk or a junkie or maybe worrying this was a scam. Thinking I won't get involved because if I do I'm going to get robbed by an accomplice hidden nearby. It was a sad fact that the more vulnerable a person was the more cynically people would regard them.

Not that anyone could have helped Jordan Radley by then.

'We need to speak to the locals,' he said. 'See if anyone heard gunshots. Nail down the time.'

'I've got door to door on it,' Ferreira told him.

She looked as perturbed as he felt but there was a focus in her eyes that he was relieved to see. The last few months he'd detected a slight remoteness in her, would catch her staring into middle distance across the office, or spot some quick shadow flittering across her face with no clear cause. And he knew what it was, what memories she was trying to push away. The guilt she was wrangling with. Or, more worryingly, her fears about the lack of guilt she was feeling.

And every time he opened his mouth to speak – to ask if she was okay, tell her it wasn't her fault – she seemed to hear the unshaped words and would head them off before he could say anything. A consequence of working together for over a decade, that you could read each other so precisely that the things that needed saying were often the ones that remained forever unspoken.

Ferreira was questioning Jenkins about trace evidence; if the killer had moved Radley's body, then they must have left something of themselves behind.

'There's chalk dust on the hems of his jeans and socks,' she said. 'So it looks like your killer was wearing disposable gloves. He probably knew about the dangers of gunshot residue getting ingrained into his skin. And he'd probably anticipated he'd have to move the body off the pavement.'

'Shootings are usually premeditated, right?' Ferreira said. 'You go to the trouble of getting hold of a gun, you aren't going to make it easy for us.'

'What about the gun?' Zigic asked.

'Small calibre,' Jenkins told him. 'Handgun, obviously. We'll need to get the bullets out before I can tell you more.'

'No sign of the weapon nearby?'

'The undergrowth is pretty tangled,' she said. 'If it's here we'll find it, but you're going to need to get some more bodies down if you want to widen the search area.'

'We're about a minute away from Stillwater Lakes.' Ferreira cocked her head to the west, towards the old knotholes that had been regenerated into a nature reserve when the brickyard closed. 'That's the smart place to get rid of a murder weapon.'

Jenkins nodded. 'Those old pits go hundreds of metres down.'

They left the tent, Jenkins promising to update them as soon as she knew anything more. As they stripped out of their suits, Zigic thought of the lakes behind them and all the secrets you could hide under a hundred metres of dark water.

'I'll call in and get a search team organised,' Ferreira said, buttoning her coat and turning the collar up against the wind shearing down London Road. 'Maybe we'll get lucky.'

The rush hour traffic was beginning to thicken and Zigic noticed how long the lines were now on either side of the lights, the drivers craning to see what was going on. He could see the inevitable phone held up at open windows, filming the featureless walls of the tent, and the flickering tape at the cordon.

He turned away and started down the narrow, high-hedged lane towards Stillwater Lakes.

There was a semicircle of workers' cottages arranged around a modest green, like something from a fenland village; the roar of the flyover buffered slightly by the thick copse the houses were arranged to face. If you could tune the traffic noise out, there was a sense of idyllic isolation to the development. The sound of birdsong faint under the engine noise.

DC Zac Parr was standing at the edge of the green, speaking with one of the uniformed officers. When he saw Zigic he broke into an odd, stiff-legged trot, black trench coat flapping behind him.

'What have you got for me, Zac?' Zigic called, going to meet him.

'Gunshots,' he said, jerking his thumb back towards one of the houses in the middle of the row. 'They didn't think it was gunshots but the lady there said she heard two loud bangs, about thirty seconds apart, around half ten last night.'

'From inside the house?'

'Outside. She had the door open to try and get her cat in before she went to bed,' Parr explained. 'I asked if she could be sure about the time and she said she'd turned the TV off just as *Newsnight* started. Went straight to the door, opened up, heard a bang. Thirty seconds later, heard another.'

'Did she call to report it?'

Parr shrugged. 'How do you know what's a bang and what's a gunshot if you're not around guns all the time?'

He was right but Zigic suspected it might be more a case of 'that kind of thing doesn't happen here'. There were a dozen things you could blame a couple of short, sharp bangs on if you didn't want to believe that kind of violence was a possibility so close to your front door.

'Then, the fella over there,' Parr pointed towards a house nearer to the road. 'He reckons he heard a car backfiring about half past ten as well.'

The times tallied.

'The woman who was outside with her cat,' Zigic said. 'Did she see anyone?'

'No.'

'Okay. We're going to need to speak to the people in the houses on the road,' he told Parr. 'And the ones across the road up the way. There can't be much foot traffic along here in the evening.'

'Yes, sir.'

'Radley's killer might have followed him from wherever he was walking home from. Either that or they knew he would take this route and they hung around waiting for him to go past. So between ten and half past, anyone sighted, we need descriptions.'

Parr nodded. 'On it.'

Zigic went back to the main road, looking for CCTV cameras on garages or houses. Knowing already that there were no council ones along here. Only the traffic cameras on the lights 300 metres further along the road. The killer had chosen his spot well. Around the corner on Club Way, there were businesses with open yards in front of them, high security fences and cameras to watch over them. Anyone loitering there would likely have been seen and recorded.

Then again, London Road was the main route in and out of the city centre, connecting the suburbs of Yaxley and Hampton to Peterborough proper, and would have been carrying fairly heavy traffic at half past ten, he guessed. People heading home from nights out or into the big supermarket on Serpentine Green to

15

do their shopping while the place was quiet. Someone must have seen something.

It was a strange place to pick, the more he thought about it. Five minutes later and Jordan Radley would have been on an isolated stretch of cycleway. No potential witnesses, no cameras. Hedgerow on both sides.

Was the killer concerned that the isolation might make *him* vulnerable, Zigic wondered. That Jordan might have got the better of him?

Chapter Three

The Radley house sat at the edge of the sprawling Hampton new town, down a quiet close built behind a hulking apartment block that separated them from the noise of the main road. They'd driven through the expensive houses already, the ones on more generous plots with denser landscaping and Georgian styling, now they were on the back end of the development, where the houses were modest and plain, hidden away like an embarrassment.

But still, it was a nice enough house, Zigic thought. It was a buff-brick and white-windowed end of terrace, narrow and tucked away into a corner, with a stretch of shared greenery in front of it and black railings demarcating the slim space between the pathway and the kitchen window. The small patch of bare earth here had been planted with a couple of spiky cotoneasters, heavy with bright orange berries that poked through the railings, a few white cyclamens dotted around them.

Upstairs the curtains were drawn but as they approached the front door, he noticed a light on in the kitchen, then movement as someone darted away from the sink.

His mother, Zigic thought. Moira Radley.

The front door opened before they had chance to ring the bell.

'What's happened to him?' she demanded, a snap in her voice but fear etched in the lines of her angular face. 'Where's Jordan?'

'Can we come in, please?' Ferreira said gently.

Moira Radley turned away from them and walked slowly, falteringly, through the cream-painted hallway, hand reaching for the newel post and then a shelf above the radiator to steady her path into the living room at the back of the house, where the television was muted and the lights were all burning. Her phone was on the coffee table next to a mug of tea that had filmed over. She sank down into the soft grey corner sofa, drew a sheepskin pillow to her chest.

She didn't look at either of them. Eyes roving over the patterned rug, as if there was an alternative explanation for their presence hidden in its geometric lines. She knew before they even arrived, Zigic guessed.

People didn't always. More than once he'd gone to a house to deliver this worst of all news, only to be immediately lectured about the lack of community policing in the area or the noise level coming from a neighbouring house. And even once he'd asked to go inside and led the person into their own home with the careful gait and mannered calm the situation always drew out of him, still they didn't catch on. Or maybe it was just they refused to face it until the final, irrevocable moment when the words were said.

He knew he shouldn't think that way but it always made him wonder how close those couples and families were.

Moira Radley knew. She knew because her son had gone out yesterday and didn't come home and that was obviously not normal for him.

Ferreira sat down next to her, perched tentatively on the edge of the sofa and for a moment he didn't think she was up to it. Saw the familiar dark cloud pass across her eyes, before she inclined her head and took a breath.

'I'm very sorry but Jordan has been killed.'

Moira lurched where she sat, hand shooting out to grab the arm of the sofa, searching for purchase, then slowly she sagged, chin into chest, abdomen into thighs, and a deep, ragged cry broke out of her, strip-throated and raw. Ferreira put her arm around her and Moira turned into her shoulder, holding her hands cupped over her face as she wept, rocking and shuddering.

Ferreira rubbed her shoulder, speaking to her in a voice so low he didn't catch the words. But he saw the strain on Mel's face, the threat of tears in her own eyes. And it was so out of character that he couldn't look at her, felt like an intruder in the moment.

Quietly he retreated into the kitchen, set the kettle to boil and found some cups, taking down and putting back the one with 'WORLD'S COOLEST GODDAMN MUM' written on it in blocky gold letters. There was a strip from a photo booth stuck to the fridge door, Jordan in what looked like a grey morning suit, wearing a pink bow tie, Moira in a jade green off-the-shoulder dress and matching fascinator, both of them mugging and pouting as the camera flashed. They had the same long face and high cheekbones, the same dark brown hair and pale skin that was lightly flushed from drink or laughter.

She must have had him very young, Zigic realised, seeing how different the Moira Radley of the photo looked to the woman in the next room. Would have been just a teenager when Jordan came along.

He opened the fridge and took a carton of oat milk out of the door, noticing a Tupperware box filled with noodle salad, a Post-it stuck to it, telling Jordan it was for his lunch.

Was he the kind of young man who got mixed up in drugs?

Zigic looked at the vegan cookbooks lined up on the window-sill, the framed photograph of a baby Jordan hanging on the wall, his eyes squeezed shut with laughter, and thought they seemed like a nice family.

But the most unexpected people could get drawn into bad company, he reminded himself. Especially if money was tight and a good son decided that his mother needed help making ends meet. A sense of responsibility could lead to all sorts of moral compromises and unwise decisions.

He made the tea and took it back into the living room, found Moira sitting upright again. She looked numb now, eyes swollen and red, a bunched-up tissue in her fist.

'How did it happen?' she asked, watching him as he sat down in the armchair near the fireplace.

'Jordan was shot,' he told her. 'Late last night.'

She glanced at Ferreira, as if for confirmation. 'No. No, that's not possible. Where?'

'On London Road,' she said. 'Near the flyover. Do you know why Jordan was there?'

19

'He would have been walking home.' A fresh wave of tears welled up and broke and she snatched a couple of tissues from the box on the coffee table. 'I don't understand this. It doesn't make any sense. Are you sure it's him?'

'His wallet was still in his pocket. His ID was inside.'

'Maybe someone robbed him,' she said, straightening as she latched onto the slim hope. 'Maybe he was robbed and they took his wallet and whoever did that got shot. It makes sense. Somebody who'd act like that.'

She looked between them. She might be right but Zigic thought it was unlikely, given the unavoidable similarity of the photos on the fridge door and the dead man's face.

'What was Jordan wearing the last time you saw him?'

'He went out yesterday evening,' she said. 'He had on his grey jeans and his Vans, a black jumper and his green parka.'

A terrible desperation in her eyes, so potent that Zigic had to force himself to meet her gaze when he told her that it was definitely Jordan.

'I want to see him,' she said sharply.

'We can sort that out,' Ferreira told her softly. 'We need to ask you a few questions though. Is that okay?'

Moira nodded.

'Where did Jordan go yesterday evening?'

'He went to the working men's club on Belsize Avenue. There was a football match on and he goes over sometimes to watch it with them.'

'With who?'

She waved a dismissive hand. 'It's a bunch of old men. Nice old men, Jordan's been going there for a few months.'

Zigic knew the place. A rickety old club with white pebble-dashed walls and a flat roof, built decades ago for the staff of a local engineering firm. The kind of place that had felt like an anachronism even in the nineties when his grandfather and father had occasionally dragged him along to play pool or watch a match. A room full of men drinking pints from glass tankards and talking about the political actions of people long out of power.

He'd hated it. The endless barracking and banter, the sense of being completely adrift in the wrong element. Picked on for his clothes and his haircut and the words he used. 'Sound like you've swallowed a dictionary, lad.'

'It's members only, isn't it?' he asked now.

'I thought it was strange too,' she conceded with a wan smile. 'But he started going over there in the summer, he was talking to them about their mental health.'

'Did Jordan work in the NHS?' Ferreira asked, clearly struggling to make sense of this.

'No,' Moira said. 'It was for his college work to begin with, then he started to get to know them and they sort of took to him, got friendly. I think …' She frowned, eyes watering again. 'Jordan never knew his dad, and my dad and me didn't get on, so he didn't see much of his grandpa, I think they kind of filled that gap for him.'

She blew her nose, apologised reflexively.

'Was Jordan studying in town?' Ferreira asked.

'At Peterborough College, yes. He's in his third year. Journalism.' A warm smile. 'He was doing brilliantly. Just … so, well, I was so proud of him. Nobody in my family ever went to university before. Not even my sister and she's really smart. She always says Jordan got his brains from her.' Another faint smile, warm but quickly gone. 'He wanted to go to UEA. He pretended he didn't but it was only because he knew we couldn't afford it and he didn't want me to feel bad because I couldn't do that for him. If he'd gone there he'd still be alive now.'

She broke down again, turning her face towards the wall as she cried.

'I'm sorry.'

'It's okay, Moira,' Ferreira said, patting her hand. 'Take your time.'

She wiped her face on the sleeve of her jumper.

'How did Jordan get on with his classmates?' Zigic asked.

'Good. Fine,' she said. 'It's not like school, is it? You're not with them all the time.'

'Was there anyone in particular he was close to?'

'Not really. No one he mentioned. But he'd moved past them a bit.' She reached for her tea, held onto the cup without drinking.

'How do you mean?'

'Jordan was doing some work at the *ET* already. Then he got this article published in the *Big Issue* last month.' Her face lit up. 'He hadn't even finished his degree and he was getting in the papers. That's what he was like. He worked his socks off to get on. He was always saying how tough it was to get a good job in the media if you didn't have contacts.' She turned to Ferreira. 'It's all posh kids. Daddy's friends giving them an introduction, that sort of thing. Jordan knew he was going to have to make something happen for himself and he went out and did it.'

'What was the article about?' Ferreira asked, and Zigic heard the slight lift in her voice, the stirring of instinct.

'The blokes at the Club,' Moira said. 'All about how they were coping after losing their jobs at the Greenaway factory. That kind of thing. They really opened up to Jordan. And you think, men like that, that generation, they don't talk about their feelings, do they? I know my dad never did. But they trusted Jordan with some really heavy stuff.' She got up from the sofa. 'I've got a copy somewhere.'

'How was he doing at the *ET*?'

'He was enjoying it,' she said. 'He didn't want to stay there forever but he knew it would be good on his CV.'

'Had there been any trouble with what he was writing for them?' Ferreira asked.

Moira pulled a box file off the bookshelves, paused as she went to open it. 'What do you mean trouble?'

'Anyone get angry with his articles?'

'Is that why you think he was shot?' she asked, all the energy bleeding out of her again. 'Like that woman in Malta? They blew her up.'

'It's far too early to speculate,' Zigic said, giving Ferreira a warning look. 'We're just trying to get an idea of what was going on with Jordan.'

He couldn't believe that whatever the young man was writing about for the local paper would actually lead someone to shoot him, but these were strange times and threats to the press were becoming an everyday occurrence. Social media opening journalists up to the lunatic element in a way that was unthinkable even ten years ago when the worst they had to deal with were occasional belligerent emails or angry letters.

'Was Jordan seeing anyone?' Ferreira asked.

'He was too busy for a girlfriend,' Moira said airily.

Somehow Zigic doubted that, but even the most devoted son needed a secret or two from his mother.

'What about friends? Is there anyone in particular he might have confided in?'

'He was working so many hours all of his old friends from school sort of fell by the wayside,' Moira said regretfully. 'And uni isn't like school. That's what he said, you're *friendly* with people but you're not really friends with them.'

Another hint of doubt crept in and Zigic wondered if Jordan was keeping things from his mum or if she was keeping something from them.

'Was Jordan having trouble fitting in there?' Ferreira asked.

'No,' she said, with a shrug. 'Jordan got on with everyone, that's just the sort of boy he was. Talk to anyone. Ever since he was little.'

'But he wasn't making new friends,' Ferreira prodded.

'He was there to study,' Moira said, defensiveness creeping into her voice.

'Was there anyone he mentioned not getting on with?'

'No, he didn't talk about any of them much.' Moira held the copy of the *Big Issue* out to Ferreira. 'Here. It's the only one I've got.'

'I'll take a photo, then you can keep it here,' she reassured her.

Moira found the article and cleared a space on the coffee table, placed the magazine carefully in front of her and smoothed the pages down with a kind of reverence that struck Zigic hard in the chest.

'Would it be okay if we had a look at Jordan's room?' Zigic asked, as Moira took the magazine back and replaced it in the box file, revealing a brief glimpse of the press clippings inside.

'Top of the stairs,' she said, staying where she was, kneeling on the floor, her fingertips brushing the cover of the magazine.

Chapter Four

Jordan Radley's bedroom was done out like a minimalist Scandinavian hotel room. White-painted walls, a single wooden bed neatly made with a knitted blanket at the foot and a sheepskin rug perfectly placed to take his feet when he swung them out in the morning. A few black-framed prints on the wall: a London skyline, an old-fashioned typewriter and a quote printed in a simple font: 'Comfort the afflicted, afflict the comfortable.' In one corner of the room stood a narrow canvas wardrobe with its front rolled down, and under the window, a black-painted desk with an unused ruled notepad and a pot of freshly sharpened pencils next to it. No corkboard or folders full of clippings to show them what he'd been working on when he was killed.

Zigic could give her all the stern looks he liked. When a journalist got shot on the street, you started with their work, Ferreira thought. Especially when that journalist was a twenty-one-year-old boy who hadn't lived long enough to piss off many other people.

'Where's his laptop?' Zigic asked, opening the drawers and closing them again quickly. 'No tablet or thumb drives either.'

'Wardrobe?' Ferreira folded up the front and hooked it in place, finding his clothes just as precisely arranged as the rest of the room. Everything rolled and stacked on the shelves, arranged by colour, nothing in the hanging space except a black suit in a plastic protector and a couple of summer-weight jackets, shoes lined up below. 'No sign of a laptop in here.'

'His chargers are still plugged into the wall,' Zigic said. 'Phone or tablet and laptop.'

'No sign of them in the living room.' She lifted a few items of clothing, checking Jordan hadn't hidden his devices under them. 'What about the kitchen?'

'Not in there.'

He looked around the room with a mistrustful air. Probably thinking of the state of his own bedroom at that age, she thought. Her brothers' had been hellholes. Discarded towels and dropped clothes littering the floor, magazines and spent socks under the bed, posters thrown up haphazardly on the walls and ceilings, the back of their doors; anywhere with space to take cars and tits and footballers. Everything drenched in a miasma of body spray and testosterone.

Jordan Radley was clearly a very particular young man.

'Maybe he took his laptop out with him,' Zigic suggested.

'To watch football?' Ferreira asked. 'Why would he do that?'

'They're not here.' He opened the drawer again, sifting through the contents.

Ferreira went back downstairs, found Moira Radley back on the sofa, television turned off, staring at the blank screen, an expression of deep and terrible loss on her face so severe that for a moment Ferreira couldn't bring herself to speak.

'Moira,' she said gently, making the woman start. 'Do you know where Jordan's laptop is?'

'In his room.'

'It's not. Did he take a bag with him when he went out?'

'No, just his phone. He didn't need anything else. He was going to watch the football.'

Her voice had flattened into a monotone. Somewhere in the back of her mind she must know what these questions implied but that was a distant concern right now.

'What about his house keys?' Ferreira asked, beginning to pull things together. 'Did he take those with him?'

'He always does,' Moira said. 'My shift started at eight, he wouldn't have been able to get back in without them.'

'Is it possible he forgot them?'

Moira dragged herself up, limbs heavy-looking, and shuffled into the kitchen, to a small wooden rack with keys written on it. Only one set there, attached to a pink pompom.

'They're not here,' she said, perplexed. 'He always leaves them here. I drummed it into him since he was little. Leave them on the hook then you won't lose them.' She brushed past Ferreira, out of the room and up the stairs.

Ferreira followed her into Jordan's bedroom, where Zigic was squatted down, looking under his bed.

'It should be here,' she said, almost to herself, going to the desk. She opened the drawers and closed them again, checked down the back. 'Where's his messenger bag?'

'Are you sure he didn't take it with him?' Zigic asked.

'I'm positive.' Moira turned to them. 'I came in and brought him his washing just before he left. His laptop was on his desk and his bag was right down there by the side of it, where he always kept it.'

'Can you have a look in his desk and tell us if anything else is missing?' Zigic said. 'Hard drives, USB sticks, things like that.'

'He's got loads of the things,' Moira told him, opening the draws and rattling the contents. 'He was paranoid about backing everything up. There were two on his key ring. He had a tablet I got him for Christmas as well. They're all gone.'

Keys gone, bag gone, tech gone; there was only one explanation Ferreira could see.

'Has someone broke in?' Moira asked, her hand going to her throat.

'It's too early to say but I think we should have forensics come in and have a look just in case,' Zigic said, carefully ushering her out of the room without appearing to do so. As they went downstairs, he asked her if anyone else had keys to the house.

'Just my sister for emergencies,' she said, unwilling to sit down again. She stood with one foot on top of the other, gazing around the living room as if it was tainted. 'It doesn't look like anyone's been in. Don't they usually trash the place?'

'It depends what they're looking for,' Ferreira said, getting another warning glare from Zigic.

But he was underestimating Moira Radley if he thought she wasn't putting all of this together herself. Ferreira could see the cogs turning even through her grief. She wanted answers, a logical explanation, anything to distract herself from her terrible loss.

He started towards the door, said, 'I'll check with the neighbour.'

Ferreira waited for the sound of the door closing, hearing it stick on the first attempt, a soft curse from Zigic before he shoved it open and slammed it hard, shaking the walls.

'Do you know what Jordan was working on?' she asked.

'You think that's why he was killed,' Moira said, a new steeliness coming into her voice. 'He doesn't but you do.'

Admitting it would be a mistake, Ferreira reminded herself. Moira Radley was in a delicate state right now, looking to them for information they didn't have and shouldn't share even if they did. Anything she said, any hint of direction she gave the grieving mother, would potentially shape Moira's thoughts about Jordan's murder and that was a dangerous thing to do. Because once she'd fastened on a reason, she might conceal facts that conflicted with it, innocently try to give them what she thought they wanted to hear rather than what they actually needed to know.

And there was always, lingering in the background, the possibility of Moira sharing this theory with the wrong person. Jordan's murderer getting to hear about it and feeding them false information when they came to question him.

She was already thinking *him*, couldn't stop herself. The gun and the moving of Jordan's body, slight as it was. This didn't feel like a woman's crime.

'It's too early to speculate,' Ferreira said, the standard line, the flat delivery. 'I know it's hard to hear that and I know you need answers, but it's really important that we all keep an open mind. And that you tell us everything you possibly can about Jordan's life so we can try and speak to everyone we need to.'

Moira stared at her. 'Please don't patronise me.'

'This doesn't feel … usual,' Ferreira said carefully. 'You've told us Jordan was studying and working and there was no trouble with anyone, no enemies. So we have to keep an open mind, okay? Because either it's someone very well hidden or it's a part of his life he hadn't told you anything about.'

Moira bit her lip, said nothing, as Ferreira waited for a reply.

'You seem like a very good mother and you and Jordan were obviously close.'

A hitch in Moira's breathing, a gasp swallowed down.

'So I have to think, what would he feel a need to keep from you?'

'He was a good boy,' Moira said firmly.

'I believe you.'

Did she?

In her gut, yes, but she knew it wasn't as infallible as she'd like to think.

'Was Jordan worried about anything?' Ferreira continued.

'Jordan worried about everything,' Moira said, eyes lighting up. 'Climate change, Universal Credit, the Windrush families, animal welfare, Brexit. I mean, he *cared*. That was the kind of boy he was. Ever since he was little. If he saw someone in pain, it was like he was feeling it himself.'

The cynical part of Ferreira heard the note in Moira's words and she understood where it was coming from, would have done the same in her position. My boy was a good person, we are good people. Help me. Find who killed my son. Don't let this slip.

But she saw pride there too and realised that the version of Jordan Moira wanted her to believe in was the one Moira truly believed in herself.

'Was that why he chose to study journalism?'

'He thought that was how you made the world better.' Moira shrugged, like it was simple. 'Tell the truth, show people what's happening.'

'And what truth was he telling?'

'I don't know what he was working on,' she said, regret in her tone. 'He didn't like talking about stories until he was finished them.'

'But he was working on something?'

She nodded. 'He was excited about it, whatever it was.'

'He didn't give you *any* indication at all?'

29

'He said, "This is the one, Mum."' Moira wrapped her arms around her middle. 'Jordan was sure all he needed was one brilliant story and that would be him on his way.'

'Where?'

'Out of the *ET*, out of Peterborough, I suppose.' She pressed her knuckles to her mouth, blinked away tears. 'I kept hoping he wouldn't find it. I didn't want him to leave. Kids go to London, they never come back.'

Five minutes later, standing outside the house, smoking a cigarette, Ferreira was thinking about what Moira had said. The big story, the one that would kick-start Jordan's career. What would he do to find it? How far would he go and into what treacherous territory?

Jordan was obviously smart enough to realise how the odds were stacked against him, how thick the class ceiling above his head was. Journalists on local papers did sometimes manage to move up to the nationals, but Ferreira knew enough about the changing nature of the media to realise it wouldn't be easy to make that leap without contacts or a good degree from a prestigious university. Pluck and tenacity weren't enough any more. Maybe they never really had been.

It would need to be something impressive to get his foot in the door.

Something with interest to people beyond Peterborough.

She wondered what he'd got himself into. How badly those involved might want to silence him.

Zigic came out of the neighbouring house.

'Sounds like someone let themselves in late last night,' he said. 'Before eleven apparently but he couldn't give me a more precise time.'

'Is he sure?'

'He said the front door woke him just as he was nodding off and it does make a hell of a bang, so I'm inclined to think he's right.'

Ferreira took a deep drag on her cigarette. 'So, our killer shoots Jordan, steal his keys, then comes round here and lets himself in to steal his laptop and drives ...'

Zigic kicked at a small stone on the pavement, seemingly uncomfortable about the development.

'It could be a robbery,' he said, sounding more hopeful than certain.

'What do you think a second-hand laptop's worth these days?' she asked incredulously. 'You think it's worth buying a handgun and shooting someone for a couple of hundred quid? At most.' She shook her head. 'Come on, you know what this is just as well as I do.'

'We can't jump to conclusions, Mel,' he warned.

'Moira reckons he was working on a big story. Something that had got him very excited.'

'Did she say what it was?'

'She doesn't know.'

Zigic rubbed his beard, uneasy-looking. 'Then we need to find someone who does.'

Chapter Five

A sharp wind cut across the park behind the Greenaway Club as they climbed out of the car, bringing with it the sound of children playing on the swings. The club was a squat, pebble-dashed building with skinny metal windows set well above eye level; nothing to distract you once you were inside, no easy indication of how late it had got and that maybe you should be at home now.

Two hundred metres away, down the bottom of the road, hidden by a row of terraced houses was the old Greenaway Engineering site. Five years ago it had been a thriving manufacturing business specialising in automation systems, entering its sixth decade in Peterborough. A rare success story in surviving globalisation and one financial crisis after another. Over 150 men had worked at the place, highly skilled, highly paid, doing the kind of jobs Zigic's friends had been pushed towards by their parents. When he was at school the training programme was always oversubscribed and the company would turn up on careers day, making big claims about the long-term prospects for employment with them.

More than four years ago all that changed.

The company was sold to a German rival for an undisclosed sum. Promises made then too. Zigic remembered the owner, Marcus Greenaway, being given the front page of the local paper to insist that no jobs would be lost and that the venerable old firm started by his grandfather would remain in Peterborough for generations to come.

Within days the factory gates were locked. The workers on the wrong side, protesting at the injustice, knowing they'd never find another role at their age, that the years they'd given to the place counted for nothing as the new owners cleared out the tooling in the big old sheds. The intellectual property spirited away more subtly.

Now there was nothing left of the place.

The site was in the process of being redeveloped. Two blocks of flats already finished, their thrusting spires dominating the skyline, dwarfing the old Edwardian terraces in the foreground. A third tower alongside them, all metal still, waiting to be clad in brick and something that would pass for wood from a distance.

Every time the former Greenaway workers came to the Club, they would see the buildings and be forced to confront what they'd lost again.

Zigic was surprised any of them could face it, wondered how strong the camaraderie of the group must be for them to return again and again.

'It makes even less sense that Jordan was hanging out here when you look at it.' Ferreira eyed the flaking paintwork and the felt flapping where a strip had come loose on the flat roof, the hanging baskets full of plastic flowers. 'Would you have come here when you were Jordan's age?'

'Not if it could help it,' he said. 'But I suppose he got a story out of them and it was obviously a big deal for him career-wise. Maybe he felt like he owed them something after that.'

She gave a non-committal murmur and followed him through a recessed porch that smelled of disinfectant and into the main room, a broad white box with a sprung floor highly polished under the strip lights that hung from the suspended ceiling. It was the Club he knew from childhood, right down to the burgundy velvet banquettes along one wall and the mahogany-look bar in a distant corner. The cold smell of damp was imperfectly masked by room freshener, and somehow, a faint whiff of old ashtrays.

He'd been expecting to find it empty at a little after 10 a.m., but there were a dozen or so elderly ladies in loose-fitting workout gear milling about and chatting, readying themselves for what he guessed was a sit-down aerobics class, judging by the chairs arranged in ranks, facing the long wall and an old-school boom box. Its owner was dressed in a brightly patterned onesie, talking to a sixty-something man with a swirl of wavy grey hair and silver-framed glasses too small for his rounded face.

'That'll be Humble,' Ferreira said. 'His photo was in Jordan's *Big Issue* article.'

Bruce Humble stood with his arms folded as he listened to the aerobics instructor, nodding and smiling, giving the impression, even from ten metres away, of forced politeness. He was barrel-chested and flat-stomached, dressed in jeans and polished tan brogues, a sky-blue shirt with white collar and cuffs.

Humble looked away from the instructor as they approached, excused himself and came over to meet them. The professional half-smile stayed plastered on his lightly tanned face until he saw the ID Ferreira was holding up. He faltered, just like everyone did, brain whirring through the possibilities: an accident, a death, his family, someone else's.

'Can I help you?' he asked reluctantly.

Ferreira made the introductions. 'Is there somewhere private we could have a chat?'

'Of course. Follow me, please.'

He led them to a small room behind the bar, the toilets opposite, stock room next to it. A sheet of paper tacked to the door said, 'Bruce Humble – Manager'.

'New job?' Zigic asked, gesturing at the makeshift nameplate.

'No,' he said. 'I've been here three years now. I keep meaning to get a proper sign made up but it feels a bit of a waste when there's only me on staff.'

'Did you work at the factory before?'

'I was in the sales department, yes,' he said tersely. 'I used to come in and help out the old fella who ran the place before me. Then when he retired the board of trustees asked if I'd want to come on full-time.'

'How did the Club come to survive the sale of the factory?' Zigic asked.

'Mrs Greenaway senior had it all tied up separate in a trust,' he explained. 'She wanted to be sure we had this place even if everything else went.'

34

Humble led them into his office. It looked like it hadn't been touched since the early eighties, with green-and-cream striped wallpaper under a fleur-de-lys border and a leather-topped desk surrounded by mismatched office chairs, where his laptop sat closed next to a takeaway coffee steaming gently in the sunlight coming through the high window.

'Now, what can I do for you?' Humble asked, waving for them to sit.

'Jordan Radley,' Ferreira said.

Humble started, eyes widening with concern. 'I know him, yes. Has something happened to him?'

Not has he done something, Zigic thought. Humble immediately assuming he was a victim rather than a suspect in a crime.

'Jordan was killed last night.'

'Fucking hell.' He let out a shocked huff, pressing himself back in his chair. 'Sorry, excuse my language.' A quick glance to Ferreira. 'How did it happen?'

'We're still piecing together the details,' Zigic said. 'But Jordan was shot while he was walking home.'

'Shot?' Humble's face went slack. 'God almighty, that poor boy. Why?'

'We were hoping you might be able to help us with that,' Ferreira told him. 'Jordan was here yesterday evening, is that right?'

Humble nodded. 'He was.'

'Why?'

'The same reason everyone else was here; he was watching the football.' Humble put a trembling hand to his mouth. 'I'm sorry, I don't understand this.'

'How did he seem to you last night?'

'Normal.' Humble shrugged. 'I mean, he wasn't spooked or anything. He was chatting away, watching the match. Just ... normal.'

'How long had he been coming in here?' Ferreira asked, notepad out.

'A few months,' Humble said, watching her write. 'He got in touch with me awhile back about coming in and talking to some of the lads. He was a student at the college, doing journalism. Did someone tell you that?'

'We've spoken to his mother.'

'She must be in bits.' Humble shook his head. 'Poor woman.'

'She mentioned an article Jordan wrote about you and some of the members,' Zigic prompted.

'Yeah, that was how it started. He wanted to interview some of the lads so I sounded them out for him, asked who was happy to talk to him. Most of them didn't want any part of it. They're a great bunch but talking about their feelings for a newspaper … wasn't going to happen.'

'How about the men who did talk to him?' Ferreira asked. 'How did they feel about the finished piece?'

'Good, yeah,' he said, forced lightness in his voice. 'Think they were happy to get some of it off their chests, you know?'

'Anyone not happy about it?'

Humble came forward in his seat, brought his big hands down on the desktop. 'Jordan was very sensitive to their situations. He changed their names, protected their privacy. But I don't see what that's got to do with him being shot.'

'We're just trying to get an idea of who Jordan was friendly with here,' Zigic said smoothly. 'This is an unusual place for a young man to hang out.'

'Not really.'

'Are there many kids his age using the Club?'

'Some of the blokes bring their sons along now and again,' Humble explained. 'But, yeah, alright, I suppose they're not the same stamp as Jordan. To be honest with you I didn't expect to see him in here again after he'd done the article but, I don't know, you talk to people about their darkest moments, I reckon that creates a bond, don't you?'

Zigic nodded. 'Who was he friendly with?'

Humble gave them names, Ferreira writing them down. Three men: Lionel Ridgeon, Steve Gurney, Richard Caxton.

'Were they in last night as well?' she asked.

'Yeah. I doubt they'll be able to tell you anything more than I can, though. We were all together most of the evening. Had a few drinks, bit of a laugh, that was it. Same as every other night. I can't –' A wobbly breath escaped from his mouth. 'I just can't believe this is happening.'

They gave him a moment, the sound of music starting up in the main room, bright and poppy, the instructor's voice even brighter over the top of it as she took her class through their paces.

Humble stared at the scarred green leather set into the desktop, his thumb running back and forth over a deep gash turned black with age.

'What time did Jordan leave?' Ferreira asked finally.

'Just after ten, if I remember right.' He squinted, thinking. 'It cleared out pretty quick after the final whistle. Lionel and Steve chipped off, Jordan was still talking to Dick about something or other, then Dick left about ten, and I had a word with Jordan before he went. Can't have been more than five or ten minutes after.'

'What were you talking about?'

'Jordan was giving me some advice about our social media presence. I've been trying to get more people in. The running costs here aren't crazy but we could do with bringing in a bigger crowd at the events. Jordan was more tech savvy than me.'

It didn't sound like the kind of conversation you could have in five minutes, but Zigic let it go, knowing there would be another opportunity to ask Humble more questions.

'Has there ever been any trouble with Jordan here?' he asked.

'Of course not,' Humble said scornfully. 'It's not that sort of place. Most of the lads come here because there's never any trouble. You go out in town, you never know who's going to kick off. We're like a family, all know each other, go way back. I wouldn't tolerate any trouble.'

'Did you see anyone hanging around when Jordan left?' Zigic asked, getting an immediate shake of the head.

'I was in here clearing up. Must have been a good half an hour doing that, then I kicked out the stragglers, locked up and went home.'

'What about CCTV? I noticed you've got a camera on the front door.'

37

'Doesn't work,' Humble told him. 'Went on the blink a couple of months back when we had a power cut. I've not managed to find someone to fix it yet.' He shrugged. 'Funds as they are. CCTV's mostly a deterrent, right?'

'Until there's a crime and we need the footage, yeah,' Ferreira said, making another quick note. 'We're going to need a list of your members. Everyone who was in last night.'

'Alright.' Humble opened his laptop and booted it up. 'But, like I said, there wasn't any trouble.'

For a moment they sat in silence, as he found the list and sent it to a printer on the shelf beside his desk.

'What did Jordan talk about when he was in here?' Ferreira asked.

'The usual stuff,' Humble said, turning to check on the printer. 'But he didn't really get a word in edgeways with the lads, to be honest with you. Dick was always going on about politics and that. He's a right old Trot and nobody wants to listen to it in here, but Jordan was that way as well, so they had that in common. Dick'd be going on about the good old days, the union, the strikes. Reliving his youth.'

It didn't sound like the makings of a big news story to Zigic. Doubted it was the kind of thing Jordan Radley might be murdered over.

'Dick's going to take this hard,' Humble said. He whipped a few sheets of paper from the printer. 'Do you want me to mark up who was in last night? Would that be the easiest way to do it?'

'If you wouldn't mind.' Zigic watched him scan down the list of names and addresses and phone numbers, placing a small red star next to the right ones. 'Did Jordan ever talk about his work?'

'Yeah, matter of fact he was talking to Dick about it last night,' Humble said, not looking up from the paper. 'He was saying how the waiting staff were being messed about by management. Not getting their tips, that sort of thing. That's what set Dick off about the union. Saying Jordan should get them to organise.' He tutted. 'Pie in the sky, but that's Dick all over.'

'What job's this?' Ferreira asked. 'His mother said he was at the *Evening Telegraph*.'

Humble handed her the marked-up list. 'He was there, yeah. But he does a few shifts at the Old Mill out Yaxley way. He was only part-time at the *ET*, one day a week, and you know what that kind of work pays.'

Withheld tips didn't sound like a big story either.

'What about his job at the *ET*?' Ferreira pressed. 'What did he say about that?'

'Not much,' Humble replied. 'He didn't seem to think much of the place. But he was an ambitious kid and they had him doing reports on council meetings, stuff like that. I remember him saying he'd written a couple of articles they wouldn't run for some reason, but I don't know what they were about.' Humble turned to Zigic, sceptical-looking. 'You don't think he was killed because of something he wrote?'

'It's too early to say.'

The words already feeling like a lie rather than the evasion they usually were.

'Did he mention a girlfriend?'

Humble smiled. 'Yeah, Steve had that out of him. He's a bugger for it, can always smell when someone's loved up.'

'Who is she?'

'Woman he worked with at the Mill,' Humble said, brows going up. 'Older woman. Steve ribbed him over that for a good while.'

'Did he tell you her name?'

'No, he was very mysterious about her. I half thought he was making her up to get Steve off his back to tell you the truth.' Humble gave them a slightly apologetic look. 'I'd always figured Jordan was gay. But then me and the wife went over to the Mill for lunch one weekend and there was this stunning-looking woman there and I thought, that's who she is. But my wife said maybe Jordan just had a crush on her. So I – and it wasn't very tactful of me, my wife's always telling me I'm like a bull in a china shop – I mentioned that Jordan recommended we try the tomahawk steaks and she blushed right down to her blouse.' He opened his hands up wide. 'I said to my wife, told you so.'

39

Zigic thanked Bruce Humble for his help and they walked out back through the aerobics lesson, a Kylie Minogue song worming its way into his ear, the chorus looping still as he pulled out of the car park onto Belsize Avenue, thinking of the girlfriend Jordan hadn't told his mother about and all the men who'd taken a gun and shot their ex's new bloke.

Jordan walking home, minutes away from a far more isolated spot on the lane that ran right up to his front door. Was this a killer who couldn't wait that long? Couldn't control themselves? Had looked at his back and seen a target and pulled the trigger?

CHAPTER SIX

It was beginning to drizzle when they pulled into the car park at Thorpe Road Station, the building's long, low façade looking even duller than usual under the grey light. A few people were milling around outside, two uniforms escorting a sullen woman with her hands in cuffs up the front steps into the crowded reception area.

Since the city centre station on London Road had closed down last summer, they were taking the added workload with no more staff and no more space. Ferreira wondered how many minor crimes weren't being reported now that the process involved a long walk or a drive across town. Had that been a factor in the decision to close the station down; massage the crime figures by nudging people away from coming forward? Essential cost-cutting they'd been told at the time, much needed money going into the coffers, and she was sure the hotel being built on the old site next to the Magistrate's Court had made someone money. None of it seemed to flow into their budget though.

The cuts were biting hard. Three years ago, Hate Crimes had been 'reabsorbed' into major crimes, sending her and DI Zigic and DC Bobby Wahlia back downstairs into the general pool of detectives. Since then they'd found their workload increasing as officers who retired or took transfers went unreplaced. Civilian staff were quietly reduced. There was talk of forensics being outsourced to a private lab, the plans on hold for the moment, but only because of the recent scandal about a private facility and a staff member who'd faked his credentials, springing dozens of convicted criminals from prison when the story hit the news.

Ferreira pushed that thought away, the fallout from the scandal still a raw wound she had resolved not to pick at, to not even acknowledge if she could help it.

For a month afterward she'd been confined to desk duty, while the official inquiry ran its course. Then three months of fortnightly visits to a psychiatrist who listened more than he spoke but somehow managed to probe her more thoroughly than the detectives who'd carried out the investigation. She'd felt a sense of triumph when he signed her off, releasing her back to her own internal resources, feeling like she'd beaten him. Six hour-long sessions and she'd stuck to the lie DCS Riggott had formulated for her, built on the bones of the lie she'd told him. Both of them aware of the cost of telling the truth.

The lie was so completely discussed and analysed that she was beginning to believe it herself now. Told it to Zigic and Billy as well, because it had to be that way, no matter how much she wanted to come clean to them both.

But she knew how they would look at her if they knew what she'd done. Zigic would be horrified, would try to hide it, tell her there was no other way. But she would see what he really thought, knew he'd never fully trust her again. Billy would be sanguine. Say she did the right thing and mean it and then maybe she wouldn't ever trust him again.

Neither reaction would be comfortable to deal with.

Safer to pack it all away. Forget it ever happened.

Ferreira ran up ahead of Zigic and shoved through the weighty stairwell door into the office, where she saw a board already set up for Jordan Radley's murder.

There was a lot of white space waiting to be filled under an image DC Keri Bloom had pulled from social media. Jordan's hair neatly barbered, heavy-framed glasses pushed up his nose. He was dressed in a navy-and-white checked shirt with a buttoned-down collar fastened at the neck. He looked older, more serious. The man Moira had said he wanted to become; a man with important things to say.

Bloom was tapping a marker pen against her knuckles, studying the provisional timeline she'd mapped out on the board.

Unlike Radley, Bloom always seemed younger than she was, with her pixie-cut hair and an endless array of blouses with Peter Pan collars, an intense and eager air around her that the job didn't seem to be blunting.

'You can add Jordan leaving the Greenaway Club around five past ten,' Ferreira told her, as Zigic disappeared into his office. 'And I've got a list of people who were there last night that we're going to need to get to.'

Ferreira stuck the list to the board, not sure which column the men belonged in yet. Suspects, persons of interest or witnesses. Until they'd plotted out the addresses they were returning home to and managed to pin down the times they left the Club, it was impossible to say.

'Where's Zac?' she asked, glancing towards DC Parr's desk.

'On his way back in,' Bloom said. 'Door to door along London Road didn't yield any witnesses unfortunately.'

'It was always a long shot,' Ferreira said, thinking of the distance of the houses from the locus, the lack of clear sight lines from windows. 'If we do get a decent witness it'll probably be someone who was driving past.'

Bloom bounced lightly where she stood. 'I've called in the traffic cameras. They're around 200 metres away but the arrangement is good for us,' she explained. 'Four cameras covering the main road and turnings, so they should cover the paths.'

'Let's keep our fingers crossed then,' Ferreira said.

'It's a strange place to choose to shoot someone.' Bloom screwed her nose up. 'Do you think … is it possible he was shot from a car?'

'Drive-by makes sense if he was into drugs,' DC Rob Weller piped up, spinning his chair away from his desk towards them.

'We don't know this is drugs-related,' Zigic told him, coming out of his office with his coat and jumper gone, shirtsleeves folded back as if the afternoon was going to involve a lot of heavy lifting.

'But it's a shooting,' Weller said.

'People get shot for other reasons besides drugs. And nothing we've heard about Jordan Radley so far suggests any involvement with any kind of criminality. He was a student at Peterborough

43

College, he was working part-time at the *Evening Telegraph* and doing shifts at the Old Mill in Yaxley. If he was a drug dealer he certainly went out of his way to avoiding looking like one.' Zigic sat down on the edge of an empty desk. 'Rob, you need to call in Radley's financials. See if there's any income we can't account for. Extravagant spending habits, vices. Check his mum's too.'

Weller nodded. 'Yes, sir.'

DC Parr came into the office, shucking off a rain-spattered anorak. 'What have I missed?'

'Nothing yet,' Ferreira said. 'Get over here.'

Zigic went on. 'The issue we have right now is that Radley's killer stole his keys and used them to gain access to his home, where it appears he cleared out every piece of tech Radley owned. We have no sign of his phone at the scene, so presumably that was taken off him after the murder, too.'

'So this is a robbery?' Weller asked, frowning.

'No,' Parr said, glancing at Ferreira. 'Radley's address wasn't in his wallet, was it?'

She shook her head. 'Not as far as we know. All the ID he had on him was still intact and there was no address on any of it. Driver's licence would have given it but he didn't have one. So I think we have to assume his killer already knew where he lived.'

'Doesn't mean it wasn't a robbery,' Weller said, unwilling to have a second theory shot down in as many minutes. 'He's a student. They have good tech. Say he bought a three-grand Mac. That's worth fifteen hundred quid second-hand.'

'And if that's all that was taken, you might be right,' Ferreira said. 'But USB drives are pennies and they were all taken as well.'

She waited, looking at them in turn, seeing who would say it.

'There was something on the drives,' Weller said, straightening in his chair. 'Radley's a hack. Has he been nosing around in some-one's business and they've gone for him?'

'He's working on the *ET*,' Zigic reminded them.

Ferreira heard the edge of desperation in his tone, wanting to damp down Weller's sudden enthusiasm before it infected anyone else. He would rather this was drugs-related, she knew. Easy to explain, unfortunate but expected. 'County lines' was one of those phrases respectable citizens glided over in papers and disregarded on the news. Something which belonged to a world separate from their own even when it started to come closer to their streets.

But a twenty-one-year-old journalism student getting murdered over a story he was working on …

'Journalism is supposed to be the most dangerous job in the world now,' Bloom said regretfully.

'Yes, in the *world*.' Zigic stood up. 'Not in England and definitely not in Peterborough. And we need to keep in mind that Jordan Radley wasn't stalking the corridors of power, trying to expose corrupt politicians and corporate shenanigans –'

'As far as we know,' Weller said.

Zigic shot Ferreira a pointed look as if this was all her fault, his officers following the early leads they had to its logical conclusion. The same conclusion he'd reached but wasn't ready to fully admit to himself.

'Jordan had published one article in a magazine,' he said. 'And that was about the male mental health crisis. So, we're going to keep an open mind.' He turned his attention to Bloom. 'Keri, can you get hold of Jordan's phone records?'

'Yes, sir.'

'We're at a major disadvantage without his devices, so we're going to have to try and plug that gap. We know he was seeing a woman he worked with at the Old Mill – but he appears to have been very secretive about her.'

A murmur from Weller. 'She'll have a boyfriend then.'

Zigic ignored him, went on. 'The post-mortem is scheduled for late this afternoon, so we might get some movement then. Preliminary forensics should be in around the same time.' His face went stern. 'Until then I want us to pull together everything we possibly can about Jordan Radley's life.'

CHAPTER SEVEN

Back at her desk, Ferreira started to read the article Jordan had written for the *Big Issue*. It was a double-page spread, a photograph of the Greenaway Club taken in autumn sunshine, another of Bruce Humble seated in a circle with half a dozen men, the angle of the photograph subtly obscuring their features, but you would recognise them if you knew who they were already, she thought. The pseudonyms hadn't really ensured their anonymity.

Bloom had been right, it was heavy stuff.

'Allan' talking about how his life had fallen apart when he lost his job. He'd always worked and wanted to keep doing so.

> The job centre was no help. It's all box ticking and do this course and do that course, report here twice a week or we'll stop your benefits. And the benefits not worth having. I was on eight hundred a week before that and they expected me to get by on next to nothing. I couldn't pay my mortgage. My wife was terrified we'd lose the house. She took on a second job. We had to borrow off her mum just to keep the lights on. It was humiliating, having to go begging to someone like that. I've never done that in my life. I started work at sixteen and I've always been able to look after my family. Now it's like I'm nothing. I'm *worth* nothing.

Ferreira took a sip of her coffee, imagining what it would have cost 'Allan' to speak so openly. The weight on his shoulders that might have lifted temporarily with the catharsis. But once the interview was over, once the words were actually out, the problem was still there.

'Peter' describing the dispiriting experience of dealing with an employment agency.

There's this boy, barely old enough to shave, telling me there's no call for my skills in Peterborough. Telling me I need to get some more experience on my CV. I'm fifty-four, I was a bloody fabricator. That's a specialised job, right? And what do I get offered, shelf stacking. Minimum wage, zero-hours contract, no benefits, no security. I say to him, what do you think I am? I'm not looking for a bit of pin money to take down the bingo, I've got to keep a roof over my head. Bloody shop work. I did a three-year apprenticeship learning my craft and you expect me to go and work in bloody Budgens. And you know what he said to me, this little scrote, 'Think yourself lucky, most people would be happy to do this job.'

As she read on she noticed a theme developing, the fury, the shock of finding themselves in a world that didn't need or respect the skills they'd spent a lifetime developing. 'Humiliation' cropping up again and again as these men took jobs they didn't want to avoid being labelled as scroungers or layabouts, told themselves they took the jobs so they could keep looking themselves in the eye. But the precarity of their lives was plain to see. Rent and mortgages to pay, families still looking to them for support. Homelessness only ever a couple of short steps away.

Jordan Radley had captured the keen sense of helplessness, the shock of having their lives completely upended. It was another kind of grief, she realised, grieving for the certainty and security they'd taken for granted before.

'I can't retire until I'm sixty but I don't think I'll make it that far,' 'Tom' said.

The way things are going I'll work till I drop. We lost the house a few months after I got laid off. We were mortgaged up to the hilt and I couldn't find another job that'd cover the payments. My wife left. Then the kids moved up to Doncaster after her. I'm in a bloody bedsit now and I can hardly afford that on what I'm earning. I worked thirty years, did everything right, got a good trade, pulled all the overtime I could, and I've still ended up on the scrapheap. My daughter wants to help me out but she's struggling enough without me to worry about. Her Universal Credit's all messed up and she's got loans everywhere she can't pay back. I told her, don't worry about your old dad, I'll find something. I can't tell her how bad it is. Some days I only have one meal. My doctor's over the moon I'm losing weight, he says it's good for my arthritis. 'Whatever you're doing, keep it up,' he said. And I could have laughed in his face. 'Whatever I'm doing'? I'm starving to death.

Was this why Jordan Radley hadn't walked away from the Club once the article was written? They'd opened up to him, showed him the faces they kept hidden from everyone else, even their families, and he'd felt a responsibility not to be like the people at the benefits agency and the employment agency and the public they encountered in their new jobs. Had Jordan wanted them to feel like they still mattered in the world?

No wonder Moira was so destroyed. She'd raised a good man and now he was gone.

Out the corner of her eye Ferreira noticed DI Greta Kitson going into Zigic's office. She was the resident authority on the drugs trade in Peterborough, so Zigic was clearly trying to nail down whether Jordan Radley was involved or not. The possibility was very slight, she imagined, but they had to know for certain.

Ferreira reached across her desk to Murray's, careful not to knock over her pen pot or the framed photographs of her sons, reaching for the Mason jar of chocolate cookies she'd brought in on Monday morning. There were four left and she guessed Colleen wouldn't miss one.

She ate it, reading the rest of the article, the flavour dulling on her tongue as 'Colin' explained that losing his job was the final straw.

I'd tried already. Not long after my wife died. But it didn't work. I wasn't in a good way. I had insomnia, I couldn't eat,

48

I could barely talk. It was like moving through this thick grey fog all the time. We'd spent all our savings on carers because I wasn't going to have her going into a home. At the end there was nothing left. All I had was my job to keep me going. Then that went and I thought, fuck this. What's the point? I saw my mates taking these shitty jobs, getting talked down to, getting abuse off everyone, I had the dole office telling me I had an attitude problem because I didn't want to go and work in some meat-processing place out on the Fens. I wasn't going to live like that. So I tried again. More pills this time. I wasn't messing about. But, I don't know what happened, I panicked, I suppose. Called an ambulance. They pumped my stomach, cleared me out. The doctor asked what happened and I told her I got confused about how many I'd taken. She never questioned that anyone would take forty pills by accident. They don't care. People like us, we're a burden, right? Surplus to requirements and better out of the way. Don't ask questions. Don't offer help. Go home, sort yourself out.

Ferreira exhaled slowly, wondering if these were the same men Jordan Radley was with last night. They seemed too ground down for violence, more likely to damage themselves than anyone else.

She closed the page, found Jordan Radley's Twitter account, began to scan his timeline.

The last tweet he posted – a couple of hours before he died – was a photograph inside the Greenaway Club taken from the back of the room, showing a crowd of men all facing the big screen TV as the football played. Around two dozen men there but he'd framed the shot to make the cavernous room seem smaller and more intimate, the gathering larger than it really was. She saw Bruce Humble standing near the screen, face in profile, mouth open as the shutter clicked.

With the lads at the @greenawaywmc #coys

Further back and there were more tweets mentioning the place, more photographs of darts matches and pool games, but mostly it was his own work he was pushing. The article in the *Big Issue* had got good engagement, plenty of likes and retweets, but when she opened up the replies, she saw the predictable mix of support and ire.

Comments about the men needing to pull themselves together and man up. Jokes about suicide, people saying they should be happy they'd got jobs, they didn't know how lucky they were. A few were gloating that they should have known this would happen when they voted Brexit. Who did they think would end up doing those menial jobs when the immigrants were sent back?

But it was mostly support. Links to charities for male mental health and the Samaritans, groups working to help older men get back into work. A few journalists from northern newspapers commending the piece and Jordan for getting the word out about the problems of underemployment and precarious labour. He thanked every one of them, didn't engage with the trolls.

Interspersed with his own work were links to other articles on similar subjects and she saw his politics emerging and how his interests were projected to the world: community centres closing and libraries under threat, articles in the *ET* about proposed new developments and funds promised to upskill working-class kids, good-news pieces on green spaces and cycleways and arts events in the city.

There was very little personal stuff on there and she wondered if he was curating his image with one eye on his career, saving his private life for less public channels. The only non-work tweets were photographs he'd taken around Peterborough: details of old buildings hashtagged #lookup, sunrises over the River Nene and street vendors on Cathedral Square, exhibitions at the museum on Priestgate and an evening he'd spent at the Key Theatre watching a live stream of a play from the West End.

Anyone looking to hire him would be happy with what they saw, she thought.

Back to early autumn now and she stopped at a flurry of tweets directed to the university, the chancellor cc'd in as well as a lecturer called Simon Unger. There were photographs of a gathering at a pub near the campus on Oundle Road, links to a piece from the *Guardian*, another from a Berlin newspaper about the same subject.

Ferreira swore, pushing away from her desk, and went into Zigic's office.

'I think we need to go to the uni,' she said.

'Why?'

She started to explain and he was on his feet before she'd told him half the story, a fierce look in his eye as he charged out of his office.

CHAPTER EIGHT

Peterborough University's main campus sat behind a broad green on Oundle Road. The building's original brutalist façade had been reworked into something more contemporary, covered in bright cladding and with a striking canopy extending over the entrance. It was the building they put on the prospectus, the one that dominated the website, but the journalism department wasn't housed there and Zigic wondered how the students felt once they found out they were actually going to study in an ugly orange-brick office block at the edge of the city centre.

Inside it had a grimly institutional air that extended to the poky office Simon Unger led them to on the third floor. Its white walls were covered in posters and notices, mocked-up front pages and a few framed articles from his own days as a reporter, Zigic noticed as he went to take a seat in front of Unger's cluttered desk. It had the feel of an old hack's domain, a relic from an era when things still needed to be on paper to be real.

Unger was that generation. Fifty-something, with small eyes behind large tortoiseshell glasses, a long, sallow face that he rubbed absently as he worked through his shock at Jordan Radley's death, the usual response of someone who knew a murder victim but wasn't particularly close to them, the platitudes and disbelief all couched in the language of a newspaper report. The man must think in sound bites, Zigic thought, as he watched him push his fingers back through his greying blond hair, leaving it standing tufted on his head.

'Such a waste,' Unger said finally. 'Most of the students I have to deal with want to be lifestyle writers or entertainment journalists; they think they're going to have this ridiculous life jetting off around the world interviewing celebrities. But Jordan had somehow got this notion that journalism could actually change things. God knows where a boy his age picked up an idea like that.' Unger smiled faintly. 'I kept trying to bring him back down to earth. A lot of the job with kids like Jordan is getting them to understand that investigative journalism is expensive and time-consuming, and the way the media landscape is now there's virtually no market for it. You're competing with every other stupid thing on people's phones and their phones are reprogramming their brains so they can only think in short snatches. Long form is niche. It's niche *within* niche.'

'And then he went and got an article published,' Zigic said.

Unger chuckled. 'Yep, that undermined my warnings somewhat. The really good ones are always only going to do what they want. Jordan was like that. Great instincts, sharp eye for detail and empathy. You can teach a lot of things, you can show people the tricks, but genuine empathy is what elevates stories.'

'What was Jordan working on when he died?' Ferreira asked.

'For me or for himself?'

'Both.'

Unger frowned. 'I don't know what he was working on independently.'

'Wouldn't he discuss that with you?'

'Rule one is you protect the story until it's ready to go,' he said. 'Jordan had just had his first national piece published, and whatever he was working on away from here, my guess is he was aiming high with it. He felt like he was building momentum at the *ET*, then the *Big Issue* comes along, so if he was working on something – which I'm sure he was – it would be something he hoped would look impressive on his CV.'

'And what about his degree work?' Zigic asked.

'Well …' Unger knitted his fingers together across his stomach. 'The last project I set them was an investigative piece about the effects of austerity in Peterborough. They were working in groups of three but Jordan did most of it, I think.'

'Why do you think that?'

'The piece his group turned in was about the slashing of the budget for day centres for adults with learning disabilities. That was pure Jordan.' Unger's face twisted. 'Robyn wants to be a travel writer and Harry thinks he's going to be a sports reporter, so I doubt they contributed much.'

'Would this be Harry Bracewell?' Zigic asked.

Unger stiffened slightly in his seat, then nodded.

'And why would you set Jordan and Harry a task together given what happened?'

Unger shifted his weight, glanced at Ferreira, then back to Zigic, looking more nervous than he should be, Zigic thought. Unless there was more to the story than Ferreira had been able to piece together so far.

'I believe in constructive dialogue,' Unger said carefully. 'And I thought the best way for them to overcome their differences would be to work together on a project. We're too much in our little bubbles. That's why the world's in the mess it is right now. We shut out any dissenting voices that threaten our sense of self. We retreat into the assumed rightness of our individual morality and we become dangerously inflexible.' Some colour had come into his face, excitement in his voice. 'Journalists are supposed to be neutral. You have to approach any story from a neutral position or else you're not a reporter, you're a propagandist.'

'Not much room for propagandising in sports reports,' Ferreira suggested.

He didn't reply, jaw clenching.

She nodded. 'So, Jordan was too inflexible for your liking, not Harry?'

'I thought it could become a problem for him in the long term,' Unger said, back to picking his words. 'He was very set in his politics and they were not moderate.'

'And you thought Harry Bracewell could give him a fresh perspective?'

Unger put a hand up defensively. 'I wanted Jordan to under-stand that just because he didn't agree with a person, it didn't mean he could ignore them and their arguments.'

'And which of Harry Bracewell's arguments did you think Jordan could benefit from listening to?' Ferreira asked icily. 'The one about the great replacement theory or the one that says it's time to deport all second- and third-generation immigrants?'

A queasy look crossed Unger's face and he turned pointedly away from Ferreira, eyes on Zigic now, as if hoping he would prove a more receptive target.

'Harry is very young –'

'So were the Hitler Youth,' Ferreira snapped. 'Harry Bracewell invited a speaker from a banned organisation onto campus and when you were informed you defended his right to express his political beliefs.'

'I believe in free speech,' Unger said defiantly.

'Young Country are a hate group,' Ferreira told him. 'You weren't defending *free* speech, you were defending *hate* speech. At a university with a multicultural student body, you decided to throw your weight behind someone who was bringing in recruiters for a far-right organisation that has been banned in Germany and will likely be banned here very soon.'

'Did you go to their meeting?' Zigic asked him.

There was a calculating look in Unger's eyes and his fingers moved slowly down his tie. Probably trying to remember whether he'd been photographed, who else they might ask, if they suspected this was a factor in Jordan's death and would pursue it far enough to reveal whatever lies he was clearly considering telling.

'I did go along, yes,' he said finally. 'But only because Jordan and some of the other students had raised concerns and I thought it was best that a representative from the university was there to check that things didn't get out of hand.'

'And what would you have considered "out of hand" behaviour to be?' Ferreira was at the edge of her seat. 'Nazi salutes? Desecrating a synagogue?'

His eyes narrowed. 'This is exactly what I'm talking about. If we lose our minds every time someone expresses an opinion we disagree with, we just push them underground. And they fester and multiply in the dark with nobody to hold them to account. I encourage constructive criticism and reasoned debate because that's how you counter dangerous ideologies. You don't no-platform them, you put them on stage and force them to justify their positions.'

'But Young Country weren't taking part in a debate,' Zigic pointed out. 'They were holding a rally in the back room of a pub.'

'Or maybe you held them to account,' Ferreira said. 'Did you challenge them?'

'I was observing,' he said flatly.

Zigic noticed Ferreira slide back in her chair, the admission bringing a hint of a satisfied smile to her face.

'This is ridiculous.' Unger threw his hands up. 'What has any of this got to do with Jordan's murder? It was months ago. Harry and he managed to work together in a perfectly civilised fashion afterwards. There was no hint of trouble between them.'

'Didn't you find that strange?' Ferreira asked. 'Jordan called for Harry and all the other students involved to be expelled from their courses. You don't just forget something like that.'

'Apparently Harry did.'

Zigic glanced at Ferreira, saw her winding up for another go, but he thought Simon Unger had shown them who he was, exactly where his loyalties lay.

'Where can we find Harry Bracewell?' he asked.

'He and Robyn were in the cafeteria about twenty minutes ago,' Unger said, relief in his tone. 'You passed it as you came in.'

Zigic stood up, Unger matching him, coming around the desk to open the office door, as if he wanted to be absolutely sure they were leaving.

Ferreira took her time, lingering by the desk, eyes moving over the surface as she tapped her still-open notebook against her thigh. Unger was watching her, hand tightening around the door handle.

'Is there something else I can help you with?' he asked.

Ferreira turned back to him. 'Yes, where were you last night between 10 and 11 p.m.?'

'Am I a suspect?' he asked incredulously, looking once again to Zigic. 'Are you seriously asking me for an alibi?'

'I seriously am,' Ferreira said. 'Do you have one?'

Unger's shoulders lifted up around his ears defensively. 'Well, I was at home.'

'Alone?'

He folded his arms, shifted his weight between his feet. 'As a matter of fact, yes, I was alone.'

Ferreira made a tutting noise, wrote something in her notebook. 'So you can't account for your whereabouts at the time Jordan Radley was murdered?'

'I've just told you where I was,' Unger said coldly.

Zigic slipped a card out of his pocket and handed it to Unger. 'If you do think of anything that might be helpful ...'

The door slammed the moment they were in the corridor but neither spoke until they were in the stairwell, heading down to the ground floor.

'You don't really think he's a suspect?' Zigic asked.

'No, just messing with the prick.' Ferreira shot him a quick, faint grin, no real pleasure in it now they'd done with Unger. 'But he was at that Young Country meeting for some reason and I don't believe for one second that it was in a professional capacity.'

'Me neither.'

They walked through the deserted reception area towards the café. It was a high-street chain fitted awkwardly into a space not designed for it and Zigic wondered if there was anywhere now beyond the reach of identikit coffee places. How long would it be before the canteen at Thorpe Wood Station was turned into a Starbucks?

'Over there under the shitty painting, that's Bracewell,' Ferreira said. 'Which one do you want to take?'

Zigic saw her face harden, posture straightening and knew who she wanted to speak to.

'I think we'll do this together.'

CHAPTER NINE

'Harry Bracewell?'

Bracewell snapped to his feet, alerted by the officialdom in Zigic's tone. He looked between the two of them, curious but open and as Zigic made the introductions he reached out to shake their hands, firm and measured, meeting Ferreira's eye and giving her a warm smile.

He was around six two, slim and well turned out in jeans and a wool jumper, hair neatly styled, features on the unremarkable side of handsome. He introduced his girlfriend, Robyn Shaw, and she followed his lead, a quick hello, a weaker shake. A petite and pretty blonde with her hair in a fishtail plait, wearing a sweater dress with thick tights and flat ankle boots.

They were the kind of couple older people would look at and think seemed nice. And if it wasn't for what she'd found on Jordan Radley's Twitter page, Ferreira might have thought the same, walking in here. But she knew what he really was. The kind of young man who wanted a united white Europe, gunboats in the Mediterranean and the return of the death penalty, women in the kitchen, men in charge. More dangerous than the previous incarnations, because his organisation had realised that their agenda was better pursued with stealth than force. That youth and an appearance of respectability might succeed where decades of street-fighting football hooligans had failed.

'How can we help you, sir?' Bracewell asked, waiting for them to sit before he did.

A power move or genuine politeness, she wasn't sure.

'One of your fellow students was murdered last night,' Zigic said. 'Jordan Radley.'

Robyn gasped. 'No, poor Jordan.'

Ferreira felt the young woman's eyes on her but kept her attention fixed on Bracewell as he arranged his face into a grave expression.

'I'm very saddened to hear that,' he said, almost sounding like he meant it. The tone right but the words too mannered. 'How did he die?'

'He was shot,' Zigic said.

'Barbaric,' Bracewell muttered, reaching for Robyn's hand and turning towards her. 'Are you okay, darling?'

She nodded, squeezed his hand. 'I'll be alright, I just need a moment.'

'How well did you know Jordan?' Zigic asked.

'Quite well, I suppose,' Bracewell said, rubbing Robyn's knuckles with his thumb as she stared dazed at the tabletop in front of her. 'We'd been on the course together for two and half years or so. We didn't really socialise with him but I always found him quite friendly enough. And we'd worked on a few projects together. Mr Unger understands how important collaborative working practices are so he tends to set rather a lot of group tasks.'

Confident, Ferreira thought. His accent local but educated, probably a Kings school pupil. Just like her and Zigic and whole lot of other immigrant kids. She wondered where exactly Bracewell had gone off the rails. If it started at home or if he'd been radicalised online like so many other extremists before him.

'Jordan had drifted slightly this last term,' Bracewell said. 'I think he was finding it rather difficult to keep up with his peers. Financially, I mean.'

Confident and superior, speaking like a man twice his age.

'Jordan's family weren't particularly well off,' he went on, voice dropping as if he was sharing some terrible secret. 'It's a big problem for students from his socio-economic background. The fees are one thing, everyone expects those, but it isn't until you're actually at university that you realise how important the networking is. You have to put yourself out there and you have to be able to pay your way if you're going to cultivate the right contacts.' He frowned. 'That was obviously an issue for him.'

Ferreira thought of her own university days in Cambridge. Always aware that she didn't quite fit in. Never allowed to forget it by people who sounded just like Harry Bracewell.

This wasn't Cambridge though, even if Bracewell didn't seem to realise that.

She wondered why he wasn't studying somewhere more impressive, where his elocution and his attitude would have been a better fit. If maybe his own socio-economic background was similar to Jordan Radley's and he was trying to hide it.

She knew that Young Country didn't want working-class members. They pulled their ranks from the educated and the affluent, the potential influencers and leaders of the future, people capable of manning the barricades of the culture war they thought they were fighting.

Bracewell was talking about the last project he and Robyn had worked on with Jordan, doing a passable job of sounding concerned about the closure of adult care facilities. Next to him Robyn had pulled herself together and nodded along as he spoke, not interrupting, watching him for cues. A surrendered wife in the making, Ferreira thought.

'The problem with having such a well-sprung safety net is that we've diluted the provision of care for people like that who really need it.' Bracewell looked at Ferreira. 'Don't you agree?'

She ignored the question. 'How did you find working with Jordan?'

'We worked well together,' Bracewell said simply. 'I like to think I'm a team player.'

'Robyn?'

The young woman nodded. 'It was very interesting. I hadn't met people like that before.'

'Like what?'

'Who were suffering so badly,' she said, a little ache in her voice. 'It was very sad.'

Behind them the coffee machine hissed and spat, a young man at the counter flirting loudly with the guy serving him, raising his voice to make sure his compliments reached their intended destination. Bracewell looked towards him, a brief flicker of disgust wrinkling the skin around his nose.

'Was there anyone on campus Jordan didn't get along with?' Zigic asked.

Bracewell knitted his fingers in between Robyn's.

'In the interests of openness I should tell you we had a … disagreement a few months ago.' Bracewell sighed. 'It was what I would call an intellectual divergence.'

Of course you'd call it that, Ferreira thought.

'What was it about?' she asked.

'Jordan was a radical socialist. Virtually a communist.'

He made a vague gesture which Ferreira took to mean 'you know the type', clearly expecting them to be more right than left as members of the police. She wondered if he'd listened to their names as he was introduced. If he thought that Zigic's suggested he'd found a potential ally, given the rise of Young Country in Serbia and Croatia. And what *she* thought would hardly matter.

'I admired his conviction,' Bracewell said affably. 'The greatest problem facing Western Europe at the moment is apathy. Apathy and ignorance. You could at least debate with Jordan.'

'And what did you debate about?' Ferreira asked him.

'We had a disagreement about no-platforming.' Bracewell shrugged. 'I was involved in an off-campus event and Jordan took exception to the speaker. I invited him to come along and engage with our guest, put his challenge to him directly. But instead Jordan launched an attack on me and the other students involved. He attempted to raise an online mob to pressurise the university into banning the event and having me excluded.'

'That sounds like slightly more than a disagreement,' Zigic suggested. 'How did you feel about it?'

'It's only to be expected,' Bracewell said, eyes dropping regretfully for a moment. 'We have a culture of outrage in this country. Especially in universities. Jordan saw something he didn't like and decided to try and use online outrage to make it go away. I wasn't surprised. I wasn't even offended. It's par for the course.'

'That must have made it awkward for you in class,' Ferreira said. 'How did you manage to work together on a project after that?'

Bracewell smiled, giving her the full wattage. 'Like I said, I'm a team player.'

'And you'd won anyway?'

'I will admit that did help. But I wasn't going to rub it in. It's not in my nature.'

They could have pressed it and if she'd been alone she might have done, but Zigic had made it clear they were going to tread lightly in the first instance. Which meant he'd already pegged Bracewell as a suspect.

'You can't think of anyone who might have wanted to harm Jordan?' Zigic asked. 'Any arguments? An ex maybe?'

'Jordan was a bit of an outsider,' Bracewell said. 'I can't imagine he was close enough to anyone for them to want to kill him.'

'And girlfriends?'

'Not that I know of.' Bracewell turned to Robyn. 'Do you know who Jordan was seeing?'

'No, sorry.' She made a regretful face at Zigic. 'I wish I could be more helpful. He was working at the *Evening Telegraph*. Maybe he had friends there.'

Zigic took out a card and handed it to Harry Bracewell, gave another to Robyn. 'If you think of anything else.'

'Of course.' Bracewell slipped the card into the pocket of his mobile phone's case. Robyn held onto hers, flexing it between her fingers.

'And while I have you both,' Zigic said. 'Where were you between ten and eleven last night?'

Bracewell nodded. 'Because Jordan and I had a disagreement.'

'We ask everyone,' Zigic told him. 'Makes it easier to rule them out.'

'The Queens Arms,' Bracewell said. 'They have live music on Monday nights. I can't remember exactly when we arrived but around seven thirty, I think. Then we left around eleven.' He smiled faintly, as if this wasn't quite real to him. 'Plenty of witnesses, Inspector.'

CHAPTER TEN

The offices of the *Evening Telegraph* were quiet when they arrived a little after 2:30 p.m., half a dozen people at their desks, finishing up their final tasks before heading home. Or maybe this was just the day shift, Zigic thought, wondering if a whole new group would arrive later to keep the online edition updated. Moderate all those furious exchanges that happened below the line.

He hardly ever bought the paper now, wasn't sure who did, and there was an air of despondency around the place. The certain knowledge that these jobs were not forever, that the news had changed, become faster and shallower and somehow, inexplicably, less important as the world became more complicated.

It wasn't somewhere he expected an ambitious young man like Jordan Radley to want to be, but it was the only option he supposed. A good thing to have on his CV as he attempted the vertiginous climb from working-class lad in a provincial city to the glittering heights of London and the nationals.

The editor had come down to meet them in reception, already knew Jordan had been killed, briefed by the press officer a couple of hours earlier.

As they passed between the desks, heading for Geri Colman's office, Zigic noticed a copy of the paper sitting on an empty chair, Jordan Radley's face beaming off the front page. Not the image they had on the board back at the station, but instead one lifted from his social media. Smiling and happy, a young man cut down in his prime.

It was what they needed the public to see. His byline photo was serious and maybe even a little stern. This would induce witnesses to come forward, Zigic thought hopefully.

Geri Colman pointed them towards the seats at her desk, went around the other side and flopped down into her own chair. She looked dishevelled from the day, blouse creased at the elbows, auburn hair hanging limp around her full face.

'It's so senseless,' she said, her voice low and husky, full of the cold she'd warned them about when she'd refused to shake their hands. 'Was it a random attack?'

'We don't think so,' Ferreira told her.

'I just can't imagine anyone wanting to kill Jordan. He was such a little sweetheart. Everyone here loved him.' She looked through the glass wall of her office to the newsroom beyond. 'He only came in one day a week, but he'd become part of the team. We're going to miss him.'

'What kind of stories was Jordan working on?' Ferreira asked.

'I gave him a fair degree of freedom,' Colman said, reaching for a packet of cough sweets on her desk and popping one in her mouth. 'A lot of what we're doing these days is jumped-up PR, to be honest with you. I don't have the staff or the budget to go out and investigate properly any more. And even if I did, it isn't what people want to read.' She sighed. 'I don't know what they want any more. Rightmove killed our property pull-out. Tinder killed our personal ads. Fucking Gumtree ... We can't even shift copies to people who've got their wedding photos in because they've got a hundred other shots on Facebook and Instagram and every-where else.'

She sucked loudly on her sweet, the scent of medicated cherries filling the room.

'Jordan wanted to write big stories,' she said, tucking the sweet into her cheek. 'And there are still biggish stories in Peterborough if you're prepared to do the legwork.'

'Had he found one?' Ferreira asked.

'Not yet. Not that he'd tell me about anyway,' Colman said. 'But they're all like that. Like little squirrels, hoarding their leads and their sources.' She smiled affectionately. 'I always know when something's in the offing though. Jordan was excited. He'd gone furtive on me.'

The same they'd heard from his mother. The big story. The one.

Except from what Moira told them, he had no intention of settling for a front page in the *ET* when he finally nailed it down.

'Is there anyone here he might have told about it?' Ferreira asked. 'Someone he might have gone to for advice?'

Colman shook her head. 'They don't work like that. There are only so many good stories and you don't share. Not if you can help it.'

'But Jordan was a newbie. Surely he didn't have the experience or the contacts to put together a big scoop?'

Colman grinned at Ferreira. '"A scoop".'

She smiled back. 'Okay. But you know what I mean. It must take years to build up contacts. Jordan must have needed some help.'

'If he did he never asked for it.' Colman looked thoughtful. 'I got the impression he thought asking for help was cheating. You see that with the young ones when they come in. Think they have to do it all themselves. It's arrogance, I guess. Arrogance of youth, all that.'

'Was Jordan arrogant?' Zigic asked, thinking of what Simon Unger had said about him, not sure how much he believed the lecturer's version of Jordan Radley now.

'He was *confident*,' Colman said. 'But it was justified and it wasn't … unattractive. He had a way with him. People liked him immediately. They didn't even know why. That's how you get stories. Being able to make people open up and talk to you. Instant connection.'

'And had he made any special connections here?'

'A girlfriend you mean?' She shook her head. 'Jordan was the youngest here by ten years.'

'We've heard he appreciated the older woman,' Zigic told her.

'If only I'd known.' Colman laughed throatily, subsided into a sigh and a sad smile. 'Joking, Inspector. I'm older than his mother I imagine. How's she coping? I was thinking I should go around and see her.'

'Maybe wait a couple of days,' Ferreira suggested. 'She's not doing great.'

'I can imagine.' Colman shuddered. 'God, my girls … I wouldn't be able to take it.'

On the desk her phone began to ring and she ignored it, the sound an insistent trilling she kept talking over.

'Shooting though, that's hardly the expected thing, is it? Sounds targeted.' There was a shrewd look in her eye and Zigic reminded himself that she wasn't just the editor of a slowly failing local daily, she would be stringing for the nationals and anything he let on beyond what the press officer had already shared might end up quoted anywhere. 'Did you find the gun?'

'You know we can't discuss operational matters,' Zigic told her. 'We'll keep you updated, but for now I need you to help us. Had Jordan mentioned being threatened by anyone?'

Colman shook her head. 'Nothing beyond the usual crap on social media. All my people get that. I tell them to ignore it.' She shrugged. 'What other option do we have?'

'You could report it,' Ferreira suggested. 'We can take action if the threats are serious enough.'

Colman snorted. 'If you investigated every time someone threatened to burn our offices down, you'd never close another case. Christ, even my football guy gets death threats if he doesn't cover the latest POSH game with the proper degree of respect. They're headcases, Sergeant. Nothing better to do than tell people who don't know they exist what they think of them.'

Zigic didn't like how dismissive she was about it. Wondered why she couldn't conceive of the threats as anything more than a nuisance.

'Jordan has been shot,' he reminded her. 'And if he's been the target of persistent and credible threats, we need to find who was behind them.'

'Did he mention anyone in particular who'd got to him?' Ferreira asked.

'No,' Colman said, vaguely chastened-looking. 'It's different for that generation. They live online. He didn't even mention getting crap, I only know he did because I follow him on Twitter and I see some of the reactions to his pieces. But if there was a serious problem I think he would have told me.'

Zigic wasn't so sure. The impression he was building up of Jordan Radley was of a self-contained young man who compartmentalised his life. His mother not knowing about his girlfriend, his lecturer not knowing what he was working on, his editor unaware too. He was wondering if anyone would be able to tell them what Jordan had been doing in the weeks before he died. Show them a route that led to credible suspects.

'We need to have a look at his desk,' Zigic said. 'And we'd like to have a quick chat to your staff while we're here.'

Colman stood up. 'Of course.'

They followed her back into the newsroom, heads cocking as they passed, everyone aware who they were. Zigic recognised faces from press briefings, knew a couple of the people by name but wouldn't call them acquaintances. Twenty years ago, when he was starting out, coppers and hacks all drank together in the same pub, swapping war stories and sharing information, sometimes deliberately leaking information at their superior's behest, more often letting something slip after they'd been bought a few rounds. It had always been a strained relationship, covertly adversarial, unpleasantly symbiotic.

But times had changed. As the paper's circulation shrank the information they could provide became less and less valuable. The post-work pub culture was falling away too. Drinks too expensive, shifts too long, people actually wanting to get home to their families in a way the previous generation hadn't. Now the press officer did the dirty work and everyone knew where they stood.

Jordan Radley's desk was tucked away against a thick pillar at the centre of the room, a small flat-screen TV hung there, silently showing rolling news. His desk was as ominously tidy as the one in his bedroom. No framed photos or homely touches, unlike the desk next to his, which was scattered with small clusters of crystals and a white china Buddha. Nobody at it but the computer screen was showing a half-written interview with a comedian who was apparently playing the Cresset at the weekend. Nina Keyes on the byline.

'I'll go do the questions,' Ferreira said quietly.

He sat down in Jordan's chair, three drawers to his right, three open shelves to his left. The shelves contained nothing but old editions of the *ET*, unused notepads and printer paper still wrapped. The top drawer was all stationery, the second was empty and the third full of chocolate bars and a copy of the October edition of *Vogue*.

'That's mine, sorry,' a woman said, sliding into the seat next to him, a mug of steaming coffee in her hand. 'I kind of overflowed my storage and Jordan didn't leave his stuff here so he let me have his drawers as well.'

'When was the last time you talked to Jordan?' he asked.

'Monday,' Nina said, blinking rapidly. 'Yesterday. It doesn't seem possible that he was here twenty-four hours ago and now he's dead.'

She didn't seem particularly cut up about it but the news had circulated before they arrived and Zigic supposed the worst of the shock had passed for Jordan's colleagues. And maybe Geri Colman had slightly overstated his presence in the newsroom. How close could you get to anyone coming in one day a week? And only for a couple of months at that.

'How did he seem to you?'

'Normal.' Nina shrugged, taking a Twix out of the drawer. 'He asked about my weekend, I told him about the show I'd been to. I asked what he'd been up to and he said he'd been working. He has another job. Waiting tables.'

Across the room Zigic saw Ferreira standing talking to an older man with sandy hair and a slight paunch.

'What was Jordan working on?' he asked.

'Something about a proposed expansion of cycleways,' Nina said. 'It's in today's edition if you want to read it.'

Not something that would get Jordan murdered, Zigic thought. Although it would probably attract complaints given the anger a certain subset of motorists seemed able to raise about anything related to cyclists.

'How about otherwise? Did Jordan tell you about the big story he was investigating?'

She shook her head.

'Geri mentioned that he might have been getting threats about his articles,' Zigic said. 'Do you know about that?'

Nina rolled her eyes. 'You'd be amazed what we get hassle about.' She turned back to her computer, went into her emails. 'Listen to this. "Your review of the Black Horse at Elton was disgusting. Fifty pounds for dinner! Stop writing about places for all the bloody London commuters and try thinking about us locals. You don't live in the real world, you privileged bitch."'

She frowned. 'See, there's literally nothing you could write that somebody won't complain about.'

But Zigic was looking at the message still. 'Is that your private email account?'

'No, it's my *ET* one,' she said. 'We have to put them at the bottom of the articles so people can get in touch and give us feedback.'

Zigic called over Geri Colman, rising as she approached. 'We need access to Jordan's work email. Can you open that up for me?'

Colman's brow furrowed. 'I can't, no. It's password protected. But I can call in our IT bloke and have him sort it out.'

'Could you, please.'

'He isn't in the building,' Colman said. 'We can't afford permanent IT support, he's freelance.' Her phone was in her hand. 'Let me call him and see how quickly he can get over here.'

Zigic thanked her, thanked Nina Keyes for her help and moved onto the next run of desks, asking the same questions of the man who did the sports coverage and the woman who did the births, deaths and marriages, but found that neither of them knew Jordan Radley well enough to have been confided in. Ferreira was still talking to the guy with the paunch and when he went over to them, the man was in the middle of explaining how Jordan Radley had taken over the city council coverage after another staff member retired.

'It's deadly boring stuff,' he said, shoving his hands into his pockets. 'I was on it for a while and I don't think I got a single worthwhile story from it in six months.' He looked at Zigic. 'The problem is they don't decide anything in the public meetings, you know? It's all fixed way before it gets anywhere near the public domain. Meetings in restaurants and quiet backhanders on the golf course. I tried telling Jordan that but ... well, he was a kid, wasn't he? Didn't know how the world worked yet.' He shrugged. 'Another idealist. We get them now and again. In here playing at Woodward and Bernstein.'

'He obviously saw something there to keep him at it,' Ferreira suggested.

The man glanced away towards Geri Colman, standing at the window on her phone – 'Well, when *can* you fit us in?'

'The real problem,' the man said, lowering his voice, 'is the advertising revenue. We're on the bones of our arse here and the only thing keeping the printing press running is the ad space we sell to local developers. Geri isn't about start running any stories that might piss them off.'

Geri Colman started towards them and the man slipped back to his desk.

'We're looking at later on this afternoon,' she said. 'He's on another job but he's promised me he'll be over before close of business at five. Sorry, but that's the best I can do.'

'We appreciate your help,' Zigic said. 'I'll send someone over once your man's been in.'

With Jordan Radley's tech stolen from his home, this might be the only window onto his professional life they had. He prayed that there would be something useful in the emails on the *ET*'s system.

CHAPTER ELEVEN

'So I've just been up to Anti-Terror,' Ferreira said, coming into his office and closing the door behind her. 'Had a chat with Amit. They're aware of Harry Bracewell. Apparently they weren't until it all kicked off at the uni and Jordan flagged up the Young Country rally but they've been keeping an eye on him since then.'

'And?' Zigic asked.

'And he's exactly what he looks like, an aspiring player who's trying to worm his way inside by recruiting on campus.' Ferreira sat down opposite him. 'Young Country started a big push into academia here at the beginning of term. Public schools, universities. Utilised members they'd attracted via private online forums. Vetted them in person then brought them closer by promising to send speakers to the most promising locations.'

'Peterborough being promising?'

'We're a multicultural city,' she said archly. 'Of course we're a promising target for the far right.' Disgust flashed across her face momentarily. 'We've already got one martyr for them to rally around, haven't we?'

She hadn't mentioned it for so long Zigic had hoped she'd somehow managed to put it aside. But he supposed that was always going to be impossible with the scars that remained on her body. A neo-Nazi vigilante they'd finally run down to a basement bomb factory, catching him with an explosives vest already strapped to his body. Ferreira had seen it a split second before he did. Pushed him out of the way and taken the force of the blast as she turned to run. Weeks in hospital, months in physical therapy, years since then and new traumas to supplant it but this one went deep with her.

71

'Bracewell's getting more central to the UK set-up,' she said. 'Amit reckons the threatened no-platforming at the uni created a lot of attention and they thrive on spectacle.'

'But is he dangerous?' Zigic asked and immediately realised his mistake. 'I know he's dangerous. I mean, is he someone who could get hold of a gun and shoot Jordan Radley?'

'Young Country is committed to change by stealth. Ostensibly they're anti-violence. But they're running training camps, and weapons are part of it apparently.' She drew her fingers back through her hair. 'There's already chat in their less exclusive private forums about Jordan's death.'

'Saying what?'

'Surprisingly, they're more concerned about how this is going to affect their image than anything else,' she said. 'There's talk of an upcoming profile in some men's mag and they're worried this will make them too hot to cover.'

Zigic swore. 'Is that where we are now? Neo-Nazi fashions spreads?'

'Apparently so,' she said. 'And they're called nipsters. Nazi hipsters.'

'Fucking hell.'

'Yeah.' She leaned back in the chair, looking weary. 'What are you doing?'

'Preliminary forensics have just come in,' he told her, trying to shake off the misanthropic torpor he felt threatening to descend after her debriefing. 'Not much to go on unfortunately but Kate's flagged one interesting thing.'

'What's that?'

'Jordan was shot with a converted replica.'

Ferreira straightened up sharply. 'That changes things, then.'

'I don't know,' he said, still trying to work it through himself. 'Buying an illegal handgun is a matter of having the right contacts but converted replicas generally come from dealers too, don't they?'

'There's videos on YouTube showing you how to convert a replica.'

'But you have to be capable of doing it,' he pointed out.

'How hard do you think it is?'

'It can't be that easy or we'd see people getting shot with them every other day.'

She didn't seem convinced. 'This opens up the possibility of it being something more personal.'

'His tech was stolen,' he reminded her.

'And if you wanted him dead for a personal reason entirely unconnected to his work, wouldn't going in and stealing his laptop and stuff muddy the waters?'

She was right. A smart killer might take that route. But was Jordan's murderer that smart? He'd been shot on the side of a relatively busy road, albeit at a quieter time of night. Anyone could have seen it happen.

Murders were occasionally made to look like robberies, a cheap attempt to throw them off the scent. But in that case Jordan's wallet would have been the obvious bit of misdirection. Not taking his keys and going to his house.

'The killer needed to know where he lived,' Zigic said, saying it out loud to understand the logic. 'And they would have needed to know his mother was working nights and not at home.'

'You're assuming they wouldn't have gone through her as well,' Ferreira said darkly. 'Did forensics get anything from the bullet?'

'No prints,' he said. 'And there's no rifling because it's a conversion. So even if we found it we wouldn't be able to definitively tie the weapon to the crime.'

'If we find a converted replica in someone's house, I think that'll be compelling enough for a jury.'

Zigic seriously doubted that the killer would have kept hold of the gun.

He ran through the rest of the findings with her. The lack of trace evidence on Jordan's body, just the chalk on his hems and ankles from the gloves the killer had worn, the same compound used by a manufacturer who supplied generic products to a dozen different supermarkets and DIY stores, no route for them there.

'Anything at the scene?' she asked.

'It's a high traffic area,' he said, with a shrug. 'Keri's working her way through the CCTV on London Road but the cameras don't cover the paths as well as we need them to, so if the killer went there on foot we're relying on a witness.'

'What about cars passing during the time frame?' Ferreira asked.

'She's made a list. We're looking at twenty-six vehicles in a five-minute stretch around the time the nearest houses report hearing gunshots.'

'That's not many.'

'Half ten on a Monday night,' he said. 'End of the month. Who's got money to be going out then?' Through the internal window he could see Keri Bloom concentrating on her computer screen, already tracking down the owners of those twenty-six vehicles. 'You'd have thought if they saw someone getting shot, they'd have come forward already.'

'People don't. You know that.'

'We'll go to them, then.'

Ferreira stood up. 'What do you want to do about Bracewell?'

'Check out his alibi. See about getting CCTV from the Queens Arms if they have it.'

'You do realise that he might be involved without actually being the person who pulled the trigger,' she said as she opened the door. 'We're not looking at one arsehole with a grudge against Jordan here. He's part of a terror network.'

'I know, Mel. I understand how serious this is.'

As she went out, DCI Billy Adams came in, the briefest touch to the small of her back as they passed in the doorway, and Zigic noticed that she didn't stiffen when he did that at work any more. It had been a tough adjustment for her, he thought, and if Adams was a better sort of man, he would have respected her desire to separate their home life and their professional life, but Zigic suspected he couldn't help himself.

Adams looked tired, with dark shadows under his eyes and sickly pallor to his skin. There was an uncharacteristic weight hanging around his shoulders. More than a year since he'd dragged Zigic into an off-book investigation that had put them on the wrong side of DCS Riggott, threatened both of their careers and taken them into territory that could have seen them

74

both locked up. The punishment Riggott doled out had been both subtle and harsh. He'd left Zigic untouched, but hit Adams – his former protégé – where it hurt most: confining him to his office, laying endless strategic tasks on him to make sure he rarely made it out into the field.

Now he haunted the office. Waiting for Riggott to retire and be replaced by someone who might let him loose again.

He leaned against the internal window, hands in his pockets. 'Alright, Ziggy, where are you at with the Radley murder?'

There was a report mostly written on his computer and he almost told Adams that he would have to wait for it, but it felt petty to shut him out.

'We're struggling slightly without his phone,' Zigic admitted. 'But things are starting to become a bit clearer.'

He explained about the trouble on campus, Harry Bracewell's far right connections, the Greenaway Club and the men there who Zigic didn't think were suspects but couldn't quite disregard yet. The break-in. The girlfriend. The infuriating hints towards a 'big story' Jordan was working on but which they couldn't seem to crack.

'Have you talked to Radley's contact at the *Big Issue?*' Adams asked. 'If he was working on something major and looking to place it, stands to reason he'd start with contacts he already had.'

Zigic nodded, thinking it wasn't a bad idea. 'We'll do that.'

'I was just looking over Kate's report,' Adams said, crossing his arms. 'What's your thinking on the converted replica?'

'Right now I'm more concerned about identifying a motive,' Zigic said, feeling the familiar stirring of irritation that always emerged when he was called on to justify his investigative techniques to Adams. 'That seems a better use of time than trying to track down a gun that's designed to be untraceable.'

Colleen Murray called across the office, 'Boss, got something.'

Adams turned sharply. 'What's up, Col?'

She looked awkward as she came into the office, apologetically gesturing towards Zigic. The skin around Adams's eyes tightened in a flinch he wasn't quick enough to hide; the sting of being

75

reminded that Colleen wasn't his right hand any more. That he didn't need one in his new position.

'Jordan's mum just rung me,' Murray said, positioning herself to include Adams. An act of politeness tinged with pity. 'Sounds like we might have Jordan's laptop after all.'

'How?'

'She reckons the one that was taken in the break-in was a temporary loan. Some old thing his auntie lent him,' Murray smiled triumphantly, 'while Jordan's was in the shop.'

Zigic stood up, feeling a surge of energy running through him.

'Why's it in the shop?' Adams looked dubious. 'What's wrong with it?'

'Our tech guys can figure that out,' Zigic said, refusing to let him dampen this moment of progress. 'Call around and see if you can track it down, Col.'

She sketched a salute at him. 'On it.'

'Looks like you got lucky,' Adams said, drifting towards the door after her. 'Again.'

Zigic held down the comment he wanted to make, let the snipe go. If it had been the other way around and Riggott had cut him down, leaving Adams unscathed, he'd probably be bitter too.

But that was the risk that came with being the favourite. When you fell from grace the drop could be fatal.

CHAPTER TWELVE

Ferreira stood at the window, looking down onto the station's front steps where Zigic was giving a statement to the press. He looked awkward, even from behind, and she knew how much he hated doing this, how his customary quiet confidence tended to desert him under the arc lights. To his credit he'd never tried to delegate the responsibility and she was grateful for that.

Zigic was hoping this appearance would bring out the witnesses they'd so far failed to identify. Jordan Radley was a sympathetic victim, the photograph the press officer had chosen showing him smiling and inoffensive-looking. They'd spent ten minutes discussing the choice and Ferreira hadn't agreed, wanted to use his byline because she thought it was more representative.

'Smart people are unsympathetic,' the press officer said matter-of-factly. 'And journalists are hardly the most popular of people right now.'

Ferreira went back to Jordan Radley's board, started to add the findings from the post-mortem.

Jordan had been in good health, no sign of previous violence on his body.

Two gunshots; centre of the back and back of the head. The first would have been fatal within minutes, but his killer hadn't wanted to risk survival.

It was an execution, she thought, stepping back from the board so she could take it all in together.

Logically she knew they were into the territory of diminishing returns right now. That gone six o'clock it would be better for everyone to go home, eat something, get some rest and return here bright and early, minds sharpened and ready.

But it was difficult to walk away in the first twenty-four hours. Especially when you didn't feel like you'd made enough progress.

With some cases the first day yielded more information than you could easily cope with, filling the suspects columns and bringing to light multiple persons of interest, a mess of conflicting witnesses and potential motives and a tangle of infuriating cross-currents you'd spend the next week or month or sometimes even longer, painstakingly unpicking. And when they were in the thick of a case like that, she always yearned for simplicity.

This was not going to be one of those cases, she was beginning to suspect.

Twenty hours on from Jordan's murder and their investigation already felt like one destined to be dominated by absences.

No weapon. No witnesses. No clear motive yet.

The staff at the *ET* were professional acquaintances rather than friends and she expected it to be the same situation with the men at the Greenaway Club. Couldn't imagine him having genuinely bonded with anyone thirty years older than himself.

With a few hours to get over the initial shock, his mother had been able to give them a list of friends he'd mentioned from uni and from his job waiting tables at the Old Mill, but she didn't have phone numbers or surnames so that was going to take longer than usual to follow up.

They still needed to speak to the girlfriend, Ferreira realised, cursing herself for letting it slip her mind. She would stop on the way home from work.

Murray had tracked down Jordan's missing laptop at least, but that wasn't quite the breakthrough they'd hoped it to be. The tech department had it now, along with a note from the repair guys at the shop, warning that it was completely knackered. The tech guys were confident they could recover Jordan's files but couldn't promise what state they'd be in.

The emails from the *ET* hadn't arrived yet either. At five they'd had an apologetic call from Jordan's editor, saying her IT chap hadn't been able to make it, but that he had promised he would be there first thing tomorrow morning.

Not long after that, Jordan's other editor, from the *Big Issue*, returned Zigic's call, equally apologetic, no idea what Jordan was working on. He'd told Jordan to stay in touch after his first article, offered advice and help with contacts that Jordan had never taken him up on. The same story they'd heard from Geri Colman at the *ET*, Jordan wanting to do it all by himself.

Zigic came back into the office, digging his thumb into the knot of his tie.

'Okay, quick debrief,' he said, approaching the board. 'Rob, anything in Jordan's financials?'

Weller jerked away from his computer, almost knocking over the can of Red Bull set next to his keyboard.

'No sign of anything suspicious yet, sir,' he said. 'He's predictable. Wages in from the Old Mill, money out to his mum. For rent I guess. He doesn't have enough disposable income to get up to much he shouldn't. No large amounts of cash in or out. I don't know how he was living to be honest. Can't have been having much fun.' He swivelled slightly in his chair. 'The only thing I can see that's out of his routine is a payment to the Trainline site on November 16th.'

'Do we know where he was going?' Zigic asked, a stirring of interest in his voice.

'Can't tell from his bank statement,' Weller told him. 'We'll need to find the ticket or the confirmation messages.'

'Or ask his mum,' Murray suggested.

'What about his mother?' Zigic asked Weller.

'Same story. They're both in their overdrafts for about half the month. Looks like they're struggling. But ...'

'Who isn't,' Parr interjected. 'He's interning at the *ET*, right?'

'No sign of a wage from there,' Weller said. 'Must have been an intern.'

Ferreira had assumed he was on the payroll but it made sense. Not even finished his degree. Only going into the office one day a week. They would get whatever they could out of him, explain how good it would look on his CV, keep him on until he got a better offer or realised he was worth more than mere 'exposure'.

Zigic nodded, immediately dismissing the idea of a financial component to Jordan's murder. 'What about his phone records?'

'Still waiting,' Weller said. 'But we've got his laptop now, that's where the interesting stuff's going to be, right?'

Zigic gestured at Bloom. 'Keri, what about the drivers you've pulled from CCTV on London Road?'

'I've managed to speak to a few of them but I don't have anything to report yet. Sorry.' She frowned as if it was her fault people had seen nothing. 'I've left messages with the others so we might get lucky.'

Zigic rolled his tie up and tucked it into his jacket pocket.

'Zac, the men from the Greenaway Club?'

Parr scratched his head. 'I've not done them all yet but we've got a few hits. It's mostly petty stuff: drink-driving, speeding, possession. Old convictions by and large. One of them did a few years for actual bodily harm back in the late nineties, got into a fight with a taxi driver, broke his jaw. The last year or so he's been cautioned a few times for aggressive begging, shoplifting. He's no fixed abode.'

'Who?'

'Daniel McLeary,' Parr said, reading from the sheet on his desk. 'Then we've got Steve Gurney. Lot of fighting in his twenties but he goes respectable until 2008 when we've got an altercation with a bloke over a parking space. Gurney knocked a couple of the bloke's teeth out. Suspended sentence because it was six of one, half a dozen of the other.' He flipped to another sheet. 'The most recent conviction among them is Lionel Ridgeon. Bit of an odd one, this. He was done for harassing a neighbour back in early 2017, fairly minor stuff to begin with. Came off the back of some noise complaints he'd made about the neighbour playing loud music at all hours. Eventually he seems to have cracked and cut off the neighbour's electric supply.'

'Were they at the Club last night?' Ferreira asked.

'Both of them, yeah.' Parr nodded. 'But we've got them in trouble more recently as well. There's a whole cluster of offences in 2015 after the factory closed down. Harassment, criminal damage, trespass, assault.'

'Busy boys,' Weller muttered.

Parr slid the piece of paper closer to himself. 'You'll remember this, Col.'

Murray looked momentarily perplexed. 'Oh, yeah. All that shit with the owners?'

Ferreira glanced at Zigic, saw he was just as confused as she was. But they'd still been in Hate Crimes in 2015, removed from the day-to-day activities down here, remote from what was happening in the parts of Peterborough where the men who worked at the Greenaway factory lived. She remembered the closure of the factory, protests at the gates, placards and angry faces. Had no idea charges were ever brought against the men.

The same men Jordan had interviewed for the *Big Issue*. On the scrapheap, struggling with the new reality they found themselves living in.

'It got pretty nasty,' Parr said gravely. 'They were over at the boss's place scaring his wife and kids. Smashed his car up. Went after the solicitors who did the deal for him. Graffitied their office.'

'What was the assault charge for?' Zigic asked.

'McLeary had a run-in with one of the security guards at the site.'

'All their stuff was still inside,' Murray said. 'The men wanted to get back in and collect it but they were barred entry. The firm put private security on the gates and they got heavy-handed.'

Ferreira heard the sympathy in her voice, the disgust in Parr's; made a note to bear their personal opinions in mind when they went to speak to these men.

'So, who was involved in all this?' she asked.

'The ringleader was Bruce Humble,' Parr said.

The amenable manager of the Greenaway Club. Helpful but guarded, she'd thought as they sat in his office, and now she knew why. He wouldn't be a fan of the police. Would have sat there balancing his personal dislike for them against his desire to see Jordan's killer caught.

Or, she realised, was he thinking about what would happen when they ran the list of names he gave them through the system? Already worried about how it would come back on him.

Ferreira went over to the board and picked up a marker pen. 'Who else?'

'Steve Gurney,' Parr said, reading from the sheet. 'Richard Caxton, Gary Walker, Peter Lynch, Lionel Ridgeon, Salvatore Graziano, Daniel McLeary.'

The board filling up suddenly.

'According to the list you gave me, they were all at the Club last night,' Parr said. 'So they've obviously stayed close.'

'Who was lead on this?' Zigic asked.

'Sawyer,' Murray told him.

A brief moment of uncomfortable silence, eyes dropping, feet shuffling.

DI Carol Sawyer, who had gone off sick at the end of 2015 and never returned. The cancer which was supposed to be in remission reasserting its presence with a swiftness nobody saw coming.

'Sawyer was lead,' Murray said, giving him a pointed look. 'But Riggott was keeping a very close eye on it all.'

CHAPTER THIRTEEN

Zigic met Greta Kitson in the corridor as he was heading for Riggott's office. She looked tired out, the case she was working obviously weighing heavily on her. One woman dead, two more suffering from serious infections arising from Botox treatments procured at a local beauty parlour run out of a converted garage. Nobody on the staff trained for the job, the chemicals they were using bought online from a supplier in Hungary who was denying any responsibility.

The press were circling, just the kind of story they loved. Vanity punished, before and after photos to really ram the horror home. The dead woman's family were calling for action, demanding the parlour's owner be dragged back to Peterborough from wherever in Europe she was currently lying low, having disappeared mere hours after Kitson and DC Lear visited her home. Kitson was taking the heat for not arresting her immediately, even though the full extent of the woman's guilt wasn't known at the time.

Extra pressure from Riggott was the last thing she needed.

'What kind of mood is he in?' Zigic asked in an undertone.

'I've soaked up the worst of it,' Kitson whispered. 'You want to get in there before he recharges.'

The door was open but Zigic knocked anyway.

'Don't stand on ceremony,' Riggott said. 'I'm not the fucking pope.'

He was pulling his suit jacket on, standing at the centre of the office, the only thing in it that still looked the same. Riggott had cleared out months ago in readiness for retirement, stripped the photos off the walls, the professional trappings he'd gathered over three decades packed up and sent home or thrown away.

Then the woman who had been due to take the job had resigned suddenly from the force for reasons unspecified and so the boss remained. Even the family photos were gone from his desk, Zigic noted again, and he wondered why Riggott hadn't at least kept them during this strange in-between period as he waited for a replacement to arrive.

Zigic moved to sit down, stopped when Riggott put his hand up.

'Let's away to the pub, I've had a bollockful of this place today.'

It was the last thing Zigic wanted to do at the end of a long shift. It was pushing seven now and he knew Anna and the kids would have eaten without him but still he'd rather be at home with them than staring down a session with his boss. Riggott was getting sentimental as the end approached, wanting to talk over old glories, rehash the wins of his career in his better moods, bitterly regret the failures as the drink got hold of him. Neither option was much fun for his audience.

Zigic reluctantly drove out of the station car park behind Riggott, followed him along the parkway and towards Ailsworth, hoping they were actually going to a pub. For a moment he had a terrible feeling Riggott was going to keep driving until he reached Zigic's house at the edge of the village, invite himself in and settle down there for the evening.

Zigic breathed a sigh of relief when he pulled off the road outside the Prince of Wales.

Inside, the post-work crowd had thinned out already and it was mostly regulars in, sitting at the bar not talking. A couple were eating dinner, a suited man working on his laptop at another table. A fire was burning in the inglenook, Sky Sports News muted on the big screen, music playing low.

'Sit yourself down, Ziggy, I'll get these.'

Zigic went to an out-of-the-way table, the heat from the open fire barely reaching him, a thin draught cutting in around the old metal windows. He texted Anna to warn her that he'd be even later than he'd expected to be last time he texted.

Riggott came over, already looking more chipper than Zigic would have liked. As if this wasn't work. Whiskey for himself, vodka for Zigic, both doubles.

He was going to be walking home, he realised.

'Nice wee pub this,' Riggott said. 'Used to drink down the road at the Oak when we were living in Sutton.'

Zigic nodded, wanting to get to business but knowing he couldn't launch straight into it. He listened as Riggott talked about the pub where he lived now, good menu but no atmosphere, the locals didn't use it much, and there were always gangs of walkers in, dressed up like toddlers with their wind-slapped faces and their muddy hiking boots.

'You see the mad bastards skipping through the village like the von Trapps.' He sipped his whiskey. '*Singing*. You believe that? I blame fucking *Countryfile*.'

'We get a few here,' Zigic said, just for something to say.

'Sure, it's no way to spend your retirement that.' Riggott loosened his tie, leaning back in the creaky wooden chair. 'Work your whole life then spend the end of it pissing behind bushes and stomping through cow shit.'

Zigic smiled faintly. 'You won't be taking up hiking then?'

'Golf, bar, death, that's my retirement plan.' Said in a joking tone but his face serious. 'You ever think about what you'll do when you're out?'

He did think about it, more so as the years went by and fifty started to become a number he couldn't ignore any more.

'Get an allotment,' Zigic said. 'Learn to make beer. Read *The Iliad* finally.'

'The horse did it,' Riggott told him. 'Saved you a job there.'

'Thanks.'

Riggott raised his glass and took another drink. Zigic swirled around his vodka, the smell of it metallic and the taste flat.

'Typical I don't get a peaceful send-off,' Riggott said. 'Fucking city awash with dodgy Botox and then you go and bring me a murdered journalist. You and Greta are going to put me in the ground between the pair of youse.' He stared into his drink. 'This fucking world. I'll be glad to be out of it.'

'It's no worse than it's ever been. We're just getting less tolerant of the shit as we get older.'

'Never had a hack shot in the fucking back before,' Riggott snapped, seeming to have forgotten where they were.

The barman watched them for a few seconds, before he turned away to serve a couple of women in suits who'd come in.

'This isn't the Peterborough I know.' Riggott took another drink, placed the glass very deliberately on the beer mat. 'What is it, then? What did the poor wee fucker do to get himself executed out on the street?'

Zigic leaned forward across the table. 'We're looking at an altercation with another student on his course.'

Quickly and quietly he explained about Harry Bracewell and his links to Young Country, saw Riggott's jaw clench.

'There are other leads but this is the only sign of trouble we've been able to find so far.' Zigic took another sip of his vodka, palate acclimatising. 'We've got his laptop now but whoever killed him broke into his house and stole everything related to his work.'

Riggott's eyebrow went up, a glimmer of the old hunter coming through the melancholy. 'We're going to be needing another drink.'

Zigic went to the bar, ordered a second round, thinking of limiting them to singles but he knew it was unforgivable to come back with less than you'd been sent for. Further down the bar two of the locals were talking about the shooting, saying it would be drugs, Peterborough was all junkies now, the kids had too much money and nothing better to do with it than get out of their heads.

Not like in their day.

At the table Riggott had slipped his jacket off, sat with his elbows on the table, hunched forward, all predatory angles.

'So what was your wean working on?' he asked, as Zigic sat down again.

'Tech should be able to give us the files tomorrow morning. But several people we've talked to have said Jordan was excited about some big story he'd found.' He explained about the article Jordan had written for the *Big Issue*, what his lecturer had told them about his political bent. 'I'm guessing whatever he was looking into is going to be controversial.'

Riggott steepled his fingers around the rim of his glass, muttered, 'Aye, plenty of that in town these days.'

86

'One thing we're trying to figure out is why he was hanging around the Greenaway Club,' Zigic said. 'He wrote a piece about the men there but he's stayed in touch with them. He was there watching football last night.'

'And you've run them through the system and found out what a bunch of shady bastards they are.'

Zigic nodded, glad that they were getting down to it now. 'There was some trouble with a protest at the Greenaway factory, right?'

'Sure, it was a sight more serious than a protest,' Riggott said darkly. 'Threats, intimidation. A group of them were harassing their old boss and his family.' Zigic waited, watching Riggott think it through. 'But they'd lost their jobs overnight. Their whole livelihoods gone.'

'Can't have been easy for them.'

'No.' Riggott rubbed his face, eyes losing focus momentarily. 'Same happened to my old man. Place he was at went under. Put him out on his arse at fifty. Old fucker didn't know what to do with himself. Couldn't get another job. Nothing to fill his day except drinking.' He frowned, a twitch of anger around his nose. 'Drank himself to death in five years. Would have done it faster if he'd had the money.'

He would have been the same age Riggott was now, Zigic realised. And maybe that was weighing on him, surviving his father but staring down the barrel of retirement with nothing to fill his time. Money was no object to him if the drive towards self-destruction was already present.

'Are they dangerous?' Zigic asked.

Riggott sighed. 'They were fair wild. That real fucking impotent rage, you know? Greenaway didn't help himself how he treated them. Sold their jobs out from under them after he'd stood hand on heart and swore there wouldn't be any redundancies. Day after the papers were signed the gates are locked for good.' Riggott put his hand up. 'I'm not condoning what they did, but I can't say as I don't understand it.'

'They were put down pretty aggressively,' Zigic said, thinking of the charges that could have been cautions, the others given short stretches inside, tags when they came out. Criminal records wouldn't have helped their employment prospects.

'Greenaway was in tight with the Chief Constable,' Riggott said, reaching for his drink. 'These lads turn up at his house and vandalise his car, he doesn't call 999, he calls the big man and the big man calls me out of my bed and it's made crystal fucking clear that we're to go heavy on this. "Nip it in the bud", right?'

'And it worked?' Zigic asked. 'They stopped?'

'Aye, it stopped,' Riggott said. 'But only because Marcus Greenaway died. Wasn't much point in having a go after that.'

Zigic felt a prickling sensation at the back of his eyes, the murky thrill of anticipation as he saw a potential new line of enquiry click together with tantalising ease.

'Hold your bollocks, Ziggy,' Riggott warned, seeing his expression. 'It was an accident. Stupid bastard crashed his helicopter into a field.'

But the prickling remained, almost a sting now.

'Are you sure it was an accident?'

'I am *absolutely* fucking certain,' Riggott said. 'Sure, I thought the same thing that's getting your dick up about now, but the crash report came back clean and the AAIB don't get that shite wrong. The chopper hadn't been maintained properly, he'd been skimping on maintenance, and some dinky wee part or other failed. It was a known fault on that model; they've been dropping out of the sky hither and yon.'

Riggott believed it. Zigic could hear it in his voice. And he knew that any shadow of doubt would have sent him hurtling after Bruce Humble and his gang.

But still …

'Air crash investigators don't make fuck-ups,' Riggott insisted, an impatient edge in his tone. 'Especially when some rich bastard's widow is looking to sue the manufacturer for a seven-figure sum. Mrs Greenaway brought in two independent investigators to try and overturn the AAIB's report and she got nowhere with it.' He drained his glass. 'If there'd been any question of tampering, we'd have dragged Humble and his boys in triple fucking quick, believe you me.'

Zigic sighed, the prickling clearing, the new line of investigation disappearing from the version of Jordan Radley's murder board he carried around in his head.

'Course,' Riggott said, rising from the table, wallet in his hand. 'If the boy Radley's reaction to the story was anything like yours, he might have put some people's backs up just asking questions about it.'

CHAPTER FOURTEEN

'Are you sure you're alright?' Jackie asked, looking up from her book, eyes probing above the chrome line of her reading glasses. Every inch the schoolmarm and usually it would excite Humble, her appearance of sternness. Take him back to Miss Leggatt, with her tight skirts and the blouses you could see her bra straps through. But not tonight.

'I'm fine,' he said. 'Honestly.'

'I think it might help if we talk about it,' Jackie insisted, closing her book but keeping her finger in the page. 'You're still in shock right now, but talking will help. I promise.'

Explaining it to him like he was one of her troubled students. Calm and measured and a bit cold. Not how she really felt, he knew that. It was a defence mechanism she used at work to insulate herself from all the terrible things those poor kids told her. The problem was she couldn't turn it off sometimes.

He didn't need that.

Not tonight.

She'd let him be during dinner, eaten on their knees in front of the TV rather than at the table in the conservatory. When the news came on he realised he couldn't swallow the food in his mouth. Had to go and spit the fish pie out into the kitchen sink, saying he'd found a bone in it.

He returned to find the screen paused on Jordan's photograph. The boy looking so fresh-faced and happy. Not the serious young man Humble knew, all earnest opinions and professional empathy.

'We should listen to this,' Jackie said.

And so they'd sat through the speech by DI Zigic outside Thorpe Wood Station. The detective looked different as well, straighter and more official in a suit he hadn't been wearing when he came to the Club. Under the arc lights he was a different beast entirely and if Zigic had looked like that this morning, maybe he would have handled him differently. He'd let himself be put at ease by the scruffy beard and the slightly too long hair and the casual clothes.

After everything he'd been through, he should have known better than to underestimate these people.

Humble had felt bile rising in his throat, had swallowed it down and sat watching the screen without seeing it any more, ears buzzing with white noise. Thinking of the last time he'd seen those brown-brick steps in front of the station, strong fingers holding his hands where they were cuffed behind his back.

The white noise had refused to fade as he scraped the remnants of his dinner into the dog's bowl and stacked the dishwasher and made tea and found biscuits and put on some documentary about the greatest feats of engineering in Industrial Revolution Britain. All of them crumbling now or long gone or converted into luxury apartments for young professionals.

Just like the Greenaway factory. Torn down and replaced with blocks of flats.

His untouched tea went cold and he knew Jackie was watching him from the armchair next to the fire where she liked to sit on wintery evenings. He wanted her with him on the sofa. To be able to reach out and hold her foot, be anchored by her presence. But it was best that she was there, he realised, as one documentary gave way to another, because if he touched her she would feel his racing pulse and then she would *know* he wasn't alright at all.

'It's okay to be upset,' she said. 'It's perfectly natural when someone you know dies.'

'I just need to be quiet for a little bit,' he told her, as softly as he could manage. Worried she could hear the tremble in his voice.

Reluctantly she went back to her book but he could feel her eyes on him, could hear the words she wanted to say, sitting unspoken between them.

And more than anything he wanted to be able to confide in her. Thought that if he let it out then the terrible hollowness in his stomach, the ache in his chest and the band slowly tightening around his temples, might go away. If he could just share his fears with her, then she would say, don't be stupid. You always did have an overactive imagination.

But he couldn't tell her.

Because what if she agreed with him?

What if she told him to go straight to the police? This was serious. It was murder. Someone he'd known and liked had been shot and he owed it to Jordan and the people who loved him to come clean. She would make him get in the car right away. Would drive him across town and march him into the station herself.

She knew the police had been to see him already, but she was less interested in what they'd asked him than in what they'd told him about Jordan. She was struggling to process the shock herself, he thought. Had never met the boy but he'd talked about him often enough for her to feel like she knew him.

She knew he was nice and clever and that things like this weren't supposed to happen to people like that.

She thought it was random.

'Do you want another cuppa?' he asked, standing abruptly, sending his fuzzy head spinning.

'I shouldn't have any more caffeine,' she said. 'I won't sleep.'

'Cocoa then?'

She smiled. 'I'd love one.'

In the kitchen he poured milk into the small enamel saucepan they only ever used for cocoa, set it on a low heat and stood over it, watching the perfect white surface beginning to shimmer.

He remembered the hot chocolate he'd been making the last time the police came for him. Letting his granddaughters sneak marshmallows out of the bag on the worktop while Jackie shouted at him from the living room not to spoil them.

Then the knock on the door.

Insistent in the way only the police knocked.

He was expecting it but not on a Sunday. Not really thinking they would come for him at home like this. But he should have known better.

The detective at the door was short and thin in a grey trouser suit, her hair scraped back off her face. Two heavyset uniformed officers behind her. Clear what would happen if he kicked off. As if he would. Man of his age, standing there with his granddaughters by his side and his wife calling to ask who it was, was it her parcel?

He'd gone meekly, hating himself for how submissive he was.

He'd pictured the moment, told himself to stand up straight and look them in the eye. Make no apologies, give no excuses. He was in the right. Morally if not legally. And even if they wouldn't understand that he would remember it.

Because by then all he had was his pride.

The neighbours were on their front steps, watching it all play out. The girls' confusion, Jackie's protests and demands for an explanation that the DI gave her in a voice loud enough for the people three doors down to hear it.

'Your husband is under arrest for harassment.' Then looking at the girls and plastering a smile on her face, she went on, 'You should take them inside. It's too cold to be out here.'

Later there had been tears and recriminations. Jackie packing a bag and going to her sister's for a few days, which became a few weeks. The one good thing he'd managed to keep hold of, a strong marriage to the only woman he'd ever loved. Blew that over what? Money. Pride. Solidarity.

None of it worth a thing without her.

And now he was in the same position again.

Hiding things from Jackie.

Lying to the police.

Waiting for the knock on the door.

DAY TWO

WEDNESDAY

CHAPTER FIFTEEN

'I hate that shower,' Billy said, coming into the kitchen. 'You have to run around in it to get wet.' He grabbed the cafetière and poured a cup of coffee. 'I'm sure it was supposed to be a power shower when we bought the place, wasn't it?'

'You think they took it out and put that old thing in when they left?' Ferreira asked, smearing honey onto her toast.

'I wouldn't put it past the sneaky bastards.'

She watched him go into the fridge, coming out with the bowl of bircher muesli he'd made the night before. He took the plate off the top and frowned at it like he hoped it had turned into something more appetising while he was sleeping.

'If you want a new one we'll need to find a plumber,' she said, as he sat down across from her at the small glass table. It was the right size for the space in front of the French doors at the end of the galley kitchen, but he had plans for an extension that, when they could afford it, would span the entire back of the cottage, had already picked out an eight-seater stripped oak table with black metal legs and matching benches.

It would be woefully unfashionable by the time they got around to doing the work, Ferreira thought, reflecting on the current state of the lounge, a mishmash of his old furniture and the few things she'd brought from her flat. The walls still the viscerally upsetting shade of egg-yolk yellow as when they moved in six months ago.

That first weekend they went out and bought paint samples, carefully applied them to the chimney-breast wall in neat squares; the off-black he wanted next to her choice of oxblood red, both sitting awkwardly alongside the compromise colour of malachite green. By now she was sick of them all, was wondering if she could buy a mirror big enough to cover them up completely and just accept the coagulated yellow that reminded her of an unfortunate stain on an ugly tie.

Maybe she could rebrand it in her head. Call it ochre or aconite or mineral yellow.

At least the kitchen was decent though. Off-white walls and glossy black units like she'd had at her flat, with wooden floors and recessed lights. The garden beyond the French doors were full of morning sunlight, songbirds in the overgrown foliage that was beginning to wilt and turn as winter came on.

It had been a good move coming here to Elton, she reassured herself. Even if the practicalities had been terrifying. All the paperwork that marked an irrevocable pooling of responsibility.

None of this was the life she thought she'd wanted but somehow they had drifted into it. And somehow she was actually happier with him that she was without him.

She ate her toast and scrolled down her tablet, reading through old articles Jordan Radley had written for the *Evening Telegraph*. Nothing particularly controversial there.

Across the table Billy was eating with grim determination, looking out into the garden. He was like this in the mornings now, quieter and more contained, like a kid dreading going to school. All the old energy and bravado bled away.

If Riggott didn't go soon she wasn't sure how much of Billy would survive. If Riggott left a bad report for his replacement and the situation continued as it was now, she suspected Billy would quit.

He was doing important work, locked away in his office, but he couldn't accept that strategic policing was just as vital as the cut and thrust of solving cases as they came in. Riggott had him doing analysis of potential hotspots for money laundering in Peterborough, identifying businesses whose publicly held accounts didn't seem to match their profile or footfall. Billy not even getting to go and stake them out. That job was done by

CCTV cameras and ones they secreted in nearby buildings, occasionally a couple of plain-clothes detectives getting involved on the ground.

Eventually there would be a report and it would go over to financial crimes. Out of his hands. No glory when the arrests were made, none of the pleasure of taking the criminals he'd identified into an interview room and breaking them open.

He topped up his coffee, held the pot over her cup.

'I've had two already,' she said, pulling it away.

'You don't need the caffeine as much as I do.'

It felt like an invitation but she knew better than to take it. Any questions about his work this close to the beginning of shift would see her arriving late, dragged into a frustrating and circular discussion about what he'd done wrong and how Riggott shouldn't be punishing him like this. The unfairness. The pettiness. Then Zigic would come up and she would find herself defending his role in it all. And then things would get really heated.

'I better get dressed.'

Twenty minutes later they were walking into the office, everyone else in already, the room buzzing with bright voices prepped to take on the coming day. It wasn't always like this and Ferreira was reassured to see how invested the team were in this case, thought it was something to do with Jordan Radley's youth and the inexplicable violence of his death. But perhaps it was also because this case already felt significant, the kind you wanted to work on when you signed up.

Billy peeled off and went over to DI Kitson, wanting an update on where she was on her Botox death case. Ferreira made for Zigic's office, seeing through the internal window where he sat at his desk with his head in his hands.

'What's wrong with you?' she teased.

He looked up slowly, like his skull was carrying extra weight, his eyes impressively bloodshot.

'I went to the pub with Riggott last night,' he said.

She smiled. 'Well, that'll do it. Think you can manage to get through the briefing?'

'If everyone uses their indoor voices, yeah.' He reached for the mug of coffee on his desk. There was a packet of aspirin next to it and a spent chocolate wrapper.

'You've got caramel in your beard.' She pointed to her own face. 'Right there.'

He wiped his hand down his chin. 'Got it?'

'Yeah, you look totally together now.'

Zigic rose from his chair in stages, bracing himself against his desk. He picked up his coffee and went out into the main office, calling in a traumatised voice for everyone to gather around as he walked over to the board.

Slowly the chatter fell away and all faces turned towards him. There were a few raised eyebrows and supressed smiles at the sight of him. Zigic never turned up for work like this, was unforgiving of anyone who did, and the amusement was palpable in the room.

'You alright there, Ziggy lad?' Riggott called from the back of the office, fresh-faced and chipper-looking, the night's hard drinking metabolised entirely.

Zigic nodded at him and Ferreira saw the boss grin, could see the satisfaction he took being able to drink his officers under the table still.

'Okay.' Zigic turned and looked at the board. 'So, we should be getting into Jordan's laptop sometime today but until then there's plenty to be going on with. Mel, you went to talk to Jordan's girlfriend last night, right?'

'"Girlfriend" is probably making it sound more serious than it was,' she said. 'Turns out they're work friends with benefits. She's got kids, no man about, so doesn't sound like we've got jealousy as a potential motive.'

'Did she know what Jordan was working on?'

'No,' Ferreira said, remembering the woman telling her how surprised she'd been when she saw Jordan's photo in a copy of the *Big Issue* in her GP's waiting room. 'She knew he was working at the *ET* but she didn't think anything of it. He didn't talk about his work with her. I got the impression it was just a physical thing. Convenient piece of younger man, you know?'

'What about threats?' Riggott asked. 'Enemies?'

Ferreira shook her head. 'As far as she was concerned he was just a nice, quiet guy who she had sex with once a week after their shift ended.'

'Dead end then,' Zigic said, striking 'girlfriend?' out on the board as he took a sip of his coffee. 'Today's focus is going to be on the men from the Greenaway Club. We've got nineteen of them present the night Jordan was murdered. Eight of them have criminal records related to harassment and intimidation against the factory's former owner, Marcus Greenaway.'

'Does that make them suspects though?' Weller was tapping a pen against the arm of his chair. 'Jordan didn't have anything to do with the factory, did he?'

'First, stop making that noise,' Zigic told him. 'Second, Marcus Greenaway died in an air crash not long after the factory was sold.'

Murmurs and straightening spines and Ferreira felt the same sharpening sensation.

'That's why Jordan was hanging around the place then,' she said. 'He thought there was another story to be had?'

'No,' Zigic said. 'The crash was thoroughly and repeatedly investigated and it was definitely accidental. No criminal investigation required, no question of foul play.'

'But did Jordan know that?' Weller asked, raising his pen to strike his chair again but catching himself before he did. 'If Jordan was asking questions about the crash, it could easily have spooked the person responsible into killing him.'

'It was an *accident*,' Zigic repeated. 'It isn't a potential motive in Jordan's murder, it's just something we all need to be aware of in case it comes up.' He looked at them each in turn, the effect blunted by his reddened eyeballs. 'We're talking to these men because they were with Jordan the night he died. Some of them were his friends and he might have confided in them about being threatened or scared of someone.'

'What about their records?' Parr asked slightly testily. 'We know they're a bad lot. Chances are, Jordan's done something to get on the wrong side of one of them and he's wound up dead.'

'There's a world of difference between slashing car tyres and shooting someone in the back,' Zigic said.

Parr frowned. 'He's a clean-living, studious kid. Where else was he going to run into a killer?'

'Harry Bracewell.' Ferreira pointed to the board, the mugshot still sitting alone in the suspects column.

Zigic turned to Murray. 'Col, I need you to go over to the Queens Arms and check out Bracewell's alibi.'

'No problem.'

'And the friends Jordan's mum mentioned,' he added.

She nodded.

Ferreira half listened as Zigic went back to the Greenaway men, dividing up the list of names between the team, keeping back the three who Humble said were friendliest with Jordan for them to go and see this morning. She was thinking about Bracewell again, the reading up she'd done on Young Country last night while Billy cooked dinner. The important information had come from Anti-Terror but she'd been curious about their public profile, whether Jordan had been discussed at all.

Nothing. Not a mention on any of their social media. No posts from Harry Bracewell since nine o'clock Tuesday night when he'd taken a photograph of the band he'd gone to see at the Queens Arms. Some folk rock duo she hadn't heard of and she was surprised that it was his taste, but then what was more white than folk music?

Zigic began to wrap up the briefing, eyes flicking away quickly as Riggott left the office. He gave Bloom a few words of encouragement as she returned to the list of drivers who'd passed the crime scene, then gave Weller his orders for the day, making sure he understood exactly what was expected of him.

Weller asked a couple of questions in a brisk voice, somehow managing to sit at attention.

It was getting embarrassing now, how badly he wanted to impress Zigic. A few months ago, Weller had dropped the suits and serious ties he'd always worn for work, started dressing in dark jeans and smart jumpers, bought a short wool coat and

Chelsea boots, mimicking Zigic's look so overtly that Murray had started calling him 'single white male'.

Zigic pretended not to notice but Ferreira was sure it was working against Weller. Almost told him to cut it out, that imitation was no way to earn respect, but decided against it. Because he did seem to be working harder than before.

'Alright,' Zigic said, coming over to her desk, still slightly queasy-looking. 'Bit of fresh air, I think.'

Chapter Sixteen

Steve Gurney lived in Stanground in a 1930s semi-detached house around the corner from Zigic's parents. It was nice area, full of elderly people who had originally moved there in the seventies and eighties and more recent residents drawn by the village feel within close proximity of the city centre. Not an affluent area, but stable, somewhere to get your foot on the ladder and start a family.

Gurney's place was opposite a run of forlorn-looking shops that seemed to change hands on a yearly basis; the Polish supermarket still going but he wasn't sure how they would manage as their customers started to leave Peterborough. It wasn't an exodus, not yet, but he'd noticed the change since the EU referendum, the pace increasing as people failed to gain the right to remain or decided they didn't want to be in a country that had rejected them.

He knew Ferreira's parents hadn't been granted settled status yet, that they'd signed their home and business over to her brothers in case the worst happened. Her own status was sorted, the process smoothed over by her job, but she'd complained the whole way through it, furious that she had to justify herself after twenty-two years in the UK.

She went on ahead of him, ignoring the front door and walking down the side of the house, aiming for the sound of banging and a radio playing, through an open gate into the small back garden.

He followed, feeling the ground slightly more certain under his feet now that the coffee and the aspirin were kicking in. The daylight was no longer unbearable through his sunglasses. Another hour or two and he might feel human again.

The patio doors were open and Steve Gurney was on his knees in dusty work gear and protective pads, sorting strips of dark wood laminate into piles. The room had been emptied of its furniture, a third of the floor already refinished. The lines between the boards didn't look quite true to Zigic but he wasn't at the stage of hangover recovery where he trusted his eye.

'Steve Gurney?' Ferreira asked, warrant card held up to him, as she switched off the radio. 'DS Ferreira, DI Zigic. We'd like to have a word with you, please.'

'This about Jordan?' He stood up, patting down the front of his camo-print combats. A lean guy with a tanned face and tattooed arms hanging out of his T-shirt. Fifty-two, Zigic knew from his record, but younger-looking with his curly black hair untroubled by grey. Out of a bottle, Zigic assumed.

'How do you know about Jordan?' Ferreira asked.

'Bruce gave me a bell yesterday afternoon. Couldn't believe it when he told me. I said to my Hazel, I never had Jordan down for drug stuff. You never know though, do you? Our youngest were mad on it for a few years but we never knew what she were doing.' He scratched his ear. 'They're good at hiding it, junkies. Crafty.'

'What makes you think it was drugs?' Ferreira asked.

'He got shot, right? What else is it gonna be?'

The same thing they'd assumed at the scene. A knee-jerk reaction that nothing they'd heard since supported.

'We don't think it was drugs-related,' Zigic told him, getting an unconvinced look in reply.

'Did Jordan mention having trouble with anyone?' Ferreira asked.

'He weren't that sort of lad,' Gurney said, gentle mockery in his voice. 'There weren't a bad bone in his body.'

'That doesn't mean he didn't have enemies.'

'Where would he get enemies from?' Gurney asked dismissively.

'His work at the paper maybe,' Ferreira suggested. 'What did he tell you about that?'

'He never said much to me about it. Bruce might know. They were tight.' Gurney reached for an open can of Coke sitting on the mantelpiece, took a quick swig. 'Can't see him talking about his writing to any of the blokes, be honest. They were always ribbing him about being a smart arse. Not nasty like, just banter. He was clever, we could all see that. Curious, you know?'

'About what?'

'The world.' Gurney gestured vaguely towards the open patio door. 'History, politics, that sort of stuff.' He shook his head. 'You couldn't have got me to even *read* a paper when I were his age. Girls and cars, that were all I were interested in.'

'And fighting,' Ferreira said.

'Yeah, I've got a record. But what my record don't tell you is I never went looking for trouble.' He nodded at Zigic. 'You'll know what it's like. When you're the biggest bloke in the pub, some little shit always wants to try and prove himself by putting you down.'

'I think you were drinking in the wrong pubs,' Zigic suggested.

Gurney shrugged. He wasn't a big man by Zigic's reckoning, five ten, lean but solid, a bit of bulk across his shoulders. A generation ago he might have looked like an impressive target for someone with a complex, now he was just a middle-aged guy who kept himself in trim.

'What time did you leave the Club on Monday night?' Ferreira asked.

'Straight after the end of the match,' Gurney said. 'I wanted to get an early start in the morning.' He pointed up. 'I've had the bathroom to tile and it's a right ball-ache. You don't get in on it first thing, you'll never do it.'

'You moving?'

His face brightened suddenly. 'Spain, yeah. Sell this place up and get out of Peterborough. It's not the place it used to be.'

Zigic saw Ferreira's jaw flex, knew exactly what she was thinking.

'Did you see anyone hanging around the Club?' he asked.

'No, it were dead,' Gurney said. 'Jordan were still there when I left anyway, so I wouldn't know if someone were waiting for him or anything like that.'

'How did you get home?'

'Walked.'

'Long way to walk home.'

He shrugged. 'Fifteen, twenty minutes.'

'And what time did you get in?' Zigic asked, aware of Ferreira making notes next to him and Gurney watching her do it.

'Ahh, I dunno.' He blew out a long breath, thinking. 'My missus got home a coupla minutes after me, I can give you her number if you wanna ask her.' He took his phone from his pocket and read it out, giving them an approximation of an alibi before they had chance to ask him for one. But they never trusted the spouse's word. 'Fifteen minutes walk from the Club. Match ended at 9:45.' Gurney waggled his head as he did the maths. 'Say ten past 10, summat like that.'

Ferreira looked up from her pad. 'And what route did you take?'

'Same one as always,' Gurney told her, a little edge in his voice now, knowing he was a suspect but not prepared to acknowledge it.

He'd learnt his lesson, Zigic imagined. Enough convictions on his record to understand that cooperation was the wisest course of action.

He described the route for them, getting tetchy as he drew closer to home.

They would look for him on CCTV, see if his story checked out. He should have been home before Jordan was shot and it was a quick drive to the crime scene if he'd wanted to make it, Zigic thought.

Ferreira continued questioning him on times and whereabouts, if anyone left the Club the same time as him, who was still there when they departed, who did he last see Jordan talking to. Gurney shrugged apologetically when he couldn't tell her.

'I weren't looking. I never knew he were going to get killed, did I?'

'Is there anything Jordan mentioned in the last few weeks that struck you as odd?' Zigic asked.

'I tune all that political crap out. What's the point of getting wound up about summat the likes of us can't change?' Gurney shook his head. 'He were a nice kid but he hadn't got a bloody clue how the world works.'

'But you took part in the article for the *Big Issue*,' Ferreira said.

He looked down sharply to the worn toes of his trainers. 'That were different, weren't it? No one gives a shit about men's problems. We're supposed to keep it all to ourselves. Even if it kills us. You know suicide kills more men than road accidents? Jordan said it shouldn't be like that. He got it. Least I could do were tell him about my … stuff.'

'How did you feel about the article?'

'Never read it,' Gurney said, lifting his gaze again but not making eye contact.

'Why not?'

'Didn't wanna see what I'd said and find out I sounded like a wanker. My missus read it, she reckoned Jordan did us proud.' Gurney pressed his lips together. 'She said she never knew I'd been feeling like that.'

When he finally met Zigic's eye there was defiance there, a challenge to mock, to see him as weak. But Zigic didn't think that. He knew how hard it would have been for someone like Gurney to open up to someone like Jordan. All the while knowing that people he knew would read the article. That he would face their judgement. Handing the magazine to his wife must have felt like a momentous act for him. *Here are the things I couldn't tell you.*

'Was anyone unhappy about the article?' Ferreira asked.

'How do you mean?'

He was stalling, Zigic thought, seeing Gurney's eyes lockdown.

'Did any of the other men who took part not like how they came across in the article?'

'Not that I heard.'

Ferreira shifted her weight between her feet, scenting the same unwillingness that Zigic did.

'We saw the reactions on social media,' she said. 'It can't have been easy reading complete strangers insulting you all like that.'

He tutted. 'I don't look at bloody social media. I'm not a fourteen-year-old girl.'

'Nobody in real life mentioned it?' she asked. 'People you knew away from the Club?'

'Few people, yeah. But nothing out of order.'

'They recognised you from the photo,' Ferreira said.

He nodded. 'I figured that, yeah.'

'But Jordan promised he'd hide your identities.'

'He did his best.' Gurney turned away from them, kneeled down at the last row of laminated boards and reached for the next one on the pile. 'Look, I need to be getting on. I promised her ladyship I'd be done with this today.'

Ferreira shot him a questioning look and Zigic gestured towards the door, thanked Steve Gurney for his time and left a card on the mantelpiece, sure they wouldn't hear from the man again.

Not unless they found a reason to come back for him.

Chapter Seventeen

Bruce Humble sat in his car outside the Polish supermarket on Oakdale Avenue, eyes dead ahead, willing himself to blink out of existence. Or at least become temporarily invisible.

He wanted to look and see if Zigic and the woman were coming over to him, but he felt sure that if he did they would feel his eyes on them. Then they would stop and turn and see him, start to wonder why he was sitting there opposite Steve's house, if there was something going on.

Stories being prepared, times straightened out, lies decided upon.

They would take him in. Not in handcuffs this time but under suspicion. And he wasn't sure he could stand it again. He gripped the steering wheel and stared at the Peterborough United sticker in the back window of the car in front of him, one corner peeling away. Counted to ten, then twenty, then fifty, willing them gone.

There was no sign of the detectives.

They were inside with Steve now but he couldn't think about that.

Carefully he manoeuvred himself out of the parking space, drove around the block and back onto the main road, hands still tight on the wheel, eyes refusing to blink. He drove through Stanground proper and into the old village, turned down onto the Fletton Marina development, a few spots of rain hitting his windscreen as he pulled up outside Lionel's house.

Lionel had the garage door open, music playing as Humble got out of his car. The neighbours wouldn't like it, he thought, but Lionel was a law unto himself.

Never used to be like that but he was different these days and Humble wasn't sure if it was Patti who'd changed him or if it was

110

the brush with death that had brought them together. Seeing him working away in the garage, crouched down putting a new wheel onto a bright orange off-road bike, it seemed impossible that he'd ever found himself in such a hopeless place.

Lionel sang along to the music in his thick fen accent, nodding in time, pausing occasionally to tap out a dull rhythm on the bike's chunky tyre with his spanner. He was wearing shorts despite the weather and a fleece jumper, his greying ponytail coiled in the hood.

Was he wrong bringing this to Lionel's door? Letting his nerves and his overactive imagination get the better of him?

Of all the people he could have talked to about this, Lionel was the least capable of dealing with it.

Humble thought of him laying in the hospital bed, the smell of vomit and charcoal still on his breath, tubes going into his nose and his arm. He remembered how pale he'd been, almost see-through, half-starved before he took the overdose. His system so thoroughly compromised that his doctors weren't sure he'd make it.

He'd been like that for three weeks, no visitors but Humble and Dick Caxton and a woman from a local charity who called on patients without family. She'd been there once when Humble arrived, reading to Lionel from a copy of the *Mirror*, and he almost told her Lionel's paper was the *Sport* and that hearing that crap would likely drive him deeper down. But she was nice and a little bit lonely herself, recently widowed and looking for something good to do with her time. She was still there when Lionel finally came around.

Patti.

Who, it turned out, Lionel had been at school with, had a mad crush on but was never brave enough to tell her.

Three months later he moved into her place. Two after that they got married on a beach in Barbados, a spur-of-the-moment decision while they were on holiday.

She'd turned Lionel's life around for him. Brought him out of the grief and depression, got him working again, helped set him up in the bike repair business he ran from their garage.

Lionel looked up from the bike, blinked then smiled.

111

'Ay up, buh, what brings you round?'

'The police are at Steve's,' he said, without meaning to. Blurted that out instead of the small talk he was going to start with.

Lionel straightened up, pulled a rag out of his pocket and wiped his hands clean.

'Can't say as I'm surprised,' he said. 'Jordan were over at the Club, course they're going to want to talk to us lot.'

'I think they reckon one of the lads killed him.'

Lionel gave him a funny look and he knew why. He'd always been the level-headed one. At work, whenever there was a problem, he'd be the one to fix it, to go to management with their grievances and get an accommodation.

'You reckon they're right about that?' Lionel asked, leaning back against his workbench.

'I don't know. No.'

Saying it but not meaning it.

Last night, laying awake in bed with Jackie snoring softly next to him, he'd been playing through the conversations they'd had at the Club. Weeks of talk, all different subjects, Jordan interested, full of questions.

Probing them.

'I wouldn't put it past Steve,' Lionel said thoughtfully.

'Why would he do that?' Humble demanded.

As if he hadn't been thinking the same thing.

Lionel shrugged. 'He were pissed off about the article, weren't he? I mean, it were alright for me. Patti knew what'd happened, she knows how I can get. No shame in it for me her seeing the thing all in black and white like that. But Steve ...'

Humble stopped, his hand on the bike's wheel, rough under his palm.

'Hazel wasn't very happy with him.'

'She was embarrassed,' Lionel said. 'All that buckering crap she got at work about it. Women won't stand for having their failings rubbed in their faces.'

'It was hardly her fault,' Humble protested.

'Nup, but that's not the way she were looking at it,' Lionel said. 'There's all her mates going on as how she weren't seeing to him right. And you think on now, if she were saying that to Patti, then, God knows, what she were saying to Steve about it.'

Humble knew exactly what she was saying.

Steve had told him, one night in the Club after last orders, just the two of them sitting with whiskeys and their darts forgotten on the table.

Steve almost in tears because Hazel wasn't talking to him. He'd given her the article because he couldn't bring himself to actually say the words to her. I'm depressed. I hate my life. And that was the first she'd heard of it. Didn't know he'd spoken to Jordan, had no idea all of this was about to be public knowledge. The identities disguised but not as well as they needed to be to guarantee the men's anonymity.

Hazel raging and crying. Telling him he'd humiliated her. What was wrong with him? Why couldn't he talk to her if it was *that* bad. If he hated his life *with her* so fucking much. Why didn't he go to the doctors? Call the Samaritans? Why the hell had he aired their dirty linen in a *magazine*?

Hadn't he caused her enough grief already?

'But they're alright now,' Humble said tentatively. 'You want that sort of thing out in the open.'

'Not that open.'

Humble swore. 'No. He wouldn't.'

Lionel frowned, giving him a look that said we both know he would. We both know what kind of man he is. Steve always the first to throw his hands up, even if he wasn't always the instigator. Unable to meet angry words with just words.

Had he been festering this whole time?

Feeling like he'd been conned into speaking the truth. That he'd opened himself up and got nothing for it but more pain. While Jordan was lauded as a 'sensitive chronicler of the working man's emotional hinterland'.

Those exact words. And Humble remembered how he'd sneered when he read them on Twitter. Some left-wing London journalist who seemed to think the 'working man' was a different species. Some quaint curio to be turned this way and that, examined and explored and written about by people who knew his own soul better than he could know it himself.

It wasn't Jordan's fault, he reminded himself.

Jordan was more one of them than not. He'd had the best intentions and it wasn't his fault that there had been fallout.

'What do we do?' Humble asked quietly.

Lionel came across the garage, hard-faced suddenly. 'We don't *do* nothing. We don't *say* nothing. Steve's our mate and we're not grassing him up.'

'But –'

'No, buh,' Lionel said, softer now but even more insistent. 'We're just talking now, you and me. We don't know owt. We didn't see owt. And if we go starting giving the police ideas about Steve, you can bet your balls they'll make sure they find summat that'll stick.' Lionel backed away again, pointing at him. 'You know what them bastards are like, Bruce. You remember, same as I bloody do.'

He did.

The protest at the factory gates broken up with batons. Men in their sixties being dragged across concrete.

Then the arrests.

The questioning.

DI Sawyer with her scraped-back hair and her gaunt face, sitting across from him in an interview room, playing sympathetic but only for as long as she thought the tactic might work. Then she turned. Asking him how long he thought a man his age would last in prison? If he knew the kind of people he'd be banged up with. Did he want his daughter having to explain to her kids where grandad was? Did he want those girls walking into a visiting room and seeing what the place had done to him?

Wanting him to turn on his mates.

Name the ringleader. Blame anyone except himself.

But he'd been at the heart of it and he wasn't going to put that on anyone else. Knew that in the other rooms the men he'd stood with would be just as firm in their refusal to cooperate.

Because all they had by that point was each other.

And you didn't grass.

114

CHAPTER EIGHTEEN

Last time they'd been to this house the occupants were migrant workers. A three-bed terrace cut up into four bedsits. The roar of the parkway barely thirty metres from the back wall, the fire station on one side, a tyre fitters on the other. No other houses for a good 300 metres. Constant noise and exhaust smell, the rooms cramped and badly insulated, furnished with single beds and lone armchairs. Sinks in corners and hotplates on sideboards. They'd been looking for a young woman who'd been reported missing, had word that her boyfriend was staying in the HMO, but by the time they got there he was gone and nobody could tell them where the woman was, if she'd even been there.

That was five years ago.

The room visible through the open door was just the same, as was the odour of contained bodies and stale cooking, with not even a fresh coat of paint on the walls, but the woman telling them Dick Caxton wasn't at home had a Peterborough accent and an English name.

The look was familiar, Ferreira thought. Worn down by long hours, unhappy at being woken as she tried to sleep off her night shift, suspicious of their presence and what exactly they wanted with Caxton.

'Dick's not in any trouble,' Zigic assured her. 'We just need to ask him a few questions. Do you know where we could find him?'

The woman sniffed, seemed to decide that helping would get rid of them quicker than refusing. 'He works at the Metro down on Oundle Road.'

In the car again, Zigic said, 'Looks like Caxton's fallen on hard times.'

'It's probably how most people who work retail jobs live now.'

'Jordan's mum works at the big Tesco.' He pulled out quickly onto the main road, filling a brief gap in the relentless traffic coming off the parkway. 'She isn't living in one room like that.'

'She had him to help her cover the bills,' Ferreira pointed out. 'God knows what'll happen to her now.'

The line between relative security and destitution was getting thinner, she thought. Two wages and you could keep your head above water. One and you sank. The last few years she'd struggled herself to meet the rent on her flat and her car payments and the ever rising costs of her utility bills and all the debt she'd somehow managed to pile up without being able to point to even one thing and say, 'That's where all my money went.'

Moving in with Billy had eased the pressure. Now her half of the mortgage cost less than what she'd been paying in rent and she'd been shocked when they sat down and worked out the cost of running the place. Every bill smaller than she'd expected, the benefits of cohabitation right there on paper.

She joked about it. Said, 'If I'd realised how much I was saving, I'd have moved in with you ages ago.'

And it was funny because they both knew their relationship was in the right place to take that next big step, but afterwards she'd thought of all the people who stayed with someone they didn't like, never mind love, because of financial constraints.

'Ridgeon lives round here, right?' Zigic asked.

'On the marina,' Ferreira told him, snapping back to reality.

She found the address and directed Zigic to a burgundy-brick house buried at the bottom of a 1980s development of boxy detached places with neatly tended front gardens and sparkling windows. Mostly retirees there judging by the amount of cars in driveways at 10 a.m. This was a far more affluent area than Dick Caxton had washed up in, with Neighbourhood Watch stickers and warnings on the lamp posts about dogs fouling the pavements. Barely a three-minute drive across Stanground's patchworked housing estates but a world away. An appreciable step up from Steve Gurney's place too, and Ferreira wondered at the difference in the men's circumstances.

The garage door was open as Ridgeon worked on a mountain bike inside. He was a wiry man in his early sixties, with an ale-drinker's paunch stretching his khaki fleece and a long grey ponytail that Ferreira recognised from the photo in Jordan's article. Another man who'd be easy to identify if you knew him.

Ridgeon came to meet them on the driveway as Zigic made the introductions.

'I were just nipping in for a cuppa,' he said, in a thick accent of the kind Ferreira hadn't heard since she was a kid living out on the Fens. 'You want one?'

'I could use a coffee,' Zigic said.

'Rough night?' Ridgeon asked, with a twinkle in his eye. 'Say no more, buh.'

They followed him through the back door into a glossy white kitchen with pink things scattered around; kettle and toaster, tea towels and saucepans all candy-coloured and sparkling clean. Lionel Ridgeon looked wrong in it, standing at the sink, scrubbing the bike grease off his hands, combat shorts hanging low on his hips and a hole in the toe of his left sock where he'd kicked off his trainers.

Ferreira watched him as he talked about Jordan's death. The same shock that they'd heard from everyone. The senselessness of it. Peterborough not the same. The world going to hell.

A natural reaction, she supposed. Especially for people of Ridgeon's generation who were settling into the idea that they had lived through a golden age of peace and prosperity that was long gone now.

The kettle came to a boil and he poured it over coffee grounds in a pink enamel cafetière, brought it to the table with cups and sugar and a carton of milk. He unzipped his fleece as he sat down, revealing a faded AC/DC T-shirt.

Zigic started with the logistics of the night and she made notes as Lionel Ridgeon told them when he'd left the Club and the route he took home.

117

The same questions they'd put to Gurney, about the evening's conversation and whether he'd seen anyone hanging around the Club, and they got the same replies. But then why would someone hang around in plain sight if they were going to follow Jordan home?

'Did Jordan ever discuss his work with you?' Zigic asked.

'Now, you'll want to talk to Dick for that,' Ridgeon said. 'Dick Caxton. Him and Jordan were always going on about politics and the like.' He poured their coffees. 'I never could make head nor tail of what they were on about. Dick were saying about how our phones listen to us and tell the government what we're thinking. He always were a bit of a conspiracy nut.'

It wasn't exactly a conspiracy, Ferreira thought. But depending on where Caxton got his information from, he could still be a nut.

'Jordan were a good lad, though. He'd sit there patient as you like and listen to the daft old sod rambling on.'

'Did Dick take part in the article Jordan wrote?' Zigic asked, sugaring his coffee.

Ridgeon nodded. 'Dick's not been having it easy.'

'How about you?'

'Yup, you sign me up, buh, I said. I know how hard it is for fellas to go for help.' He curled his hand around his cup. 'Men are conditioned not to, that's what Jordan reckoned. They tell us when we're little lads not to cry. That's for girls. They tell us, you keep it all in like a proper man. But it's poison doing that. That's why so many of these young 'uns now are acting all aggressive. Going and doing themselves in.' His thumb brushed across the rim of the cup, eyes dropping. 'I tried it. After my wife died. There weren't no point being here without her, I thought. I don't know if it were grief or depression or whatever you want to call it.'

Ferreira recognised the story from the article. Strange putting a face to the man. She wasn't sure what she'd expected but Lionel Ridgeon seemed pretty together now, his life good. None of the financial concerns the other men were experiencing. But then again grief didn't respect your monetary comfort or the closeness of your friends and family.

'I wanted other lads to know there's no shame in feeling help-less,' he said. 'I reckoned if a big fella like me's prepared to come out and say it, they'd see it were normal.'

'What happened after the article ran?' she asked.

'Search me,' he shrugged. 'Hopefully a few blokes saw it and it figured out they didn't have to keep it all bottled up. They got help or what have you. That were the point of it, right?'

'How did the others feel about it?'

'Same as me, far as I know.' He sipped his coffee.

'All of them?' Ferreira asked, watching him carefully, seeing his gaze slide across the tabletop and settle on a point on the floor a metre away.

'Far as I know.'

'Steve Gurney suggested that not everyone was happy with how they'd been represented,' she said carefully.

'Did he?'

'Was Steve not happy about it?'

'I reckon his wife weren't too pleased about it.' Ridgeon kneaded the back of his neck. 'But we agreed to it. We knew what we was doing.'

'It's different when it's out in the world for everyone to see, though.'

'It were a good article,' Ridgeon said, answering a question she hadn't asked, and she saw the desire to deflect, his reluctance to point the finger at one of his friends. Or maybe to suggest Jordan had stitched them up.

You didn't speak ill of the dead, after all.

CHAPTER NINETEEN

In Old Fletton they stopped at a hole-in-the-wall bakery for pastries and takeaway coffee, Zigic seeming to need yet more caffeine to lift him out of the final lingering effects of his hangover. Ferreira had only been out with Riggott a handful of times, always ended up drinking more than she could handle. She wondered what they'd talked about for long enough to get Zigic in this state. It couldn't have just been the case.

An update came in from Parr while she was eating her plum Danish and she put him on speaker, resting her phone on the armrest between them.

'Anything useful, Zac?'

'Nothing so far,' he said. 'I'm three down and none of them had anything to do with Jordan.'

'They weren't involved with the article then?' Zigic asked.

'No, sir. Consensus seems to be that Jordan was a bleeding heart liberal. Or a whinging, lefty snowflake, take your pick. All of them said he was tight with Humble and Caxton. They mentioned Ridgeon and Gurney too. Sounds like they're a bit of a unit.'

'Anyone see anything Monday night?'

'Nothing out of the ordinary.' A car horn sounded at Parr's end. 'They've all given alibis but my gut is they didn't have anything to do with Jordan, so I can't see why they'd have taken against him strong enough to kill him.' A metallic voice asked for his order. 'I'll call when I know something.'

He rang off abruptly and Zigic frowned at the dead screen.

'We should have gone for a drive-thru, you know.'

Ferreira looked at the ragged nub of Danish in her hand. 'Yeah, this isn't great.'

'Dick Caxton, then.'

A couple of minutes later, Zigic pulled into the small parking area in front of the Tesco Metro and they went in. A couple of people were milling about, a young man behind the counter, an older one stacking cleaning products on the shelves in the far corner.

Dick Caxton was tall and gaunt in his blue uniform, head shaved but the shadow of a receding hairline showing under the lights, his movements those of an older and more frail man. Fifty-one going on sixty, Ferreira thought, and not a healthy sixty.

'Mr Caxton?' Zigic asked.

He paused a moment, fingertips touching the bottle of washing-up liquid he'd just slotted into place. 'You the police?'

Zigic made the introductions, said, 'We'd like to ask you a few questions if you have a minute.'

'Popping out, Wes,' Caxton called across the shop, before he turned towards them. 'Best go out back, alright?'

He led them through a door marked 'Staff Only' and into a small yard cluttered with collapsed cardboard boxes, dominated by two large green bins padlocked against theft.

Ferreira wondered how often they were broken into that they needed locking, how bad things were for the locals that bin diving was a possibility.

'Do you know who killed Jordan?' Caxton asked, as the door closed behind them.

'It's still very early,' Zigic told him.

Caxton took a packet of tobacco out of his trouser pocket and began to roll a painfully skinny cigarette. Ferreira thought of his room at the HMO and the man in Jordan's article who had to be him; losing weight because he couldn't afford to eat more than once a day. She knew there were people who'd say he should quit smoking if he was struggling to buy food. Knew those people had never been truly poor or they would understand how it was the small pleasures that got you through the day.

121

Again Zigic took him through the standard questions while she noted the times and the route he'd taken home. He'd caught a bus on the street around the corner from the Club, heading in the opposite direction to where Jordan had been shot. If he really was on the bus. He'd left before Jordan though and they were already assuming his killer had laid in wait for him.

He answered the questions in a tired monotone, with very little emotion on display, and she'd expected more from him given what the other men had said. If Caxton and Jordan had been friendly, shouldn't he be cut up?

But then, it was a day and half on and you could get a lot out of your system in thirty-six hours.

Unprompted, Caxton said, 'We're becoming a society that hates the truth. We don't recognise it when we see it and when we do recognise it we don't like what it says about us.' He gestured towards them with his cigarette. 'And that's just the ordinary people. The elites hate the truth even more because when it *does* get out it shows them up for what they are. Fucking … robber barons, stealing the country out from under the people and blaming whatever scapegoat suits their narrative. Foreigners, Jews, Muslims. Journalists. Enemies of the people, right?'

Here finally was the emotion, a sense of helpless rage. His feelings about Jordan's death sublimated into a rant, more comfortable that way. Less immediately painful, Ferreira thought.

They let him go on.

'You know being a journalist is more dangerous than being a soldier? There are tens of thousands of journalists in prison around the world right now. And we'll go the same way if we're not careful.' He let out a humourless laugh. 'Shit, we're already there. Poor kid like Jordan, speaking truth to power, goes and gets shot. How are we any better than fucking … Iran?'

'Because we're going to catch whoever killed him,' Zigic said firmly.

'Do you know what he was working on?' Ferreira asked.

Caxton's eyes lost focus briefly, perhaps he was back in the Greenaway Club, voicing these same sentiments with Jordan. 'We

122

talked a lot about politics. The blokes in there aren't interested. Most of them hadn't voted for years. Not until Brexit and Boris, that got them out.' He smiled bitterly. 'You can't tell them. They don't want to hear it.'

'But Jordan did?'

'He understood why we're in this mess,' Caxton said appreciatively. 'We talked a lot about the unions. How it was back in the day before it all went to shit. I've tried talking to them here about joining up but they don't think they need it. They're all convinced this is a temporary job but I ask you, what the hell else are they going to find in Peterborough? I was earning eight hundred a week *clear* at Greenaway's. Holiday pay, sick pay, money going into my pension. Now look at me. There's nothing out there for me. There's nothing for them. No training, no opportunities.' He shook his head. 'Poor bloody kids. They're born on the scrapheap and they don't even realise.'

'Jordan was getting on okay though,' Ferreira prompted.

'Banging his head against the class ceiling.' Caxton took a drag on his cigarette. 'Yeah, he was getting somewhere but he was working his bollocks off for it. One day at the *ET*. Unpaid, mind. Waiting tables four nights a week. All while he's trying to study. It shouldn't be like that.'

Sadness welling up in him now, pinching the skin around his eyes.

'We're wondering if Jordan was killed because of something he was working on for the paper,' Ferreira said. 'Did he mention a story to you?'

A flicker of pride crossed Caxton's face. 'Oh, yeah. He had something big in the pipeline.'

'What was it about?'

'I don't know, but his blood was up.' Caxton took another drag on his rollie. 'Knowing Jordan it would have been something contentious. That's what he was interested in. Getting to the stuff them at the top didn't want exposing.'

'Them who?' Ferreira asked. 'The council?'

'The council's not the top,' Caxton said dismissively. 'Jordan would have wanted the bastards who pull their strings.'

Zigic was frowning at him and Ferreira wondered if he was buying Caxton's story. A part of her had reservations. Surely if Caxton and Jordan were so close, so neatly aligned in their political beliefs, he would have been the natural person to confide in over what he was investigating?

Were they really close? Or had Caxton, lonely and ideologically at odds with his old workmates at the Greenaway Club, latched onto Jordan as an intellectual ally?

'Did you take part in the article he wrote?' Zigic asked.

Caxton cocked his head. 'Yeah, I did.'

'And how did you feel about the finished thing?'

'I thought he did a grand job,' Caxton said. 'But he was a clever kid so I never expected anything else from him.'

'We've heard some people weren't quite so happy about it.'

Caxton's face darkened. 'McLeary.'

Daniel McLeary. One of the men DC Parr had flagged already. A history of violence. Involvement in the protests at the Greenaway factory, which had seen him arrested. Homeless now and getting in trouble for begging and shoplifting. Still showing up at the Club though, trying to maintain a link with his old life, Ferreira thought.

'What happened with McLeary?' Zigic asked.

'It was something of nothing,' Caxton said, shuffling where he stood, put on the back foot by the sudden change in Zigic's tone. Not information gathering any more, questioning. 'McLeary got sacked a few days after the *Big Issue* came out. The lads at the garage where he was working saw it, put two and two together about him being a member of the Club. So when his boss lets him go, Danny convinces himself it's because of the article.' Caxton looked at his rollie, didn't go to inhale. 'Load of rubbish. He got the sack because he was working on the black and those jobs never last above a few weeks.'

Zigic stared at him. 'What did McLeary say to Jordan about it?'

'Nothing.'

He was lying, Ferreira thought, hearing the hitch in his voice. He'd said too much and now he was regretting it. He wouldn't trust them. Not someone with his beliefs.

'Where can we find McLeary?' she asked.

'He's homeless,' Caxton said. 'I don't know where he's dossing but he hangs around on Cathedral Square in the day. If the weather's nice.'

It wasn't today, but they'd start there.

'Danny wouldn't have hurt Jordan,' Caxton said, as they started back into the shop. 'He gets a bit worked up but it never lasts. Angry one minute, your best mate the next, it's just how he is.'

Unpredictable, Ferreira thought.

Uneven.

Dangerous enough to ambush Jordan Radley and shoot him in the back?

CHAPTER TWENTY

Zigic found a space on St Peter's Road, parked in the lee of the cathedral's high stone wall, and they walked through the old blue-tiled arcade towards the square, passing two homeless men wrapped in sleeping bags and blankets against the wind that cut up the narrow passageway. Cold there, but out of the worst of the weather. One man was asleep, getting some rest while it was safer to do so, and Zigic wondered where he would stay that night. If he'd be out in the open or if there was a room waiting for him in a hostel. They were closing down at an alarming rate and private rentals becoming scarcer. Landlords unwilling to take a risk on them and trust that they would pay up on time now the rent didn't go directly into their bank accounts. The cynical part of him wondered if that had been the point of Universal Credit, marginalising people already struggling. The 'hostile environment' being extended now it had proved so successful against immigrants.

'Zac's been given McLeary's name as well,' Ferreira said, pocketing her phone as they reached Bridge Street. 'One of the blokes he talked to reckoned McLeary was complaining about getting sacked. Sounds like he was pretty upfront about blaming Jordan.'

'Did he confront Jordan about it?' Zigic asked.

'Not that the bloke knew,' she said. 'Or maybe he just thought better of mentioning it.'

Cathedral Square was quiet. The rain had abated but the sky was threatening more, a chill wind blowing across the broad and open expanse between Queensgate Shopping Centre and the bars and cafés opposite, where the tables on the pavement sat empty behind their cordons. The few shoppers about moved quickly and determinedly, but he noticed a cluster of men sheltering under the open-sided Guildhall.

'McLeary's not there,' Ferreira said quietly, as they drew closer.

She took out her phone and found his photograph, asked the men if anyone knew him, getting shakes of the heads and vaguely disgruntled 'no's. Lying, Zigic thought, but he wasn't surprised and didn't blame them. Next time it might be a copper coming looking for them and McLeary denying all knowledge.

'We could try some of the hostels,' Ferreira suggested.

'Humble might know where he's staying.'

'He didn't mention anything about McLeary being in the article or him being pissed off about it, so I think we have to put Humble down as non-cooperative on this point.'

She was jumping to conclusions already.

'He might not have known about it.'

Ferreira shrugged, still looking at the men as she rolled a cigarette. 'Billy says there's a bloke on the market who was done for selling converted replicas. Might be worth talking to him while we're here. Jepson – did you work that case?'

'Yeah.' They started off up Long Causeway. 'He can't have been out of prison long. He got twenty years for selling a converted replica to a man who shot his ex-wife with it. When we arrested the guy he gave Jepson up in the hope of getting leniency. His house was like a weapons factory when we raided it.'

'He was doing it in his house?' Ferreira asked.

'He wasn't the sharpest tool in the workshop,' Zigic told her, remembering how shocked Jepson had been when they smashed his front door in, sitting there in his living room, watching cartoons with a handgun on the coffee table, waiting for the buyer to arrive, a plastic food bag knotted around a cluster of home-made bullets.

The market was even quieter than Cathedral Square when they passed under the iron gateway. Zigic couldn't remember the last time he'd been on it. When he was a kid they'd come down and his dad would buy bunches of bare-rooted wallflower plants wrapped in damp newspaper, stopping and talking to every other stallholder, shaking their hands and asking after their families.

The endless, tedious conversations he'd stood listening to. Then when he got older, he and his sister would go to the second-hand book stall and he'd browse the imported comics while Katarina hunted through the Point Horrors.

The bookseller was still there, but nobody was buying today and he could smell the sweet tang of overripe fruit on the greengrocer's before they reached it, walking past more stalls that were shuttered than open. A guy was doing mobile phone repairs and SIM unlocking, another had endless racks of waterproof jackets and plastic shoes, handbags he saw Ferreira screw her nose up at.

'Did you come here when you were a kid?' he asked.

'Yeah, Mum always complained about how crap it was compared to the ones back home.'

'My nan did that too,' he told her. 'And she was pretty deaf by then so they all got to hear about it.'

Ferreira laughed. 'I bet you just died of embarrassment.'

He had. Even the thought of it now brought a flash of heat to his face.

'Billy said Jepson's selling work gear,' she said. 'Or that's what he's using as a front these days anyway.'

They found Jepson's stall at the far edge of the market, sited between two vacant pitches. A burger van was parked a few metres away, wafting out the scent of frying onions and greasy meat. The remnants of Zigic's hangover told him it was just what he needed to settle his stomach, but the part of him that had sobered up vetoed the idea.

Prison had been hard on Jepson, he saw, as they got closer. He'd kept his compact shape but his face looked roughened up, deep lines running down each cheek, heavy bags under his eyes. He had wind-chapped skin and thinning grey hair in an undercut thirty years too young for him.

'I remember you,' he said, putting a hard eye on Zigic.

'Then you'll know why we're here.'

'I don't do that any more.' Jepson gestured at the knock-off DeWalt boots boxed up in front of him. 'This is my line now. Good for giving suspects a kicking. Only twenty pound a pair.' He turned to Ferreira. 'We do ladies too.'

'You think these would make it past Trading Standards?' she asked, turning one over between her hands.

'Is that what you're going to threaten me with?' Jepson laughed incredulously. 'Read the label. DeValt. All as legit as they need to be.'

'And how's business?'

'Not much footfall,' he said, looking around at the conspicuous lack of customers at the surrounding stalls.

'What about your other business?' Zigic asked.

Jepson shook his head. 'Told you, I don't do that any more.'

'Prison straighten you out?'

'I'm not going back inside.' He blew into his hands. 'This about that old boy that got shot?'

'Now why would you think that?'

'Because you're here,' Jepson said, stiffening slightly. 'So I imagine he was shot with a converted replica and you're going to ask me if I'm up to my old tricks.'

'And are you?' Ferreira asked, tossing the boot back into its box.

'Would I be out here freezing my balls off if I was?'

'It's a good front,' she suggested. 'And an easy place for interested parties to come find you.'

'There's no money in that game any more,' Jepson said. 'Any idiot with a vice and a drill and a bit of common sense could work out how to do it off online videos.'

Ferreira gave him an indulgent look. 'I think you're selling yourself short there, Mr Jepson. From what I hear it's a highly specialised skill.'

'I'll take all the flattery you want to give out but I can't tell you what I don't know.' He shrugged inside his donkey jacket. 'Chances are that gun came off of some shady bastard on the dark web.'

'Is that where you're selling yours now?' Zigic asked.

Jepson grinned at him. 'Son, I've only just got the drop of Grindr. The dark web's well beyond me.'

Zigic remembered him during questioning. Not a hardened criminal, just a man with a marketable skill and lack of basic morality. With his house full of weapons and kit, denial had never been an option, but he didn't try the no comment route, didn't excuse his actions. Accepted his complicity in the woman's death.

Which had made the case easier at the time but it meant that now Zigic had no idea whether he was lying or not. Simply didn't know what that looked or sounded like.

His gut feeling was that Jepson was playing straight with them.

'So who should we be talking to?' Ferreira asked him.

'Search me.' Another slight shrug. 'I've been inside for the last ten years, remember. It's not like I'm in some gun dealers' WhatsApp group.'

On the nearest stall a cannonball-shaped man in a red anorak was watching and listening and Zigic realised that if Jepson was still dealing he wouldn't be carrying anything on his own stall. An accomplice nearby would be sensible. But they had no warrant and no real cause to start overturning people's businesses.

'A young man has been murdered,' Ferreira reminded Jepson, an impatient edge coming into her voice. 'Shot in the back. Executed on the street.'

'I told you,' Jepson snapped. 'I'm done with all that. I learned my lesson. That's what you wanted, right? It's what I was supposed to do while I was banged up all those fucking years. I *learned* I didn't want to lose another day to that place.' The colour was rising in Jepson's ravaged face. 'I'm still on licence, for fuck's sake. How stupid do you think I am?'

Fear in his face where Zigic had hoped to see guilt. And he knew how often the former masked the latter, but didn't think it was now. Not with this man.

'If you hear anything …' he said.

Jepson wiped his mouth. 'I know where to find you.'

Chapter Twenty-One

Daniel McLeary went up in the suspects column, his mugshot from four months previous showing a sallow-faced man with grey stubble and very green eyes, one of them smudged brown where an old bruise was slowly fading. Fifty-seven but older-looking. Like so many of the men from the Greenaway Club, Zigic thought; the stress of the last few years telling hard on them. Previously comfortable lives knocked off course, the debilitating effects of stress and depression, the sleep-robbing anxiety of bills they couldn't pay and roofs that might not stay over their heads.

Even Lionel Ridgeon, who had evidently found a fresh start with a new woman after his wife's death, carried a shadow around him. The grief that had driven him to attempt suicide still lingering, always present, Zigic guessed.

'We need to track down McLeary,' he said.

Ferreira nodded, looking at the board. 'I'll call Bruce Humble, see if he can tell us where he's staying at the moment.'

'And the benefits agency,' he suggested. 'They must have a last known address if nothing else. Maybe uniform as well. If he's been shoplifting and begging, they might know a bit more about him than what we've got on his file.'

Thinking that if McLeary had killed Jordan Radley, he could have left town already. Nothing to keep him here.

Thinking as well that a man with his lack of financial resources would find it hard to come by a gun. But there were ways, he supposed. Replicas were cheap after all and McLeary had been working at a garage until recently, meaning he might still have access to the kind of tools you'd need to make a conversion. Assuming he had the skill level.

131

And Zigic was convinced it took real skill, despite Jepson's flippant assertion that anyone could do it if they watched a couple of online tutorials.

He'd tried that when Anna bought a new light for the dining room. Googled the process and read a bunch of posts on DIY forums that said you didn't need an electrician if the wires were already in place. Click this link, get these tools, piece of piss.

The light was in the garage now, swaddled in bubble wrap, waiting for a professional to come and deal with the mess he'd made.

Parr came in as he was pouring a cup of coffee, knowing he shouldn't because he was jittery enough already, but also that if he didn't the delayed crash would hit him even harder.

'Couple more blokes mentioned McLeary,' Parr said, throwing his waterproof over the back of his chair. 'Sounds like he could be handy with his fists when he wanted to be.'

But fighting was different to shooting someone. A whole new order of magnitude and the more reports they got back of McLeary's temper the more Zigic began to wonder about it. If his reputation was just a distraction.

If all the men at the Greenaway Club were.

Zigic went into his office and pulled up the files from the harassment and criminal damage charges back in 2015, wanting to see how the men they'd spoken to acted when they were suspected of crimes they had definitely committed.

As he read the interview transcripts he heard DI Sawyer's throaty voice as if she was in the room with him. Calm and even, probing when she saw cracks, letting the men talk themselves into trouble.

Zigic had half expected to find a series of denials or no comments but all of them were open about what they'd done. Admissions followed by lengthy justifications. Every one of them mentioning the jobs they'd lost.

Bruce Humble saying, 'You should look into the sale of the factory if you want to investigate a real crime.'

Similar from Dick Caxton: 'That's it, right? One rule for the rich another for the rest of us. Those bastards stole everything from us and you did *nothing*. We wreck a couple of hundred quid's worth of car tyres and you drag us out of our houses like murderers.'

'What would you have done if it were your job?' Steve Gurney demanded. 'Wouldn't be yours though, would it? No, you're sitting pretty at the taxpayers' expense.'

They weren't. None of them. A 20 per cent real-terms cut in police wages since 2010 and who knew what would be left of his pension pot by the time he retired? Never mind the youngsters like Bloom and Weller. Zigic knew that there were uniforms at the station working second jobs already, had read news reports about coppers resorting to food banks to feed their families.

Nobody was sitting pretty.

He dragged his attention back to the transcripts.

The heat of the situation was burning off the pages as Zigic read on. He kept thinking that there was none of this heat around the men now. That if Jordan had got on the wrong side of one of them, shouldn't they be seeing this same anger?

If *this* level of rage had led to slashed tyres, then how would Humble or Gurney behave if they'd been angry enough to murder Jordan Radley?

When he tried going further back, to interviews for Steve Gurney's run-in with another driver in a Sainsbury's car park and to Daniel McLeary's fight with a taxi driver, he found the same indignation blowing up around them. Both men acting like they were the victims.

Lionel Ridgeon was different though and as Zigic read through the statement he'd given to DC Lear, he heard a ground-down and weary man speaking.

'My wife'll be lucky to see out the month. I'm not having her spending her last few weeks listening to what that bastard calls music blaring through the bloody walls at all hours.' A fair comment, Zigic thought, and any half decent neighbour would have considered the impact he was having on those living next door during such a difficult time.

Ridgeon didn't play the victim but even Zigic struggled to judge him for cutting off the neighbour's power supply.

Until he saw the details of how Ridgeon had achieved that in Lear's report. How he'd waited until the neighbour had gone to work and then broken into the house, located the fuse box in the cupboard under the stairs and disconnected it with a professional electrician's precision, before replacing the unit so that it appeared untampered with. He would have got away with it if not for the well-concealed nanny-cam the neighbour had set up to monitor the activities of his cats while he was out.

A non-confrontational approach, he thought. A smarter one than he might have given Ridgeon credit for.

Zigic picked up the phone and called the tech department, asked for an update on Jordan's laptop.

'It'll be the end of day. Sorry, but I can only work with what I have in front of me.'

As he put the phone down Colleen Murray knocked on his door, hair damp and beginning to frizz around her face, beige raincoat darkly speckled.

'Anything from Jordan's work friends?' he asked.

'Nothing useful,' she said. 'He was good with the customers, made decent tips. Didn't shirk his responsibilities or miss shifts.' She wiped away a few strands of dirty blonde hair plastered to her cheek. 'No trouble to report with other staff members or customers. It's a nice sort of place, all old folks and families. Hardly rough arse central.'

'And Jordan was friendly but distant, right?'

She nodded. 'Same everywhere we're going, you have to ask yourself why.'

'I got the feeling he was biding his time,' Zigic said, remembering what Jordan's mother had told them. How ambitious he was, how badly he wanted to get out of Peterborough. 'If he thought he was going on to better things, I suppose he didn't want to get close to anyone.'

'You don't get to choose that though, do you?' Murray asked. 'You work with people, you get matey with them. It's inevitable. It's just familiarity. Even if you've got bugger all in common, spending that much time together you end up bonding. No matter how annoying they are.'

'Is that a subtle way of saying you want moving away from Mel?' he asked.

Murray smiled. 'No, but if you could get her to stop eating all my biscuits, I'd appreciate it.'

'You think there was something amiss with Jordan?' he asked.

Murray screwed her face up. 'I'm wondering if he might have been a bit of a user.'

'Or he was socially awkward?'

'You can't do his job without highly developed social skills,' she pointed out. 'Anyway, I went to the pub where Harry Bracewell was on the night of the murder.'

'And?'

'The bartender remembered him and his girlfriend. I think he remembered the girlfriend a bit better.' She patted the handbag slung across her front. 'I've got the footage from the camera on their main door, so I'll go through and see if we can fix a time for them leaving.'

Zigic got up and went out to the main office, over to the board where a map of the surrounding area was tacked up.

'Where's the pub?' he asked.

Murray pointed to a spot on Oundle Road. 'Bit of a walk to the crime scene.'

'How long do you think?' He traced the route with his finger-tip, through tight-packed suburban streets, all twists and turns. 'Fifteen minutes?'

'If he was moving fast, yeah.'

'He's a young guy,' Zigic reminded her.

'Ten or fifteen minutes then,' she said, retreating to her desk.

Zigic stared at the map, plotting the route in his mind, the side streets not covered by CCTV, the shortcuts Bracewell might have taken, how easily he could have secreted himself in the bushes near the locus. Nobody noticed bland-looking young men on the street.

Across Murray's shoulder he saw her computer screen filled with a shot of the entrance of a pub. A yellow-tinged lantern light in the deep tiled porchway. Heavy double doors glazed with bullseye glass, the interior glowing through it.

He watched people arriving in fast-forward. The time code showing a little after 7 p.m. Murray sitting hunched and focused as the clock shot past 7:30, slowing and going back when Bracewell and his girlfriend arrived, both dressed in dark clothes. Night camouflage.

'You can do this yourself if you want,' Murray said without turning around.

Zigic took the hint. Went back into his office and waited.

CHAPTER TWENTY-TWO

An hour of calls got Ferreira nowhere and she wondered if she was being fobbed off because she'd done this on the phone rather than going around Daniel McLeary's possible haunts in person. It was easy to lie to a disembodied voice, less so when you had to meet its owner's eye. But these people had no reason to lie to her, she reminded herself, as she put the phone down once more, dropping it into the cradle harder than she meant to.

She'd told everyone the same thing.

'One of Danny's friends has died and we need to get some background. We were hoping he could help. Do you know where I could find him?'

Apologies and old information were all she got for her trouble. Daniel McLeary hadn't been staying at any of the hostels she tried and the woman at the benefits agency told them McLeary wasn't in receipt of Universal Credit or anything else for that matter. She tried the soup kitchen on Fitzwilliam Street and found the number had been disconnected.

After that she went downstairs and talked to a few of the uniforms who recognised him from previous run-ins. She had his photo circulated and was assured that they would keep a special eye out for him.

Bruce Humble's phone went to voicemail when she tried it.

A little after three, she got a call from Geri Colman at the *Evening Telegraph*, more apologies but at least this time there was information at the end of them. The IT guy had done his bit and Jordan's emails were ready for collection.

She sent Parr over for the flash drive and waited, pacing around the office, always returning to Jordan Radley's board where Harry

Bracewell stared out of the suspects column at her. More than just wishful thinking now that Colleen had ripped apart his alibi.

CCTV from the main entrance of the Queens Arms had shown Bracewell and his girlfriend arriving a little after half past seven. Just as he'd said when they asked him for an alibi.

Two hours later they left again.

Earlier than he'd claimed but was it long enough to be suspicious? Thirty minutes' difference between alibi and reality. Barely a fifteen-minute walk between the pub and the crime scene.

Assuming he'd had the gun on him already and that he was cool-headed enough to go from a pleasant evening of live music to executing a fellow student on the side of a main road with no preparation time in between.

A sociopath could do that, she thought, looking at his image on the board and the point on the map that marked his address. Imagining how easy it would have been to walk home with his girlfriend and then go out again and wait for Jordan Radley.

As she was rolling a cigarette the Google alert she'd set up for Jordan's name pinged, sending her to a statement from the National Union of Journalists.

> We are shocked and saddened to hear of the murder of Peterborough journalist Jordan Radley. Jordan was at the beginning of what promised to be a successful career, marked by his already well-established skill as a reporter and investigator, as well as his dedication to supporting those on the margins of society. In what is becoming an all too familiar case for crusading journalists in the United Kingdom and around the world, Jordan was shot in a cowardly act of violence.
>
> His killing is a stark reminder of the ongoing threat of gun violence in this country and of the rising tide of animosity towards members of the press and the need for solidarity and strength in these dark times.
>
> Our thoughts go out to Jordan's family and friends.

Ferreira closed the page.

A short while later Parr returned, handed her a thumb drive and went to make himself a cup of tea. 'You want one?'

Three other people around the office said yes and he slumped where he stood.

'I'm okay, thanks,' Ferreira told him, returning to her desk as he grudgingly fulfilled the other orders.

Jordan's inbox was empty.

She swore lightly to herself. Wondered if Colman had been through Jordan's emails already, looking for some fresh angle she could spin into another front-page story. Or to see if there was anything that she might have wanted to delete before it got to them.

No way of knowing now.

They should have taken Jordan's computer when they were at the newspaper's office, she realised. Had extended the editor a professional courtesy she didn't deserve because they had been so thoroughly drilled that you were always to keep the local press onside.

Ferreira prayed that they hadn't lost something vital for their act of misplaced respect.

But no, didn't this look just right for Jordan?

She thought of how fastidious he seemed, the tidy desk at home with nothing superfluous left out. What they knew of him so far suggested a mind that abhorred clutter and when she went to the deleted messages she found a week's worth waiting to be emptied.

Clicking through, they were all perfectly innocuous. People getting in touch to ask him to cover their stories about bin collections and unruly hedges, a man whose cat had gone missing and a woman wanting Jordan to help raise awareness of her crowdfunding for a statue of a local musician, which was some-how failing to gain traction. The email read like the woman was on something but Jordan had sent a polite reply suggesting that social media might have wider reach for her target demographic than an article in the local paper. He'd replied to most of the messages, sending links to groups who might be able to help, faultlessly polite and patient.

Nothing there that might have got him killed.

Into the saved messages next.

She'd been expecting all of the emails to relate to articles he'd written for the *ET* but quickly it became clear that most weren't. This was the only public address she'd found for Jordan online so she supposed it was inevitable that this was where the bulk of the long-form vitriol was sent.

As she scanned them she wondered why he was saving these ramblings. None was overtly threatening but they were hardly the kind of thing you'd want to come back to and reread: people calling him a snowflake and a libtard, accusing him of being in the pay of the Labour party and the Russian government and George Soros.

Ferreira thought of Harry Bracewell and his extremist buddies, wondered if any of these had originated with them.

People were angry that he'd covered an event at the city mosque, the same person popping up to complain about misandrist bias in his choice of quotes across several articles; did he realise 70 per cent of his quotes were from women when they were only 51 per cent of the population. Telling him women wouldn't fuck him just because he pretended to care about the shit they were taking. Calling him a beta and a cuck, a little bitchboy.

She felt her own anger stirring as she read on, checking the email addresses and finding them generic and seemingly random, addresses unlikely to lead back to identifiable people.

Ferreira rubbed her eyes, returned her attention to the screen, kept clicking, vaguely aware of Kitson coming back from a press briefing and heading straight into Billy's office. She wondered how long Kitson would be able to put up with his micromanaging. Whether she'd eventually complain to Riggott and have him rein Billy in.

If Riggott cared enough to get involved in office politics any more.

He was largely absent from briefings these days, less constructive in his criticisms and less forthcoming in his support. The Walton incident had broken something in Riggott, she thought. And quietly, in some corner of her soul she didn't want to prod, she was judging him for playing the victim. Three innocent people had died, one irredeemably guilty person had died, and she …

Ferreira blinked a few times, pushed away the memory of Walton lying in a pool of blood, the rasping sounds of his breathing. But as she went back to Jordan's emails, her tongue slid along her bottom teeth, finding the implants that looked real enough but still felt alien inside her mouth, the patina too slick, the sound they made when she clicked them slightly off-key.

She took a breath, opened another red-flagged email.

'Shit.'

There were no words, just a photograph; a lean-faced, grey-haired woman in her late forties, her expression grim, eyes haunted.

Ferreira went into Zigic's office, found him in the middle of a conversation with his wife. He put up an apologetic hand and she waited in the doorway as he carefully transcribed the shopping list he was being given. Saw 'wine' at the top, underlined twice.

'What have you found?' he asked, as he put his phone down.

'Somebody sent Jordan a photograph of Anna Politkovskaya,' she said. 'Russian journalist, shot dead by –'

'I know who she is, Mel.'

'She was shot with a converted replica. Did you know that?'

'You think the killer sent him that?' Zigic asked, uncertain sounding. 'Like a warning?'

'It's an unusual choice of weapon, right?' She paced the narrow space in front of his desk. 'We've not really thought about why that particular method, have we? But it's weird. Even you have to admit that.'

He nodded but she could see the reluctance on him still, written in the tilt of his shoulders and the line of his upper lip.

'There's an element of spectacle about it,' she said.

'You're still thinking Bracewell?'

'I'm thinking it looks like more than a straightforward murder. Kate said it back at the scene: "execution style". And that's exactly what it looks like. A public execution. Maybe that's why he was killed right next to a main road, because this wasn't just about Jordan Radley, it was about saying, "We can get to you anywhere."'

Zigic shook his head. 'Mel, this is serious enough without us reading some deeper agenda into it.'

She scowled at him. 'Jordan Radley was sent a photograph of an assassinated journalist less than a week before he was *executed* with the same kind of weapon. You don't think this might be significant?'

'It's a death threat,' he conceded. 'Of course I think it's significant.'

'And Jordan saved the email, just like he saved all the nasty shit people sent him.'

'Get it over to tech,' Zigic said wearily. 'See if they can trace the sender.'

'That's the longest of long shots,' she told him. 'These people are more careful than that.'

'So you don't want to check it out?' he asked.

'I'll send it,' she said. 'But I think we need to bring Bracewell in. He's lied about his alibi. We've got an half an hour where we can't account for his movements. Don't you want to put that to him?'

Zigic rubbed his beard. 'Half an hour is a tight time frame.'

'It's long enough,' she insisted.

'No,' he said, shifting straighter in his chair. 'It isn't. Half an hour is easily explainable as misremembering. If you want to make this about Bracewell, you're going to need something more substantial than that.'

CHAPTER TWENTY-THREE

The afternoon was wearing on towards shift end and Ferreira felt a nagging irritation every time she looked at Harry Bracewell's photograph on the board. A sensation she could put down to irritation at Zigic for not backing her theory but they'd been here before on other cases and he'd given her leeway on longer shots. Putting her in the uncomfortable position of having to consider whether this one was beyond his tolerance for a reason. If maybe she was letting her dislike of Bracewell cloud her judgement.

His attitude was insufferable, his beliefs repugnant, but as she'd looked over and again at the brief clip of security footage from the doorway of the pub on Queen's Road, she saw nothing to suggest a man bent on committing murder in the following thirty minutes. He'd looked a little drunk, with his arm draped heavily around his girlfriend's shoulder and feet dragging as if he was fit for nothing but his bed.

A particularly organised murderer might have spotted the camera and known it would be integral to his future alibi. Acted the part for it, to throw them off the scent. But as much as she wanted to believe that, she couldn't seem to convince herself.

At the front of the room Zigic was explaining that they would be returning to the crime scene tonight at ten to interview potential witnesses. Volunteering her just like that, but there was nothing she could do about it.

Determinedly she finished the energy bar she'd bought from the vending machine, eyeing the jar of biscuits on Murray's desk and thinking about the trip to the gym she would have to cancel tonight. A class booked that she'd still have to pay for, but there was no way she'd manage to fit in dinner and an hour of spin and still have the time and energy to join Zigic on London Road in what promised to be sub-zero temperatures, for however long he thought was necessary.

It wasn't their job really. Could easily be delegated, but Zigic always liked to lead from the front, make sure his junior officers never felt that the grunt work and tedium fell solely on them.

'Rob, where are you at with the phone records?' Zigic asked, turning to Weller.

There was a bundle of paper on his desk, the top sheet covered in strips of highlighter pen.

'Jordan used his mobile a *lot*,' Weller said. 'I'm tracking down the numbers but it's going to take awhile yet. The geographical ones aren't too much bother, a lot of them are companies.'

'What kind of companies?' Ferreira asked.

'Solicitors' offices, architects, charities, that sort of thing.'

'He's calling around for stories,' Zigic said. 'Are they in clusters?'

Weller flipped through the pages. 'Yeah, I suppose so. He's calling an architect, then a housing charity, then a hostel.'

'He's looking for quotes,' Ferreira said, remembering the article she'd read on the *ET*'s website about the homeless hostel being bought up and the site redeveloped. 'If he was working on some big story when he was killed, then his contacts for it are going to be in his call logs.'

'What's the most recent set of calls look like?' Zigic asked.

Weller scrambled through the sheets and Ferreira saw Zigic's expression harden.

'When somebody's been murdered you start with their final phone calls,' Zigic told him, an uncharacteristic edge to his tone.

'Sorry, sir.' Weller kept his eyes on the papers, turned to the last page, which was completely untouched. Not a scrap of pen anywhere on it. 'I'll get on this now.'

Zigic went into his office and closed the door.

For a second Ferreira considered going and saying something, but Weller was in the wrong and it wasn't as if Zigic had torn a strip off him.

She went back to Jordan Radley's emails from his account at the *Evening Telegraph*, the photo of a dead journalist still open on her screen and finally she closed it.

There was nothing else from that email address. Most of the people who contacted Jordan seemed to be frequent complainers. She imagined them feeling like they were putting him in his place, that they got some thrill from knowing the sight of their address would make him angry or nervous.

She wondered how Jordan had really felt about these people. Impossible to know for sure but saving the emails suggested they had got under his skin.

Was Jordan scared? Is that why he'd created this hate-filled archive? Perhaps he thought that one day it might be important that the record was there. That he suspected one of these people might be unhinged enough to move from the online world to the real one.

She thought of Daniel McLeary, the man from the Greenaway Club with the axe to grind. His photo in the suspects column alongside Harry Bracewell. She knew they needed to track him down as a matter of urgency but when she checked her phone, there were no callbacks from any of the people she'd contacted about him. Not even Bruce Humble who, out of everyone, had a personal link with Jordan and an interest in finding his killer.

She tried Humble again, getting sent to voicemail after four rings. Humble seeing her number and rejecting the call.

What was he hiding, she wondered.

For a while she lost herself in Jordan's emails, didn't realise how long she'd been there until Weller came over holding the sheet of phone records.

'I've found something,' he said, slightly apologetic. 'Jordan called this number three times in the ten days before he was killed.'

She looked at the number he'd highlighted. Seven calls, all around midday. The durations ranging from eight minutes to twenty-five.

'First call on October 27th,' he said, reaching out to turn the pages back. 'Then a week later multiple calls during the day that weren't answered.'

Ferreira looked at the spread of them, trying to figure out what Jordan had been up to.

'Could this be the story?' Weller asked.

'They picked up eventually,' Ferreira said, seeing an hour-long phone conversation on November 17th, started just after 8 a.m. 'Have you traced the number?'

'It's a private home,' he told her. 'Over in Bretton.'

She smiled, started towards Zigic's office. 'Good work, Rob.'

CHAPTER TWENTY-FOUR

It was a low-rise block on a gentrifying estate to the north of the city, the place renovated since the last time Zigic had been there a year or more ago. Stretches of white-painted cladding were now fixed to the façade and wrapped around the sides, bright and burnished under the low, late afternoon sun.

Ferreira pressed the buzzer for flat 2A but the door didn't open. She tried one after another until the main doors opened, letting them into a narrow vestibule with green-tiled walls and a painted concrete floor, then up a stairwell to the second floor.

Sheila Yule answered the door in her pyjamas and dressing gown, ash blonde hair in a tousled bob and cobalt blue spectacles dominating her face. Almost hiding how tired she was behind them.

'Mrs Yule, could we come in for a few minutes?' Zigic showed her his ID even though she didn't look at it. Almost nobody did. 'It's about Jordan Radley.'

'I'm on shift soon,' she said, walking away from the open door. 'You'll have to be quick.'

They followed her into a chilly living room at the front of the flat, the large picture window overlooking the dense screen planting that separated the block from the dual carriageway beyond, dampening the noise to a low thrum. The room was neat but dated and Zigic imagined Sheila Yule and her husband had decorated it when they first moved in then not touched it since. Striped wallpaper, a patterned carpet under a patterned rug, a china cabinet filled with figurines and family photos in gilt frames.

She sat down in a burgundy velour armchair near the electric fire and picked up a half-eaten bowl of porridge.

'Sorry, but if I don't eat now I'm going to be starving all night.' She gestured with her spoon. 'Sit. Go on, ask your questions.'

They sat on the sofa and Zigic felt a disconcerting sense of having lost time somehow; Sheila Yule having breakfast while what must have been a recorded episode of *This Morning* played on the television. She muted the sound but left it running as the presenters hosted a phone-in about toxic friendships. He glanced towards the window, where the sun was setting behind the trees, just to reassure himself that it was actually late afternoon.

'Are you on night shift?' Zigic asked.

'I'm a home care nurse,' she said. 'Six tonight till eight tomorrow.'

'We'll be as quick as we can then,' he assured her. 'What was the nature of your relationship with Jordan Radley?'

'I didn't have a relationship with him,' she said. 'I knew him, but not very well.'

'Do you know what's happened to him?'

She nodded, spoon going still in her porridge. 'Terrible thing to happen to a nice young man like that.'

'You and Jordan were in regular contact in the days before his death,' Zigic said, letting her know they knew and that there was no point denying it. 'Can you tell us what you were talking about?'

She put her bowl aside, reached for a mug of tea on the low table between them. 'Jordan wanted to know about my job. How it worked, that kind of thing.'

'Why?'

'For a story, I suppose. He *was* a journalist.'

'Why would Jordan think you'd be able to give him a story?' Zigic asked. 'Is there something wrong at the place you work?'

'I dare say it's no worse than anywhere else.' She shrugged. 'And it's not like people don't already know what a mess the social care system's in, is it? You could say it as many times as you like, it's not going to make it any better.'

'Is that what you told Jordan?'

'More or less.' Sheila sipped her tea, evading his gaze.

'It took you a long time to tell him that,' Zigic pointed out. 'You were in contact for weeks before his death. Seven calls, Sheila.'

'He was a bit pushy,' she said, shoulders lifting around her ears.

'How did Jordan make contact with you?' Ferreira asked, and he heard the challenge in the question, knew that she'd noticed Sheila click into defensive mode.

'He called me up out of the blue and said he needed to find a carer for his nan and that someone had recommended me.'

'Who?'

'That's the first thing I asked him.' Sheila put down her tea and picked up her porridge again, the smell of it sweet and milky. 'He told me he couldn't remember the woman's name but it was someone who came into the restaurant where he worked.'

Jordan had been lying, Zigic thought. Dangling an opportunity in front of Sheila Yule, maybe guessing that she would need money and hoping the need might overcome her initial suspicions.

'I told him I could only work through the agency,' Sheila went on. 'I have to be available whenever they call me in for a shift. I can't register with a second agency and I can't take on private work. If I'm not on the end of the phone when they call, I get the sack.' She looked into her bowl. 'I told him I couldn't afford to lose my job. But like I said, he was a bit pushy and I agreed to meet with him because he said his nan was important to him.' She frowned. 'He sounded emotional.'

Putting it on to draw her out, Zigic thought. He wondered at how easily it had come to Jordan. If that made him a good journalist or a bad person – or if the two went together.

'And when did you realise he didn't actually have a job for you?' Ferreira asked.

'We met in a café over the way,' Sheila said. 'He was upfront about it once I was there. He told me he was interested in what was going on in social care and he needed someone like me to give him the facts.'

'How did you feel about that?'

'I wasn't happy,' she said, the memory heating her voice up before she brought herself back down. 'But I could see that he had good intentions. He was stupid if he thought anyone else would care but it was nice that he did.'

'What did you tell him?'

'I didn't have anything to tell.' She put the bowl down again. 'He asked me some questions about my shifts and the kind of people I care for. Was the company good? Did they hold back my money? But that's not a story, is it? Carers get treated like dirt and their bosses dock their wages whenever they get the chance.'

'Did Jordan want more?'

'I don't know.' She wrapped her dressing gown around herself. 'Yes, I mean, he wanted a story and I couldn't give him one.'

'How did he react when he realised it had been a waste of time?'

'He thanked me for talking to him and left the café,' she said.

For a few seconds there was nothing but the hum of the TV set as Sheila Yule watched them, waiting for the next round of questions, the hope that it was over now palpable.

'So what were you talking about on the phone?' Ferreira asked.

Sheila nudged her glasses up her nose. 'The same thing.'

'For hours on end?'

'It wasn't hours,' she said dismissively.

'Cumulatively it was,' Ferreira told her. 'Forty minutes here, twenty minutes there. You talked to Jordan for a whole hour on November 17th. That's just over a week before he died, Sheila.' Ferreira on the edge of the sofa now. 'What were you talking about?'

'I've told you already.'

'What do you think's going on here?' Ferreira asked, voice dropping. 'Jordan has been murdered. Shot twice to make sure he never got up again.'

Sheila Yule knew how serious it was, Zigic saw. She drew her dressing gown even tighter around herself, knuckles going white on the fabric, knees pressing hard together.

'You clearly maintained contact with Jordan after that initial meeting,' Ferreira said. 'And we know he was working on a big story when he died. Did you give him that story?'

She was terrified, Zigic now realised. Had been from the second they walked in maybe.

'We can protect you,' he said. 'If you and Jordan were involved in something that got him killed, we can keep you safe.'

'I don't know what he was doing,' she said firmly.

'If something you told him led to his murder, then you owe it to Jordan to come forward,' Ferreira pressed.

Sheila Yule couldn't look at her, stared at the floor in front of her feet.

'His mother is devastated,' Ferreira said. 'She needs to see whoever killed her son behind bars.'

'I don't know anything,' Sheila snapped, standing up sharply. 'If I knew I'd tell you. But this is nothing to do with me.'

She stormed out of the room and they followed.

'I know you're scared,' Ferreira said. 'And you're right to be, but keeping quiet won't keep you safe.'

The door to the bedroom stood open, a blue nurse's uniform laid out on the foot of the bed.

'I'd like you to leave now,' she said fiercely. 'I've told you everything I know.'

Zigic held a card out to her. 'You can get me on these numbers any time. Day or night. If you change your mind about helping us, I want you to call me.'

Reluctantly she took it and showed them out.

Zigic wanted to stay and try to talk her around but she was scared, he knew, and fear didn't listen to logic or appeals for assistance; it went straight to say nothing, make yourself small, run as far as you can.

If they were going to draw her into helping them, they would need more than the bald facts of Jordan Radley's murder.

CHAPTER TWENTY-FIVE

'Billy's sulking,' Ferreira said, taking a drag on her roll-up. 'I think he was actually angling to come out and help with this tonight.'

Zigic made a non-committal noise and looked along the path towards the row of shops 300 metres away where a few teenagers were hanging around. The light and their laughter closing the distance between the crime scene and the continuation of ordinary life.

Ferreira tucked her chin down into her scarf. 'If he knew how fucking cold it was, he'd realise how lucky he is staying at home.'

'Riggott won't be there forever,' Zigic said.

'He's going to leave word for his replacement though, isn't he?'

'Probably,' Zigic conceded, rubbing his hands together for warmth. 'Doesn't mean they'll take any notice. Not if they're any good at the job. You don't rock up at a new post and let your predecessor's old feuds get in the way of managing your team.'

They both knew that was exactly how it worked, though. A quiet drink at handover, point out who the troublemakers are, who can be relied on to cover your back, who has a drink problem or a gambling problem. A new DCS arriving at a station cold needed that knowledge if they wanted to hit the ground running. Policing was so tightly budgeted and time constrained now that you couldn't afford to take your time and suss out each individual officer for yourself.

And God knows Riggott had dirt on all of them.

She took another drag, refusing to think of what her report would say. The damage he could deal her if he chose to.

Riggott, with all his dubious behaviours in the past, would walk away into a peaceful retirement, leaving them to face a superior officer who would know all their secrets and the leverage it created. Never mind that this last mess, out of all of the ones they'd found themselves in over the years, was Riggott's fault more than anyone else's.

A pizza delivery van slowed as it passed them but didn't stop. The driver looked towards the yellow incident board placed on the pavement where Jordan Radley had been shot. Lots of drivers had slowed in the last twenty minutes but it was idle curiosity, she thought. The usual ghoulish desire to see what had happened on a road they knew well.

There was a second board on the other side of the road, two uniformed officers working the pavement.

10:15 now and they were coming up to the time Jordan Radley had been shot.

A few locals had been past, stopped and answered their questions before asking a few of their own, everyone wanting to know if they were safe to walk home or bring their dog out before they went to bed. So far nobody reported seeing anything amiss on Monday night.

People were creatures of habit and everyone they'd spoken to reported coming through here at the same time every night. Knocking off work the same time, their dog whining at the door at ten on the dot.

'Anna wasn't happy about it,' Zigic said. 'We've just got to a crucial bit in *Fauda* and I know she's watching it without me.'

Ferreira shook her head. 'Totally unacceptable behaviour.'

'I wouldn't mind but she'll watch it on her own, then when I need to catch up, she'll sit there telling me everything that's about to happen.'

'You should change the Netflix password before you go out,' Ferreira suggested.

He smiled. 'Is that what you do?'

'I *may* have done that while we were watching *Ozark*.'

'I don't know if that's a dick move or a power move.'

'Same thing, right?' she said. 'But it works.'

A few more people came and went. None had seen anything.

10:30 now. She thought of Jordan Radley approaching the place where he would die. Wondered if he felt it. Some presentiment. An itch at the back of his neck, an urge to turn and look behind him. A survival instinct people told themselves was akin to superstition. Something we didn't need any more. That we'd evolved out of.

She thought of his mother, Moira. At home now, maybe watching the clock as it ticked around and past the forty-eight-hour mark. Two days without him that must have felt like years.

At 10:32 they got a hit.

A woman in an oversize black waterproof and stout boots came out of one of the new houses across the road, a small brown dog with her that yapped at the cars as they waited for the lights to change. The dog dragged her over the road, straining at the end of its leash with a determination barely contained by the fluorescent harness it wore.

'You know you aren't going to go until you get to the trees,' she said. 'Come on, Lyra.'

Zigic smiled as she approached them, the dog disappearing into the undergrowth, just a flicker of white-tipped tail wagging.

'She's very curious,' he said.

'She's a bloody nightmare.' The woman nodded towards the incident awareness sign. 'I didn't know if I should bother you or not but now you're here ...'

Ferreira straightened, thinking that she should and that waiting until you happened to run into a pair of coppers on the street was no way of assisting a murder investigation. But Zigic was taking charge of this one.

'Did you see something?' he asked.

'I don't know if it's relevant.' She glanced towards her dog. 'I couldn't say for certain what time it was so I don't know if I'm telling you something useful or if I'm just suggesting a perfectly innocent person might be involved in a murder.'

'What did you see?' Zigic asked.

'There was a man here,' she said. 'On Monday night when I brought Lyra out to go doo-doo. He was just back there where the greenway starts. Near the houses.'

'What did he look like?'

'I didn't want to make eye contact with him.' She turned to Ferreira. 'You know how it is when you don't know someone's there and then suddenly they just are. It spooked me, to be honest. I didn't know if he was a flasher or something, so I put my head down and kept walking.'

Zigic asked her to show them exactly where the man had been and they followed her back along the path a few metres, the dog reluctantly tagging along.

'There,' she said. 'Nearly in the bushes. I only noticed him because Lyra started barking at him.'

Ferreira could see why she'd been unsettled. It was a dark spot, outside the scope of the nearest street light. A natural hollow in the hedge, perfectly person-sized, with a straight sight line to the path.

The man would have seen Jordan coming, she realised, as she walked to the centre of the path and looked back, but Jordan wouldn't have seen him.

'Do you have any idea what time this might have been?' Zigic asked.

'Not long after ten. Maybe five past, I suppose.'

Ferreira glanced at Zigic, saw the urgency on him. Wanting desperately for this woman to have seen something. The danger now was that if he pressed her, it would cause her to elaborate, wanting to please him because she seemed a nice, decent woman who would want to help the police solve a terrible murder. The enthusiastic eyewitnesses were often the ones who derailed cases.

'Can you tell us anything about how this man looked?' he asked.

'I only saw him for a moment.' Her voice began to waver, eyes straying back to the gap in the hedge.

'Height?'

'Normal height,' she said. 'He wasn't overly tall or overly short. Just ... normal.'

Ferreira cursed internally, thinking of Harry Bracewell coming in at six foot two and skinny with it, so that nobody would call him 'normal height'. Not enough to entirely rule him out but she felt him slip out of the frame.

'What was this man wearing?' Zigic asked.

'Dark clothes,' the woman said. 'Very nondescript. I remember that I couldn't see his face properly, though. I think he was wearing one of those snoods or a scarf pulled up like this.' The side of her hand cut across her nose. 'And I couldn't tell you what colour hair he had so I think he must have been wearing a hat.'

She couldn't say any of those things with a reasonable degree of certainty, Ferreira thought, but what she could tell them was a start.

A man had been waiting here for Jordan Radley to walk by. He'd hidden himself from view. Possibly dressed to blend into the shadows.

Zigic thanked the woman and took her details before she walked away, the dog trotting on ahead of her, barking at some new agitant.

'What do you think?' he asked. 'Not a flasher, right?'

'Probably not.'

'And probably not Harry Bracewell either.'

'No,' she said grudgingly. 'I doubt it. Not if this is the bloke we're looking for.'

They approached the gap in the hedgerow. Ferreira switched on her phone's torch and ran the beam over the ground, seeing a couple of cigarette butts and the silver foil wrapper from a stick of gum, the ground damp-looking, soft.

'Footprints,' she said.

Zigic peered close then straightened again. 'We need to get forensics down here right now.'

DAY THREE

THURSDAY

Chapter Twenty-Six

The first forty-eight hours were up but the pace of the investigation showed no signs of flagging. Everyone was in well before briefing was due to start at eight, the smell of coffee and pastries dominating the office, the box that Zigic had brought in with him was decimated now, only a single sad-looking doughnut left when Ferreira arrived. Parr was standing there with a half-eaten lemon yum-yum in one hand, clearly wondering if he needed the extra sugar rush.

'Okay, we've got a lot to get through today,' Zigic said, walking to the front of the room. The same sentiment as yesterday and no less true, no less urgency in his tone. He explained about the witness they'd found at the locus last night. The vagueness of her description but, 'It's a start. We know whoever killed Jordan was waiting for him and that he took some measures to hide his identity. We'll circulate the description – such as it is – and maybe it'll jog someone's memory.'

'Might be someone else got a better look at him,' Murray suggested.

Zigic nodded. 'We'll be going back to the scene tonight. Same routine. See if we can find a second eyewitness.' He stepped aside, indicating the photo of the spot where the man had been loitering. 'Forensics have been through and we've got a cluster of size nine footprints.'

'Industry standard,' Parr muttered, then bit into the doughnut, jam oozing out, which he caught on the back of his hand.

'We've also got a few snagged fibres. Might come to nothing, especially in such a high traffic area, but that spot was off the beaten track and there's no real reason for anyone else to have been there.'

It wasn't the kind of evidence the CPS or a jury would be impressed by but in an interview room it could be enough to help chip away the defiance of a suspect who was protesting their innocence. Forensic traces always seemed to put a bigger scare into suspects than they really should.

'Where are we with the CCTV, Keri?' he asked.

Bloom wrinkled her nose. 'I've managed to speak to all of the drivers but nobody saw anything. Now we know the killer was standing right there, it seems implausible that someone didn't see him though.'

'It's a bad sight line off the road,' Ferreira told her. 'Partially obscured and he was wearing dark clothing.'

'The good news is we finally have the data culled from Jordan's laptop,' Zigic said, scratching his eyebrow. 'The slightly less good news is that due to the damage to the motherboard, it's not archived by date or file type or any of the usual markers we'd use to start sifting through it. So it's going to take a bit more dedication to get through it all and find out what Jordan was working on.'

'I can start on that,' Bloom said, sounding like she was savouring the challenge.

'Good stuff.' Zigic pointed at Parr. 'I need you on that too, Zac.'

'Sir.'

Murray nodded towards the board. 'What about Bracewell?'

'Out of contention,' Zigic said. 'We've got size nine footprints and a medium-height suspect sighted at the scene – Bracewell is six two and a size twelve.'

'You know what they say about men with big feet,' Parr said, grinning at Murray. 'Not a viable suspect given the forensic evidence at the scene.'

She rolled her eyes at him.

'Now, Sheila Yule.' Zigic turned and looked at the photograph on the board pulled from her driving licence, showing her with longer hair and a more easy-going expression than she'd had at the flat yesterday afternoon. 'Rob, what have you found?'

160

Weller stood smartly, went to the board, and Ferreira noticed Zigic trying to hide a vaguely bemused half-smile as he stepped aside to let him have the floor.

'The company Jordan was apparently digging for dirt on is P&N Medico,' he started.

'They used to be Pickman Nye,' Ferreira added, glancing up as she was rolling a cigarette. 'We know them.'

They'd run into the firm years ago, back when they were supplying migrant labourers of dubious legality to the farming and food-processing sectors. On the up even then, with an office in the Cathedral precincts and contracts with the city council. An extensive rebrand a few years ago had turned them into P&N Medico.

They were a favourite of the local NHS trusts and the various groups that supplied home care and nursing staff to the bigger elder-care facilities, Weller said, giving them background they didn't need because he clearly wanted Zigic to see that he'd been working hard.

'We've got isolated incidents involving P&N staff,' he went on, feet spread wide, hands moving as he talked. 'Theft from patients being the main issue. A couple of accusations of assault that were quietly dropped.'

'They paid off the families,' Murray said, dunking a biscuit in her tea.

'Probably,' Weller agreed. 'One of the families turned in hidden camera footage so it wasn't up for debate that the assaults occurred and we pressed ahead on that charge after they tried pulling the complaint.'

'It sounds like Jordan was onto something with them,' Bloom said. 'Is it possible one of the families contacted him with a tip-off?'

'Pay-offs normally come with non-disclosure clauses,' Murray told her.

'However he got to the company, there might be a story there,' Weller said, voice rising slightly, reclaiming control of the floor. 'And they're turning over enough to make any problem go away.

Companies House shows they have over two million at the bank as of the end of the last tax year.'

'That buys a lot of silence,' Murray muttered.

'Do we have any evidence of Jordan making contact with the company?' Zigic asked, sitting on an empty desk with his arms folded.

'Nothing in his *ET* emails,' Ferreira told him.

'Nothing in his phone records either,' Weller conceded. 'But if he was in the early stages of building a story, he wouldn't contact them, would he?'

'We need to find out how he really got onto Sheila Yule,' Zigic said. 'She wouldn't or couldn't tell us but he didn't pick her name out of thin air. Get in touch with the families we know about and see if they know her. Or if she was mentioned in the original case notes.'

Weller nodded. 'Yes, sir.'

'What do we know about Sheila Yule?' Ferreira asked.

'No criminal record,' Bloom said, spinning around her yellow diamond engagement ring. 'I've put in a call to the Care Quality Commission to see if they've had any reports about her, though. They usually get dealt with in-house, don't they?'

Ferreira nodded.

'What about family?'

'No children,' Bloom said, frowning. 'She divorced her husband three years ago and he died last winter.'

'How?'

'I'll find out. But he was seventy-four, so …'

'It was a bad year for winter flu,' Murray told them. 'Five of them went in the home where my dad is.'

Zigic straightened up away from the desk and walked over to the board, Weller retreating to his chair as he moved in. Ferreira noticed Bloom giving him a quick nod of encouragement.

'The priority right now,' Zigic said, 'is finding anything in Jordan's files that links to Sheila Yule or background on what he was looking for at P&N Medico. We know they've got secrets and it sounds like Jordan was aware of that too. So how did he find out? Who was he talking to besides Sheila Yule? And what did these people tell him?' His face took on a serious cast. 'This woman is scared. She doesn't want to talk to us, so we're going to have to find a way round her or something that's going to compel her to come clean on what she was doing with Jordan.'

'Do you think she's in danger?' Bloom asked.

'If Jordan *was* killed over the story she gave him, or if someone believes she gave him it, then, yes, she's in danger, Keri. So the faster we find a way to bring her in and get her side of the story the better.'

Chapter Twenty-Seven

Four families had reported staff from P&N Medico to the police in the last two years. The most serious accusation, backed up by video footage, showed a heavyset nurse looming over a frail man in an armchair, shouting at him for leaking through his pad.

Zigic had to stop the footage, felt himself welling up with rage and sadness at the sight of it. Thinking of how the man's son must have felt when he checked the video file. How worried he must have been to place cameras in the house to begin with.

And how he'd tried to withdraw the complaint, presumably after being offered a payment by P&N Medico.

It seemed inconceivable that hush money would make you look the other way on something so horrific. Knowing that without the prosecution they'd mounted the nurse would likely still be working, doing the same thing to someone else's vulnerable loved ones.

He wondered how much Sheila Yule could conceivably know about all this. The staff would talk amongst themselves he imagined but most home care jobs were carried out by people working alone and from what he could make out it was a high-churn profession. Half an hour visits booked, but maybe as little as fifteen minutes inside the house. Then onto the next one. For up to sixteen hours per shift. Very little opportunity to compare notes with the other nurses.

A patient might have told her, he realised. But getting access to P&N's client list would be almost impossible without a compelling reason.

How Jordan made contact with Sheila was their main concern.

Or, he realised, how she might have made contact with him.

Now Jordan was dead they couldn't prove who instigated the conversations. No guarantee that any of it played out how Sheila had suggested. She was scared enough to say just about anything to get them out of the flat yesterday afternoon, he thought. And she wouldn't get any less scared until they arrested whoever had killed Jordan.

Bloom knocked on Zigic's door, opened it immediately.

'Sir, I think we've found something.'

Gratefully he left the case files and went into the main office. He found Ferreira sitting in Bloom's seat, intently focused on a file opened on the screen, swearing softly to herself. She looked up as he approached, eyes lit.

'What is it?' he asked.

'Keri's found an AAIB report.'

He blinked at her. 'What do you mean?'

'The Air Accidents Investigation Branch. It's the official report into the crash that killed Marcus Greenaway,' Bloom told him, a thrill in her voice. 'It seems like Jordan was looking into it before he died.'

Ferreira was still reading, scrolling fast.

'What does it say?'

'Exactly what we've been told,' she said, sounding disappointed. 'The model was notoriously unreliable. It's got one of the highest failure and fatality rates of any civilian helicopter on the market.'

'Part of the stabilisation system failed,' Bloom added. 'They put out a report last year advising additional checks on the control shaft after a similar accident but obviously that was far too late for Marcus Greenaway.'

'Send it over to me, would you?'

He went back into his office, opened the file and began to read. The basic details were laid out at the top; the date and time of the crash. The location he'd taken off from at Holme Airfield, a private strip at the edge of a picturesque little village just south of Peterborough. The destination Marcus Greenaway never reached, another private landing strip outside Cambridge. He'd crashed in a field two miles south of Holme, barely a hundred yards away from the A1, perilously close to eight lanes of fast moving, densely packed traffic.

The model and the registration number of the helicopter.

Occupants 1/Fatalities 1

Marcus Greenaway flying himself to a meeting?

His flight experience logged at just under 200 hours, which could have been a factor in him not recognising that something was wrong with the machine, Zigic supposed. A more experienced pilot might have spotted the issue before he took off. Stopped and got out and called someone qualified to deal with it.

Ferreira came into his office, put a cup of black coffee down next to his keyboard and retreated to the chair opposite with her own.

'You can't have read all this yet,' he said.

'I've read as much as I need to. Open and shut.'

'Well, just hold off on the theorising until I've finished, will you?'

He kept reading. Felt himself speeding up as his eyes skimmed over pages of technical specification that he didn't understand. Details of the flight controls and the structural integrity, the state of the engine. Seeing mention of the control shaft that Bloom had already picked up on being blamed for the accident.

The weather and ground conditions on the January morning had been described in detail even though they seemed immaterial. It was form, he guessed. The investigator following their process, making sure no corners were cut, no possibility left unexplored. Not when a man had died and his family had been left behind with questions that demanded answers.

And, according to Riggott, a large insurance claim against the manufacturers in the pipeline.

'You can just skip to the end,' Ferreira said. 'That's where the verdict is.'

Zigic paused at the pathology section.

An aviation pathologist reviewed the post-mortem report on Mr Greenaway and concurred that the accident was not survivable. Mr Greenaway was said to have been drinking on the night before the accident, which may have contributed to his being unaware of early warning signs of loss of tail rotor control.

Maps after that. Elevation levels and a lot of technical details that meant nothing to him.

'Is this why Jordan was hanging around the Club?' Ferreira asked, seemingly struggling to convince herself it was. 'He's pulled the report, but there's no story in it. There must be something more to it than this?'

'He was obviously interested in the crash but that isn't the same thing as investigating it.' Zigic sipped his coffee. 'He might have been researching the background to the factory for the article. Maybe he came across the crash report and downloaded it just in case. Until we know what other info he had about the factory, we can't say whether this was the focus for a story or just … random crap on his hard drive.'

'He did mention the sale in the *Big Issue* piece,' she said. 'So he was obviously researching around the place. But there wasn't anything about the crash so he obviously didn't think it was relevant.'

Zigic thought of how dismissive Riggott had been about the accident, mentioned it more like he was sharing gossip than suggesting a potential line of investigation.

'There was no criminal case,' Ferreira said. 'It must have looked innocent from the off, right?'

'Riggott reckons the Greenaway family threw their clout at the Chief Constable while the harassment was going on,' he told her. 'My guess is they'd have been screaming for blood if they thought there was even a glimmer of a chance the crash was sabotage.'

Ferreira looked thoughtful. 'This could just be nosiness.'

'Spectacular deaths are going to attract even the most ideologically driven reporter. That's basic human nature.'

'And it *is* the bloke who fucked over Jordan's new mates at the Club.' She tapped her knuckles against the arm of the chair. 'You'd want to know how that bloke died after you'd heard so much bad shit about him, I reckon.'

Zigic nodded. 'It tells us something anyway. We know that Jordan wasn't finished with the Club. The crash was a dead end but maybe he found out something that wasn't.'

'We've got several members with criminal records and violent tempers,' Ferreira reminded him, as if he could have forgotten. 'Plenty of scope for Jordan getting on the wrong side of someone.'

'What about Daniel McLeary?' Zigic asked.

'Uniform are looking out for him. I've left word at his regular haunts.' She sounded doubtful of their prospects of finding McLeary, and Zigic understood it. They'd been here before, chasing down men who disappeared between the cracks.

She sighed. 'You still going through the P&N stuff?'

'Yeah.'

'Grim?'

'Grimmer than even I expected.'

'And that's just the cases they didn't manage to silence before we were contacted,' Ferreira said. 'How many more payouts have they made that we don't know about?'

Zigic thought of P&N's fancy headquarters at Lynch Wood, the very public donations to local arts centre, not to mention their banners all over a recent fun run around Ferry Meadows in aid of a charity supporting the elderly. No company shelled out that much cash unless they had something to hide. Buying goodwill in advance of inevitable exposure.

'It seems like the kind of story Jordan would have wanted to write,' Ferreira said. 'You look at his articles so far, it slots right in.'

'More so than "tycoon in fireball death plunge"?' Zigic asked.

She smiled and he knew they shouldn't be joking about it.

'What do you want to do about this with P&N?' She nodded towards the paperwork on his desk. 'Go pay them a visit?'

His turn to smile. Of course she wanted to storm around there and start rattling cages. But P&N were too smart for that and if she wasn't so frustrated with their lack of progress, he knew she would see that.

'Sheila Yule's who we need to speak to,' he said.

'She won't talk.'

'She talked to Jordan,' he pointed out. 'If he found a way to get through to her, then I'm sure we can do the same.'

CHAPTER TWENTY-EIGHT

Later that morning, uniform brought Daniel McLeary into Thorpe Wood Station. They had picked him up at a spot popular with day drinkers near the market.

Ferreira had him put in Interview Room 2 with a sandwich and a cup of strong, sweet tea. Gave him just long enough to get through them before she returned with Zigic in tow.

McLeary gave them a disgusted look as they walked in, his green eyes bloodshot under thick blond brows a shade or two darker than what remained of the long and straggly hair sticking out from under his baseball cap. There was stubble on his cheeks, a smudge of old bruising around one eye that was older than Jordan's murder. When Zigic asked about it he said there were some nasty little shits in Peterborough.

'Nobody to look down on 'cept a homeless man.'

He finished his tea as they took their seats. Ferreira set up the tapes, the turning spools picking up the sound of him tapping his fingers arrhythmically against the table, jumpy but she wasn't sure if it was experience of the room or something more specific behind the nerves.

Zigic began with the usual questions they'd asked all the men from the Club: what time he arrived and when he left.

McLeary told them he'd left during the second half of the match, wasn't feeling it.

'Why not?'

'Too much like the old days,' he said, looking away from them, toying with the cuff of his hoodie. 'You get settled in there, it's easy to forget how fucked your life is once you walk out of the door again.'

Zigic asked where he went afterwards and what route he'd taken. McLeary answered with no hesitation.

'I'm dossing with a mate in Woodston for a bit. Sleeping on his sofa.' Giving the address before he was asked for it, knowing the routine. 'He can tell you where I was if you don't believe me.'

They would check. She expected the man to lie for McLeary but you could never be sure. McLeary was living the kind of transient life where friends and enemies were made quickly and sides were switched even faster.

'Did you speak to Jordan on Monday night?' Zigic asked.

'No, he was with Humble and that lot. I was with Sal and them.'

'How did you get on with Jordan?'

McLeary shrugged. 'He seemed an alright lad. I didn't have much to do with him, tell you the truth. Young kid like that, got nothing in common.'

'Except the article he wrote about you,' Zigic reminded him.

'About *us*,' McLeary said. 'Weren't just me.'

'But you're the only person who wasn't happy about it.'

McLeary said nothing. Knew better than to answer a statement.

'Why were you annoyed about the article?' Zigic asked.

'I weren't.'

'We've been informed otherwise.' Zigic locked his hands together on the table and Ferreira saw McLeary stare at them rather than meet his eye. 'Several of your clubmates have stated that you were livid about the article. You got grief for it at work and then you got sacked. Your friends say you blamed Jordan for losing you your job. What did you say to him about it?'

'Nothing,' McLeary insisted, shooting him a filthy look. 'What was the point? I'd lost my job. It were a shit job at that. I'd find another.'

'Have you found another?'

'Not yet. But I will.' McLeary sounded defiant but Ferreira could see how thin his bravado was. 'And I'm not the only person who were unhappy about the article.'

He waited without elaborating, a sly expression on his tired old face.

Zigic stared him down, amused-looking, before he eventually asked. 'Who else was as angry as you then, Mr McLeary?'

'Steve.' McLeary nodded. 'Steve Gurney, you've talked to him? Big, ugly bastard, right nasty temper on him.'

Just like you, Ferreira thought. Wondering how many times the men had clashed while they were working at the Greenaway factory, sure that these two hard cases would need to establish which of them was the alpha dog.

'Word round the Club is Steve's old woman blew her fucking top over that article Jordan wrote.' McLeary checked his mug, found a mouthful of cold tea still inside and drank it down. 'Threatened to leave him over it they reckon.'

'Who was saying this?' Zigic asked.

'People.'

'Which people?'

'I'm only telling you what I heard,' McLeary said, putting his hands up. 'Apparently Steve's missus were getting grief off of the girls at her work, saying she wanted to throw him out and get a proper bloke instead of that whinging headcase. Seems to me they were only saying what she were thinking herself, though. Wouldn't have threatened him with leaving otherwise, would she now?' He shrugged. 'Couldn't believe it when I saw Steve sitting there, laughing and joking with Jordan. Matey as you like. Not the Steve Gurney I know, that.'

'Maybe he's mellowed,' Ferreira suggested.

'Not fucking likely.'

'Who do you think killed Jordan?' Zigic asked.

The question seemed to catch McLeary off guard. He stuttered and stumbled around a reply. 'I don't know. How would I know? All I know's that I never did it. Shot, weren't he? Where would I get a gun? My benefit got stopped two months ago. Five minutes late to appointment and they've cut me off until March. I'm fucking skint. If I had a gun I'd rob a bank, not shoot some kid.' He put his hands up again. 'That's a joke. I'm joking.'

'It's not a very funny joke,' Ferreira said, as severely as she could.

McLeary looked chastened. 'Sorry. Look, Jordan were a nice kid. He didn't deserve that happening to him.'

Ferreira could see what Dick Caxton had meant about McLeary. How fast his moods changed and how legitimate each switch seemed. She'd seen a lot of people put on acts for them in here but she didn't think this was a performance.

Not that it made McLeary any less of a suspect. Anyone who flashed hot and cold like this, who seemed not fully in control of their emotional responses, made her nervous.

Then again, Jordan's murder hadn't been a spontaneous act and McLeary struck her as a spontaneous man. Would he have the forward planning skills to locate a gun and follow Jordan home once to find out where he lived, then go ahead and lay in wait for him? Would McLeary be patient enough for that kind of murder?

'Why do you think Jordan was hanging around the Club?' Zigic asked.

'Search me. Must be better places for an old boy his age to go.'

'We know Jordan was working on a story when he died,' Zigic said. 'Did you hear anything about that?'

'We talked a lot of shit when he was interviewing us for the article.' McLeary whipped his baseball cap off, scratched his head and resettled it lower on his brow. 'We was at it for hours. Only so much you can say about your fucking health problems and money problems when Jordan keeps asking you how you feel.' McLeary steepled his hands in front of him, back straightening, voice lightening. '"And how did that make you feel?" It was all he ever said. You'd tell him about your wife leaving after you lost your job. "And how did that make you feel?" Then you'd tell him you'd got a grandkiddie you'd never seen cos your son didn't want owt to do with you. "And how did that make you feel?" On and on like a broken fucking record.'

The anger was stirring through him now. Colour rising in his face, arms and shoulders going taut under the layers of clothing. He was a bigger man than he looked, Ferreira realised. Not broken by his situation. Not yet. Still some fight left in him.

But enough to kill Jordan?

She wasn't sure.

'Did my head in,' he said. 'You've got Dick blaming his arthritis on genetically modified tomatoes. And there's Lionel crying because he tried to kill himself – *twice* – but he's still fucking here, right? Yeah, *poor* Lionel. With that hairdresser he's gone and shacked up with. No chance of him ending up on the street while he's keeping her happy. There's Jordan nodding and frowning, like he cared.' McLeary laughed suddenly. 'Only time I saw Jordan flinch was when we toasted to the crash.'

'What?'

McLeary waved a dismissive hand. 'Thing we do whenever we get together. Toast that bastard's death.'

'Marcus Greenaway?' Ferreira asked, trying to sound casual.

'The man who fell to earth.' McLeary grinned, shook his head. 'Alright, it's dark. But after what he did to us you can't blame the lads for taking their pleasure where they can.'

'And Jordan didn't approve?'

'They're delicate little flowers, these young ones,' McLeary said, bitterness creeping into his voice. 'But he got it when Bruce told him what went on. Karma, Jordan called it.'

'What did Humble tell Jordan?' Zigic asked.

McLeary's eyes sharpened and Ferreira was expecting a dismissal, but instead he leaned forward slightly. 'He said Greenaway got what were coming to him. Act of God, call it what you like. But he got in that helicopter and it crashed. Killed him outright.'

'Was Jordan interested?'

'Course he was. Something like that, wouldn't you be?' McLeary glanced at Ferreira. 'Jordan started asking all these questions. How'd it happen? Was it an accident?'

'Was it?'

'You tell me, you're the police.'

'The air accident investigation people seemed to think so,' Ferreira said.

He snorted. 'Must have been then.'

'And what do you think?'

'I think it didn't get us our jobs back,' McLeary said hotly. 'But it made a lot of people happy, seeing that bastard get his comeuppance.'

CHAPTER TWENTY-NINE

'Do you believe him?' Ferreira asked, as they went back into the office.

'About the toasting, yes.'

'Doesn't mean anything though, does it?' He could hear the stirrings of uncertainty in her voice. 'Greenaway fucked them over, it's only natural they're going to take some degree of pleasure in his death.'

'What's this now?' Riggott asked, turning from the conversation he was having with DI Kitson. He was in the opposite corner of the room but somehow he'd heard them, ears pricking up, eyes shrewd as he weaved between the desks.

'We've just been talking to Daniel McLeary,' Ferreira explained. 'He insinuated that someone at the Club might have been involved in Marcus Greenaway's crash.'

'He's trying to take the heat off himself,' Zigic said. 'He lost his job over Jordan's article. He's got good reason to want us anywhere else but near him.'

Riggott folded his arms, looking between the two of them as if he suspected they were hiding something from him. 'And what's he been saying about the crash?'

'Jordan Radley had a copy of the AAIB report,' Zigic told him.

'But it's a dead end,' Ferreira said. 'We know it was an accident. We've got no reason to think Jordan had any more than a passing interest in what happened.'

'It was more than a passing interest,' Parr said.

Riggott turned on his heel and went over to him. 'What have you found yourself there, Zac?'

Parr stood up, his hand passing fast across his desk, sweeping a few crumbs onto the floor before Riggott got to him.

'I've found a bunch of photos of Holme Airfield on Jordan's laptop.' He gestured at the screen. 'I thought he might have pulled them off some website or other but then I checked and they were taken on October 2nd. On an iPhone 10.' He glanced at Ferreira. 'That's what Jordan's phone was, right?'

'Yeah.'

Zigic looked on as Riggott flicked through the photos, wishing he could ease his boss aside and examine them at his own speed.

The images had been taken on a cloudy day, the main hangar looming large, its door thrown open, revealing several aircraft inside and a man milling around in the doorway. Then the runway and the fields surrounding it.

'Our intrepid Mr Radley took himself over to the airfield then,' Riggott said, straightening up away from the desk. 'Seems to me yon wean sniffed out a story after all.'

'It does explain why he was hanging around at the Club,' Parr added.

'There's no motive here,' Zigic said reluctantly. 'It doesn't matter what Jordan thought or what questions he might have been asking. The crash was an accident so there's no suspect for him to put on the defensive.'

'You want to take a chance on that, Ziggy lad?' Riggott cocked his head. 'Because I'm not seeing much progress on your other fronts.'

'Jordan was investigating abuses by social care staff working for P&N Medico,' Ferreira said. 'We've got a nurse who works for them in close contact with Jordan in the weeks before his death.'

'It looks like she might be a whistleblower.' Zigic spread his hands wide. 'She's too scared to talk to us right now, but we're working on it.'

Riggott walked out of the office, making it clear they were to follow him into the relative privacy of the corridor where the only witness was Colleen Murray, debating with the vending machine.

'Sure, you know I'm not one to go telling you how to run your case,' Riggott said, sounding like he actually believed it. 'But you want to keep in mind here, the Greenaway family will kick up the almightiest fucking hell if it turns out youse two missed a chance to avenge their late lamented son.'

'The crash was an accident,' Zigic said. 'You told me that yourself. And there's no logical reason to think it had a bearing on Jordan's murder.'

'Aye, you'll get no argument from me on that score. But it'll look good on you to have that written down in a nice, tidy report.'

Riggott strode away up the corridor, leaving no space for further discussion.

Zigic watched him go, wanting to follow and challenge him but knowing there was little point. The boss had spoken.

'I can go on my own,' Ferreira said. 'Let you get on with the P&N stuff.'

Zigic sighed. 'No, he's going to want a blow-by-blow report. I'd better come with you.'

They drove out of the city centre and past the restaurant in Yaxley where Jordan Radley had worked, through the prettier, older part of the village and onto the fenland beyond it. Water lying in the fields and flooding the short tracts of sparse woodland, the drier acres pure black, a few hunkered-down cottages scattered about. Neither of them spoke. Ferreira on her phone while Zigic concentrated on navigating the steeply cambered road full of humps and ruts where the peat underneath it had swollen and shrunk away again, leaving the tarmac awkwardly deformed.

As he slowed for the flashing speed-warning sign at the edge of the village, Ferreira put her phone away. A few seconds later she pointed to a grand Georgian manor house behind a high slate-topped wall and a pair of impenetrable-looking wrought-iron gates.

'That's where Marcus Greenaway lived,' she said. 'Fair bit of security by the look of it.'

'Makes sense given the harassment.' Zigic heard the lack of interest in his tone and knew he should be putting his full focus on this.

But he was still thinking of Sheila Yule and the families who had dropped charges against P&N Medico carers. Weller had been on the phone to someone when they left the office and Zigic wanted to know what he'd found, his gut telling him that was where they would find Jordan's killer.

Remembering how scared Sheila was. Sure she had good cause.

He turned onto Holme Airfield, slowing as he approached the corrugated-steel main hangar. The doors were open just as they had been in Jordan's photos of the place, but from this angle Zigic saw a much smaller building bolted onto the side, an office, he guessed. As he pulled up alongside two other vehicles, a compactly built man came out, the wind snapping at his trousers, stirring his thinning sandy hair around his scalp.

Ferreira was away fast, pulling her coat on as she walked up to the man as he entered the hangar, her ID out.

'Do you work here?'

'I'm the owner,' he said. 'Michael Browning. Can I help you?'

'DS Ferreira, DI Zigic.'

Zigic nodded to Browning, saw the suspicion on his face already.

'A young man called Jordan Radley came here in early October,' Ferreira said. 'He was looking into an accident at your airfield.'

Browning crossed his arms, mouth setting into a hard line. 'Yes, I remember him. And I'll tell you what I told him. Marcus Greenaway was a very good friend of mine and his death was a great loss to the village. Nobody here wants all of that raking up again.'

'All of what?'

'His death was an unfortunate accident,' Browning said firmly, refusing to play along with Ferreira's innocent act. 'The Daedalus is a notoriously troubled machine and the AAIB cleared us of any wrongdoing in the accident.'

'Is that what Jordan was interested in?' she asked. 'The machine's safety record?'

'I explained to him that all the information he needed could be found online,' Browning told her. 'He was a hack, he should have known that.'

'Have you had other journalists approach you?' Zigic asked.

Browning's shoulders slumped. 'We were overrun with them after the accident. I had enough of it at the time, I wasn't going to entertain some jumped-up muckraker now. It was almost four years ago, for God's sake. The last thing the family needed was all of that bringing up again.'

'We believe Jordan Radley was investigating the possibility that the crash wasn't an accident,' Ferreira said.

Browning nodded. 'And I set him straight. If he kept believing it after he'd seen the report, then he was either an idiot or a chancer.'

Zigic noticed a stooped man in a set of navy overalls pass along the back wall of the hangar, heading to a light aircraft with its engine exposed, a toolbox on the floor underneath.

'Now,' Browning said. 'Unless there's anything else ...'

'Jordan Radley was shot dead on Monday night,' Ferreira told him.

A quick frown. 'I'm very sorry to hear that. But if you'd excuse me, I have rather a lot of work to be getting on with.'

Michael Browning went out of the hangar, moving faster than he had before, not a backward glance as he headed into his office. Assuming they were leaving, Zigic thought, assuming the same thing himself, but Ferreira was already gone. She was walking between the parked planes and the sagging rotor blades of two other helicopters, making for the man in the overalls.

'Never saw him,' the man said, giving the photo on her mobile a cursory glance.

'He was here in early October,' Ferreira pressed. 'Asking questions about Marcus Greenaway's crash.'

The man had his hands inside the plane's engine, his attention fixed on it, but Zigic wasn't sure if he was actually doing something in there or just avoiding dealing with Ferreira.

She wasn't going anywhere though.

'Were you responsible for servicing Greenaway's helicopter?'

The man nodded.

'So you missed the problem with the tail rotor?' Ferreira asked.

'They're unreliable,' he said flatly. 'I told Mr Greenaway he should've upgraded to a better machine, but he knew best.'

'Did you tell that to the AAIB, Mr Pyle?'

'I did.'

Pyle still wasn't looking at her. He reached into his toolbox for a can of WD-40 and shook it up.

'This young man,' Ferreira went on. 'Jordan Radley. He believed the crash wasn't an accident.'

'And what would he know?' Pyle asked.

They left him to his work, Ferreira shooting him an irritated look as they headed out of the hangar and went back to the car.

'He could have been a bit more helpful,' she said. 'If I didn't know it was an accident I'd like him for sabotaging Greenaway's helicopter.'

CHAPTER THIRTY

The gates were now open at the Greenaway house when they drove past and Zigic debated with himself for a few seconds before turning the car around in the gateway to a sprawling and untidy farmyard.

He pulled into the driveway of the house. It was a broad red-brick manor with tall sash windows and a stone portico, a coach house to the right, and stabling to the left. There was a black Range Rover parked up at the front door, a woman climbing out.

Zigic drew up next to the vehicle.

'That'll be Rachel Greenaway, then,' Ferreira said.

She was middle-aged with glossy brown hair and large sunglasses pushed back onto her head, dressed in the usual rural uniform of jeans and sensible boots and quilted jacket. She slammed the back door on the Range Rover and started towards them as they got out of the car.

'What do you want?' she demanded.

Zigic flashed his ID.

'Rachel Greenaway?' he asked.

'Yes.' She tucked her hands into her jacket pockets. 'What's this about?'

'We're investigating the murder of a young man called Jordan Radley.'

The briefest flicker of annoyance across her face. 'The journalist.'

'We have reason to believe he was asking questions about your husband's death,' Ferreira said.

Zigic cringed internally at her bluntness, wanted to remind her that this woman had been widowed. That the distance of nearly four years didn't reduce their responsibility to treat her with a degree of care. That the kicking her husband had given the men at the Greenaway factory didn't reduce it either. He suspected it was the latter rather than the former behind Ferreira's lack of delicacy.

'Had Jordan been to see you?' she asked.

Rachel Greenaway nodded. 'He didn't get quite as lucky as you did. The gates were closed when he came. I was out here doing a bit of tidying up in the borders and he started shouting questions at me from the path.'

'What did he ask you?'

'He wanted to know about the accident,' she said, eyes drifting further away from them, to a distant corner of the garden. 'Was I satisfied with the official report? Did I believe it was an accident?'

'And did you?' Ferreira asked.

'Of course I did,' she said sharply. 'The AAIB know their job. If I thought there was any question of criminal negligence at the airfield, I'd have sued.'

'Did you tell him that?'

She nodded, jawline hardening. 'That's when he started saying just the stupidest things. Claiming there had been a break-in at the airfield a couple of weeks before the accident happened and saying he believed it was cover for someone to tamper with Marcus's helicopter.'

Zigic saw Ferreira trying to hide her interest, felt a low thrum stirring through himself.

'It was absolutely ridiculous. I knew that.' Greenaway took her sunglasses off her head and folded them away into her pocket. 'But I won't say it didn't unnerve me. As soon as I'd got shot of him I went over to the airfield and talked to Mike Browning about it – he owns the place – he assured me there hadn't been a break-in and there was no question of sabotage.'

'Did you believe him?' Ferreira asked, her expression indicating that she didn't.

There was a pause before Rachel Greenaway answered. 'I could see why Mike might lie about it. If there was a break-in and some damage occurred during it that he hadn't reported or rectified, then he'd be liable and he must have known I'd sue him out of existence. But ...' She bit her lip. 'Mike and Marcus were good friends, they'd known each other since school, and I doubt very much that Mike would have done anything to endanger Marcus's safety. Never mind his business. The airfield is his whole life.'

'Did Radley mention who told him about the break-in?'

Rachel Greenaway leaned against the side of her Range Rover. 'No, but he'd been to the airfield and there's only Mike and Francis Pyle working there.'

'Did you ask Pyle about it?'

'No. I spoke to Mike,' she said. 'It's impossible getting any sense out of Francis.'

Jordan Radley spinning a story, Zigic thought. Pulling the same trick he'd tried on Sheila Yule, finding something that would draw her in, the right emotional lever to get in front of her, and open up the story he was interested in.

'Did Radley say who he thought might be responsible for this break-in?' Ferreira asked.

'No. He was too smart to make that kind of accusation.' She pushed herself away from her vehicle again. 'He was fishing. I worked in the media before I married Marcus so I know how this goes. We're coming up on the four year anniversary of the accident and he was looking for a story to sell. If he could manipulate me into giving him a quote about suspecting sabotage, then it's "weeping widow believes husband's tragic air death was murder".' Her nostrils flared. 'He'd tried the same thing with Anthea, my mother-in-law. She gave him short shrift apparently. But that's how the press works. Harass whoever you have to for the sake of the story.'

Zigic frowned. So far nothing they'd seen in Jordan Radley's body of work suggested this was the kind of story he was interested in pursuing. No political undertow, no marginal group to give voice to.

Then again, Jordan had been here and to Marcus Greenaway's mother. He'd been to the airfield asking questions. He was clearly up to something and if it seemed out of character, maybe that was only because they hadn't built up a true picture of his character yet.

'Jordan Radley went to the airfield on October 2nd,' Ferreira said slowly. 'And your husband died in January. That seems a long way out to be working on a story about the anniversary of the accident.'

Greenaway gave her a sharp look, as if she'd spoken out of turn, and Zigic saw Ferreira stiffen at the assumption of superiority the look carried.

'Jordan Radley had been talking to some of your husband's former employees,' Ferreira carried on. 'Or, given what happened with the factory sale, victims.'

'That wasn't supposed to happen,' Greenaway said, a glimmer of what might have been regret in her eyes. 'The buyers promised they wouldn't take the company abroad.'

'Then how *did* it happen?' Ferreira pressed.

'I don't know. I wasn't involved with the sale,' Greenaway insisted, more defensive now. More guilty-sounding. 'Marcus's father had been propping the company up for years out of his own pocket. But he just couldn't maintain its viability in a global market. How could he hope to compete with countries who don't have workers' rights or environmental restrictions to worry about?'

Zigic wondered if she really believed what she was saying or if this was a well-worn justification honed in the aftermath of the sale. Thinking of the firm's order book, which had been transferred to the buyer's plant in Germany. Its reputation as an industry leader in the presumably cut-throat sector of automation development and manufacture.

'Of course,' Rachel Greenaway sniffed. 'Once the sale was finalised all of that was forgotten. Everything the family had sacrificed to keep the factory open for the previous ten years was ignored.'

185

Ferreira eyed the house and Zigic felt the same question rising up in him: just what had she sacrificed? He remembered the bedsit Dick Caxton was living in and Lionel Ridgeon's suicide attempts. Steve Gurney's home lost and his self-respect along with it. Daniel McLeary living rough.

150 men in Peterborough had all lost something more than money; they'd lost their sense of pride and belonging, the ability to turn back at the end of the day and look at the factory gates and believe that they had made something useful and important during their shift.

That *they* were useful and important.

It was easy to see how that kind of loss might turn someone to violence, Zigic thought.

But he still didn't believe it.

The accident report was as concrete a piece of evidence as you could ask for in a murder investigation.

And yet ...

Something was tugging at his gut.

A vague sense of having been lied to. Or at least, of not being told everything there was to know by the men from the Greenaway Club. Everyone saying what a nice kid Jordan was, what a smart young lad. None of them mentioning the crash or Jordan's interest in it.

Because they didn't know what he was doing?

Or because they didn't want it to be looked at again?

Chapter Thirty-One

'Okay everyone, gather around, please.'

Zigic strode over to Jordan Radley's board as Ferreira slung her bag under her desk, feeling the same irresistible impetus she saw in Zigic as he clapped his hands at Weller, telling him to get his earbuds out and pay attention.

'Did you find something at the airfield?' Parr asked, a hint of smugness in his tone, but he'd earned it, Ferreira thought.

Zigic nodded. 'We did.'

'Knew it.' Parr grinned. 'Marcus Greenaway was murdered, wasn't he?'

'For the time being we're treating the crash as an accident,' Zigic said, trying to keep them all grounded but the optimism in his voice told its own story. 'The AAIB report is the authority on the matter until we know better. However, it now appears that they weren't in possession of the full facts when they made their judgement.'

All eyes were on him. Murray leaning forward slightly in her chair, Weller head cocked and waiting, Bloom's face set in rapt concentration.

'A fortnight prior to Marcus Greenaway's fatal accident there was a break-in at Holme Airfield.' Zigic pressed his palms together as eyes widened and heads nodded, letting them process what it meant for a couple of seconds. 'The main office was rifled and the petty cash box was taken. The burglars then proceeded to force their way into the hangar and steal £2,000 worth of tools.'

'Were any of the machines damaged?' Murray asked.

'Browning, the owner, insists not,' Zigic told her.

She frowned. 'And he didn't tell the AAIB about this?'

'No. And he didn't report it to us either.'

Murray sucked air through her teeth. 'Dodgy, very dodgy.'

'His line was that the break-in was irrelevant,' Zigic went on. 'The robbers knew what they were looking for. Took the most expensive small items they could get their hands on and scarpered.'

They'd pressed Michael Browning on it during their second visit, there in the small and chilly office, surrounded by photographs of antique planes and snapshots of his previous life in the RAF. Browning maintaining the line.

'Targeted break-ins aren't unusual at rural businesses,' Bloom said hesitantly.

'But the owners not reporting them is,' Murray countered. 'They know we don't have the resources to get involved but they still need a crime number for their insurance, and two grand isn't an amount you'd write off for the sake of a phone call, is it?' She gave Zigic a pointed look. 'He's lying.'

'Even if he didn't think we'd do anything he should have told the AAIB,' Parr said. 'Say he doesn't want to make an insurance claim because he's worried about putting his premiums up. Fine. But someone dies, you stump up whatever information you've got.'

'Unless you've got something to hide,' Murray said darkly.

Weller shot forward in his chair. 'There *was* damage to the machine, yeah?'

The team were breaking it down just as Ferreira and Zigic had done on the drive back into the city. Turning it around, checking the angles and the possible motivations and coming to this same conclusion.

Something was not quite right about Michael Browning.

'One theory,' Ferreira said, 'is that Browning had his mechanic quietly make the necessary repairs without alerting the owners.'

'Stuff getting smashed up isn't good for business,' Murray said. 'Especially the kind of business where you're minding rich people's expensive toys.'

Ferreira nodded. 'And we've got Marcus Greenaway's widow threatening legal action against whoever was responsible for her husband's death. Giving Browning a *really* good reason to keep his mouth shut when the AAIB investigator arrives.'

'And when Jordan showed up,' Zigic added.

'Sorry.' Bloom blinked rapidly at him. 'How did Jordan know about the break-in? Why would Browning admit it to him if he kept it from the AAIB?'

'It didn't come from Browning,' Ferreira said. 'The mechanic, Francis Pyle, told Jordan.'

'So, Pyle isn't involved?' Weller asked. 'Why 'fess up if he was?'

'It's way too early to make that call,' Zigic warned.

'Jordan did seem to have a way of getting things out of people,' Ferreira reminded them. 'And until we know a bit more about Michael Browning and Francis Pyle, we can't guess at why Pyle might have talked to Jordan.'

'What about the security system?' Murray asked. 'Place like that, it's got to be high spec.'

'Browning insists he set it when he left the night before,' Zigic said. 'But he also says it hadn't been tripped when he got in the next morning.'

'So, he forgot to set it?'

'Or the burglars overrode it,' Parr suggested.

'That's a possibility,' Zigic replied. 'But we don't know how many people had the code. Pyle would know it. Maybe some of the owners, too. Browning admitted he hadn't changed it since the system was fitted.'

'Convenient,' Parr grumbled.

'Zac, you're on Browning,' Zigic said, gesturing at him. 'Col, Francis Pyle. Anything in the run-up to the crash and anything since. Neither of them could give us a decent alibi for the time Jordan was shot.'

'And a mechanic could probably convert a replica pistol like that.' Weller snapped his fingers.

Zigic shot him a faintly irritated look, more for the action than the suggestion, Ferreira suspected.

'What about the blokes who broke into the place?' Parr asked, eyes on the list of names on Jordan's board: the men from the Greenaway Club. 'Maybe the theft was cover for sabotage.'

'Maybe,' Zigic conceded.

Another possibility they'd batted back and forth as they headed back into the station.

'If we're saying a mechanic could convert a replica pistol, then we're also saying an engineer could sabotage a helicopter,' Parr went on, face hardening as he kept his attention on the board. The same disgust Ferreira had noticed whenever the men from the Club came up.

'We've got security camera footage from the break-in,' Zigic said. 'The quality isn't up to much but it's with the techies now and hopefully they'll get us a better look at the men responsible.'

'If Browning didn't report it, why keep the footage?' Bloom asked.

'He said he'd kept it in case the burglars hit them again and he needed to hand it over,' Ferreira told her, the explanation sounding just as strange as it had on its initial telling.

Bloom made a low, disbelieving sound. 'For *four years?*'

Ferreira shrugged. She'd known it happen before, people holding on to evidence meaning to do something with it, then forgetting they had it, putting the crime aside and moving on with their lives until it became important again.

There were two warring explanations for acting that way. Thinking it was probably nothing or knowing it might actually be a big deal. She couldn't figure out which side Browning came down on. Not yet.

'What's the other theory?' Murray asked, looking at Ferreira across the desk.

At the front of the room Zigic folded his arms. As defensive as he had been when she first suggested the possibility. Leaving it until they were pulling into the station car park so he'd have less time to disagree with her.

'It's not so much a theory as a point of interest,' Ferreira conceded. 'After Jordan went to the airfield he approached

190

Greenaway's widow, Rachel, and his mother, Anthea. It sounds like he questioned both of them over the crash.'

'And what did they say?' Murray asked.

'The wife, not much,' Ferreira told her. 'The mother … we've got to find out.'

Chapter Thirty-Two

Anthea Greenaway led them through her home, soft shoes silent on the flagstones, passing doors standing open on a grand dining room to the left and a drawing room done out in oxblood and busy swags to the right, into a broad, high expanse of cream-painted cast iron and glass. In most houses it would be a conservatory, Zigic thought, but here you would have to call it an orangery. There were a few citrus bushes heavy with fruit in lead planters among the profusion of greenery still lush and shining-leaved thanks to the heating he felt rising from the floor. The space was unpleasantly humid, as if everything had been very recently misted, and had an aroma of damp soil.

Despite the balmy temperature Anthea Greenaway was in wide wool trousers and two jumpers that swamped her diminutive frame, and when she showed them to the wicker seats set among a jungle of luxurious palms, he noticed a paisley blanket tossed aside with a copy of *The Lady*. Anthea would be of an age where the cold began to creep stealthily into your bones. Late seventies, he guessed. Sharp-eyed and sharp-boned, her white hair smoothed into a chignon. Every inch the grande dame of a grand local family.

'Please.' She gestured for them to sit. 'Tea, I think.'

She left the orangery and Zigic saw Ferreira casting an unimpressed eye over the place. Impossible not to compare it with the bedsit where they'd searched for Dick Caxton or the modest semi where Steve Gurney lived, a house you could drop into this room and still have space left over.

This wasn't money from the sale of the factory, though. It was much older.

A minute later Anthea returned empty-handed and took her seat across from them at the low, glass-topped table.

'Now,' she said, folding her hands demurely in her lap. 'What is it you'd like to talk to me about?'

'We're investigating the murder of a young man called Jordan Radley,' Zigic told her, taking out a photograph. 'We believe he'd been to speak with you sometime in October, is that correct?'

She gave the photo a cursory glance. 'That's correct.'

'Why did he approach you?'

A long blink, lips pursed. 'Several years ago I lost my son Marcus in a helicopter crash. This young man was of the opinion that it wasn't the accident we'd all been led to believe.'

'What evidence did he offer to support his theory?' Zigic asked.

'There was no evidence,' Anthea said regretfully. 'Nothing that would pass for evidence in criminal proceedings, but he'd discovered there had been a burglary at the airfield Marcus used a fortnight before he died. Mr Radley was of the opinion that the two events may have been connected.'

'There was no mention of a burglary in the official report,' Zigic reminded her. 'We have no record of one being reported either.'

'Nevertheless.'

'Your daughter-in-law seemed to think Jordan Radley was lying about it to get a reaction from her,' he said.

Anthea didn't respond and Zigic could see the force of will involved in remaining silent. Suspected it was the daughter-in-law she was holding her tongue over rather than Jordan.

'Did you believe there had been a break-in?'

She nodded. 'I can't see that the young man had any reason to lie to me and I believe I'm a sound enough judge of character to know when someone tries to.'

'The AAIB ruled the crash an accident,' Zigic said. 'Did you not agree with the verdict?'

Anthea looked down at her hands – a discreet diamond ring and a perfect pearl-coloured manicure – her fingers twitching thoughtfully.

'At the time, I was satisfied with the investigation.' She looked up and met Zigic's gaze steadily. 'I will admit that my first instinct on hearing what happened to Marcus wasn't quite so measured. When you lose a child …' Her bright blue eyes hardened. 'That pain demands someone be punished. But it was an accident. And once you accept that, the pain becomes something you have to deal with within yourself.'

She hadn't dealt with it, Zigic thought. Not fully. And maybe she never would. Just like Moira Radley would never be able to move past losing Jordan. Like no good parent could.

'Who did you think was responsible?' Ferreira asked.

Anthea turned towards her, face stiffening. 'The mechanic, of course. It was his responsibility to see to Marcus's safety when he flew. The fact that the helicopter failed was down to his negligence or incompetence.'

'The AAIB report states that it was a known fault in the machine,' Ferreira pointed out. 'They didn't lay blame on the mechanic or the airfield.'

'No, they blamed Marcus,' Anthea said acidly. 'He may not have been the most experienced of pilots but allowing a helicopter to be flown by *anyone* when there was a developing fault speaks to irresponsible management of the airfield and a mechanic who wasn't performing his duties with due care and attention.'

A woman in chinos and a black polo shirt emerged from among the plants with a wooden tray bearing a white teapot and cups and saucers rimmed with gold. They were getting the good china, Zigic noted, wondering what, if anything, that meant.

'Thank you, Marta.'

The woman withdrew discreetly and Anthea asked how they took their tea, pouring three cups and placing theirs in front of them.

Zigic thanked her. 'Did you share these thoughts with Jordan Radley?'

Anthea nodded. 'He was of the opinion that Marcus's helicopter may have suffered some damage during the break-in.'

'Just Marcus's machine?' Ferreira asked.

'He didn't speculate.'

'Why would someone breaking in to steal petty cash and tools cause that kind of damage?'

Anthea glared at her. 'I couldn't say. Devilment?'

'Or maybe Marcus was targeted deliberately?'

'Why would anyone want to harm my son?' she asked, her voice heating up slightly.

'It must have occurred to you,' Ferreira said, 'that Marcus and your family had suffered an escalating campaign of harassment following the sale of the factory. Surely you considered the possibility that the crash was a continuation of that?'

'No,' Anthea said sternly. 'I did *not* consider that.'

'150 men lost their jobs,' Ferreira reminded her. 'Several of them went to prison for their part in the harassment. You seriously didn't wonder, at any point, whether one of those men was involved?'

'They were good, honest men,' Anthea Greenaway said, with a vehemence that surprised Zigic. 'What they may have done in the heat of the moment following the loss of their jobs does not make them capable of murder.'

'You knew them well enough to make that judgement?' Ferreira asked.

'Greenaway Engineering was one of Peterborough's oldest and largest companies,' she said proudly. 'Our employees were decent, respectable men and we always did them the courtesy of treating them as such.'

Not exactly answering Ferreira's question.

'Until Marcus sold out,' she said.

Anthea sank back in her chair. 'Marcus didn't want to sell the factory. His father entrusted six decades of hard work to him. He raised Marcus to understand that his first responsibility was to the people who'd allowed the business to thrive and his second responsibility was to maintain it in a fit state to be passed on to his son.'

Her eyes lost focus and Zigic willed Ferreira to remain silent, let the woman say whatever was sending those ripples of thought across her pale and powdered face.

'Sadly Marcus lacked his father's business acumen,' she went on faintly. 'He was handed one of the few British engineering firms to have weathered the vagaries of globalisation.' Anthea looked at Zigic. 'Greenaway was a market leader, that was why we survived for so long where others failed. Peerless research and development, excellent standing in the industry. Our patents alone were worth millions and would have allowed the company to continue for another ten years even if no further innovations were achieved.'

Sounding less like the grande dame now and more like the CEO of Greenaway Engineering, someone Zigic could easily imagine accompanying her husband on the rounds of networking necessary to keep a business on top, impressing the right people, advising from the modest distance expected of women of her generation. He wondered if the factory would have been sold under her stewardship.

'So what went wrong?' Ferreira asked, more gently this time.

Anthea sighed. 'Marcus wasn't interested in engineering. He joined the firm to keep me happy but it was never his dream. After his father passed, he started to delegate too much control to the wrong people until finally I put my foot down with him and told him to stop playing at being the leader and actually be one.' She looked away from them, staring regretfully towards the garden beyond the orangery's tall windows, the grass dropping away into a distant woodland. Anthea frowned. 'Marcus managed to lose almost two million pounds in eight years.'

'But that was recoverable, surely,' Ferreira said. 'Old firm, strong reputation, any bank would have been happy to shore you up.'

'They would have, yes.' Anthea's face darkened. 'But Marcus decided to sell a stake to a private investor instead.' She gave a thin smile, utterly devoid of humour. 'You've met my daughter-in-law, I believe?'

Zigic nodded.

'Her brother, Hugo Docherty.' She looked at them as if she expected the name to mean something, but it didn't. 'Within a month Marcus dismissed the entire top management and most of the middle tier. Then he parted ways with the legal firm we've used since 1960 and took on Docherty's woman.' Disgust sharpened her nose. 'Every value we instilled in Marcus as a boy amounted to nothing once Docherty wrapped his tentacles around him.'

'So Docherty was responsible for the sale?' Ferreira asked, an edge returning to her voice.

'The asset stripping began almost immediately,' Anthea explained, her hand curling into a small, bony fist. 'He even tried to close the working men's club and redevelop the site it sat on. Fortunately my father-in-law had placed it in a trust and I managed to protect it, but Docherty seemed to take that as a personal affront.' She grimaced. 'That was the turning point. If he'd had any compunctions about manoeuvring Marcus into selling, they disappeared that day. Docherty would have destroyed the company just to spite me.'

For a moment nobody spoke and Zigic thought of the men who'd lost their jobs, collateral damage in a power play between two people they probably barely knew. Anthea Greenaway with the burden of history and responsibility heavy on her shoulders, hampered by it as she tried to fight off someone absolutely unencumbered by these same values, focused first on the money and second on the win.

And Marcus Greenaway, the ineffectual figurehead, caught between them. Unequal to the position, even by his mother's telling.

'If Docherty was the driving force behind the sale, why did the harassment focus on Marcus?' he asked.

'Oh, Hugo Docherty was too smart to show his face,' Anthea said vehemently. 'Marcus had him dripping poison in one ear and Rachel drooling it into the other. Don't let her fool you, Inspector Zigic, she isn't the simpleton she appears to be. They're virtually *feral*, the pair of them.'

Not a description he would have used about the woman in the quilted jacket and the expensive boots, standing in front of her Georgian pile.

'Once it was over and done with Marcus regretted it, of course.' Anthea shook her head angrily. 'He was so naïve he believed Docherty and Rachel when they assured him that the buyers would keep the factory running and nobody would lose their jobs.' Fury flashed across her face. 'Oh, the arguments we had over that. I told him he was being lied to. I accused him of not caring.' She pressed her fingers lightly to her cheek, skin heated even through her make-up. 'But he *did* care. He was so guilt-stricken he didn't even want to call you when his car was vandalised outside his own home with his children looking on. He didn't want to create any more trouble for the men. But, of course, Rachel insisted.'

Easier to believe that of Rachel Greenaway, remembering her attitude as they'd pulled up onto her driveway.

Zigic tried not to let the woman's dislike colour his own thoughts, reminded himself that there were currents stirring through this family that he knew nothing about. And with a mob at your home, who wouldn't call the police?

Anthea looked pensive. 'I lied to you earlier, my first instinct when Marcus died wasn't to look for someone to punish. It was to wonder if he'd killed himself.'

Another long moment of silence fell as she appeared to gather herself, straightening in the chair again and reaching for the china pot to freshen her tea.

'How much of this did you share with Jordan Radley?' Zigic asked.

'Everything.' Anthea lowered her cup to the saucer with a gentle chime. 'If he was going to write a story about Marcus, I wanted him to have the truth.'

CHAPTER THIRTY-THREE

'This is the big story then.' Murray dipped a biscuit into her tea. 'If Jordan got to Greenaway's mother, he was definitely chasing something down.'

Ferreira nodded, wondering if they should be opening up a new board for Marcus Greenaway's death. It felt premature still but she could see the shape emerging, an inevitability to it. The accident now not quite as innocent as it had initially seemed when Zigic first told them about it, the break-in raising the spectre of sabotage or at least hidden damage that might have contributed to the failure of Greenaway's helicopter.

Something for Jordan Radley to stumble across.

A cover-up.

Serious enough to get him killed?

'The weird thing is, she seemed more interested in excusing Marcus's part in the sale of the factory than discussing the circumstances around the crash,' Ferreira said.

'Maybe it's a bit raw still,' Murray suggested.

'I don't know, she was pretty controlled about it all.' Remembering Anthea Greenaway's ramrod poise and bland good manners. At the time she'd put it down to that British stiff upper lip she'd heard so much about over the years but rarely saw any actual evidence of. But now she wondered about how the woman's back went up when Ferreira mentioned the sale. How *that* was her button. 'The way Anthea Greenaway tells it, Jordan just turned up on her doorstep one day and asked if he could talk to her and she let him in. No preamble, no explanation, she opens herself up to some random local journalist.'

'And you don't trust her?' Murray asked, faintly amused.

Ferreira crossed her arms, shrugged. 'I'm surprised at her response to a doorstepping.'

'She lost her son,' Murray reminded her. 'Probably she was happy to have someone sympathetic to listen to her talk about him.'

'I doubt she's short of sympathetic friends. Her circle's hardly going to have ostracised her over closing down the factory, are they?'

Now it was Murray's turn to shrug.

'Have you found anything on the mechanic?' Ferreira asked.

'He's clean. Superficially anyway. I'm still having a dig about.'

Ferreira turned to Parr. 'Zac, what about you?'

'Browning's owned the airfield since 2004,' Parr said. 'The local paper made a big song and dance about him saving it from closure when the previous owner retired. Must have been a hefty chunk of money to buy something like that but no sign of where it came from. He retired out of the RAF and moved right in on it.' He propped his elbows on the desk. 'I'm trying to get hold of someone at the AAIB to check if there's anything that didn't make it into the official report.'

'Any other problems at the airfield?' Ferreira asked. 'Break-ins, accidents, whatever?'

'Nothing,' Parr told her. 'It looks like a well-run, well-respected place. They've done some fundraising for the village church and they have those 1940s weekends a few times a year. No suspicion of it being used for criminality.'

'Doesn't mean they're not dodgy,' Murray said.

Drugs, Ferreira thought. Private airstrips the easiest way to bring them in, circumventing the usual customs checks. Not just drugs. Cash. Weapons. People.

'Check out Browning's financials, Col.'

'Will do.'

'Are we going to ignore the obvious explanation then?' Parr asked, now standing near the board with his hands shoved in the pockets of his grey suit trousers, looking irritated.

'Zac's got a bone up his arse about something,' Murray muttered.

'We're not asking the big question here,' he insisted, keeping his eyes on Ferreira.

'What's that?'

'We're saying Greenaway's helicopter might have been *damaged* and Browning and/or Pyle covered it up, right?' Rocking onto his heels. 'Why aren't we thinking Greenaway's helicopter was *sabotaged* by someone specifically? He's been the victim of a prolonged harassment campaign. The men responsible are engineers of one sort or another.'

They had considered it. On the way back, Ferreira and Zigic had picked around the gaps in Anthea Greenaway's story, discussing what she'd wanted to tell them and what she succeeded in drawing attention to by studious avoidance.

The men from the Greenaway Club she'd defended at the merest provocation.

'We don't know enough about the break-in to make that call yet,' Ferreira warned. 'Browning has denied any damage occurred and until we can prove otherwise we can't let ourselves get bogged down in a theoretical. Prove the damage then we can start speculating who caused it and why.'

'Jordan thought the break-in was cover for sabotage.' He pointed at the board, 'He told Rachel Greenaway that exact thing.'

'Jordan had the luxury of believing whatever suited him,' Ferreira explained. 'We don't. We deal in evidence, remember. Not whatever's going to make a good story.'

Parr snorted. 'You feel sorry for them.'

'My feelings get left at the bottom of the station steps,' she said firmly. 'The same as yours are supposed to be.'

'Yeah, right,' he grumbled.

'Yes,' she snapped. '*Right*. Think about it, Zac. Jordan had befriended these blokes you've got down for murder. Do you think he'd really be digging for some story that'd get them banged up?'

He crossed his arms. 'We don't know what he might've been up to. And he *didn't* run a story about it, did he? Maybe he found something that implicated his new pals and *that*'s why the story hits a dead end.'

Ferreira shoved her hand back through her hair, exasperated with his unblinking commitment to this pet theory. He'd been incubating it since the very first mention of the Greenaway factory. Parr's sympathies lying in the wrong direction but she knew she wouldn't shake him from them.

'Find me something beyond your gut and we'll look at it,' she said. 'Alright, Zac? Go for it.'

He turned away, returning to his desk with a satisfied expression. Sat down smartly, smoothing his tie with one hand and reaching for his mouse with the other.

Ferreira supressed a frustrated sigh.

On the board the men from the Greenaway Club stared out at her. Their mugshots showed bold and open faces, the photographs taken directly after their arrest outside Marcus Greenaway's house in Holme Village. Nobody was ashamed or looking scared, all remained defiant in the face of the camera, certain of the rightness of their actions.

She thought of what they'd done. The first protests outside the factory's locked gates, then the attacks on the solicitors' office and the Greenaway home, the car tyres slashed and the windscreen shattered.

These men weren't hiding. They weren't looking for revenge taken from the shadows. They wanted to expose Marcus Greenaway for what he'd done to them.

Were they really the kind of people to withdraw and plot a murder that would pass for an accident? Were they even capable of it? Despite Daniel McLeary's description of the group toasting Greenaway's death, she doubted it.

And, as his mother Anthea told them, Marcus was not the driving force behind the sale.

Those men would be aware of Hugo Docherty's involvement, Ferreira was sure. Bruce Humble's role on the board of the working men's club would have brought them into contact, given him an early red flag about how Docherty intended to squeeze a return from his investment in Greenaway Engineering by tearing the place down and building all over it.

Had Docherty been harassed too, she wondered. Docherty was by far the more logical target for revenge. But had he taken it quietly? The price of doing business?

'Oh,' Murray said sharply. 'I called Jordan's mum.'

Ferreira turned away from the board. 'How's she doing?'

'Her sister's with her, seems like that's helping.' Murray frowned. 'Much as anything's going to in that situation. She wanted to know what was happening and I told her we're making progress.'

The only option available.

'But I asked her if she knew where he'd been booking train tickets for this month,' Murray said, voice lifting. 'And Moira reckoned he went over to Leicester trying to get an interview for a story.'

The Trainline order on Jordan's bank statement. Slipped between the cracks as they trawled through all the chaotic information dumped on them from his laptop.

Ferreira hadn't even written it on the board.

'Did Moira know what story it was?' she asked, making a note now. 'What was the date, Rob?'

'November 18th,' Weller answered, quicker than she expected him to.

Murray's eyebrows went up, just as shocked. 'Moira didn't know what the story was but she said Jordan went to Leicester for it in person because he couldn't get anywhere with them on the phone.'

At his desk Weller started scrambling through the call logs from Jordan's mobile. 'There's a Leicester number on here somewhere. Hold on.'

What could have taken him there, Ferreira wondered. Some fresh lead on Marcus Greenaway's crash or an altogether different story shaping up?

'Do P&N do business in Leicester?' Murray asked. 'You reckon we should get in touch with the Leicestershire lot and see if they'd had any trouble with P&N staff?'

Ferreira nodded, glancing at Sheila Yule's photograph on the board. A person of interest still. Withholding information from them but out of fear, Ferreira thought, not guilt.

'According to their website P&N Medico cover East Anglia and the East Midlands,' Bloom told them.

'It's not P&N. It's not even medical-related.' Weller turned his screen so Ferreira could see it. 'Drury Prior, they're an environmental management consultancy.'

'And what do they do when they're at home?' Murray asked.

Ferreira read the page across his shoulder. 'They provide consultancy and expert advice on all matters pertaining to the management of contaminated land.'

'I'll call the office, yeah?' Weller asked, reaching for his phone and putting it on loudspeaker.

Ferreira nodded, listening to it ring as she clicked through the pages of Drury Prior's website, finding a lot of words and not much solid information, but she supposed this was the kind of business that was mostly carried out in private. Nobody wanted to feature in a gallery of developments built on previously contaminated soil.

The phone kept ringing and Weller grimaced at her as a recorded message clicked in. She killed the call before he could say anything. Took out her mobile and tapped in the other number on their contact page.

She paced around the desks as she waited, half expecting this number to go unanswered too.

'Hello?'

She stopped. 'Hello, this is DS Ferreira with Peterborough police, who am I speaking to, please?'

A pause, the sound of wind filling it. 'David Prior, can I help you with something?'

'Mr Prior, we're investigating a serious crime and your number has come up, would you be available to speak to us?'

'I'm near Peterborough right now,' he said, a hint of reluctance in his voice. 'I'm doing a site inspection.'

'What's the address?' she asked. 'We'll come to you.'

She made a note of it and thanked him before she rang off. Went into Zigic's office just as he was coming out, explained what they'd found.

'Riggott wants me in his office,' he said.

'Can't it wait?'

'When has he ever been able to wait?' Zigic said. 'Go talk to Prior. I'll deal with this.'

He trudged out of the office and she saw Weller looking at her expectantly.

'Alright, Rob. You're up.'

CHAPTER THIRTY-FOUR

'I don't get it,' Weller said, as they crossed the A1, heading into open countryside. 'I get wanting to be a journalist, I suppose – travelling the world, interviewing famous people – but the stuff Jordan was writing about, nobody cares about that.'

'Some people do,' Ferreira pointed out. 'He was getting stories in the paper.'

'The local paper.'

'You don't just rock up at *The Times* and say, hey, I'm a fucking brilliant reporter give me a job immediately.' She slowed as she approached the edge of Elton, a moment of dislocation as she remembered she lived in this quiet, stone and thatch, hunkered-down little haven now. 'You especially don't get to do that if you're some kid from Peterborough whose mum works at a supermarket.'

'Then why didn't he write about stuff people are actually interested in?' Weller asked, watching the fields swipe past from behind his sunglasses.

'Like what? Celebrities and all that shit?'

'It's what the people want,' he said.

'Rob, the people want to drive drunk and dump old fridges in areas of outstanding natural beauty, do you think we should let them do that?'

He snorted. 'Bit different, isn't it?'

'Not massively, no. If you don't put the truth in front of people, how will they ever know what's going on in the world?' she asked. 'If all people read is stupid magazines about which soap star has cellulite and what footballer's bought a pet tiger, you soon get to a point where companies do whatever the hell they want and governments lie to the electorate and before you know it you've got –'

'Brexit?' He grinned.

'A compromised democracy.'

She was already regretting bringing him. This was the first time she'd taken him out on a case, the first time she'd heard him offer any opinion at length, and he was making her feel very old and very serious and she didn't appreciate that one little bit.

Should have brought Murray, she thought. If nothing else the drive would have given her an opportunity to get the lowdown on Colleen's new bloke. She'd been infuriatingly discreet about him so far. All Ferreira knew was that a friend had set them up on a blind date and that he was a retired geography teacher. 'Not an old bugger, though,' Colleen had said. 'He took early retirement. He's still got plenty of go in him.'

If Colleen kept shtum much longer Ferreira was going to resort to the nuclear option and invite her and the ex-teacher around for dinner. She didn't want to be the kind of person who held dinner parties but if that was what it took …

Weller was going again. 'I just don't get why anyone would want to spend their whole life writing about depressing crap.'

'Maybe he felt a sense of duty to the public.' Ferreira sped up as the road began to rise, following the rolling swells of the Leicestershire wolds. 'Getting to truths people don't want revealing. It's kind of the same as what we do except the crimes aren't as obvious as the ones we deal with. A good journalist gets in *before* someone dies. Like what you've been looking into at P&N Medico, right?'

She glanced over at him, seeing if he was following.

'Those crimes were brought to us and P&N's money made most of them go away. Nothing we can do about it after that. But a good journalist brings stories like that out into the open where no amount of money can hide the wrongdoing.'

'Then what?' Weller asked. '*We* make arrests. What does a journalist do?'

'You *really* don't see what I'm getting at here?'

'Yeah, it's all like a higher calling or something,' he said dismissively.

For a few seconds she focused on the road, slowing again as she passed through another village, twenty miles an hour as she drove between the long rows of sandstone cottages and over the narrow bridge and onwards north.

Was there any point in pressing him on this? She'd made it as explicit as she could.

'Why did you join up?' she asked, unable to stop herself.

He shrugged. 'There wasn't much else on offer. It was this or the army. Mum and Dad said I couldn't stay at home forever.'

It figured, she thought. Explained the sense she had of him as someone clocking on and off with no deeper motivation.

'What did you want to do?' she asked.

'Be a rock star.' Weller smiled slightly and she couldn't decide if he was joking or embarrassed by his youthful naïveté. 'I was in a punk band at uni.'

'Because none of you could play your instruments?'

He laughed. 'Yeah. I'm way better now. Not good enough to quit the day job but we get some gigs.'

Please God, don't invite me to watch your band play, Ferreira thought, already decided on planting drugs in his desk and having him fired if he put her on the spot like that.

He started talking about their influences and their style and she half listened to the names of other groups she didn't recognise, hearing for the first time since she'd known him actual enthusiasm in his voice. Thinking that there was some fundamental incompatibility between being a copper and being in a band. Thinking, too, how young it made him sound.

Up ahead she spotted a sun-faded sign for a long defunct petrol station and slowed to pull in behind the navy Jeep parked on the kerb. The perimeter was secured behind high chain-link fencing but other than that nothing had been done to the site so far. The old, single-storey shop spanned the width of the land, three pumps still in place but presumably disconnected from the tank underneath them.

Exactly the kind of site you'd need a decontamination expert for, Ferreira thought, as she squeezed through a gap in the fence and walked around the side of the building, looking for David Prior. Behind it the land opened up, an acre or so, she guessed, and there at the far end, where it sloped down towards a fast-running brook, was a man taking a sample from the water and placing it in a case.

'Mr Prior,' she called.

He put his hand up, then snapped the case closed and came to meet them.

'I would have been happy to come to you,' he said.

'It's no problem,' she said lightly. 'You're obviously a busy man. The least we could do was save you the drive.' She gestured around them. 'What are you doing here?'

'Oh, just taking some samples,' he said, patting the case. 'The owners were *stunned* to discover that old petrol stations come with old petrol tanks that are prone to leaking. It's going to cost them a fortune to clean this lot up, but that's why you don't buy development properties on a whim.'

He smiled and she pulled an understanding face.

'Amateurs, right?' She brought out her phone and found a photo of Jordan Radley. 'This young man came to your office recently, what did he want with you?'

Prior peered at the screen, shading it with his hand against the low afternoon sun. 'Yes, I think he did, actually. He wanted some information about a job we'd worked on. I told him everything was in the public domain and he'd be able to find it on the local authority planning portal.' He pushed his glasses back up his nose. 'I think he said the information he was look-ing for wasn't on the portal, and I explained to him that it's company policy that we don't discuss the background to reports with members of the public.' He glanced at Weller. 'Client confidentiality.'

'Was he pushy?' Weller asked.

Prior winced. 'Polite but rather pushy, yes. He wanted to know if we handled the decontamination process and I explained that we don't do that. We just carry out an investigation and suggest a plan for dealing with any potential hazards we identify on site.'

'What job was he interested in?' Ferreira asked.

'One we did in Peterborough,' he said. 'It wasn't one of mine. My partner handled it but she's off on maternity leave at the moment.'

'How badly contaminated was the site?'

'I'm afraid I couldn't tell you.' Prior shuffled slightly where he stood. 'As I said, it wasn't one of my jobs. Sorry, you didn't say, what's this in relation to?'

'Jordan Radley was murdered a few days ago,' Ferreira told him and watched his eyes widen.

He cleared his throat noisily. 'Oh, dear.'

'So, we're going to need to see the report you did for the site,' she said. 'All of it. Not just the public domain elements.'

Prior seemed to be debating internally.

'We can get a warrant if need be,' Ferreira said.

'No, no, that won't be necessary.' He took his phone out. 'If you let me have your email address, I can dig it out when I get back to the office and send it to you.'

Ferreira thanked him, watched him type her email address into his phone, noticing how his fingers trembled.

CHAPTER THIRTY-FIVE

'You've been to see Dame Greenaway,' Riggott said, as Zigic sat down opposite him.

'We've spoken to her, yes.' Zigic held his insinuating gaze. 'I'm wondering why she saw fit to call you about it though.'

'Catch yourself on, Ziggy.' Riggott took a drag on his vape pen. 'Anthea Greenaway didn't call me. I've never met the woman. Wouldn't know her from Eve. The Chief Constable called me. From the fucking fairway no doubt, this being a weekday afternoon and fine weather for knocking his dimpled wee balls about.'

Riggott smiled thinly.

'So?'

'So, when the big lad calls asking after a case involving a member of his illustrious social circle, you want to be well fucking sure you've kept me abreast of developments so I'm not stammering away like a tube, assuring him I have my finest man on it, while he's asking me this and that and every other damn fool question I don't have an answer for.'

Zigic leaned back in the uncomfortable plastic chair.

'I was planning on debriefing you when we had a better idea if it's relevant to our case,' he said. 'Right now we've got some new details to look into but that's as far as it goes.'

'One of these new details being the incursion by persons unknown a mere fortnight before Marcus Greenaway did his best Icarus impression?' Riggott propped his elbows on the desk. 'Aye, Mrs Greenaway told the big man all about it, Ziggy.'

'She already knew about it before we arrived,' he said. 'She got it from Jordan Radley. Who got it from a mechanic at the airfield. Jordan had also told Greenaway's widow. Although neither of them saw fit to report it to us when they first heard about it six weeks ago.' Zigic heard the irritation in his voice. 'It seems like pretty much everyone around Marcus Greenaway has an aversion to cooperating with the police. Including his so-called mate at the airfield who covered up the break-in.'

'Well, they're wanting to cooperate now,' Riggott told him. 'They're wanting a sight more than cooperation in fact. Your visit's gotten Mrs Greenaway all riled up and emotional and calling the Chief Constable, who was a close personal friend of Marcus's father and the recipient of the beneficence of the Greenaway family on enough occasions for them to look upon him as their own private police officer, to be deployed in times of need.' He took another drag, exhaled a plume of steam. 'Or any old fucking time they feel like it.'

Riggott sounded dismissive but Zigic understood where it was coming from. A defensive posture against the charge the Chief Constable had no doubt thrown at him already: that he'd let Marcus Greenaway's death be put down to an accident when it should have been investigated more thoroughly at the time.

A bollocking had been administered and now Riggott needed to pass it on.

Zigic knew he should sit there and take it. But the case *had* been let slip too easily and he'd realised that the moment Riggott mentioned the crash, sitting in the draughty window of his local pub. An air crash involving a man who'd been the target of previous, recent harassment shouldn't have been written off as an accident simply because the AAIB considered it one.

'Who was liaising with the AAIB investigator on the initial incident?' he asked.

Riggott scowled at him. 'Watch yourself, son.'

'How much did you tell them about the harassment?'

'They were up my arse like a carbonated colonic,' Riggott said irritably. 'The investigation had everything we had and they came up with a verdict of an accident.'

'Did you agree with the verdict at the time?' Zigic asked.

Riggott rearranged himself in the chair, a quick, jagged movement. 'Sure, what do I fucking know about helicopters? The experts say accident, it's an accident. I wouldn't let them waltz in here and tell me my job. Who am I to go telling them theirs?'

It was a rare and dark pleasure to watch Riggott squirm and even as Zigic disliked himself for enjoying it, he couldn't bring himself to stop prodding at his boss who'd spent years relishing his position on the other side of the questions.

'But if you'd known back then about the break-in, what would you have thought?'

'I'd have had a sight more sense than to run off thinking it meant Marcus Greenaway was murdered,' Riggott snapped. 'I'd sure as hell not go stirring up the more influential members of his family into the kind of wild, conspiratorial thinking that'd get the Chief Constable crawling up my hole.'

Zigic took it placidly, hearing more desperation than defiance.

'This isn't conspiratorial thinking,' he insisted. 'The break-in is one thing. You could write that off as the burglary Michael Browning insists it was and keep calling Greenaway's death an accident, but now we've got Jordan Radley shot in the back a few weeks after he started asking awkward questions about the incident.'

'You like Browning for it?' Riggott asked, perking up.

'He's got a motive if something happened to Greenaway's helicopter during the break-in.'

'Do you want to be a wee bit fuzzier with your thinking there, Ziggy?' Riggott asked teasingly. '*Something* isn't what you mean now, is it?'

'Sabotage, then.'

'Aye, let's talk dirty, just among ourselves.' Riggott grinned. 'And who'd want to go and do a thing like that?'

'We're already looking into the men who were sacked after the factory closed,' Zigic reminded him. 'If one of them was responsible for Jordan's death, then it'll be easier to catch them for that and work backwards to Greenaway rather than the other way around.'

'Sure, it's not looking easy from where I'm sitting, son.'

'We're making progress,' Zigic insisted, feeling Riggott push him onto the back foot again. 'But we're wondering why

Greenaway would be targeted when it was his brother-in-law, Hugo Docherty, who forced the sale through.'

'You think the lads on the factory floor were privy to what was going on in the heady heights of the boardroom?' Riggott asked.

'Wouldn't take a genius to work out that the sale came less than a year after Docherty bought a stake in the company.'

Riggott nodded thoughtfully, taking another drag on his vape pen.

'Anthea Greenaway went to great pains to be sure we understood what a piece of shit Docherty is,' Zigic said.

'Aye, well, she's not wrong there.' Riggott swivelled his chair from side to side, eyes lighting up. 'Rare fucking animal, Docherty.'

'She called him feral.' Zigic remembered the look of pure contempt on Anthea Greenaway's face as she said it. 'Actually she said him and Rachel Greenaway were both feral. I figured it was snobbery.'

'Snobbery, aye, but a fair shout nonetheless.' Riggott exhaled another plume of vapour. ''Bout fifteen years back we got a call from Hugo Docherty's missus. She's bawling her eyes out, off her head, because her husband's pulled up at a set of traffic lights and two big lads in balaclavas have dragged him out of the driver's seat and bundled him into the back of a van.'

Zigic felt his eyebrows go up. 'He was kidnapped?'

'A natural assumption given the circumstances. Only by the time we get to the wife she's already saying she made a mistake, forget about it, she's sorry she wasted our time.' Riggott pointed at him. 'That's a window of ten minutes she takes to change her mind about what she reported to the despatcher.'

Zigic frowned. 'What happened?'

'She tells us it was a prank. Some of Hugo's buddies putting the shits up him. They've called her and explained everything. Awfully sorry, Officer. We threaten to charge her with wasting police time. She takes it. She's scared still but not for Hugo. Of us.'

'Was she in on it?' Zigic asked, trying to pick up the direction Riggott was hinting towards.

'No, this was all your man Docherty,' Riggott told him. 'So, we pull back but we're monitoring the situation. Two days later Docherty shows up in a lay-by on the side of the A1. Falls off the back of a lorry like a slab of dodgy meat.'

'He escaped?'

'We've got no witnesses to say either way,' Riggott said with a shrug. 'Couple of uniforms pick him up. Into the station and I go to question him about where the fuck he's been for the last forty-eight hours, who had him, what did they want.' Disgust rippled around his nose. 'I get in there and Docherty's reeking like a week-old jockstrap, he's pissed himself at some point. There's not a mark on him but you can see he's been through the wars.'

'And he tells the same story the wife did?' Zigic guessed.

'"I'm terribly sorry for the confusion, Chief Inspector."' Riggott straightened up into the performance, mimicking Docherty's voice, more plummy than Zigic expected it to be. '"Some of the chaps thought it'd be a good wheeze to celebrate my thirtieth with a surprise weekend bender."'

'"Wheeze"?'

'Aye, you ever hear that one in real life?' Riggott asked, incredulous. 'Wee shite was laying it on with a fucking trowel. And we can't prove otherwise, can we? Not with four of his mates telling us the same story when we dragged their arses on in here.'

Zigic could see the sting of it around Riggott still. A fifteen-year-old lie but he couldn't quite let go of it.

'It's possible his mates were just wankers,' Zigic suggested.

'Not one of his mates matched the CCTV footage of the men who snatched Docherty out of his car,' Riggott said triumphantly. 'And none of his mates owned a van. A van that turned out to have cloned plates.'

Zigic swore.

Did Anthea Greenaway know about all that? Had she known before her son sold out a portion of her cherished family business to Docherty?

'Now,' Riggott said, drawing his attention again. 'We couldn't prove a thing about what happened to Docherty, but general consensus among the wise old heads at the time was that Docherty's daddy made the family wealth from some very insalubrious sources and that Hugo Docherty wanted to clean up the funds once the old fella was passed.'

'So it was a warning?' Zigic asked.

'Aye, that was the thinking. "Don't get ideas above your station, lad."' Riggott shook his head. 'With friends like that your enemies need to pull out all the fucking stops, hey?'

Zigic nodded, thinking about Jordan Radley circling the Greenaway family, seeing the surface respectability and the wealth. Believing the worst crime they were capable of was selling out the security of their workers.

No idea who they really were.

CHAPTER THIRTY-SIX

'You think Riggott screwed up the initial investigation into the crash, then?' Ferreira asked, as Zigic drew to a stop at a set of traffic lights.

'He was defensive about it. That's usually a sure sign of a fuck-up with him, right?'

'There's nothing on the system about it,' Ferreira said. 'They never even opened a case file at the time. Doesn't that seem weird to you?'

Zigic pulled away over the crossing, the city centre receding behind them, Fletton's bustling suburban streets opening up ahead. 'The way Riggott tells it the Chief Constable wanted to wait until they had the official report in from the AAIB before they turned it into a criminal matter.'

'Rich guys usually get a better grade of justice than that.'

He considered it for a moment. 'And prominent families like the Greenaways get to decide how much scandal attaches to them. Riggott didn't say it but my feeling is that the Chief Constable was trying to keep things under wraps at the behest of Anthea Greenaway. An accidental death is a private tragedy. They wouldn't have wanted speculation and extra stress if there was nothing to it.'

'But they were eyeing up the circumstances still?' Ferreira asked, struggling to make what Zigic told her fit together. Riggott doing his boss's bidding was a given, even if she didn't like what it implied about their role as police officers. The Greenaways' desire to avoid a whirlwind of press speculation and local gossip was also understandable, she supposed. 'I mean, the AAIB report must have taken a couple of months to compile. Riggott should

217

have been eyeing up the main suspects and motives even if he was told to keep it under wraps.'

'You'd think so,' Zigic agreed. 'But all I could get out of him was that he'd liaised with the AAIB at the Chief Constable's instruction.'

'What did he think of Browning and Pyle?'

Zigic flicked his indicator and turned down the road to the Greenaway Club. 'Browning was a cocky wee shite and Pyle wasn't the full ticket.'

Ferreira snorted. 'You don't need to be a DCS to call that.'

'What Riggott *really* seemed to want to talk about was Hugo Docherty.'

'He's in his living past glories phase now,' Ferreira said. 'Haven't you noticed?'

'It was hardly a win. Docherty put one over on them and Riggott couldn't do a thing about it.'

She scowled. 'He wants us to knock Docherty about a bit, doesn't he?'

Zigic made a non-committal sound.

'Come on, he gives you this story about Docherty being kidnapped, completely unprompted, and there's no way that had any bearing on Marcus Greenaway's crash or Jordan's murder. So why do it? Docherty made Riggott look stupid and now he wants us to go and put a scare into him.'

'I don't know, Mel. That's a bit much even by Riggott's standards.'

'Mate, his standards are in the gutter and you know it.'

A minute later they were pulling into the car park. Full dark now with five o'clock just gone and the area was empty except for Bruce Humble's car, parked under one of the few functioning street lights. It had been a long day and Ferreira was ready to call it quits. The drive to Rutland and back was wearing on her, the sense of having been pulled in multiple directions at uncomfortable speeds, leaving her craving the sofa and a rum and something stupid on TV.

But they weren't done. Not quite yet.

The Club was deserted. Just Bruce Humble and Dick Caxton sitting at one of the small tables along the burgundy velour banquette under the stretch of high windows. Music was playing low, some sort of dad rock, and the first patterings of rain were hitting the glass. The room was too bright under the strip lights, the floor recently and highly polished, but the place still had a desolate air. The size of the room maybe, Ferreira thought. Built to accommodate the proportions of a community that no longer existed.

Humble had an orange juice in front of him. Caxton was nursing a half pint, still dressed in his Tesco's uniform, his coat hanging off his spare frame.

'Did you find McLeary?' Humble asked, rising from his seat.

'We found him,' Ferreira said.

Humble nodded towards the bar. 'Get you a drink?'

'We're fine.' Zigic gestured for him to sit again, waiting for him to do it before taking one of the padded stools opposite.

Ferreira dragged another over and sat down, Caxton watching her although there was nothing to be read in his gaze. He looked exhausted with dark rings under his eyes, his lips dry and cracked.

'Tell us about "the man who fell to earth".'

Caxton turned sharply towards Humble.

Humble blinked. 'The toast?'

Ferreira didn't reply.

'It's a stupid, sick thing that McLeary and a few of his mates do,' Humble explained, disgust wrinkling his nose. 'They started after we all heard about the accident and it's become a habit. I don't like it, but what can I do? I'm not going to ban them from the Club over it.' Humble ran his hand through his wavy grey hair. 'I suppose if you wanted to be charitable you could call it gallows humour.'

'Is that how Jordan saw it?'

'He was shocked,' Humble said. 'He didn't know what was going on. We were all sitting across the other side of the room and McLeary stands up, raises his glass and sort of shouts it out, "The man who fell to earth". And five or six of his mates cheered.

This was a couple of months back. Jordan thought it was a David Bowie thing, bless his heart.' Humble smiled faintly. 'I should have left it, really. But I didn't want him to get the wrong idea about us. I suppose I figured he'd already know about the accident.'

Ferreira hadn't been expecting this. Assumed they'd need to manoeuvre Humble around to talking about the crash and Marcus Greenaway. But perhaps he'd been anticipating this conversation ever since they first approached him with the news of Jordan's death.

'Did Jordan know about the crash?' Zigic asked.

'I don't reckon so,' Caxton said. 'He'd have only been a kid at the time, wrapped up in his A-levels. He didn't say anything, anyway. He just sat there while Bruce told him what happened.'

'And what did you tell him?'

'Only what I knew from the papers,' Humble said, shifting his weight in the chair. 'That Greenaway's helicopter wasn't up to much and some bit or other failed not long after take-off. Killed him outright.'

'Which part?' Zigic asked.

'I don't know,' Humble said. 'I only know what I saw in the papers.'

'Some part in the tail, if I remember right.' Caxton looked between the two of them, flushing quickly with embarrassment. 'I was curious about what happened. I did some googling. Common fault, the experts say.'

The song changed, a heavier bass coming in, brutal even at a low level.

'Was Jordan aware that you'd been imprisoned for harassing Greenaway and his family?' Ferreira asked.

Humble heaved a deep sigh. 'No. No, I don't think he knew about that either.'

'And what did you tell him about it?'

'Nothing.' Humble stuck out his bottom lip for a moment, pensive-looking. 'It was a bad time for all of us. I wasn't going to start talking about that. It wasn't my place to. Not with all the other lads there. I figured they'd say something if they wanted him to know but nobody brought it up.'

Caxton nodding along, hand on his half pint glass but he made no move to drink. Ferreira saw how bitten down and ragged his nails were.

'How did you feel when you heard Marcus Greenaway was dead?' Zigic asked.

'I didn't feel much of anything, to tell you the truth.' Humble looked troubled. 'We'd all gone a bit crazy after the factory shut. None of us was thinking straight. The harassment and that. It wasn't us, it was the situation. Then Greenaway died and –' Humble shook his head. 'It was too abrupt, almost. You know what I mean? We'd been fighting him all that time. Been arrested and got locked up. And then he just dies and it was like, who do we hate now?'

'We'd spent a lot of time hating that man,' Caxton added.

'But you must have been relieved if nothing else,' Ferreira suggested. 'Didn't it feel a bit like karma when Greenaway crashed?'

'No,' Humble snapped. 'It didn't. It felt like a man who was cavalier with other people's lives had been cavalier with his own and died because of it.'

'Our jobs were still gone,' Caxton said sadly. 'Greenaway dying didn't fix any of our problems.'

Ferreira wondered what Parr would make of this, the appearance of brutal honesty. She suspected he'd see guilt in it but her gut was twisting the other way. There was too much regret and resignation on display for that. It hinted towards long hours of deep reflection and the processing of the uglier feelings they'd given into.

'Did Jordan mention the accident after that night at the Club?' Zigic asked.

'No.' Humble glanced at Caxton. 'Or not to me anyway.'

Zigic shot Caxton a questioning look and he shook his head.

'Never said a word to me about it either.'

'He'd been to the airfield recently,' Ferreira told them. 'He'd spoken to Greenaway's widow about his death.'

Humble just stared at her, his expression on the uneasy side of neutral.

'And his mother,' Zigic said. 'You must know Anthea Greenaway, right?'

'She's on the board of trustees for the Club.' Humble nodded across the room towards the photographs ranged along the wall, black and white images turning gradually to colour. 'Mrs Greenaway was a great supporter. Used to turn out for big events. Back in the sixties – before my time – she'd come and judge the talent shows and give talks to the women on household economy and the like.'

Ferreira rolled her eyes at the thought of the owner's wife deigning to educate the working women.

'Have you seen her since Marcus died?' Zigic asked.

'She's been in once or twice, but I got the feeling she doesn't like coming now we're all that's left of her husband's business.'

'Can't have been easy for her,' Caxton said, turning his glass around on the scarred wooden tabletop. 'Losing her boy like that.'

A moment of silence, Zigic letting it stretch on, leaving the men to their thoughts.

'Jordan was investigating the circumstances surrounding the crash,' he said finally.

Humble frowned. 'It was an accident. There's nothing to investigate.'

'Jordan seemed to think that there was a link between the crash and a break-in at the airfield a couple of weeks beforehand.'

'Then he had an overactive imagination.' Humble leaned forward, placing his big forearms on the tabletop. 'He was a smart kid but he was ambitious, and ambitious people have a habit of bending the truth to suit themselves.'

'Come on, Bruce. That's not fair,' Caxton protested.

Zigic ignored the interruption, kept his attention fixed on Humble. 'You seem to have changed your opinion of Jordan since the last time we talked to you.'

'Yeah,' Humble nodded. 'Maybe I'm starting to see a side of him I didn't know about when he was alive. He gave us a big song and dance about wanting to discuss how tough the lads were having it after the factory closed. Acting like he cared about their problems. And they opened up to him. They trusted him with things they'd never told anyone.'

'You think he was using you.'

'I'm wondering that, yeah.'

Caxton flinched at Humble's tone.

'Using you to get to the truth about the crash,' Zigic suggested.

Humble gave him a filthy look. 'It was an accident. That's the truth.'

'Jordan didn't seem to think so.'

'Don't think I don't see what you're getting at,' Humble said gruffly. 'You think nobody ever gave any of us shit when Greenaway died? Half the people I knew were joking about one of us killing him. I didn't appreciate it then and I don't appreciate it now.'

Was this the righteous indignation of the innocent man? Ferreira wondered. Or the fear of finally being caught, sending him out swinging?

'Who among your former workmates would have been capable of sabotaging a helicopter?' she asked.

Caxton's eyes widened at the question and he turned to Humble, who flushed red to the roots of his hair.

'Greenaway Engineering made high precision automation devices. We had one of the best trained workforces in this country, meaning the world.' Humble threw his chin up defiantly at her. 'Any one of a hundred blokes could have done it.'

A few minutes later, they were back in the car.

'He was messing with us, right?' Ferreira asked.

'Either way, it's a bold move.'

'Only if he's personally guilty,' she pointed out. 'And Humble was office staff. No way he was technically capable.'

She heard the certainty in her own voice but as Zigic drove back through the rush hour towards the station, she was thinking about Dick Caxton, replaying the way his head snapped towards Humble when she asked the question.

CHAPTER THIRTY-SEVEN

It was almost 9 p.m. when Ferreira emailed over the report from Drury Prior and Zigic saw the brief look of displeasure on Anna's face as he started to scan through it.

'Okay.' He put his phone face down on the coffee table near his wine. 'It can wait until tomorrow.'

She snuggled up to him and he forced himself to ignore the itch to pick his mobile up again, settled instead back into the slightly drunk calm he'd been enjoying. A glossy financial thriller Anna had chosen was on TV. Trashy but fun, and distant enough from the realities of the law that he could enjoy the shiny buildings and the pretty people. He'd argued for a documentary on international money laundering but Anna vetoed it – just like he knew she would.

Within half an hour she was asleep and he turned the programme off, then carefully manoeuvred out from under her, slipping a couple of cushions into the gap he'd left and covering her with the blanket from the back of the sofa.

In the kitchen he poured a second glass of wine while his laptop booted up, hearing an owl shrieking somewhere across the lane.

He opened up Ferreira's email, found a short polite message from David Prior, the man she'd spoken to earlier in the day, saying he hoped the report would prove useful but please feel free to contact him if she required further explanation.

The man had been more helpful than Zigic expected.

Much more helpful than Jordan Radley had found him, evidently. Or why else had he felt the need to go to their offices in person?

The report was for a site on the fringes of the Old Fletton, where the suburb butted up against the city proper, some distance from the main cluster of recent developments, which had sprung up on the southern edge of Peterborough, but close enough to justify intensive redevelopment now.

He'd noticed the apartment blocks going up over the last year, looming over the close-built streets of Edwardian terraces and the low-rise strips of local authority housing.

Stillwater Rise.

A flicker of movement at the edge of his vision drew his attention from the screen. A small blonde head imperfectly hidden around the corner of the kitchen units. He smiled, watching as Emily dropped into a crouch and crept across the open space between the cupboard and the long pine table, her bare feet small and silent on the tile floor as she inched around a carver chair. She didn't look up, had obviously decided he was too focused on his work to notice her closing in stealthily on the chocolate cupboard.

Zigic pressed his knuckles to his mouth, stifling a laugh as she reached for the handle. Her shoulders tense. Her face set in fierce concentration.

Emily opened the door and slowly reached into the cupboard, her hand grasping too hard at whatever chocolate bar she wanted, making the packaging rustle. A high, startled noise broke out of her and she whipped around to see if she'd been caught, her freckled face set in absolute horror.

'Was that a mouse?' Zigic asked, letting his eyes widen, matching her shock. 'Is there a mouse making all that noise in the cupboard?'

He got out of his chair and crept over to her, Emily giggling. 'It was a bunny,' she said.

'The same bunny that stole Stefan's toast this morning at breakfast?'

Emily nodded.

'Well, it's too late for little bunnies *and* little to girls to be eating chocolate.' He swept her up and slung her over his shoulder, carried her upstairs as she insisted that bunnies didn't have a bedtime and they didn't have to go to the dentist, so they could eat chocolate whenever they wanted.

'But you're not a bunny, are you?' Zigic put her back into bed and pulled the covers up to her chin. 'No more chocolate raids, little mouse.'

Downstairs again he paused for a moment at the kitchen door, thinking that they really should move where they kept the chocolate. Milan and Stefan had finally accepted they couldn't eat whatever they wanted whenever they felt like it but Emily was a trickier customer than either of the boys had been. A lock on the door might work but he wouldn't put it past her to pick it. There was a sharpness to her thinking that gratified and terrified him in equal measure, but while she was so young he resolved to be proud of his quick-witted little cat burglar.

He sat down at the table, returned his attention to his laptop. Stillwater Rise.

A new development that had piqued Jordan Radley's interest.

Zigic googled the address. Ten storeys of soft red bricks and off-black windows, stretches of slate grey cladding and glass balconies, a penthouse on each of the three blocks complete with roof gardens and hot tubs under canopies. To the north the balconies would give onto the River Nene, where it bisected the city. The views to the south would be over Stillwater Lakes. Where Jordan had been killed.

'Luxury urban living for the discerning young professional', the developer's website promised, touting the lively bar scene in Peterborough, the brands available in the shopping centre and the city's rich cultural heritage. The forty-three minutes it would take to get to King's Cross Station.

According to Rightmove the flats were renting out for between £1,100 and £1,600 a month. One beds were selling for £200,000 and the price rising steeply from there.

The final phase was underway he saw. The last of the blocks rising up from the ground.

Ground that had been contaminated with a cocktail of heavy metals and other highly toxic substances, according to the Preliminary Risk Assessment in Drury Prior's report.

Not surprising, given that the site had spent the last seven decades being used for the manufacture of automation machinery, Zigic thought. All the related chemicals only becoming a problem when the owners wanted to build flats on it.

It wouldn't be the only site in the city with the same problems but the address told him why Jordan Radley had been interested in this specific tract of land.

It was the former Greenaway Engineering plant.

He sat back in his chair and reached for his wine.

Jordan wasn't finished with the Greenaways. He'd found his first story with the men who'd been made redundant, then he'd begun to look into the death of Marcus Greenaway but discovered nothing worth pursuing further than a visit to the airfield and a brief and apparently fractious conversation with Greenaway's widow and a much more amenable one with his mother.

Until he found this.

Zigic saw how Jordan's mind had been working, what he'd been taught. Identify a subject of interest and work around all the various angles until they'd been exhausted.

Except this particular subject was giving up potential stories at every turn.

The report into the land had been commissioned by the new owners. Not the German firm who'd bought Greenaway Engineering as a going concern and promptly closed it down and taken the order book abroad.

Docherty Construction.

Zigic went to the Companies House website and typed in the name, scrolled down to the section covering people with a controlling interest, finding two directors listed. Hugo Docherty and his sister Rachel Greenaway.

He got up and paced around the kitchen, drank a glass of water to drive some of wine fuddle out of his head, wondering how this new information might fit in with Jordan's murder.

Drury Prior had identified multiple toxic contaminants on the site during their preliminary report and when he clicked onto the recommendations they'd made, he found a requirement for the developers to remove topsoil and substrata down to a depth of one metre.

He blew out a slow breath. One metre across four acres of land. He couldn't even begin to visualise the bulk of material to be removed and replaced with fresh soil. Thousands of tonnes? Tens of thousands?

There was no evidence to suggest they hadn't done it but clearly Jordan Radley had his doubts. He'd been chasing down the environmental engineering firm. And they'd been evading him.

His eyes kept returning to Hugo Docherty's name on the directory.

Docherty Construction was another old Peterborough company, responsible for developing several large estates around the city since the 1970s. A family firm started by a former road-worker: poor boy done good. Searching online showed lots of coverage in the *Evening Telegraph* as Leonard Docherty gradually built his empire, following the same route that the Greenaways had, mixing with the upper echelons, appearing at events with the right kind of people, giving conspicuously to charity; Docherty favouring church roofs and whatever projects needed funding at the Cathedral. His obituary described a well-attended funeral held there, local dignitaries turning out in numbers to pay their respects.

Leonard is survived by his son Hugo and his daughter Rachel.

Had Jordan gone through this same process, Zigic wondered.

Skipping from Docherty Construction to Rachel Greenaway to the documents held at the land registry that showed the former factory site being sold by its new German owners straight back to a member of the Greenaway family at a knock-down price.

Two million.

Half what it was worth.

A fraction of what the business as a whole had been sold for. The buyers getting everything they wanted – the patents and the order book and the tooling – while the wildly undervalued parcel of land was returned to Hugo Docherty. Not the Greenaway family. The Dochertys alone would exploit the asset.

How would this have looked to Jordan? Like the kind of story he could get published in the kind of paper he was interested in working for?

This was not the tabloid splash of Marcus Greenaway being murdered. No, this was far more in keeping with Jordan's body of work, the perfect follow-up to the article he'd written about the men dispossessed after the sale of the factory.

A venerable old company sold.

A dirty deal done.

But was it enough to get him killed?

DAY FOUR

FRIDAY

CHAPTER THIRTY-EIGHT

'You look shattered, Col,' Ferreira said, as Murray lowered herself into her chair. 'Heavy night?'

'Late one,' she said, tearing open a packet of soluble paracetamol.

Ferreira smiled. 'Yeah, painkillers are a must for sleep deprivation.'

'We went round to Gordon's mates' place.' Murray took out one of the pills and tried for a moment to drop it into the mouth of her water bottle, before giving up and going to fetch a mug. Ferreira watched as she made her way back across the office, noticing how stiffly she moved.

'What the hell did you do round there?' she asked. 'Limbo contest? Judo lessons?' Murray rolled her eyes and Ferreira made a scandalised noise. 'Oh my god, you weren't swinging, were you?'

'Hilarious,' Murray grumbled. 'We were stargazing.'

Parr laughed. 'Is that what they call it now? Keys in the bowl and pick a constellation?'

'We were,' Murray insisted.

'Shit, that's worse than swinging,' Parr told her.

'Yeah,' Ferreira agreed. 'I've lost a little bit of respect for you now, if I'm honest.'

Murray swore at them, turning to make sure Parr received the full force. 'They're nice people. They brew their own ale.'

Ferreira nodded. 'That would make it more interesting, I suppose.'

'It's strong stuff.'

'Must be if it touched *you*.' Ferreira opened her drawer and tossed Murray a sachet of electrolyte powder. 'Chase the paracetamol with that. You'll be half normal in no time.'

'Reckon I prefer her like this,' Parr said, amusement still crinkling his eyes. 'All quiet and delicate.'

Murray sipped her water. 'You just wait until this kicks in, Zac. We'll see where *you're* delicate.'

He mugged a terrified face at her, went back to his breakfast. A bacon butty smothered in brown sauce, stinking up the air with its salty, fatty scent. There was a long-standing ban on bringing McDonald's into the office due to the distraction factor it caused and Ferreira was wondering if bacon sandwiches needed to be added to the vetoed list. But that was her own healthy breakfast talking, she thought; Billy having convinced her to try the raw porridge concoction he started the day with. She'd drowned it in maple syrup but even that hadn't managed to stop her tasting the *health* in every bite.

Another thing that changed when you moved in together, she thought, no more French toast or pancake stacks. Porridge. Uncooked. What next, she wondered with a sinking feeling. Camping holidays. Matching fleeces. National Trust membership.

Zigic came out of his office and went over to the board.

'Alright, everyone, listen up.' Jordan Radley's photograph watched them from across his shoulder, still the fresh-faced young man he'd been when this started, but now Ferreira thought she detected a more speculative kind of intelligence in his eyes. The kind which had got the truth about the break-in from Francis Pyle and earned him entrance into Anthea Greenaway's home. 'Today we're going to try and figure out what happened at Holme Airfield in the weeks before Marcus Greenaway's death.'

'Are we opening an official investigation?' Bloom asked.

'Not yet,' Zigic told her. 'I want to get a better idea of the situation before we commit to that. We have expert testimony that says the crash was an accident and we have no good reason right now to doubt it.'

'Apart from the break-in,' Parr added. 'And the prolonged and violent harassment campaign leading up to it.'

'Yes, Zac,' Zigic said tersely. 'We have some suggestive elements but right now they don't add up to very much. We've got footage from the airfield security.' He rapped his knuckles on a still from the footage. 'But it's not clear enough for us to make an ID. The tech department are on it but they're swamped, so in the meantime I want us to try and narrow down our possibilities.' He pointed at Murray. 'Col, where are you with Francis Pyle?'

'Nothing doing on the first pass,' she said with a shrug. 'I'm going out to the village this morning, though. Talk to his neighbours, see if anyone can break his alibi for Monday night.'

Zigic nodded. 'Good stuff. Zac, where are you with Browning?'

Parr looked at Ferreira. 'I'm onto the blokes from the Greenaway Club, right?'

'I redeployed Zac yesterday,' she told Zigic.

'If we're considering sabotage, we have to check out the people Greenaway pissed off, right?' Parr asked testily, his gaze switching between them.

Zigic screwed his face up, knowing what the implications were of saying yes.

'It's too early to commit to that theory,' he said slowly. 'If there is more to Greenaway's death than the AAIB report suggests, then potentially we're looking at a suspect pool of 150 men. Everyone made redundant could be in the frame and any of them might have killed Jordan to stop him exposing them.'

'But the blokes behind the harassment are the most likely candidates for escalating it to murder,' Parr insisted.

'You don't think they learned their lessons after they got banged up the first time?' Murray asked.

'Getting banged up probably pissed them off even more,' Parr suggested. 'The logical next step is a more violent response.'

Murray gave him a flat look. 'Is it, Zac? You think the first thing most old boys do when they get released from nick is sabotage a bloody helicopter?'

'They're engineers,' he said, with a shrug.

'For now we're keeping an open mind,' Zigic said firmly. 'If Jordan found something damning, maybe he *was* killed to cover it up. But this isn't the only story Jordan was working on and the men at the Greenaway Club are not our only suspects for the shooting.' He turned to Weller. 'Rob, you stay on P&N Medico and Sheila Yule.'

Ferreira thought of the nurse, collapsing onto her bed after another fourteen-hour shift. Too tired to be scared or too scared to sleep?

There would be more about her in Jordan's data, she was sure. All of those long phone conversations the two of them shared, conversations she claimed were about nothing, would be recorded somewhere. Innocuous-looking, unlabelled sound files containing God knows what revelations.

'We also have Jordan investigating a possible instance of land contamination,' Zigic told them, 'at the former Greenaway Engineering site, which is currently being redeveloped into luxury apartment blocks. Redeveloped by Marcus Greenaway's widow and his brother-in-law.'

Ferreira had called Zigic this morning before work to discuss the report, found he'd spent the evening doing exactly the same thing she had: piecing together the circumstances surrounding the transfer of the Greenaway Engineering site to its German owners in summer 2015, then back to the Docherty family less than six months later. She'd felt a thrill go through her as she sat at her kitchen table, seeing each new element slot into place, thinking that it must have been how Jordan Radley felt as he was building his story.

'So is the land still contaminated?' Murray asked, sitting forward in her seat, interested now. 'That's the million-dollar question, right? Some dodgy land deal's neither here nor there. Every land deal's dodgy. There had to be more to it.'

'The environmental science guys were ducking talking to Jordan,' Weller said. 'Maybe they'd sexed up the report?'

'You'd sex *down* a contamination report,' Murray pointed out.

Ferreira swore.

Murray turned sharply to her. 'Something bit your backside?'

'Jordan's girlfriend –'

'The experienced older woman,' Parr interjected.

'Her age is not even remotely relevant,' Ferreira told him. 'The girlfriend said Jordan was so desperate to earn some extra money that he'd taken a job labouring.'

'Where?' Zigic asked.

'She didn't know. She said he only stuck it out for a few days and she thought that was because he wasn't physically up to it, but –'

Zigic smiled, eyes lighting up. 'But what if he was nosing around at the former Greenaway site?'

CHAPTER THIRTY-NINE

'I looked at one of these places when I was thinking of buying,' Ferreira said, as they passed in front of the first of the new apartment blocks, craning to stare up at the sheer red-brick and black-clad facades. 'I viewed a flat in that one there. Fifth floor, overlooking the park.'

'Why didn't you buy it?' Zigic asked.

'Couldn't afford it in the end.' She leaned back in the seat. 'Turns out my wage doesn't constitute "young, urban professional" money.'

'Your new place is a bit better than this anyway,' he said, thinking of the cottage in Elton she'd bought with Adams. Leapfrogging the starter flat and the second house and going straight to most people's idea of a forever home. 'Have you made any headway on decorating yet?'

'We're doing it tomorrow,' she told him. 'But we were "doing it tomorrow" every Friday for the last six months, so ... yeah, probably not.'

The new road ended abruptly at a ring of three-metre-high boarding, Docherty Homes announcing their involvement in bold lettering around the architect's impressions of the development. The apartments looked much the same as in the drawings, except for the final tower which was still climbing towards its apex, windowless and unclad, oddly naked next to its finished neighbours, despite the complex system of scaffolding wrapped around it.

Zigic stopped at the entrance, a wide gateway protected by a mechanical barrier and a small hut.

The guard took his time coming out, put on his hard hat before he moved and motioned for Zigic to wind down his window.

'Sales office is in tower 1,' the man said. 'You can't miss the signs.'

Zigic held up his ID slightly closer to the man's face. 'We need to talk to the site agent. Where's his office?'

'Park on the right,' the man told him. 'Office is 200 yards past the standing. I'll call Gary and let him know you're on your way.'

Zigic pulled through the gates and onto an area of compacted rubble almost filled to capacity with builders' vehicles. Men were coming and going, grabbing tools and flasks, a couple of them ducking out under the barrier, heading for the burger van parked up as near as it could get to this lucrative pool of customers. The smell of frying meat was in the air as they climbed out of the car, but when they moved into the bustle of the compound, he caught the scent of diesel fumes and the powder from cut breeze blocks, the road wet with diluted sand and covered in muddy track marks from a forklift's deep tyres. The machine was beeping up ahead of them as it reversed into a loading bay as two men watched, shouting at the driver that they didn't want any more of that shit, only the good stuff.

Difficult to imagine Jordan Radley in this environment.

Zigic had tried labouring himself during his summer holidays when he was fourteen or fifteen, his dad offering him some cash in hand to go along and help him roofing. Fetching and carrying, humping tiles and rolls of lead out of the old man's van. Remembered his dad jokingly writing 'Zigic & Son' in the dirt on the paintwork as they left the house. Remembered him angrily scrubbing it out a few hours later when they discovered Zigic had no head for heights.

The site office was three PortaKabins bolted together, up off the ground on metal legs, crusted steps leading up to it. When they went inside they found four desks ranged around the space, but only one was occupied. A heavyset thirty-something man in a green fleece jumper with Docherty Construction on the chest, a big gold watch and a pair of rimless glasses too petite for his moon-shaped face. He was on the phone, and gave them a cursory glance before returning his attention to the middle distance, listening to whoever was making so much angry noise at him. Nodding, saying yes, it would get done, he was taking care of it.

A brushed steel nameplate on his desk said Gary Dewar. Near it was a styrofoam container smelling of fried food and a huge cup of takeaway coffee. A packet of indigestion tablets were already placed close by in readiness.

Dewar put the phone down, took a breath and then clapped his hands together, finally looking at them.

'The police, great. Like I haven't got enough around my arse-hole today.' He shoved his fingers back through his dirty blond hair. 'What can I do for you?'

'We're looking for information about a young man who we think might have been working here recently,' Ferreira said.

Dewar grimaced. 'What's this one done?'

'What do they usually do?' she asked.

Dewar waved away the question, peeled the lid off his coffee. 'Who are you after, then?'

'Jordan Radley.' Ferreira showed him a photo on her phone. 'He was labouring here.'

'Yeah, he was here. Beginning of the month. Don't think he lasted, though. They've not a good day's work in them, these young lads. Won't get up in the morning, want to knock off at the first sign of rain. Moan when it's too hot, moan when it's too cold. Never off their bloody phones.'

'Who was he working for?' Zigic asked.

'He was one of Sam Connor's.'

'We'll need to speak to Connor,' Ferreira said. 'Where can we find him?'

'You can't go walking around the site,' Dewar told her. 'Health and safety. I'll get him in here.'

A couple of minutes later they were joined by a short, power-fully built man in mud-spattered waterproofs and a hi-viz jacket. He took his hard hat off as he came in and tucked it under his arm, revealing short grey hair.

'Police,' Dewar said, before they could speak. 'Looking for one of your boys. Jordan Radley.'

Connor nodded. 'Saw that.'

'What's he done?' Dewar asked.

'Got killed,' Connor said. 'Shame. He had a good attitude.'

'How long was he here?'

'Three or four days. He wasn't up to the job, though. He couldn't have been nine stone wet. He tried, to be fair to him, but he was on his fucking knees by the end of the day.' Connor shrugged amiably. 'Not everyone's made for it. Most of the lads I'm getting coming to me now aren't. But there's not much out there and it's good money if you can stick it.'

'How did Jordan get the job?' Ferreira asked.

'He come up to me out at the burger van there.' Connor gestured away towards the entrance. 'Asked if I had anything going.'

'Just like that?'

Connor smiled at her. 'We're not sending rockets to the moon, we're building flats. I'll take anyone who'll turn up and give me a solid seven hours' graft.'

Zigic imagined how tough even a few days' labouring would have been for someone who'd never done it before. A slight young man accustomed to waiting tables and sitting at a desk at the *Evening Telegraph*. Jordan had wanted to get onto this site badly enough to hustle his way into a job and stuck it out long enough to find what he needed.

'Jordan was a journalist on the local paper,' he said. 'Did you know that, Mr Connor?'

'He never told me that.' Connor glanced at Dewar. The agent was watching them carefully and Zigic could see concern on his doughy face, worried about how this might reflect on him. 'I'm not surprised though,' Connor went on. 'He was obviously a smart kid but smart doesn't help much these days. My eldest's got a first in English literature, she's working in M&S now.'

'What's this got to do with him working here?' Dewar asked impatiently. 'He didn't do a full week. He's been away over a fortnight.'

'We believe Jordan came to work here deliberately,' Zigic told him. 'We think he approached you for a job, Mr Connor, because he was working on a story about the development and he wanted to get a closer look at what was happening here.'

'Nothing's happening here,' Dewar protested.

Connor eyed him up, the dislike obvious. The site agent was never popular, Zigic knew that much from hearing his father complain endlessly about jobs like this and the ineptitude of the men who inevitably ran them. Never as qualified as any of the trades but holding sway over them despite that.

'You'd better get back to work,' Dewar said, chucking his chin up at Connor. 'The NHBC woman's on her way over and if you haven't cleaned out them cavities, you can forget that day work-sheet getting signed.'

Connor's jaw clenched, a brief flash of fury in his eyes, but he took it. He fitted his hard hat back on and left the cabin.

Dewar had blackmailed him out of their way. Threatening to dock his wages if he didn't leave. Thinking a couple of coppers wouldn't know what he was doing.

'Anything you want to know about the site, you're going to have to go through head office.' Dewar started scrambling around inside his desk drawer. 'All I do is make sure the materials are here on time and they get put together in the right order.'

Ferreira took a step closer to his desk. 'Was Jordan Radley asking questions? Is that why he didn't last?'

'I never spoke to him.' He was still hunting in his desk.

'Or maybe you caught him poking around somewhere he shouldn't have been?' she suggested.

Dewar snatched up a card. 'Here. All the numbers are on there. Call head office if you want to know anything else.'

Outside Zigic scanned the site for Sam Connor, no sign of him.

'Is there something here?' Ferreira asked. 'Or is Dewar just covering his arse?'

Zigic looked at the bank of earth, fifteen metres wide, three metres high, piled up away to the northern edge of the site. He wondered if it was new, clean soil or the polluted stuff removed during excavations that would be full of asbestos and heavy metals, so toxic that he wasn't even sure it was safe uncovered like that with the rising wind blowing it across the site.

He started back to the car.

'There's definitely something here.'

Sam Connor was standing with a couple of other men at the burger van as they drove out of the compound and he put his hand up as Zigic pulled away from the barrier, making sure they'd seen him. He said something to the other men and they picked up their orders, headed back to work.

Connor moved away to the white plastic café tables – 'For Patrons Only' – choosing one that couldn't be seen from the guard hut at the entrance. Fearful of Dewar getting to hear about this, Zigic thought as they went over to him, but concerned enough about Jordan's murder to want to talk.

'I didn't want to say any of this in front of Dewar,' he began as soon as they sat down. 'Anything he knows, it'll go straight back to head office and I'll lose my job.'

'This stays between us,' Ferreira assured him.

Connor hunched forward, elbows on his thighs, hands clasped together in front of him. 'Jordan was asking questions. A lot of questions.'

'About the development?'

'No, about the site,' Connor said. 'He wanted to know what was on here before it got cleared for building and I told him it had been a factory ever since I could remember. They made machinery,' he explained. 'And Jordan said did I think the land was safe to build on if they'd been working with heavy metals and stuff like that.'

Ferreira's eyebrows went up. 'Do a lot of casual labourers ask questions like that?'

'No, but I didn't think too much of it at the time.' Connor shrugged. 'He was a smart kid and there's not a lot to keep your brain occupied when you're labouring. I guessed he was just looking around and got thinking.'

A lanky guy came over to the van and they fell silent, waiting for the man to get his order and leave. Zigic thought about what it would have taken for Jordan to rock up here and ask Sam

Connor for a job. There was an impressive boldness to it, but then Jordan knew men like Connor from the Greenaway Club. Would have known how to pitch his voice and frame his request. Just like with Sheila Yule.

'What did you tell Jordan?' Zigic asked, once they were alone again.

'You didn't get this from me,' Connor said.

Zigic nodded.

'I mean it, this is bad shit and if you say I said anything I'll deny it.' He cast a quick glance over his shoulder, checking they weren't being observed.

'We'll keep you out of it,' Zigic said. 'I promise.'

Knowing they might not be able to do that. Hating himself for saying it, just as he hated himself every time he gave his word to someone who could well find themselves in the witness box in the near future.

'Last year,' Connor said. 'June time. One of the young lads collapsed. Not on my crew, one of the groundworkers. Right state he was in.' Connor passed his hand over his face. 'Eyes streaming, gasping, choking. His boss gets him into the back of his van, drives him off to hospital. We never see him again.'

'He died?' Ferreira asked.

'No, but not far off it.' Connor bunched his hands together. 'I'd never seen anything like it. His face was like CGI or something. And we could all smell it. This ... weird, chemical smell.'

'What was it?'

'I don't know. Never smelled anything like it before in my life,' Conner said. 'But you just knew it was wrong. It smelled dangerous. I can't explain it.'

'Did it affect you?' Ferreira asked.

'I had a headache for a couple of hours. A few of us who were there did.'

Zigic thought of the research he'd done last night, googling chemicals he'd never heard of before. A litany of symptoms that seeped into his dreams so that he'd woken up at dawn unable to breathe, sat bolt upright with his hand at his throat.

'Did you report this to management?' he asked.

'Course we did,' Connor said dismissively. 'They didn't give a shit. The boss comes down and has a look around where the smell came from, told us we were imagining it. But the hole had been open a week by then.' He cast another quick look around before he went on. 'My guess is they had someone down here after we'd all knocked off and cleared the trench out. No evidence, right? Just in case.'

'What about the rest of the site?' Ferreira asked. 'Did you see any evidence of earth being removed elsewhere?'

'No, nothing.'

'And did you tell Jordan about this?'

Connor nodded. 'Yeah. I gave him the lad's number and all.'

'Why?'

'Because nobody gave a fuck when it happened and I figured maybe Jordan could do something about it.'

Zigic cocked his head. 'You knew he was a journalist when you hired him.'

'No,' Connor insisted. 'Not right away. But when he kept asking questions I got curious. I checked him out online. Found his Twitter. Saw what kind of stuff he was writing about. I told him to go and talk to Tom Geary.'

Connor's phone buzzed and he pulled it out of the buttoned pocket of his padded shirt.

'I've got to go.'

CHAPTER FORTY

'I did a bit of digging last night,' Ferreira said, as Zigic turned onto Oundle Road, running immediately into the slow traffic that always clogged up the stretch alongside the rolling green smudge of Ferry Meadows Country Park. 'I was trying to work out how much it would cost Docherty Construction to decontaminate the Stillwater Rise site.'

'Yeah, I wondered about that,' Zigic replied, braking as the lights turned red. 'It seems like something we'd need an expert to tell us, though.'

'I thought that as well to start with. But there are these calculators online that builders use to work out how much soil they'd need to cart away for any given size of development, right?' She took out her phone, where she'd made some notes. 'So, Drury Prior recommended replacing the soil down to a depth of one metre. And the site is four acres, roughly two hectares.'

'About that, yeah.'

'Which is 40,000 tonnes to be removed and carted away for safe disposal.' Zigic let out a low whistle. 'That's a minimum of 1,200 large lorry loads at around £200 per load, but you could double that for contaminated soil that needs safe disposal.'

'Are you sure about these numbers?' Zigic asked pensively. 'That's, what, 500 grand just to clear the soil.'

'I did the maths,' Ferreira told him. 'It's right. *Then* you need to bring in new soil to replace it and make the ground level back up. And that's 40,000 tonnes at a tenner a go. So add another 400 grand.' She slipped her phone away. 'We're looking at almost a million pounds to make the Stillwater Lakes site safe for development.'

Zigic let out a low whistle. 'That's a pretty significant chunk of money.'

'Kind of explains why Docherty Construction might have dodged doing it.'

'They only paid two million for the site,' Zigic said. 'I thought it was some kind of shady deal with the firm Docherty and Greenaway sold out to but maybe it's not that at all.'

'No, maybe they sold it back to them so cheap because the clean-up operation was going to cost a fortune.'

A troubled look crossed his face. 'We're assuming they didn't do the work.'

'It's a fair assumption to make,' Ferreira insisted. 'Given what we've just been told, don't you think?'

He stuck out his bottom lip. 'Let's see what Geary has to say before we get too excited about this.'

Ferreira settled back in her seat, thinking about the flat she'd viewed in the development. A large living room/dining room/kitchen, opening onto a balcony just big enough for a café table and two chairs. A poky bedroom and a bathroom with barely the space to turn around in. All of that for £200,000. Four of those flats per floor. Ten floors in the block. Three blocks in the development.

Say, £24,000,000 combined sale price.

Maybe £6,000,000 of that would be pure profit for Rachel Greenaway and her brother.

What would have happened if Jordan exposed them? Two towers already full of people, all potentially living on land that wasn't safe for human habitation. Walking along footpaths and around parking spaces bordered by toxic earth. Taking their children to the playground built on top of it, nothing but plastic membrane and some soft finish to protect them as they chased about. And the park, with its pieces of copper-toned sculpture and benches, all of that still-bare earth waiting for the landscaping to fill out.

The blocks would be condemned, surely?

Then what? Insurance claims and payouts. Bankruptcy. Ruin.

She wondered how the men at the Greenaway Club would feel if they knew what Jordan had been working on. If his time with them had sent him on this crusade against the family and its financial security. Was it personal for him? Did it feel like justice?

Zigic turned down into Alwalton Village, past the quaint pub on the corner and the stone post office, heading along a quiet, tree-lined lane. The place felt far more remote than it was. It was almost impossible to believe that the A1 was a few hundred metres away, the Peterborough showground and all its hustle and noise even closer in the opposite direction.

Tom Geary's place was the centre cottage in a long, stone and thatch row. It had a glossy black front door and a planter next to it, holding a few bright flowers. The curtains were drawn at the downstairs window. Upstairs the windows were open and Ferreira heard a vacuum cleaner running.

Zigic knocked on the door and waited. The vacuum was still going.

He knocked again.

Finally the door opened. A tall but gaunt man, dressed in tartan pyjama bottoms and a heavy jumper under a towelling robe looked back at them with an expression so completely pain-stricken it left no space for any other reaction. Twenty-nine years old, Ferreira knew, but couldn't quite accept.

'Mr Geary, I'm DS Ferreira, this is DI Zigic.' She held up her ID. 'Could we come in?'

'What do you want?' he asked, voice flattened and thin.

'We're investigating the murder of Jordan Radley. We believe you knew him.'

Geary kept his pain-numbed gaze on her. 'No.'

'You didn't know him?'

'I can't talk to you,' he said.

'But you did talk to him?' She fought the urge to move forward, walk him back into the house. Couldn't bring herself to do it to someone in his condition. 'Jordan was working on an article about the building site you were working on when you got ill, right?'

He winced. 'I told you. I can't.'

'Tom, who is it?' a woman called from inside, the vacuum cleaner silent now.

248

He didn't answer her. 'I've got nothing to say.'

The woman came fast down the stairs, a blur of neon sports-wear and long blonde hair, and appeared behind Geary, taking him gently by the arm and turning him into the hallway, speaking quietly, telling him to go and rest, she'd deal with this.

She rounded on them.

'Who are you and what do you want?'

Ferreira told her, hearing her own voice take on some snap in return. 'We're police officers and we need to talk to your boyfriend about a murder.'

'Does he look like he could commit a murder?' she demanded in a furious whisper.

'Did Tom speak to this man?' Zigic showed her the photo of Jordan Radley. 'He was investigating the site where Tom got ill.'

The woman blocked off the doorway with her arm. 'We can't talk to you about that.'

'Why not?'

'We just can't.' Nervous-looking now. 'That guy did come here and we told him exactly the same thing.'

'Jordan Radley is dead,' Ferreira reminded her. 'He was shot in the back. So, you don't get to decide whether you want to talk to us.'

The woman groaned, glanced back inside quickly, then stepped out onto the pavement and drew the door closed behind her.

'We can't talk to you because Tom signed a non-disclosure agreement with the company,' she said. 'I shouldn't even be telling you that. We're not supposed to tell anyone anything about it.'

'Why did you agree to a NDA?' Zigic asked.

The woman rolled her eyes. 'Why do you think? We needed the money. Tom's never going to be able to work again. So we took the money and agreed to keep quiet.'

'Did you tell Jordan Radley that?'

'No. I'm only telling you because you're with the police.' The woman wrapped her arms around herself. 'You're the only people who know about it.'

Zigic slipped the photo away, giving her a curt nod. 'Okay. Thanks for your time.'

'You won't say anything?' the woman asked, as they turned back to the car. 'If they find out I've told you …'

'We won't say anything,' Ferreira assured her, remembering Zigic saying the same thing to Sam Connor. The same fear on this woman as she'd seen on him.

She got back into the car and slammed the door shut, frustrated at running into another wall. This dead end was even more annoying because she knew there was something on the other side of it.

Something that the Greenaways had been so desperate to protect that they'd thrown money and legal threats at it.

And who knows what else?

Chapter Forty-One

'How do you get around a NDA?' Ferreira asked, exhaling smoke.

Billy shrugged, leaned against the side wall of the station. 'A warrant should do it. It'll take time, though. And I'm not sure you can compel the person involved if they don't want to talk. How serious is it?'

'The crime? It's industrial contamination.' She explained briefly about Tom Geary and the hush money he'd been paid by Docherty Construction to buy his silence. 'The thing is, he doesn't want to talk. If he does he'll be violating his terms. Then the money goes away and he'll probably get sued.'

'I don't fancy your chances then.' He flicked ash off his cigarette. 'What does Ziggy think?'

'That we need to find someone who'll actually talk to us,' she said, still stinging slightly from the disappointment. Not sure what she'd been expecting Zigic to do but she'd hoped for a more proactive response. 'He can see that we're getting closer.'

'You are.'

'Great pep talk, thanks.'

'Do you need a pep talk?' he asked, giving her an indulgent look.

'No, I just need to find something in Jordan's files that moves us on, I suppose.'

'If he'd got as far as identifying a victim, he must have made notes,' Billy suggested. 'And it isn't like you don't know who was behind the NDA, is it? The big question is, would they kill Jordan to stop him digging any further?'

'We don't even know *they* know that he was digging around.'

More gaps, more questions, everywhere they turned in this case. Suspects coming and going, still no sign of the murder weapon, no solid forensics, no witnesses. Weller was head down on P&N Medico, digging into Sheila Yule's employment history.

They now knew she'd moved around a few different agencies since leaving the NHS in 2015 but not why she'd left there, thanks to an unhelpful HR department at City Hospital. Weller had speculated that Jordan's story might date back that far, testing the possibility that she'd reported something at the hospital and been let go as a result, but Zigic said it was just a theory until he found something concrete to back it up.

'How does this link with the Greenaway crash?' Billy asked, scrubbing out his cigarette. 'Isn't that your main line of enquiry?'

'It's Zac's pet theory,' she said dismissively. 'And Riggott's, but that's coming *through* him rather than *from* him.'

Billy nodded. 'Keeping the Chief Constable happy.'

'Exactly.'

They went back upstairs, Billy returning to his office and the endless reams of financial data from the endless parade of potentially suspicious businesses in the city.

Parr appeared beside her desk.

'Steve Gurney's got a pilot's licence,' he said brightly, pointing to the place on Marcus Greenaway's board where he'd written down this new information, in letters larger than it deserved.

'So what?' Ferreira asked.

'So we know he has background.'

'Of what?' she demanded. 'Where during the training for your pilot's licence do you think they explain how to sabotage a helicopter?'

Parr shrugged, shoving his hands into the pockets of his trousers. 'If you're familiar with how to fly something, stands to reason you might have an idea how the engine and stuff works, doesn't it?'

'Did he fly helicopters?'

'Microlights,' Parr said.

'Zac, microlights are one step up from a fucking kite.' Ferreira waved him away. 'If you want to bring Gurney in, you need to do better than that, matey.'

She began to click through Jordan Radley's files, looking for something that could move *her* theory on. She'd already examined Jordan's call logs, hoping to find another contact with Drury Prior in them, a source he'd spoken to directly, but there was nothing. The investigation seemed to have gone quiet after he'd returned from Leicester.

Jordan had done the hard work by that point, she thought. Found this story, God knows where. Finessed his way onto the building site, stuck out three or four hard days' labouring before Sam Connor realised who he was and what he could do to expose a scandal nobody else seemed to care about.

Then Tom Geary.

Then nothing.

She thought of what Connor had said, his suspicion that Docherty Construction had quietly removed the contaminants that sent Geary to A&E. Wondered who'd done that and where they'd gone with it.

Was the soil in somebody's garden now? Taken away and mixed in with safe earth and then loaded onto a tipper lorry and sold on. Slowly poisoning some unwitting family.

How could a NDA be enough to stop that coming out?

But it was legal paperwork and that scared people, she realised. Especially when they were in Tom Geary's situation. So ill he couldn't work, couldn't even get changed out of his pyjamas, shuffling around, stunned by the pain he was in. A bad enough situation with a payout to ease the day-to-day demands of life, unimaginably worse without it.

Would she stand up and speak the truth in his situation? She wanted to believe she would but knew that was a decision you couldn't fully appreciate until you were the person facing it.

She found herself drifting away from Jordan's files, searching for Tom Geary online instead and when she did find him she wasn't sure she had the right man, couldn't believe the difference that had come over him in the eighteen months since he'd posted his last Facebook update.

The photograph was of him and his girlfriend Bryony passing through the finish line of a foot race high in the mountains on Lanzarote, holding their linked hands aloft under the floodlights. Faces lit with exhilaration.

Ferreira scrolled back, seeing more exotic locations and extreme sporting achievements. Tom and Bryony hiking in Japan, trail running in Chile, sitting around fire pits on white sand beaches, swimming with sharks. An attractive couple living an exciting life, the kind their exes would stalk across social media, she thought, imagining that even their friends would like these posts through gritted teeth.

He looked thirty years older now.

How did you price this change in a man's life?

Was his payout bigger because of what they'd taken from him or was there some official scale, some industry standard agreed by solicitors and insurers, which dictated the price of a future lost, ambitions curtailed and achievements rendered impossible? Would he get less because he was young or more because of how many more years they'd ruined for him? Would they have paid out at all if he'd died?

Ferreira stared at a photo of the couple standing on a bridge, strapped into bungee rigs, the image snapped at the split second they began to fall, delight on their faces. Absolutely no hint of fear.

One big lungful of poisoned breath and that was it.

Somebody should be punished for this. And she found that the more she scrolled the angrier she became, thinking of how Docherty Construction had destroyed Geary's life just the same as Greenaway Engineering had whipped away the security and stability of their employees. Without a thought or a backwards glance.

These people were expendable. Sign this contract, take this money, keep your mouth shut.

It was a crime that disappeared at the stroke of a pen. Never reported to them, never investigated. The unfairness of it was making her face burn up and the muscles across her back tighten and knot.

If Tom Geary's life-changing injuries were the result of a hit and run or an act of physical violence, the perpetrator would be arrested and charged and locked up. Maybe not for as long as she would like, but Geary would have his justice.

She didn't see why this was any different.

Intent mattered, but wasn't indifference a kind of intent? How was ignoring the rules any less depraved than malicious intent? Docherty Construction knew what was in that earth and they knew how dangerous it was but they *chose* to ignore Drury Prior's report; they believed the rules that governed decontamination didn't apply to them.

What was the difference between acting to take a life and not acting to save one?

Her tongue strayed to the implants next to her molars and she shrank back from the computer screen slightly, feeling her toes curl inside her boots, like they'd curled away from that pool of blood as it slowly expanded towards her.

It was not the same.

It wasn't.

She tasted the CS gas again, felt it fill her nose, metallic and caustic. Pressed her fingertips to her eyes as they began to sting at the memory. The truth she'd told no one and the lie she'd used to keep herself safe merging disconcertingly.

'I've got some drops if you want them,' Murray said.

'I'm fine,' she managed.

'You know the fags don't help.'

Ferreira nodded. 'I know.'

'They dry your eyes out something chronic. I didn't realise how bad mine were till I quit.'

She blinked a few times. Murray, holding a small plastic bottle out to her across the desk, Ferreira's vision blurring as she did it.

'Thanks.' She tilted her head back and put the drops in, felt them cold and unpleasant as they settled along her lower lid. 'That's better.'

CHAPTER FORTY-TWO

'I'm thinking,' Parr said, standing at the board with a cup of tea in his hand.

'When you announce it like that I have to wonder how often you actually do it,' Ferreira told him, looking back to her screen where she was still clicking through Jordan Radley's files.

There were photographs and ideas for articles, drafts of pieces she'd already read in the *ET*, bits of course work and the feedback he'd been given.

'I'm thinking ...' Parr said again.

'Still?'

'We can't find any sign of our bad boys from the Club going home, right?' he asked. 'And we can't find any sign of our killer coming and going from the crime scene, yeah?'

She clicked through more social media avatars and saved articles by other writers: house-plant care and money diaries and recipes for vegan cupcakes.

'Yeah. So?'

'The green lane runs right around the southern edge of Fletton, towards two of our suspects' homes,' Parr said. 'If you wanted to get from the crime scene without being caught on camera, that would be the way to go.'

'It's also unlit,' Ferreira pointed out.

'The killer might have taken a torch.'

'Fair enough.'

Parr clicked his tongue loudly. 'The killer goes to Jordan's house and clears out all his tech, right? Then he has to get home somehow.'

'Have you decided where he went home to?' she asked.

'Humble, Ridgeon, Caxton and Gurney all live around Stanground and Old Fletton,' he said slowly, and she saw him tracing his finger along the map on Jordan's board. 'Any of them could have got home via the green lane.'

'And how far is it?'

'Less than two miles.'

'Caxton's a wreck,' she reminded him. 'He's barely managing to stack shelves at Tesco's. There's no way he's walking two miles anywhere.'

'He said he took the bus home,' Keri Bloom added, watching Parr as well now. 'Although … I can't actually find him at the stop and there's a camera close to it.'

'Maybe Caxton isn't as knackered as he's making out,' Parr suggested. 'It's a good way to throw us off the scent, right? Act like he's dying on his feet but he's actually –'

'A power walker on the quiet?' Ferreira asked, thinking of Caxton struggling to stay upright behind the counter in the shop when they'd gone to question him. 'Read the article. Caxton's back's gone. He's hardly eating and he's up to his eyeballs on pain-killers. And we're not just talking about him walking two miles home, are we? If he shot Jordan he had to walk from the Club to the crime scene and then to Jordan's house and *then* double back on himself past the scene *again* and make the two-mile schlep home to Stanground.' She nodded at Parr. 'How far's that lot?'

'Do you think we should search along the green lane?' Bloom asked, picking at her salad with a wooden fork. 'If the killer did go that way home, it would make sense to dump the gun somewhere around there.'

'That's a huge search zone,' Ferreira told her. 'And it's got lakes bordering it. It's not feasible on budget constraints.'

Bloom's shoulders went up defensively.

'Just under five miles,' Parr said, turning away from the board. 'But it doesn't mean someone else couldn't have done that same route.'

'St Margaret's Road's the more likely option,' Murray said, typing away opposite Ferreira. 'No cameras on it. You'd cut through the new estate and back again if you wanted to avoid the cameras on the crossings on London Road. Bit of rough ground to negotiate near the old Phorpres House but nothing like as much.'

She was right, Ferreira realised, thinking of the car park behind the austere old building and the steep slope down to the railway line, how it rose up to the road bridge. Barely a scramble if you were wearing sensible shoes.

'Ridgeon lives on the marina, right?' Murray asked, already knowing the answer. 'That's a much shorter journey for him.'

'It's shorter for Gurney as well.'

'They're old men,' Weller protested. 'My grandad can hardly get around the big Tesco without stopping for a rest in the shoe department.'

Murray raised her eyebrow at him. 'And how old's your grandad?'

'Seventy-eight.'

'These lads are all in their fifties or early sixties,' she said.

'So?'

'You don't suddenly collapse because you've hit fifty.' Murray pointed at him. 'You're not going to get anywhere if you go profiling people based on crap like their age.'

'It does seem pretty ageist,' Bloom said gently.

Weller put his hands up. 'Why's everyone starting on me? I'm being a realist here.'

Ferreira tuned them out, while she returned to Jordan Radley's files.

More recipes. More photographs. A list of homeless shelters that had closed along with the names and numbers of people she assumed were potential contacts for quotes.

A Freedom of Information request.

'All I'm saying is that the logistics of this look more like a young person,' Weller said grudgingly.

Ferreira left the rest of them bickering away and went into Zigic's office.

'Jordan had a Freedom of Information request for rates of pulmonary disease treated at City Hospital during the last three years,' she said. 'Just men. All age ranges. I think he was searching for other people affected by the contamination on the site where Tom Geary got ill.'

'What do they show?' Zigic asked.

'A slight rise this year.'

'Hold on,' Zigic said slowly. 'FOI requests take ages to come through and he only found out about Tom Geary at the beginning of November.'

She leaned back against the internal window. 'The report's dated October 26th.'

'He didn't know about Geary then.'

'So, why was he asking?'

Zigic rubbed his beard thoughtfully. 'Maybe Geary isn't the only victim Jordan knew about.'

CHAPTER FORTY-THREE

'Yes, Jordan Radley did come to see me,' Ms Leung said, beckoning for them to take a seat, as she went around the other side of the desk in her cramped office on the second floor of City Hospital. The car park visible through the vertical blinds hanging in the north-facing window. Grey light, the distant movements of figures between the vehicles. 'I'd gone down to the cafeteria to get a coffee and he approached me there. He said he had some questions about a potential contamination incident and wondered if I could help.'

She shrugged off her putty-coloured cardigan, the deep cuffs of her starched white shirt pristine even though the rest of her seemed slightly rumpled towards the end of her shift in City Hospital's Respiratory Health Unit.

'When was this?' Ferreira asked.

'About a month ago,' Ms Leung said, reaching for her diary and flipping through thickly filled pages. 'Hold on a moment. Yes, October 29th.'

Three days after he had received the Freedom of Information report, Zigic thought, and the very next week he went and found himself a job on the building site.

'Why did he contact you?'

'He wanted to discuss a contamination incident,' she said gravely, knitting her fingers together over her diary.

'Is it usual for you to take meetings with people to discuss potential public health hazards?' he asked.

'No, it isn't. But once something like that reaches a point where the press are showing an interest – enough of an interest to approach a respiratory health consultant like me – I have to assume there's some validity to it. So I agreed to talk to the young man.'

'Where was this incident?'

'A building site in Old Fletton,' she said, verifying what they already knew. 'I gather it's almost completed. Mr Radley seemed very concerned that the builders were at risk but also the residents.'

'Did he have any evidence to back this up?'

'No.' Ms Leung shifted in the high-backed leather swivel chair. 'He showed me a report from an environmental surveyor detailing the levels of various hazardous materials on the site prior to development starting. But lots of brownfield sites are in similar states before the developers move in and make them safe. That's the purpose of carrying out environmental surveys.'

She struck Zigic as a careful and precise kind of person, guessed it came with the job once you reached this level of specialisation. Ms Leung had published several articles on bacterial lung infections, he knew from Ferreira's pre-interview prep, seemed to be something of an authority in the field.

'Do you have much experience with land contamination?' he asked.

'It's an interest of mine,' she said, then gave them a vaguely embarrassed smile. 'Strange thing to be interested in, right? But as towns and cities keep expanding and rural communities push back on developing greenbelt land, we're going to see more former industrial sites being converted into housing, and the simple fact is that many of them aren't really fit for building homes on.'

'But surely they're made safe before work starts?' Ferreira suggested innocently.

'You would think so, wouldn't you?' Ms Leung smoothed her hand back over her hair, pulled into a low bun. 'You'd hope so, anyway.'

'Jordan didn't think the one he wanted to discuss was safe?'

'The levels of contamination indicated in the survey he gave me would certainly pose a significant risk to human health,' she said, still picking her words, Zigic thought, sensing that there was more behind them that she wasn't sure she wanted to reveal yet. 'Then there was the issue of combination. Some of the heavy metals are dangerous enough on their own but when we see them combined, the risks multiply exponentially.'

Her gaze drifted across her desk, skimming the cluster of photographs in silver frames and the jade plant in a white china pot sat next to a small plastic figure of a doctor with an oversize head. Milan and Stefan had bought Zigic one just like it in a policeman's uniform and it sat on his desk next to his computer, watching him with its big, blank eyes.

'You have to remember though,' she said. 'This is the *pre-decontamination* levels we're talking about and as far as I know all the correct procedures were followed.'

'Did Jordan believe that to be the case?' Zigic asked.

Ms Leung sighed. 'No. He was adamant that the developers had, at best, cut corners and, at worst, done absolutely no remedial work.'

'He must have had proof for this?'

'He thought the illnesses were proof,' she said.

'On the FOI request he'd called in?' Ferreira asked.

Ms Leung looked at her curiously. 'Those ones, yes. But Mr Radley wanted to talk to me about one of my patients. Sorry, I thought you knew about that. I assumed it's why you are here.'

Zigic glanced at Ferreira.

'Tom Geary?' he asked.

'I can't share those details,' Ms Leung said briskly. 'You know that.'

'Can you tell us whether Jordan mentioned that name?'

She considered it for a moment. 'He didn't, no. I should clarify here. Mr Radley wanted me to give him a quote about the potential for serious respiratory illnesses arising from the level and combination of contaminants on the Stillwater Rise Apartment complex. But I told him I couldn't form an opinion without seeing what the current levels on the site were.'

'Even with a spike in rates of serious illness during the build?' Ferreira asked.

'The information Mr Radley had was one-dimensional to say the least. Yes, we've seen a rise in incidence of serious respiratory failings but the way the information is broken down doesn't allow you to take into account pre-existing conditions or lifestyle factors. For a layperson it's tempting to look at a spike and attribute it to whatever you'd like to blame, but we don't work like that.' She took a breath, reined in her exasperation. 'I made it clear to him that if he came back to me with evidence I would raise the subject with my colleagues.'

'But he didn't come back?'

'No,' she admitted. 'Regardless, I decided to monitor the situation. I've flagged the issue with the rest of the team and we're paying close attention to the occupations and addresses of otherwise healthy people presenting with sudden-onset respiratory problems.'

Like Tom Geary had, Zigic thought.

Ferreira slid forward in her seat. 'Hold on. Jordan wanted to talk to you about one of your patients?' Leung nodded. 'Who he thought had been affected by the contamination But it wasn't Tom Geary?'

Ms Leung looked down at her hands folded together on the desk.

'Was this other patient working on the Stillwater Rise site?' Ferreira asked.

'He was. I began treating him a couple of weeks earlier.' She frowned. 'Mr Radley already knew about him.'

'How?'

'He didn't say, but I assumed he knew the man as he was very familiar with the details of his death.'

Zigic started. 'The man died?'

Ms Leung nodded.

'Then you can tell us who he is,' Ferreira said triumphantly.

CHAPTER FORTY-FOUR

'What do you want?' Sheila Yule asked, rubbing the sleep out of her eyes. Her pyjama top was sitting skewed on her shoulders, her fringe sticking up in a stiff blonde wedge.

'We need to talk to you about your husband,' Ferreira said.

She opened the door the rest of the way. 'I'll go and put the kettle on.'

They went into the living room, Zigic taking a seat at the end of the sofa where a paperback had been left splayed on the arm and Ferreira watched him hunt for a bookmark to save Sheila Yule's place before he set it down on the coffee table.

Ferreira walked over to the china cabinet, looked at the small arc of photographs on the shelf. Sheila and Derek Yule on their wedding day, her very young, hardly out of her teens, Ferreira guessed. Sheila pretty and trim in a busy white dress. Derek wearing a grey suit with big shoulders and a slight sheen to the fabric, a pencil-thin tie. Barely a head taller than Sheila but holding himself like he was ten feet tall. A funny-looking guy, with a head of curly black hair and a stiff moustache. The photos around it showed them growing older together, both thickening out and settling into one another. Holiday snaps and parties, someone else's wedding. Confetti on the ground around their feet as they laughed, clinging to each other.

At some point things between them had obviously soured, judging by the fact that they'd divorced a few years before he died. But not so much that Sheila had fully abandoned him, according to what Ms Leung had said. Sheila with him at every appointment, by his hospital bedside, before bringing him home to care for him.

She hadn't changed her name, either, and that must have meant something.

Ferreira wondered which one of them had wanted the divorce. Suspected it had been Derek or else why would she have taken him in when he was dying? Acrimonious divorces just didn't play out like that.

Sheila returned with tea and biscuits. Taking the time to compose herself, Ferreira thought, because they'd pulled her out of her bed and she knew this conversation was going to be a tough one. It was one thing preparing for it in your head, knowing it might be coming, another thing altogether when the police were in your home with the facts at their disposal.

She felt for her. Knew Sheila was scared.

But they needed the truth and with Tom Geary bound under a non-disclosure agreement she might be their only chance to get to it.

Sheila retreated to the armchair near the electric fire, curled her bare feet under her body.

'How did you find out?' she asked.

'We talked to Derek's doctor,' Zigic said. 'She told us some of it but I don't think she knows the full story, does she?'

'She did her best.' Sheila wrapped her hands around her cup. 'It came out of nowhere, that's the thing. Derek had a bit of flu, he'd had his jab and got sick, like he did every year after he'd had it. Nothing to worry about, I told him.'

Ferreira came to sit down next to Zigic, Sheila watching her move.

'Then I was at work and he rang up saying he couldn't breathe properly.' She bit her lip. 'I didn't find out until later but he'd been working near a trench on the Docherty Construction site out at Old Fletton and he said there was this God-awful smell coming out of the ground. He thought he was having an asthma attack or something.'

'Was Derek asthmatic?' Zigic asked.

'No, but it can come on at any time.' She rubbed her thumb along the rim of her cup. 'Derek wasn't a doctor, he didn't know what was happening to him. He couldn't catch his breath so he thought it was asthma.'

'But it wasn't?'

She shook her head. 'I could hear him wheezing down the phone, like his throat was closing up. The worst of it –' Her brows drew together and Ferreira saw her trying to hold down the emotions welling up in her – 'the worst of it was he sounded terrified. Stupid bastard was never scared of anything in his life. He didn't have the sense for it. But he was terrified. He said, "I think I'm dying."' Her bottom lip trembled and she pressed her hand to her mouth; still wearing her wedding ring, Ferreira noticed. 'I got in the car and went over to his place. He looked half dead when he answered the door. Eyes streaming, voice going. This rattling noise when he breathed. I told him we had to call an ambulance but he wasn't having any of it. He'd always hated hospitals.' She smiled indulgently. 'Soft bugger cut the tip of his finger off once and wouldn't even go to A&E then. He just had me bandage it up and took a couple of painkillers. God knows how it never got infected.'

'He was made of tough stuff,' Zigic said gently.

'Not tough enough.' Sheila shook her head. 'Anyway, I got him in the car and drove him to A&E. The doctor took one look at him and sent him straight up to ICU.'

'Did you tell them about the smell?' Zigic asked.

She nodded. 'Nobody seemed interested. He was an old man, old men get ill. How it happens never seems to matter much. They diagnosed him with an acute bacterial infection in both his lungs. Bombarded him with antibiotics. Put him in isolation for over a week.'

'And he recovered,' Zigic said. 'Didn't he?'

'I never expected that.' Sheila looked away towards the photographs in the cabinet. 'I don't think the doctors did either. Something that serious, they'd told me to prepare for the worst.'

Ferreira wondered how she'd felt during that week. Watching the man she'd spent decades with fighting for his life. Someone she wasn't with any more but clearly still loved. If she'd made her bargains with God, if that was why she'd taken him back into her home when he was discharged. Fulfilling her side of some deal with the universe.

'Once he was well enough to leave hospital, Ms Leung kept a close eye on him. She was very good but when I tried to explain about how the symptoms started, Derek kept telling me to leave it alone, let the doctor do her job.'

'Was Ms Leung interested in how it happened?' Ferreira asked.

'She told me it was almost impossible to pinpoint the cause of a bacterial infection because we all come into contact with so many potential contaminants every day. It could be anything.' Sheila sighed. 'She got him well again, that was all that mattered really.'

Ms Leung must have been treating Tom Geary around the same time, Ferreira thought. Had she heard the same story from his girlfriend and dismissed the link? Or had Docherty Construction's lawyers got to him so quickly that he hadn't even shared the cause of his illness with his own specialist?

'And Derek moved back in here with you?' Zigic asked. 'After he was discharged?'

'It was the least I could do for him,' she said, lowering her gaze. 'He saw me through a double mastectomy. Most blokes scarper at the first sign of it, but he was a titan, bless him.'

For a moment nobody spoke and Ferreira heard a television playing in the neighbouring flat, the hollow brightness of a game show, an engine revving on the street below and a door slamming.

'He was getting better,' Sheila said, putting down her cup, tea untouched. 'I was enjoying having him here again. Even in that state he was good company. Always laughing and joking. That's why I married him.' Another glance towards the photos. 'He wasn't the best-looking lad around, but he could always make me laugh.'

Again the threat of tears crumpled her face but she pushed them down.

Abruptly the sadness shifted, her cheeks stiffening with anger.

'I got in touch with the company,' Sheila said. 'Docherty Construction. I thought, Derek's got through it but the next bloke

267

might not be so lucky. And I was thinking about all the people living in those flats. It couldn't be safe, could it?' Her hand balled into a fist on the arm of the chair. 'I wrote to them and I explained what happened to Derek – all very polite – I said I thought they should run some tests on the land because it seemed like whoever cleaned it up hadn't done as thorough a job as they should have and other people might be in danger.'

'What did they say?' Zigic asked.

'They told me they were very sorry to hear about Derek's illness but as he wasn't employed directly, it wasn't their responsibility and that the land had been thoroughly decontaminated so there was no possibility that his condition was related to his work.' Sheila drew herself up in the chair and Ferreira imagined her looking just as indignant when she first read Docherty Construction's response.

'Well, I don't mind telling you that put my back up,' she said. 'I got onto them again and I told them I wanted to see evidence that the land had been decontaminated.'

'Did you get it?'

'No. What I got was a very nasty letter from their solicitors threatening me with legal action if I persisted in my "wild allegations".' Sheila unfolded herself, leaning forwards now, anger hardening her posture. 'I thought, alright, if you want a fight I'll give you a bloody fight. I knew they were in the wrong. You don't go threatening legal action if you're innocent, do you?'

Ferreira shook her head, seeing why Jordan Radley had come to the woman. He needed a source, someone who was prepared to stand their ground publicly, come what may. And Sheila Yule seemed exactly the right kind of person for that.

'We weren't well off,' Sheila went on. 'But a friend of mine had used this no-win no-fee place in town when her tumble dryer caught fire and she said they were good. I made an appointment to go and see them, told Derek to put something smart on and come with me.' Her mouth twisted. 'But no. He wasn't having any of it. Told me to cancel the appointment and leave well alone.'

'Why didn't he want to go ahead?' Ferreira asked.

'He was starting to feel well enough to go back to work,' she said. 'He thought getting tied up in legal proceedings against them would mean he wouldn't be able to get back on site.'

'He wouldn't want to go back on site, surely,' Zigic suggested. 'He knew it was dangerous.'

'It wasn't just *that* site,' Sheila told him. 'Derek was convinced that if we kicked up trouble he'd get blacklisted. Nobody would give him a job.'

Zigic looked perplexed. 'Why would he think that? Docherty Construction are one company. They're not even that big.'

'Doesn't matter,' Sheila said regretfully. 'They all piss in the same pot. You get on the wrong side of one of them, they blacklist you and you won't get on anywhere.'

'That doesn't sound legal,' Zigic said.

'What do they care if it's legal? They all do it. Derek's cousin had the same thing. Complained to his boss about some health and safety breach on a site, got sacked, couldn't find another start anywhere. He's a window cleaner now. Fully certified gas fitter and he's cleaning windows.'

The same machinery that had silenced Tom Geary working on Derek Yule, Ferreira thought. Not so overtly in this instance but there was the fear; speak up and we'll make sure you never work again. Who could challenge that? Not a couple like the Yules with limited financial resources and limited evidence.

Not until Jordan Radley came along.

'In the end it didn't matter,' Sheila said, drawing back in the chair, turning in on herself once more. 'Derek didn't get better after all.'

They waited, neither of them wanting to prompt her as she came closer to the painful end of her story. She took off her glasses and spent a moment polishing them on the hem of her pyjama top.

'It was my fault,' she said, voice clogging. 'We were struggling for money. I could hardly manage when it was just me but having Derek here as well, all the extra costs, him not working, I ended up taking on even more shifts.'

They didn't need to hear it, Ferreira thought. Not how he died. Not exactly. But Sheila seemed to need to say it. Tear the guilt out of her chest and lay it down in front of them.

'I brought some virus home from work,' she said, eyes brimming. 'It was just … one minute he was fine and the next he was gone. It was that quick.'

'It wasn't your fault,' Zigic told her, moving to the edge of his seat but not seeming to know what to do next. 'If it wasn't for Docherty Construction, Derek wouldn't even have caught the virus. You didn't do that to him. They did.'

She nodded but Ferreira doubted she believed him. Would have been over this countless times already. Told herself she should have known better. She was a nurse. She should have been more careful. The money wasn't that important. Money she'd needed so they could eat and keep a roof over their heads.

It was always easiest to blame yourself, because you would always be available to take the punishment other people could evade.

'How much did Jordan know about all of this?' Zigic asked finally.

'He knew about the land being contaminated,' Sheila said. 'And he knew what had happened to Derek. That's why he got in touch with me in the first place. He said he was going to try and get hold of a sample of the soil so we could find out whether it had been cleaned up or not. He had a friend who worked at a charity who could test it for him. Then if it turned out it was still dangerous, we could do something about it.'

'Why didn't you tell us about this when we talked to you last time?' Zigic asked, an edge of frustration in his voice.

'Why do you think?' Sheila demanded. 'Jordan got shot. I thought it might have something to do with all this.'

Ferreira thought of all the money bound up in those three towers. The lawsuits Jordan's story would have provoked. The reputational damage.

People were killed for the contents of their wallets, for the pension they'd just collected.

Docherty Construction stood to lose far more than that.

270

'And Jordan knew about all of this back in October,' Zigic said slowly. 'How did he find out about Derek?'

'One of Derek's mates from the football told him about it apparently. They used to stand together at the POSH,' she said. 'I never met him but they'd known each other for years. Jordan got to know him somewhere or other and he mentioned it. He thought Jordan might be able to do something.'

'Who was this?' Zigic asked.

Sheila dredged her memory for the name and Ferreira willed her to find it, praying it wasn't Tom Geary, that all of this wouldn't just loop back around to the same dead end.

'Caxton,' Sheila said, clicking her fingers. 'Dick Caxton.'

CHAPTER FORTY-FIVE

'You're wanting to go after the builders now?' Riggott said, throwing a searching look up to the ceiling of his office. 'Give me strength.'

'We've got one death and one former Ironman triathlete who can barely walk to his front door unaided,' Ferreira told him, voice full of rage and frustration. 'All because Docherty Construction decided they'd rather add a few hundred grand more to their profit margin than decontaminate a site full of lethal chemicals.'

She turned to Zigic, jerked her head for support.

'It's a clear case of criminal negligence,' he said. 'And the company knows it is or they wouldn't have threatened Sheila Yule with legal action if she kept pressing them for information.'

'Not to mention the fact they've slapped a NDA on Tom Geary,' Ferreira added. 'You don't stump up for a payout and a gagging order unless there's a case to answer.'

'Jordan seems to have been getting close,' Zigic said, watching as Riggott snatched his vape pen up off the desk and took a furious hit off it.

'I don't get what the problem is here.' Ferreira twisted in her seat. 'We've got a suspicious death. We still investigate those, right?'

'What you've got,' Riggott said, pointing at her, 'is a seventy-year-old fella with a lung infection dying in the middle of the winter flu season.'

'An infection brought on by exposure to potentially fatal levels of hazardous materials on a building site where they weren't supposed to be,' Ferreira countered. 'We've got the environmental engineer's survey. What's stopping us taking some samples and having the lab run them to see if the levels are still the same as they were before work started?'

Riggott propped his elbow on the desk. 'Have you ever investigated a criminal negligence case before?'

She gave him a dead-eyed look. 'No, but I'd like to have one on my CV.'

'Well, I have and I can tell you right now they are an almighty fucking ball-ache,' he said. 'They're time-consuming and expensive and complicated as hell, and even if you manage to get the CPS to take it up, most of the soft fuckers on any given jury won't understand a tenth of what they're being told. And if all that isn't bad enough for you, the legal teams who defend them are the biggest shitehawks blood money can buy.' He took another inhale, eyes narrowing through the vapour. 'And that's before we start asking ourselves who else has their sticky wee digits in this particular pudding.'

Zigic thought of the planning application he'd read on the council website. Waved through with the barest attempt at public consultation. A handful of negative responses based on the impact on wildlife massively outweighed by supporters who wanted to see the area regenerated and affordable housing provided, saying how good it would be for the local economy in the short term – providing hundreds of construction jobs – and the long term, as the apartments attracted affluent commuters from London who would spend their city-sized wage packets in Peterborough.

Local dignitaries photographed at the groundbreaking ceremony fourteen months earlier, all smiles for the camera, chains of office sparkling under the September sunshine.

He wondered if the company had selected a piece of ground they knew to be safe for that first spade strike. Or if the big shot who'd made it found himself suddenly stricken with streaming eyes and a stinging nose, if he'd gone on to the reception afterwards, struggling to breathe.

'So you want us to ignore it?' Ferreira asked sharply. 'What, we have the budget for a dead millionaire businessman but not a dead builder?'

273

Riggott scowled at her but she was right and he knew it, Zigic thought.

'What I would like,' Riggott said, with acerbic politeness, 'is for youse two to park this revelation for the time being and concentrate on the shooting that's got our fine citizens feeling unsafe to walk the streets.'

'It's the same thing,' Ferreira insisted. 'Jordan Radley was up to his eyes in this investigation. So, for all we know, he'd gone after Docherty Construction and Rachel Greenaway already.'

'For all we know,' Riggott echoed. 'Meaning you *don't* fucking know.'

'We'll never find out if we don't pursue the lead!'

Riggott rocked back in his chair. 'Radley was gunned down on the way home from a working men's club. Sure, does that sound to you like the actions of some big bollocks construction mogul trying to head off a criminal negligence charge? Catch yourself on, Mel.'

'There are millions of pounds at stake,' she insisted.

'Behind every great fortune a great crime, aye?' Riggott shook his head. 'No, see people like that – that scale of bastard – they don't need to kill the little folk like Radley to cover up their crimes. You show me a case where some suity fucker got put away for dirty land.'

Ferreira fixed him with a hard look. 'Think about it, if this is the Dochertys trying to silence Jordan, wouldn't a lo-fi shooting with a converted replica be the perfect way to do it?'

'No,' Riggott said scornfully. 'It would be downright insane. They're aggressive and litigious and they have enough cash to wipe any amount of proletarian blood off their hands. *Money* is how people like that make problems go away.'

Ferreira threw herself back in the chair like a stroppy teenager and Zigic wished that she hadn't insisted on charging up here the second they got into the station, so blown up with the injustice of Sheila Yule's story that she couldn't even wait long enough to think through the implications.

'If they're smart enough to get that rich, then they're smart enough to try and mislead us on Jordan's murder,' she said.

274

Riggott smiled grimly. 'You know better than to think rich means smart.'

Outside in the corridor a few minutes later, Ferreira let loose a muted growl of frustration and stalked over to the vending machine.

'Have you got any change?'

Zigic dropped the few coins from his jeans pocket into the slot and waited while she punched the buttons and grabbed a Bounty bar out of the chamber at the bottom.

'You can't seriously have expected that to go any other way,' he said, as they walked back into their office, Ferreira with her mouth too full of chocolate to reply. 'Rule one, don't go to Riggott until you have a solid case.'

'You don't think his attitude might have had something to do with the fact that he's proxying for the Chief Constable and his good friends the Greenaways?' she asked.

'Riggott would love to tear down Hugo Docherty,' Zigic told her. 'So, no, I don't think that.'

It wasn't a lie, even though he heard how defensive he sounded saying it.

Riggott was leery of going after Docherty Construction because it *would* be a difficult charge to make stick. Expensive and complex and all the rest. Because the CPS were already stretched to breaking point, making decisions on prosecutions based on their odds of success more than the severity of the crimes.

They all knew that. None of them liked it. But it was where they were.

And if Ferreira was the one who had to present their cases to Peterborough's prosecutors instead of him, she might have a better feel for how they would react to the prospect of a long, drawn-out court case which would likely, at best, result in a slap on the wrists and a fine that would be negotiated down on appeal. Maybe evaded all together.

It was all so much politicking, he thought grimly, going to pour himself a coffee.

'Sir, good, you're back.' Parr appeared next to him, far more perky-looking than this point on a Friday afternoon deserved. 'I was thinking –'

'Again?' Ferreira asked, from the board, where she was adding the details they had from Sheila Yule.

'I was thinking about the AAIB report,' Parr went on, leading Zigic back towards his desk, where a BLT sat half-eaten by his computer. 'And I figured that if Jordan had reservations about it, maybe he contacted them.'

'You *were* thinking,' Ferreira said.

'So, I called them up and got talking to their press officer and it turns out Jordan *had* been in touch.' He sat down, moved the sandwich to the other side of his desk. 'She said Jordan was trying to pick holes in the report into Greenaway's crash. Apparently they get a lot of press sniffing around after high-profile incidents.'

'What did Jordan say?' Zigic asked.

'He told her he'd been in touch with an independent crash investigator who seemed to believe the AAIB were too quick to put it down to mechanical failure.' Parr gave him an expectant look and Zigic felt the enthusiasm rising in his own chest. 'He wanted their reaction to the bloke's accusations.'

'Who was the independent investigator?' Zigic asked.

Parr opened up a web page, the About Me section of a site dedicated to aviation safety. 'Chief Investigator – Alan Vickers.' The photograph showed a man in his mid-fifties with short grey hair spiked with too much, too shiny product. He stood in rimless glasses and a neat goatee in front of a display case filled with model aircraft, wearing a leather flying jacket over a T-shirt branded with the website's logo.

'He looks like he sniffs modelling glue,' Ferreira said.

'Vickers used to work at the AAIB,' Parr told her. 'So, I think we can safely assume he knows his stuff.'

'Or he's trying to undermine his previous employees,' she suggested, reaching over and clicking through a few pages on the website. 'They whole thing is just him taking apart their reports. He's obviously got an issue with the AAIB.'

'Maybe he left because he didn't think they were doing their job properly,' Parr said.

Zigic put out a steadying hand.

'Alright, what exactly was Jordan's issue with the report?'

'It sounds like Vickers told him that the lever mechanism in the tail rotor would be one of the easier parts to tamper with if you wanted to sabotage Greenaway's machine. It's got an iffy safety record so air crash investigators will just chalk it up to an expected fault bringing down another machine. According to Vickers it's almost impossible to tell the difference between natural wear to the threads and manually caused damage.'

'The AAIB's press officer told you all this?' Zigic asked sceptically.

'No, she told me about Jordan's accusations and how he'd been advised by Alan Vickers and then I found this.' Parr opened up a bookmarked page. 'Vickers posted a takedown of the report a couple of weeks ago.'

Zigic read the introduction over his shoulder. '"A local reporter has brought it to our attention that the AAIB may have dropped the ball again on a crash involving the notoriously unreliable Daedalus D55."'

'Does Vickers mention the break-in?' Ferreira asked.

Parr shook his head.

'What did the AAIB tell Jordan?'

'That they stood by their findings.' Parr shrugged. 'What else are they going to say?'

'What do you think?' Zigic looked at Ferreira standing with her arms folded, eyeing the report still open on Parr's screen. 'We've got Jordan digging in hard on this story now.'

Her shoulders lifted. 'He only gets killed over this if someone *actually* tampered with Greenaway's helicopter and I still don't see that we have any evidence to suggest that happened.'

'Apart from the break-in,' Parr protested. 'And the questions hanging over the AAIB report.'

'How far can we really trust Vickers on this, though?'

'He worked for the AAIB for fifteen years,' Parr said firmly, preparing to stand his ground. 'If this happened a couple of years earlier, Vickers would have been the one writing the report up. We'd have believed him then, wouldn't we?'

Ferreira tapped the marker pen against her knuckles.

'Right?' Parr asked Zigic.

'Yes, Zac.'

'His expertise hasn't gone away,' Parr said, a growing certainty in his voice. 'All that's changed is that he isn't on the AAIB's payroll any more.'

'That,' Ferreira conceded, 'and the fact that Vickers didn't have access to the wreckage. Which is a pretty significant hurdle for any expert to overcome.'

'Contact Vickers,' Zigic told Parr. 'See if there's anything Jordan shared with him that we don't know about.'

Ferreira went to Marcus Greenaway's board, writing up Parr's findings, and making a note that they were consulting an independent investigator.

The still from the footage of the break-in at Holme Airfield drew Zigic's eye. Two men, hunched against the camera in low light, their faces indistinct.

As Ferreira put down the marker pen, he untacked the photograph from the board.

'Alright, let's see what Caxton has to say for himself.'

Chapter Forty-Six

Dick Caxton sat at the table in his Tesco's uniform, his anorak over the back of the chair, an empty mug in front of him, alongside a sandwich packet and a chocolate wrapper. Zigic felt a pang of guilt seeing him like that, wondered how his supervisor had reacted when he was pulled off his shift a couple of hours earlier.

He looked even more gaunt under the strip light, his cheeks sunken, a patch of stubble along his jaw where he'd missed with the razor. His skin was even more sallow than it had seemed last time they spoke to him. Some of it down to the unforgiving nature of the interview room undoubtedly, but perhaps part of it grief for Jordan too.

No fear, not that Zigic could see. Just a terrible resignation written along the skewed angle of his shoulders and the way he sat hunched over with his arms crossed on the table.

'Sorry to drag you in like this,' Zigic said, as he took his seat. 'We'll try not to keep you much longer.'

'It's fine.' Caxton drew back from the table, looking uncomfortable. 'I'm happy to help.'

Ferreira set the tapes up, Caxton stating his name when she prompted him, his voice low and reluctant, nothing of the firebrand Zigic had seen in the transcripts from the old interviews with DI Sawyer.

'We've been talking to Sheila Yule,' Ferreira told him.

Caxton started. 'What?'

'Tell us how you know Sheila.'

'I don't know her.' Caxton wet his lips. 'I knew her old man. Derek. We used to see each other at the football back when I went

279

regular. We both had season tickets in the main stand. Not that I can afford that any more.'

'When was the last time you saw Derek?'

'Not since last year.' Caxton made a thoughtful face. 'Must have been October time, maybe before, beginning of the season, I reckon.'

Ferreira waited a beat, letting him think that was it. 'And how was he when you saw him?'

'He wasn't in a good way,' Caxton said carefully. 'He'd been ill. But he was getting better when I saw him. I remember he was talking about going back to work a couple of days a week. Easing himself back into it.' He looked at Zigic. 'Have you seen Sheila?'

'We have.'

Caxton nodded, realising what this was now.

'You knew how Derek got ill,' Ferreira said, the accusation in her tone making Caxton wince. 'You told Jordan all about the contamination at the Greenaway Engineering redevelopment. You put him onto that story.'

'I didn't put him onto it,' Caxton said weakly. 'We were talking about something or other – I can't remember what exactly, maybe them new houses over Corby where all the kiddies were getting cancer – and I told Jordan about a mate of mine who'd got ill working in town.'

'You told Jordan he died.'

'Yeah, but I didn't know he was going to go and do anything about it.'

Ferreira rolled her eyes. 'You were friends with Jordan. You knew exactly what he'd do as soon as you told him. This was right up Jordan's alley, yeah? Contaminated land. A death nobody else cared about. And all of it coming right back to the Greenaways. The people who took your livelihood away.'

'So?' Caxton demanded. 'It wasn't like I was making it up, was I? You've talked to Sheila, you know what happened to Derek.' He gave her a bitter look. 'Like they hadn't done enough damage to us lot. They go and build flats all over that land. Get

280

blokes working up to their arses in poison with no idea how dangerous it was. It's not me you should have in here. It's *them* bastards.'

He was right, Zigic thought. Furious and indignant, and absolutely right.

No wonder Caxton had fed Derek Yule's story to Jordan. He'd watched one lot of his friends turned over and tossed aside. It must have been hell on him seeing another man suffering for the Greenaways' greed.

'We asked you what Jordan was working on when he died,' Ferreira reminded him. 'And you said you didn't know.'

Caxton shuffled in his seat, uncomfortable under the intensity of her gaze.

'You lied to us.'

'Now hold you on hard,' Caxton said, raising his hand. 'You told me Jordan was working on some big story and you asked me if I knew what it was. Far as I was concerned I'd told him about Derek and he never said another word about it. I didn't know he'd gone off and started working on it.' His eyes widened fearfully. 'Is that why he got killed?'

'We don't know,' Zigic admitted. 'But Jordan had found a job labouring on the site. He'd taken soil samples for testing. And he was preparing to run a story on the contamination.'

Caxton frowned. 'I should never have said anything. Poor little bugger. Me and my big mouth.'

They gave him a moment.

'If Jordan mentioned anything about this story, you need to tell us,' Ferreira said.

He looked helplessly at her. 'If I knew I'd tell you. For God's sake, how do you think I feel about this?'

'He never asked you about other men you knew who were working on the site?'

A quick shake of the head but Zigic wasn't sure he was even listening to her, too lost in self-recrimination.

'They wouldn't,' he said. 'Even those bastards wouldn't kill him over that, would they?'

Zigic glanced at Ferreira, saw how badly she wanted to say yes. 'There's a lot of money at stake,' he said.

Caxton let out a stifled groan, his hand going to his back. He stood up and took a few faltering steps away from the table, lifting his right leg a little higher than his left.

'Sorry, it plays up when I don't move for a bit.'

He stopped and rubbed his back, just above the kidneys. The same pained expression making the planes of his face narrow and sharpen and Zigic wondered if he'd been giving Caxton too much credit. Was it just a back spasm telling on him so badly? Not grief for Jordan, not fear that he was partially responsible for his death?

Was Caxton even the man they thought he was? A little eccentric and unhappy, but fundamentally decent, maybe the only person at the Greenaway Club who'd truly considered Jordan a friend, rather than an oddity who'd washed up in their lives to write an article and inexplicably remained.

One thing he believed, Caxton didn't know anything more about Jordan's work on the contamination story.

Zigic gestured at Ferreira and she opened the tablet with the photograph of the break-in at Holme Airfield.

'Take a look at this for me, please,' she said. 'Tell me who you recognise.'

Caxton came back to his seat, lowered himself gingerly into it, eyes fixed on the tablet as Ferreira pushed it across to him.

'What's this?' he asked.

Ferreira blew up the image. 'Do either of these men look familiar?'

'No. Why should they?'

'We've recovered this footage from a break-in at Holme Airfield two weeks before Marcus Greenaway died,' she said. 'Now, going off the height of the door, we can say fairly confidently that neither of these men is above six foot tall. Which means we can safely rule you out.'

Caxton's mouth pressed into a firm line.

'This is the other story Jordan was working on when he died,' Zigic explained. 'And he was a good way into this one. He'd found out about the break-in, which led us to this footage, which is being enhanced as we speak.'

Caxton looked up.

'You know how good the technology is now,' Ferreira said.

'He'd also contacted an air accident investigator independent of the AAIB,' Zigic went on. 'And this expert has thrown serious doubt on the original report's findings.'

'Apparently, the part which failed and caused Greenaway's helicopter to fall to earth ...' Ferreira's eyebrow went up at Caxton as she quoted the toast, but he didn't respond, looked numb now, '... that part is *exactly* the one you'd tamper with if you wanted to take down a helicopter and have it look like innocent mechanical failure.'

'Why are you telling me about this?' Caxton's brows drew together, a deep line cutting up between them. 'I've got nothing to do with Greenaway dying.'

'No, we don't think you have.' Ferreira leaned across the table, looking casual, looking sympathetic. 'But we're starting to think that whoever *did* kill Greenaway might have shot Jordan.'

Caxton shook his head. 'It was an accident, the report said so.'

'What's a report?' she asked. 'It's one expert's opinion of how things went down. Maybe the next expert sees things differently. They're more experienced with a certain machine or they've got a lighter workload, hell, maybe they've just had a bigger cup of coffee. *Everything* is open to interpretation, you know that, Dick. You know how subjective authority can be.'

He shrank in on himself slightly where he sat.

'Jordan thought it was murder,' Zigic told him.

Ferreira nodded. 'That's why he was hanging around the Club. He was looking for Greenaway's killer.'

'No,' Caxton croaked.

'And he found a killer,' Ferreira said regretfully.

Caxton buried his face in his hands.

'Jordan liked you because you shared his sense of social justice.' Zigic ducked his head into Caxton's eyeline, waiting for him to reappear from behind his hands. 'He wasn't a boy with many friends. I suppose because he struggled to find people who thought like he did. But you and him had that bond.'

A strangled groan rattled around in Caxton's throat.

'Who are the men in the photograph?' Ferreira asked.

'I don't know.' Still hiding.

'One of them shot Jordan,' she said, sounding so certain that for a moment Zigic wondered if she knew something she hadn't shared with him. 'He shot him in the back. Then when Jordan was on the ground, choking on his own blood, he shot him in the head.'

Caxton drew his fingers down his face, held them over his mouth, fingertips pressing hard against his lips.

'I can't –' Choking off his own words.

'You can't what?' Ferreira demanded.

He shook his head, eyes closed. 'I don't know who they are.'

'If you protect them, Jordan's death is on you.' Ferreira stabbed a finger at him. 'You're just as guilty as if you put that gun to the back of his head yourself.'

Caxton stood abruptly. 'You can't keep me here. If you want to keep me here, you have to charge me with something and I haven't done anything.' The words tumbled out of him as he grabbed his anorak and tried to fit his arms into it. 'I've told you everything I know. I've cooperated with you.'

Zigic stood up, stepped aside from the table. 'You obviously need to think about this, Mr Caxton. I understand.'

'I don't know anything,' Caxton said, heading for the door.

But Zigic got there first, took the handle. 'Interview terminated 15:44.'

Caxton was breathing heavily, staring at the door. Through it. 'I want to leave now.'

'Think about Jordan tonight,' Zigic said softly. 'Think about the kind of young man he was and whether you believe he deserved to die alone on the side of the road with a bullet in his head.'

He opened the door for Caxton, kept his eyes on the man as he walked out, refusing to meet Zigic's gaze, not blinking, barely seeming to breathe as he turned away down the long white-walled corridor, a slight unevenness in his step all the way to the stairwell door.

CHAPTER FORTY-SEVEN

Thornhaugh Golf Club's reception area was done out like a Scottish hunting lodge, all leather and tartan and dark wood panelling. Loud voices and the smell of cooked meat coming from a bar nearby, well-lubricated laughter breaking out in patches as if the occupants of the various tables were competing over who was having the best time. Zigic and Ferreira kept walking, heading for the lounge where Hugo Docherty's PA told them they would be able to find him at this time of the afternoon.

The conversation in the lounge was more muted. A few tables were occupied by middle-aged men in bland golf attire and couples relaxing over coffee and copies of the *Daily Telegraph*. Zigic felt curious eyes on them as they passed, maybe trying to work out how his scruffy clothes and Ferreira's attitude had made it through the club's rigorous screening process.

Hugo Docherty was seated at a table in front of the French windows, the fairway unfurling beyond. Only a handful of figures were still out on the green as the light had begun to fade. More were hunched over their drives in the well-lit sanctuary of the driving range.

Docherty looked up from his phone as they approached, fixed a half-smile on his face and rose to greet them, hand already extended as he came around the table.

'DI Zigic.' He shook the hand, getting more pressure than he thought the introduction required and giving some back. 'DS Ferreira.'

She just nodded at Docherty and took a seat, provoking a frown that was slow to dissipate. It was still in place as Docherty returned to the leather wing chair.

Zigic had been expecting someone more formidable, given how Anthea Greenaway had described him, but there was nothing immediately 'feral' about Hugo Docherty. He was short and slight in jeans and a pale pink shirt with his initials embroidered on the pocket. Not dressed for golf but Zigic guessed the club would be more about business than pleasure for a developer. He saw the resemblance to Rachel Greenaway though. Same glossy brown hair and the same suspicious cast to his murky green eyes.

He would already know they'd spoken to her. Was likely prepared for the same kind of questions they'd asked his sister about Jordan's interest in the crash that had killed his brother-in-law. So that wasn't where they would start.

'Well now,' Docherty said, pointedly turning his phone face down on the table. 'How can I help you, Inspector?'

'We're investigating the murder of a young man called Jordan Radley,' Zigic said.

Docherty nodded sadly. 'The student who was shot, yes, I saw that. Shocking stuff.'

'We've recently learned that Jordan had taken a job on your Stillwater Rise development.' Zigic watched him carefully, saw nothing but the neutral face of a practiced negotiator. 'We believe Jordan took the job because he was working on a story about a potential contamination incident on the site.'

'The site isn't contaminated,' Docherty said flatly. 'It was when we purchased it but we undertook significant remedial work to make sure it was safe for habitation.'

'How does the clean-up process work?' Zigic asked.

'Two ways.' Docherty propped his elbow on the arm of the chair, index finger in the air. 'You can have all the affected earth removed from the site and replaced with new topsoil. But we don't do that because all you're doing is taking your problem away and handing it over to someone else to deal with, which doesn't seem right to me.' He flashed a fast, shallow smile. 'It's not worth cutting corners with contaminants. Even if you were morally bankrupt enough to. What we do is we employ a firm that come in and decontaminate the soil on site. I couldn't explain

287

exactly how they achieve that. It's somewhat beyond my expertise, but it's the most efficient way of making the land safe.'

'So if someone took a sample from the site now, it would be perfectly safe?' Ferreira asked.

'It would, yes.'

'And if it wasn't?'

'It would be a failure by the company we hired to clean up,' Docherty said gravely. 'But they gave us documented assurances that they completed their job correctly and I have no reason to believe they'd mislead us.'

'But the liability would be yours?' Ferreira pressed.

Docherty screwed his face up. 'Legally speaking ... that's debatable, and we'd certainly argue that we did everything in our power to make the site safe.'

'How much would it cost you to deal with that?'

'We carry a very hefty public liability insurance for that kind of cock-up.' He looked vaguely amused at the line of questioning. '*If* it happened. Which it didn't.'

Ferreira leaned forward in her chair. 'Then why did you make a financial settlement to Tom Geary?'

Docherty's face darkened and Zigic could see his brain whirring, turning towards the NDA Geary had signed.

'That was a decision we made based on PR,' he said slowly. 'We knew the land was safe but we didn't want the negative publicity generated by proving it to affect sales. First-phase buyers pay for the second phase of construction. We couldn't have that jeopardised. It is in no way indicative of a problem. It was an unfortunate cost we chose to incur for the greater good. And it's quite common practice.' He shrugged. 'Mud sticks.'

'And how much negative publicity would an exposé about high levels of carcinogens still present at the development cause?' Ferreira asked, relishing every word.

Docherty glared at her. 'There was no exposé because there was nothing to *expose*.'

'Did Jordan Radley approach you for comment?'

For a moment he said nothing, clearly considering his position. 'I would have to check with the office on that. I don't recall handling an enquiry but that wouldn't necessarily be something I dealt with personally.'

'What about Sheila Yule?' Ferreira lobbed the name at him. 'Do you remember how you handled her?'

'Sorry, I don't know who that is.'

'Her husband died after collapsing on your site.' Docherty looked blankly at her. 'You sent Mrs Yule a cease and desist notice when she asked for confirmation that the site was safe,' Ferreira reminded him. 'Why not show her your documented assurances?'

Another pause and Zigic felt them drawing closer to something new. Something weighty.

'My solicitor advised against that to the best of my recollection,' he said. 'She was under the impression that news of the settlement with Geary had leaked out – despite the confidentiality clause – and she believed the widow was seeking compensation where none was due.'

'Derek Yule fell ill at the same time as Tom Geary.'

'He was also almost seventy with several existing conditions and a forty-a-day habit,' Docherty insisted.

'So,' Ferreira smiled. 'You remember *something* about what happened to him.'

'I remembered the incident,' Docherty said smoothly. 'Not the name. I have a terrible memory for names.'

His first outright lie, Zigic thought. Everything else had danced around the line but that was sheer untruth and he wondered why Docherty had bothered. What exactly was different about Derek and Sheila Yule? What he was scared of?

'What did your sister tell you about her conversation with Jordan Radley last month?' Zigic asked.

'Not very much.' Docherty's shoulders relaxed and he reached over to take a sip of his sparkling water. 'Rachel thought he was trying to provoke her into saying something stupid so he'd have a story to run. But she's too smart to fall for that.'

Speaking more casually now, his face softer, eyes less intently focused.

Zigic wondered why Marcus Greenaway's death was a less perturbing topic of conversation than the Stillwater Rise development. The relief about him now was palpable.

'I mean, she was distraught at having all that brought up again,' Docherty said. 'As I'm sure you can imagine, it's been a tough few years for Rachel and the children. The last thing she needed when she was finally starting to come through her grief was some journo turn up at her home suggesting all sorts of tabloid craziness.'

'Why craziness?' Zigic asked. 'There had been a concerted harassment campaign against Marcus and Rachel.'

'Maybe it wasn't that crazy,' Docherty conceded, looking away from them momentarily, attention drawn by a man on the terrace, standing watching them through the glass as he smoked a cigar. 'They gave her absolute hell.'

'Who?'

'The workers. Marcus was away most of the time. He left Rachel to face it on her own, explain to the children what was happening. Try to make them feel safe when there were cars outside the house at night.' His face darkened at the thought. 'They'd pull up to the gates and flash their lights, rev their engines like they were going to smash through them. In the end I went and collected them all and they stayed with me and my wife for a few weeks until the worst of it had blown over. I tried to keep them safe but Rachel still had to go out.' Docherty's jaw flexed. 'Peterborough is a very small city when people have a grudge against you.'

Zigic waited for him to elaborate.

'Rachel was in M&S picking up some food and this man charged over to her and spat in her face.' His fingers went to his cheek. 'He didn't say a word. Just spat at her and walked away. Rachel was devastated. She didn't go out again for weeks after that.'

Zigic glanced over at Ferreira, saw her scepticism and felt it jarring against the certainty in his gut. The emotion coming off Docherty looked too deep to be faked.

'We don't have any record of that assault,' Ferreira said coolly.

Docherty ignored her tone. 'Rachel didn't want to involve the police. She felt guilty about what happened to them.'

Ferreira's eyebrow went up and Zigic knew she was thinking of Rachel Greenaway's high-handed attitude when they'd spoken to her. Mel wouldn't be able to give the woman credit for any finer feelings.

'What did the man look like?' Zigic asked.

'It was a long time ago.' Docherty shrugged. 'Some old guy, Rachel said. He had a ponytail.'

Lionel Ridgeon, Zigic wondered. Couldn't quite believe it of the man they'd spoken to, who'd invited them into his home and made them coffee, but he might have been a very different person four years ago. Although his appearance was distinctive enough that Zigic imagined Rachel Greenaway would easily pick him from a line-up. Especially with that rare and unfashionable ponytail.

Still, walking up to a woman and spitting in her face. It was extreme. Suggested contempt of an intensity he hadn't detected in Ridgeon's interviews from the time.

'Our father started with nothing,' Docherty went on, pride deepening his voice, as if he was the self-made man himself. 'So Rachel understood how hard it hit the chaps losing their jobs. I think she believed on some level that she deserved what they did to her.'

'Did Rachel negotiate the sale of the factory?' Ferreira asked.

'No, of course not.'

'You did,' she said. 'And yet they didn't go after you. Why was that?'

'They vandalised my solicitor's office,' he said, slightly wounded. 'And we suffered a spate of damage to our company vehicles. I couldn't prove if the damage was coordinated or who was responsible, but given the timing I'd imagine it was all part of the same venting process.'

'Why didn't you report it?'

He shrugged. 'I didn't want to pour petrol on the fire. You'd made some arrests. The men responsible were charged. I hoped, perhaps naïvely, that that would be an end to it.'

'It was an end to it,' Ferreira said.

Docherty made a thoughtful face. 'That's what I thought, but then after all this time this journalist turned up at Rachel's place, talking about Marcus's death, saying he didn't think it was an accident. Then the same with Anthea and now you're here asking me about it. You obviously have some doubts.'

'Do *you* believe the men responsible for the harassment might have been involved in Marcus's death?' Zigic asked.

'It was an accident, wasn't it?' It was Docherty's turn to study him. 'That's what the official report said.'

'We're just trying to find out who murdered Jordan Radley,' Ferreira told him. 'Where were you on Monday night between 10 and 11 p.m.?'

A quick, outraged laugh broke out of him. 'Are you serious?'

She shrugged. 'It's procedure.'

'Why would I want to kill him?' Docherty asked. 'I couldn't have told you his name if you'd put a gun to my head.'

'You don't have an alibi, then?'

'I was in London, at the Spurs game,' he said tersely. 'I can show you my season ticket if it helps and I'm sure the lads I was with have photos of us in the stands.'

The same game Jordan Radley had been watching at the Greenaway Club just before he was killed. Hugo Docherty at a safe distance, but then he wasn't the kind of man to pull the trigger himself, Zigic thought.

He was the kind who would cover his arse, arrange a solid alibi while some hired hand did the dirty work.

Ferreira wasn't letting up though. She pushed him for details, who he was with, how he travelled to White Hart Lane and where he went afterwards, what time he got home. Docherty answered her questions with a rising sense of irritation, unaccustomed to accounting for himself. Annoyed at being treated like a suspect.

Which he was, Zigic thought. Not because of anything he'd said or done during this last twenty minutes, but because of the kind of man he'd already proven himself to be. The kind whose neglect had cost one man his health and another his life.

A man who bought silence with fear and money.

And what would he do about somebody who didn't respond to either?

CHAPTER FORTY-EIGHT

'140,' McLeary yelled. His voice cut across the background chatter and the music playing, drawing the men's attention from their conversations and the ticker tape scrolling on Sky Sports News, sending them cheering at Steve Gurney's achievement.

Gurney pumped the air with his fist, looking like a man with nothing on his mind beyond whether he'd make the easy 36 checkout he'd left on the dartboard.

Humble watched from the bar as Steve walked away, letting Sal step up to the oche, Steve jiggling where he stood, impatient with the slowness of Sal's throw. He aimed three times before he would release the dart, winced as each shot hit the board a fraction off its mark.

'67.' McLeary chalked the score, faster than you'd think he was capable of, and it still amazed Humble that he had it in him. The drink and hard living hadn't blunted that part of his brain.

But he wasn't an idiot, Humble reminded himself.

Never had been.

Across the room Dick Caxton sat on the long burgundy banquette, alone with his drink and his thoughts, staring at the tabletop. He'd hardly said two words to anyone since he'd arrived an hour earlier. He was dressed in his Tesco's uniform still but Humble knew he'd come from the police station, not work.

Dick had mentioned some footage of a supposed break-in that the police had showed him. Made sure to wait until Steve turned up to drop that bombshell, watching him for a reaction.

And Steve was worried. Under the bravado he was throwing around at the dartboard, Humble could see it.

Dick had brought this shit down on them. Telling Jordan about Marcus Greenaway's accident in the first place. Telling him about the way they'd all been treated by the police during the factory protests. Giving Jordan everything he needed to stitch a story together – if he was prepared to ignore the gaps and the inconsistencies and sheer bloody stupidity of it all. Ignore the report that said it was an accident. In black and white. Signed off by an expert.

An accident.

No story there.

Enough for Jordan to get excited about though.

Lionel came out of the gents and went over to Dick, taking the stool opposite him, his back to the dartboard. They talked in low voices, faces grim, and Humble knew he should go over there but he didn't want to know what was being said.

Didn't want to be here at all tonight.

He needed some space and quiet to think things over. Couldn't get it here, couldn't get it at home. Not with Jackie watching him like a hawk, asking him if he was okay, telling him it wasn't healthy bottling up his emotions. She'd made him check his blood pressure this morning, stood over him while he did it because they'd been there before, him tidying up his numbers so she wouldn't make him go to the doctors.

210/90

Higher than it had been before and he blamed it on not sleeping properly, then having two coffees with his breakfast. She didn't challenge him, just sat down next to him and took his hand between her own, gave him a sympathetic look.

Said, 'It's okay to be sad.'

And then he'd cried.

He drained another whiskey from the optic now and threw it down, remembering how she'd rubbed his back and kissed his head, waiting for the tears to subside, then dried his face with her thumbs, staring into his eyes.

'This is your body's way of telling you to speak,' she'd said.

But he couldn't. And so he'd stood up and mumbled an excuse as he locked himself in the bathroom, knowing he needed to bring himself back under control but hating that he was pushing her away. The distance between them opening up a little more every day and he wasn't sure he'd be able to get across it again when the time came. But talking wasn't an option.

Because if he started talking where would it end?

That was why he'd avoided taking part in Jordan's article. Offered the others up like sacrificial lambs. He hadn't wanted to examine why he'd done it at the time. But now he felt everything he'd been pushing away since the factory closed, crowding in on him, all the unspoken words stacking up in his throat.

I'm not happy. I feel useless. My kids talk down to me. My friends are all depressed. I'm lying to you and I hate myself for it.

'Get your arse up, Lionel,' Steve said, bringing his hands down on Ridgeon's shoulders. 'Throw some arrows with me.'

Caxton stood up. 'I'll have a game with you.'

McLeary wiped down the scoreboard and chalked up their names as they played the bullseye for the first throw. Dick's dart landing in the 25, Steve's hitting its mark.

Humble poured himself another drink and went over to the table where Lionel had shifted around to watch the game, and sat next to him on the banquette.

'Dick's not in a good way,' Lionel said quietly. 'Them coppers have got him rattled, going on about one of the lads shooting Jordan. I says to him, Dick, buh, it's a load of old rubbish. The useless buggers can't find who did it so they're coming after us so's it looks like they're doing summat.'

'That's about what I told them,' Humble said, watching as Steve racked up another 1–40 visit.

'Trouble is,' Lionel said, his eyes on the game. 'Dick reckons Steve did it.'

Humble felt his chest tighten. 'Did he tell them that?'

'Nup, but I reckon he's working himself up to it.'

Dick retrieved his darts, stepping sideways off the oche and knocking into Steve as he walked back.

'Steady there, big man.' Steve shooting him a quick grin. 'You know you're not going to put me off like that.'

He threw again. Scored a hundred, left himself double-16. Took his own darts from the board and made a show of giving Dick a wide berth as he walked past.

'Dick, you require 170,' McLeary told him.

'I know what I fucking need,' Dick snapped.

He threw three wild darts, the third bouncing out of the board to oohs and jeers.

'25,' McLeary said loudly.

Again Dick tried to shoulder into him but Steve sidestepped him. Threw for the double-16 and missed with every dart.

'You want to be getting him home,' Lionel said. 'There's going to be a buckering punch-up if you don't.'

Did Dick know something? It was possible they'd fed him some new information. Wanting to rattle him, send him back here in this uneven state of mind and see what broke loose.

It would be about right.

The same game DI Sawyer had tried four years ago. Wanting him to turn on the others in exchange for leniency. Make her case for her.

Was DI Zigic the same?

Weren't they fucking all.

They had nothing. Four days since Jordan was killed and no arrests to show for it. The shooting of an upstanding and wholly innocent young man couldn't be allowed to go unpunished for much longer. Would start to reflect badly on the police.

Dick was the weak link. It didn't take a detective inspector to see that. He was more upset about Jordan than the rest of them, more attached to the boy. Grieving badly enough to believe whatever rubbish they fed him.

But was it rubbish? he asked himself.

If he was the police, Steve would be the prime suspect. The stuff with his wife after the article came out gave him a motive. Would they need much more than that? His record would count against him. Suggesting a man who'd know a man who could get him a gun.

At the board Steve hit the double-16 with his first dart and Humble saw Dick already shaping up for a fight as Steve turned away from the board.

Steve laughed. 'Cool your bollocks, mate, it's only a game.'

Dick strode up to him.

Humble was over to them, his arm between their chests as Steve squared up, all the humour gone out of him now.

'Alright, lads, calm down, no need for this.' He tried to prise them apart but they just moved closer.

'You got summink you wanna say?' Steve asked, accent sharpening, chin jutting.

Dick shoved into his face. 'I know it was you.'

Said so quietly nobody else in the room would have caught it but Humble did and saw Steve's eyes darken, his lips pulling back from his teeth.

'Danny,' Humble called.

McLeary ambled away from the board and threw his arm around Steve's shoulders. He wasn't strong enough to restrain him even if he wanted to and Humble could see that he didn't.

'Come on, Stevie boy,' McLeary said. 'Be a gracious winner, hey?'

'You wanna watch your fucking mouth, *mate*,' Steve growled.

Dick gave him a leery grin. 'Or what?'

Steve glared. Humble could feel how hard he was pressing forward. He shifted his feet and tried to push him away from Dick but made no ground.

'What are you going to do?' Dick asked, stepping back abruptly, looking around the room at the audience they had now. 'Batter me?'

Steve's eyes narrowed.

'You going to kill me, Steve?'

DAY FIVE

SATURDAY

CHAPTER FORTY-NINE

Sitting on the sofa in her pyjamas with a cable-knit blanket over her knees, Moira Radley looked exactly the same as she had when they'd left her house five days earlier. The curtains were drawn across the living room's French doors, the television was on but still muted, a cooking programme playing out, two chefs primping a dessert.

'Nice cup of tea for everyone,' her sister Tanya said, coming into the room with a tray and placing it on the coffee table next to a padded album open to a page of baby photos. She removed this discreetly, a sad smile flitting across her face as she closed it and slipped it onto the table's lower tier.

She was doing her best, Zigic thought, but no amount of company and gentle care could fix Moira. Only time, and that wouldn't completely heal the wound. Nothing could, not when you'd lost your only child.

He tried not to dwell on how he would feel in her position. Before he had kids he'd believed you worried less about them as they grew older but he was finding the opposite to be true, seeing the dangers around Milan and Stefan multiply with each passing year, knowing he had the same thing to come with Emily too. It would never end, he realised. Not even when they were his age or older. They would always be his babies.

Tanya retreated to the kitchen and Moira watched her go with a vague expression on her face. She was on medication now, Tanya had explained quietly when they arrived. Pills to help her sleep and others to help flatten out the extremes of her grief while she was awake. A temporary fix, which would hopefully get her through these first agonising weeks. Though Zigic wondered if she was only delaying the inevitable. Suspected that once the pills had run out the same crushing emotion would be waiting for her.

'We need to get in touch with one of Jordan's friends,' Ferreira said, using her softest voice. 'She's working for an environmental charity somewhere but we don't know the name of it. Do you know who she is?'

Moira reached slowly for her tea, seeming to struggle lining up her hand and the mug. 'An environmental charity?'

'Apparently this young woman was helping Jordan with a story he was working on,' Ferreira told her.

'What story?'

'Jordan was investigating a site in town where the land's contaminated.'

Realisation spread slowly across Moira's face. 'The place he went and did a bit of labouring?'

'That's right.'

'Did Jordan explain to you why he was there?' Zigic asked.

'No. He said he'd heard it paid well and he was trying to save up for a holiday. He wanted to go to Barcelona in the spring.' She looked into her tea. 'Why didn't he tell me what he was doing there?'

'He probably didn't want to worry you,' Ferreira said. 'A couple of the men who'd been working there had got ill. Quite seriously ill. He was probably worried you'd stop him going there.'

'I would have.' Her voice was flat but Zigic thought he could hear a stirring of heat coming through the medication. 'What happened to the men?'

'One of them died,' Ferreira told her. 'The other guy was younger so he survived it but he's never going to be himself again.'

'It was an important story,' Zigic assured Moira.

She nodded. 'Those were the ones he wanted to write.'

'Jordan took some soil samples off the site,' Ferreira went on. 'And we know from the dead man's widow that Jordan was sending the samples to a friend of his to have them analysed before he could run the story.'

'Now we just need to find the friend so we can get the results from her,' Zigic said.

Moira stared at the television, hands around her mug, face so perfectly blank that he wasn't sure if she was thinking or if she'd drifted away from the conversation.

They could hear the dishwasher being emptied in the kitchen, Tanya keeping up some semblance of normality in the house, carrying out the small tasks that grief rendered pointless but which still needed to be done. She would be grieving too he thought and maybe those small tasks were her method of holding the worst at bay.

'Lily,' Moira said finally, dragging her eyes away from the screen. 'Lily Hargreaves. They were at school together but she was a couple of years up from him. Jordan went out with her sister for a year or so. Rosie. Lovely girl.' She smiled, closing her eyes for a moment. 'She went off to uni in Southampton. She's studying law. They were perfect for each other but you know how youngsters are now.'

Zigic nodded sympathetically. 'Did they stay in touch?'

'For the first year or so,' she said. 'But Jordan and Lily got friendly. She works outside Cambridge now but she's still living in Peterborough, so it's easier to meet up.'

'Do you know where she works?' Ferreira asked.

'No.'

Lily Hargreaves. A distinctive enough name to be able to track her down.

Tanya came back into the living room, sat down next to Moira. 'Have you told them about your visitor?'

Moira shook her head.

'One of Jordan's friends came to see us this morning,' Tanya said, taking a biscuit from the plate on the table. 'Showed up at the crack of dawn with a bag of shopping. Ready meals and stuff like that. All vegan.'

'That was very thoughtful.' Ferreira shifted on the sofa, her interest piqued. 'Which of Jordan's friends was it?'

'Some old fella from that club he goes to,' Moira said.

'Richard,' Tanya added. She frowned. 'He was in a right state, bless him. Really distraught. I think he'd been crying.'

'What did he say?' Ferreira asked.

'Just how sorry he was, you know. The usual. What a lovely lad Jordan was and how sorry he was for what happened.' Tanya dipped her biscuit in her tea. 'I asked him if he wanted to come in but he said he couldn't. He was a bit awkward.'

Caxton wasn't awkward, Zigic thought. He was used to working with people and an easy talker once he got started. No reason for him to stay on the front step and bolt at the first opportunity. No reason for him to come here at all. Unless it was some ingrained sense of community spirit; that urge to feed people when they'd lost someone.

Strange that he'd chosen this morning to do it, though. Five days on from Jordan's murder. He could have found the time before now, surely.

Had the interview yesterday stirred him into action?

'He *was* friends with Jordan, right?' Tanya asked uncomfortably. 'Please don't tell me he was some weirdo.'

'No, they were quite close,' Zigic reassured her.

For a long moment nobody spoke and he took a mouthful of his tea, aware of Moira as an absence in the room, Tanya looking at her fretfully, reaching over and taking hold of her foot where it poked out from the blanket. Next to him, Ferreira's face was set in concentration. Thinking about Caxton, he'd bet. Why he'd come here and why he'd been so apologetic. If Tanya had worried he was a weirdo because she was picking up on something in his demeanour she couldn't articulate.

Caxton wasn't a weirdo. He didn't throw off those vibes at all. So what had Tanya sensed about him as he handed over a bag of carefully chosen food he couldn't afford to buy and apologised for Jordan's death?

'Oh,' Tanya said, bouncing up off the sofa. 'Jordan got a letter you might want to see as well.'

She came back from the hallway with a slim white envelope, already opened, and handed it to him. The postmark was dated Monday the 25th. Sent the day Jordan was killed.

'When did this come?' he asked, as he took out the single sheet of paper inside.

'Tuesday.' Tanya lowered her voice. 'I've only just got around to checking the mail.'

Zigic unfolded the paper, saw the letterhead of a local solicitor's firm and a few brief lines advising Jordan to cease and desist all investigations pertaining to the Stillwater Rise development. A warning that publishing his story would lead to legal action.

He handed it to Ferreira to read.

'Was he in trouble?' Tanya asked anxiously.

'The company have sent a few of these out to people,' Zigic explained. 'They're trying to hush up contamination at the site.'

'This isn't ...' She cast a quick look towards Moira, who seemed to be lost in her own head again. 'This isn't ... why, is it?'

'Probably not,' he said. 'People like this rely on lawyers and financial clout, they don't generally resort to violence.'

He said it but didn't entirely believe it. Because everything about how Docherty Construction and the Greenaways did business was violent. Not overtly, not street-level thuggery. But they displayed the same lack of regard for human life.

The kind of thinking that could easily justify murder.

CHAPTER FIFTY

An hour later, they had the findings of the soil tests Lily Hargreaves had run in the laboratory of Bosworth Life Sciences open on Zigic's computer screen. Alongside them the original report from Drury Prior. Two lists of contaminants and the levels of each of them present in the earth at the Stillwater Rise development site.

'They're *exactly* the same,' Ferreira said, looking across Zigic's shoulder. 'They can't have done any remedial work at all.'

She went around to the other side of his desk and dropped into the chair.

'When did Lily Hargreaves send these over to Jordan?' she asked.

'Saturday, November 16th,' Zigic said thoughtfully. 'So, Jordan buys a train ticket to Leicester the same day and then on the Monday – the first opportunity he has – we've got him going to Drury Prior's offices to try and talk to them about the report.'

'For a quote, probably.' She remembered how easily David Prior had stumped up the initial report, wondered if he knew anything about the samples or if his absent business partner had kept the news to herself. 'Prior made sure to tell me it wasn't their responsibility to clean up the site. They just make a recommendation and leave the developer to it.'

'Jordan didn't get a quote from them,' Zigic said. 'But he obviously put these findings to Docherty Construction or they wouldn't have bothered with a cease and desist letter.'

The letter was sitting on his desk. Evidence but only up to a point. It told them that Docherty Construction were aware that Jordan was on to them but nothing about how much further they might have gone to silence him.

Zigic sighed, rubbing his temple. 'I just don't see Hugo Docherty shooting Jordan to stop a story coming out.'

'There is *so* much money involved,' Ferreira reminded him. 'We're talking millions of pounds, right?'

'But it's not on Hugo Docherty, is it?' Zigic said. 'An outside contractor did the remediation work and signed off on the site being safe for construction to begin. They're the ones responsible.'

'Legally, yeah. But how long would it take Docherty to drag them through the courts or negotiate a settlement or whatever? Meanwhile his last tower – which is where all the profit's tied up – is going to be halted. No more sales. No more income.' She stabbed at the arm of the chair with her fingertip. 'Docherty's the one with an immediate motive. If he stops the story coming out, the development proceeds as normal. The money comes in. He gets clear of the mess.'

Zigic looked overwhelmed and she understood why. This was a long way out of their comfort zone. Crimes that weren't cut and dried, resting on obscure points of science neither of them could properly comprehend. Decisions made in private offices and boardrooms, involving governmental agencies that had teeth but only took them out of the drawer for show.

She'd done her research. Found dozens more sites around the country where similar infractions had occurred. The Environment Agency in at the ground floor, making recommendations, assuring local communities that there would be no risk to their health.

Assuming all the relevant rules were adhered to.

But what about when they weren't?

When it couldn't be proved or when nobody was prepared to look hard enough into the matter?

Every incident she'd researched went the same way. An initial flurry of action by local groups, well-meaning independent experts and retired solicitors living close by. But then the newspaper articles and blog posts would gradually peter out, no matter how damning the evidence, and all she could assume was that the victims became too fatigued to fight on. Accepted that their gardens were no-go areas and that their windows would need to be kept closed. Try to sell. Get away somewhere safer. Wait the years or decades it would take for the poison they'd inhaled or absorbed to come to the surface.

'We can't just look the other way on this,' she insisted.

'Riggott isn't going to go for raising criminal charges against them.' Zigic threw his hands up helplessly. 'And even if we could make that happen and get the CPS onside, I don't even know if it would get anywhere. Is it even a police matter?'

'A man *died* because of this. And for all we know he isn't the only one.'

'But we can't *prove* that.'

'Okay, think about it,' she said. 'Whoever killed Jordan went to the trouble to break into his house and steal every bit of tech and storage they could find. Why?'

Zigic took a couple of dried apricots from the tub on his desk. 'Because they thought there was something incriminating there?'

'Exactly. *This* report is incriminating as hell,' she said. 'If it was one of the blokes from the Greenaway Club trying to cover up this possible sabotage we're looking at, why would they take it? All the information's already in the public domain. They weren't even questioned after the crash. There's no reason to think Jordan had anything dangerously compelling in his possession.'

'You're assuming they were thinking that sensibly about what they were doing,' Zigic countered. 'And if it was someone from Docherty Construction – which I still think is a massive if – then what was stealing Jordan's stuff going to achieve? It doesn't stop us getting to Sheila Yule or Tom Geary. We were always going to get hold of this soil sample data eventually.'

'They don't know how smart we are,' Ferreira said.

He smiled faintly. 'Granted, we are pretty smart. But the same issue stands. The best way for Docherty Construction to spike Jordan's story was with money. They'd already seen that work with Tom Geary and Sheila Yule. They might not have paid Sheila off but they'd scared her off with a solicitor's letter.'

'Jordan's different though, isn't he? Journalists don't stop investigating just because some legal firm tells them to.'

'They do,' he insisted. 'All the time. And let's say, theoretically, that Hugo Docherty decided Jordan was going to stir up serious shit for him and that the only way to stop that was murdering him. Is this really how he'd do it?'

'Riggott reckons his backers are dodgy as hell, remember? If his money's coming from criminal contacts, then a shooting is pretty route one.'

'Criminals who can bankroll multimillion-pound property developments don't shoot people in the street, Mel. It draws too much attention. And with a replica gun?' He shook his head. 'No, if someone *smart* wanted Jordan dead, we'd be investigating a hit and run or a street robbery that had ended badly. The kind of case we don't expect to be able to close one hundred per cent of the time.'

She sighed, feeling the momentum dropping away in the face of his certainty.

Zigic scratched his beard. 'I think we're on a hiding to nothing with this one. You need a motive for Hugo Docherty to be behind this and I just don't see it. Jordan's caught them out and the solicitor warned him off. You don't send that letter and create a trail of evidence if you're going to have Jordan shot the next day, do you?'

He was right, as much as she resented admitting it to herself.

'Alright,' she said sharply. 'It wouldn't make any sense. But even if they're not responsible for Jordan's death, they *are* responsible for Derek Yule's.'

Zigic slumped lower in his chair. 'Agreed, but if we want to stand any chance of doing something about that, we need Riggott's support and to get that we need to give him a scalp.'

'For Marcus Greenaway?' she asked. 'What if there isn't one to give?'

'Aren't you wondering why Caxton put Jordan onto Derek Yule's death?' Zigic knitted his fingers together in front of him. 'Jordan's getting curious about Greenaway's accident, then suddenly he drops it to concentrate on the contamination?'

'The contamination's more his kind of thing,' Ferreira said, shrugging.

'And yet Caxton neglected to tell us about it when we asked him what Jordan was working on.' He opened his hands up. 'So,

309

what if Caxton fed him the story specifically to drag him away from Greenaway's death?'

'Because he was getting too close?' she asked. 'How would Caxton know that? Jordan didn't even tell his mum why he got that labouring job. No way he was debriefing Caxton on every bit of progress he was making.'

'Everyone finds somebody they want to confide in eventually.' He shoved another piece of fruit into his mouth.

Ferreira thought of how Caxton had responded to the image of the break-in at the airfield. He'd lost it in the interview room and she cursed herself for pushing him too hard too fast, knew that if she'd given him space and time, he might have talked himself into admitting the truth.

'We can't do anything else today, anyway.' Zigic stood up and switched his computer off. 'And you've got painting to be getting on with, right?'

She'd left Billy covering up the furniture in the living room with dust sheets; two tins of malachite green emulsion sitting on the hearth alongside the new trays and rollers he'd bought.

'Who won on the colours?' Zigic asked, as they went out through the main office.

'Nobody. We compromised.'

He gave her a stunned look. 'I didn't think you knew how to compromise.'

DAY SIX

SUNDAY

CHAPTER FIFTY-ONE

'Do we have to do this today?' Zigic asked, as Anna snapped open a second bin liner and placed it in front the wardrobe. She was dressed for action, in leggings and a loose shirt, her hair tied up in a high ponytail. The Anna of Action look that always sent a bolt of dread through him.

'I can sort it out by myself if you'd prefer,' she told him.

'No way.' He got up from the bed. 'You're not safe in my wardrobe by yourself.'

Anna rolled her eyes. 'Five years and you're still annoyed about that bloody jumper.'

'It was my favourite one! And you killed it.'

'The washing machine ate it,' she insisted, folding her arms.

'It *only* ate my jumper?' he asked. 'Not the rest of the load?'

Anna looked into the wardrobe at his jumbled clothing, unable to meet his eye. 'I'm not going to apologise again.'

'Why would you need to apologise if it was an accident?' he asked, seeing her flush at his teasing tone. 'You'd never make a criminal, darling.'

She gave him a wicked smile. 'Of course I would. You're a detective inspector, you'd just have to cover for me.'

'After what you did to my best jumper?' he asked incredulously. 'I'd throw the book at you.'

She shook her head, smiling vaguely, and pulled out a teal blue crew neck. 'This can go, right?'

'What's wrong with it?'

'You shouldn't wear teal with olive skin. It makes you look washed out.'

Zigic took it from her. 'But it's warm.'

'The cuff's gone,' she said, sharp eyes fastening on the hole in the ribbed knit. 'You can't go out in it.'

'I'll keep it for gardening.' He tossed it onto the bed. 'That's the keep pile.'

Anna let out a muted groan. 'Some of this lot has to go, you're encroaching on my half of the wardrobe.'

'Your two-thirds of the wardrobe,' he corrected her.

She gave him a warning look and dragged an armful of knitwear out. 'These aren't even folded up. You *never* wear them.'

'I might.'

'You wear the same half dozen jumpers all the time.' She held up a mustard one. 'This has still got the tags on. And it's full of moth holes. Can we get rid of it?'

Grudgingly he nodded and she dropped it into the bag at her feet.

Another three went in quick succession. Washed out. Damaged. A misjudged purchase. He forced himself not to take them out of the bag again.

Onto the shirts.

'I can't believe you bought a Nehru collar.' She shook her head. 'Where was I when this happened?'

'It's a grandad collar. And you were with me,' he lied. 'You said it looked sexy.'

'Yeah, sexy grandad is a look I *love* on you.'

He grinned. 'You don't think I'm going to be sexy when we're grandparents?'

'My eyesight will be terrible by then. It won't matter what you look like.' She grabbed the waistband of his jeans and planted a quick, hard kiss on his lips. 'As long as everything still works you'll be fine.'

The charity shop bag filled up fast, the bin bag slower, and they were debating whether he'd ever wear any of those suits again when his mobile rang. He backed away from the wardrobe, reaching for his phone where he'd left it on the bedside table.

'I'm watching you.'

Anna held her hands up, pulled an innocent face.

'We've got a situation,' Ferreira said.

'What's happened?'

She told him, speaking quickly and precisely, the sound of her footsteps as she spoke, then the car door slamming and the engine starting.

'You want me to pick you up?' she asked.

'Yeah. Thanks, Mel.' He rang off, attention snapping back into the room as Anna stuffed a pair of too-tight grey jeans into the charity bag. 'Can we finish this when I get home?'

'Sure.' She pressed her hands together. 'Promise I won't touch anything else until you get back.'

Three minutes later, Ferreira arrived and Zigic got into her car, praying that there would be something of his wardrobe left when he returned. If not, it would mean waiting until Anna inevitably fell asleep on the sofa tonight and retrieving the bags from wherever she stashed them.

'Should we have seen this coming?' Ferreira asked anxiously.

'I don't think anyone could have seen this coming,' he reassured her.

'We were close though,' she said, the first stirrings of anger and self-recrimination straining her voice. 'If we'd pushed harder. I don't know ... if we hadn't let ourselves get distracted.'

'We weren't distracted, we were following other lines of enquiry.' Up ahead he spotted the ambulance parked in front of Dick Caxton's place, two patrol cars alongside it. 'Let's see what happened here before we start blaming ourselves.'

They got out of the car, into the spiked energy of the crime scene. People on the opposite side of the road were standing looking over, vehicles slowing to see what was going on. The paramedics were talking to one of the uniforms, waiting until they were given the all clear to take the body away. SOCO was en route, the coroner's Alvis parked up nearby. Everybody aware that this was a suspicious death. Caxton's proximity to Jordan Radley making it so even if the other circumstances didn't raise questions.

The neighbour they'd spoken to when they first visited the house a few days ago was watching them from her window and she ducked back sharply when Zigic made eye contact with her.

Uniform had already talked to her. She insisted she'd heard nothing, seen nothing, but they would speak to her again. Properly.

On the stretch of exhaust-stained verge alongside the house, Steve Gurney and Lionel Ridgeon stood waiting. Gurney was smoking a cigarette, while Ridgeon looked stunned, one foot braced against the low kerb, his hands in his jeans pockets.

'What happened?' Ferreira demanded, as she walked over to them.

They both stared at her, neither wanting to answer.

'Well?'

Gurney gestured towards the house with his cigarette, voice hoarse when he spoke and Zigic caught a faint whiff of vomit coming off him. 'The door was unlocked when we got here. We went inside and ...'

'He were just there,' Ridgeon said, eyes unfocused, staring into the long grass. 'On the sofa. Dead.'

A queasy look slackened Gurney's face. Zigic stepped back slightly, expecting him to throw up again, but he turned his head and spat into the road.

'Did you touch anything?' Ferreira asked.

'I checked for a pulse,' Gurney said helplessly. Zigic noticed the blood on the cuff of his bomber jacket. 'I didn't know he were dead.'

They were in shock. They needed half an hour and a cup of strong tea and somewhere to sit down before they'd be in any fit state to be questioned properly. Zigic called over PCs Trent and Green, told them to drive the men to the station and make them comfortable.

He watched them go, shuffling alongside their escorts and letting themselves be put into the back of separate patrol cars. As they pulled away, the coroner emerged from the house, shrugging out of the top half of her coverall, revealing a brightly coloured sports top.

'Spin,' she said. 'I was on my way to a class when the call came.'

'What are we looking at?' Zigic asked.

'Single gunshot wound to the head. Probable suicide.' She frowned. 'With the usual caveats, of course.'

'Time of death?' Ferreira asked.

'For now I'd say twelve to fourteen hours, but again –'

'The usual caveats.'

Zigic thanked her and followed Ferreira back to her car, the boot popping as they reached it: bodysuits and shoe covers inside.

'We should probably wait for forensics,' he said, as he stepped into his coverall.

'There's been so much traffic in there already I don't see what more damage we're going to do.'

They went through the door at the side of the house, heading into a tiny hallway that served the two downstairs bedsits. Caxton's was at the back, the door standing open. The smell of contained body and twelve-hour-old death seeping into the corridor, musty and meaty, catching in Zigic's nostrils, filling his mouth.

Dick Caxton sat on the brown velour armchair slumped over to the left, a bullet hole in the side of his head. The gun lay on the floor at his feet, black and lethal.

Ferreira blew out a long, slow breath, eyes fixed on Caxton's body. Smaller and more frail than he'd looked alive, Zigic thought. A broken-down, beaten-down man reduced even further, brought to a moment of darkness so complete that he'd taken a gun and killed himself.

Caxton was dressed in a pair of paisley pyjamas, one pale, swollen-toed foot bare on the carpet, the other in a tan moccasin, and Zigic imagined him turning in early, trying and failing to sleep. Wrestling with his demons. Getting up again and then ...

'I'm pretty sure that's a converted replica.' Ferreira squatted down next to the chair and took a photograph of the gun on her phone. 'It looks kind of insubstantial.'

'Would you be saying that if we weren't searching for one already?'

'Maybe not,' she conceded. 'But it's too coincidental for that not to be the gun that was used to kill Jordan, right?'

He nodded. 'So, Caxton's the shooter?'

'I guess so.'

But she didn't sound certain and he felt the same reluctance as he looked at Caxton's body, thinking of his bad back and his chronic pain. Of how he'd visited Moira Radley yesterday morning with apologies and food.

'Did seeing Jordan's mum push him over the edge?' he asked.

'Guilt-induced suicide?' Ferreira was looking under the bed now, careful not to touch anything. 'You think he needed to apologise to her before he topped himself?'

'Some people like to clean their slate before they do it,' he said. 'Go with a clear conscience.'

'A half-arsed apology and a bag of ready meals is hardly going to send you to your maker clean.' She straightened up, went to the small white sink and looked into the medicine cabinet above. 'He was on a *lot* of medication. I'm surprised he could stand up.'

Zigic thought back to their last interview with Caxton, the pain he was in, physically and emotionally. How close to the edge he seemed. Or maybe he was recasting the man's demeanour now. It was easy to decide you'd seen desperation and defeat when you were looking at the body of a suicide. With no note they could write whatever explanation they wanted onto his actions.

'We were wondering why he gave Jordan the contaminated land story,' Ferreira said, moving to the sideboard. 'Makes sense now, doesn't it?'

'You think Caxton was responsible for Greenaway's death?'

'If he was then it stands to reason he'd want to nudge Jordan away from investigating that and move him onto something else.'

'Caxton was too tall to be either of the men at the airfield break-in, remember?'

'The break-in might not have anything to do with the crash,' she suggested. 'You said it yourself, rural businesses get targeted by thieves all the time. And there *was* stuff stolen. What if we've got too focused on that and it's actually nothing to do with the crash?'

'Then when did the helicopter get damaged?'

She shrugged. 'At another point in time. The boss man's not going to be checking his CCTV every day, is he? He only kept the footage we have because he arrived to find his locks busted and two grand's worth of kit gone. If whoever damaged Greenaway's helicopter broke in without leaving a mess behind, there's no reason for anyone to look at the CCTV, is there?' She put her hand up. '*And* anyone who's got the skills to successfully sabotage a helicopter isn't going to struggle to pick a lock, are they?'

'No,' he conceded, looking at the pile of library books on the floor next to Caxton's bed: Piketty and Klein and Chomsky. Imagined him trying to understand the underlying reasons why his life had gone the way it had, wanting to know it wasn't just him, that maybe somebody knew how to stop it.

'Look at this,' Ferreira said.

He went over to the chimney breast, saw that the sheet of plywood that had been screwed over the decommissioned fireplace was loose. The four screws at its corners were still in place but not fixed back as tight as they should be.

'I think there's something behind there.'

'Don't touch it,' Kate Jenkins said, standing in the doorway, suited up with her case in her hand.

'It looks like somebody took the board off,' Ferreira told her. 'Can we open it up?'

'Can you wait?' Kate asked, putting her case down. 'Stupid question, of course you can't wait.'

She called in her assistant Elliot and they got out of the way while the board was photographed. Close-up shots were taken of each screw, the paint flecks on the dark carpet around it, cordoned and numbered and photographed again before they were removed as well, dropped into plastic vials for later examination.

Once that was done, Kate carefully pulled the sheet of board away, the sooty scent of long dead fires blooming into the air.

Jenkins let out a low whistle and Zigic moved forward, trying to see what was in the void behind the board.

'What is it?' Ferreira asked impatiently. 'For God's sake, Kate!'

'Stay where you are,' she warned. 'Elliot, come and get a couple of shots of this.'

Zigic forced down the urge to move again. He glanced at Ferreira and saw her spring up onto her toes, trying to find a sight line between Kate and Elliot, frustration on her face as he methodically photographed the inside of the fireplace.

'You're winding us up now,' Ferreira said.

'I'm just trying to do my job here, Mel.'

Finally Jenkins got to her feet and turned to them, holding a tan leather messenger bag.

'Is that Jordan's?' Ferreira asked.

It was crumpled and dusty but Zigic saw the logo on its front and the distinctive multicoloured strap Moira Radley had described when they realised Jordan's was missing from the house.

'It's his.'

Jenkins opened it up. Inside was a silver laptop and a grey felt tablet-sized case; the items stolen from his bedroom after he was killed. She nodded towards Caxton's body.

'Seems like you've found your shooter then.'

CHAPTER FIFTY-TWO

Lionel Ridgeon had pulled himself together since they'd last seen him. The numbness replaced with a twitchy unease that sent his gaze skimming around the room as Ferreira set up the tapes.

His clothes had been removed when he arrived at the station, bagged and tagged, and taken to Kate Jenkins's lab to be examined, leaving him dressed in a plastic coverall, his feet bare under the table.

Every time he moved the plastic crackled and he winced at the sound. He hadn't complained though, didn't make a show of asking why they'd done this to him like some people did.

But he wasn't a suspect, Zigic reminded himself. Wasn't acting like one either.

Some people did in the aftermath of a suspicious death. Would get indignant at having their fingerprints taken and their DNA swabbed. Raise hell over being stripped of their clothing. And sometimes it was because they were guilty and they knew the means to prove that were being lifted from their bodies. Sometimes it was just the loss of control. Their innocence making them protest at being treated as if they'd done something wrong.

'What were you doing at Caxton's place?' Ferreira asked.

'We were going to take him over to the football,' Ridgeon told her. 'He's been worked up lately. Me and Steve reckoned it'd do him good to get out of that place for a bit.'

'Whose idea was it?'

'Steve's,' Ridgeon said. 'They'd had a bit of a set-to at the Club on Friday. He didn't want to leave it festering.'

'What had they argued about?'

'Dick were pissed up something fierce. He'd been knocking back them painkillers of his like Smarties. All over the buckering shop he were.'

It wasn't an answer.

'Did he start it?' Ferreira asked. 'Or Steve?'

'You can never tell with them two,' Ridgeon said glumly. 'Always at one another, like a couple of old women. It were usually something of nothing, though.'

'One of them must have been the instigator,' Ferreira pressed.

Ridgeon looked uncomfortable. 'They were having a game of darts and Dick was getting riled up. I thought it were just messing, you know. Dick putting Steve off of his throw because he's not a bad arm at darts is Steve and Dick's never been much cop.'

Ferreira cocked her head. 'It wasn't about the darts though, was it?'

'I dunno.' Ridgeon shrugged. 'Dick's not been himself since what happened to Jordan. And, like I say, he'd had a few too many.'

'What was said?' Ferreira asked.

'I couldn't tell you,' Ridgeon insisted, his voice taking on a clipped edge.

'What did Steve tell you about it?'

'Only that Dick were giving him lip about going on like he were the big bollocks. The usual rubbish.'

There was more to it but they would get to the truth when they questioned Steve Gurney, Zigic thought.

'If I'd known the sort of state Dick were in, I'd have gone round there to see him before.' A pained look crossed Ridgeon's face. 'I reckoned he weren't right but I never would've thought it were this bad.'

'He'd taken Jordan's death badly,' Ferreira said.

Ridgeon nodded. 'Grief's an ugly bastard. I've been there myself. You get so as you recognise the warning signs. Dick were grieving but he never had people to help him get through it. He had his daughters but they're away up north and I don't think he talked to them much before they went even. We should've been there for him.'

Ferreira gave him a moment and he stared at the tabletop, hands folded together there. Thick fingers, broad palms, rimes of oil under his short, square nails.

'What happened when you got to Dick's place?'

Ridgeon took a steadying breath. 'We buzzed his room but he never answered. The old woman upstairs let us in. We banged on his door but he never answered that neither. Then I tried it and it weren't locked.' He looked at Zigic. 'I thought, eh up, summat's amiss. You don't go leaving your door open in a place like that.'

He paused and Zigic could hear his breathing, getting ragged and short.

'We goes in and Dick's in his chair. He looked *wrong*. I were looking at him and I knew summat weren't right but it were like my brain weren't having it.' He waved his fingers at his temple. 'Steve had a sight more about him. He goes over and looks for a pulse, that's when we knew what he'd done.'

'When did you notice the gun?' Ferreira asked.

'Steve did. I couldn't see it where I were. I could see there were blood but I couldn't –' He squeezed his eyes shut. 'Did Dick kill Jordan?'

Ferreira glanced at him and Zigic nodded. No point keeping the facts back at this point. Kate Jenkins had called before they walked into the interview room, told them the gun Caxton used looked like a match for the one that shot Jordan Radley. A converted replica. The right calibre. No way to match it from the bullets because replicas didn't have rifling in their barrels. But she would recover whatever DNA she could from the weapon itself and hopefully that would tie it to Jordan's murder.

'The gun Dick used to kill himself was a converted replica,' Ferreira said. 'The same kind that was used in Jordan's murder.'

Ridgeon's eyes snapped open again. 'That don't mean he did it. Maybe he went and bought the gun for himself.'

'We also found some items in Dick's room that were stolen from Jordan's home after he was killed.'

Ridgeon swore softly to himself, buried his face in his hands and rubbed his skin so violently that when he took them away again his cheeks were burning red through his coarse grey stubble.

'I should've phoned you up yesterday,' Ridgeon said.

'Why?' Ferreira asked.

'Friday night, before all that with Steve, Dick goes – out of nowheres – he goes to me, "I killed him." And I says, "What the buckering hell are you on about, buh?" And Dick turns and he looks at me like he never knew I'd been sitting there, talking to him for the last ten minutes.' Ridgeon winced. 'Then he starts going on about this story Jordan were doing. Some building site or other where a mate of Dick's got sick. He said he told Jordan about it and that's why he got shot. Because he were going to say summat about the builders.'

Ferreira frowned at him.

'What did you think to that?'

'I were relieved,' Ridgeon told her. 'For a minute there I thought he were telling me he'd killed Jordan himself. But then he says that about the story and I thought, thank Christ.' He lowered his head, shoulders hunching up. 'But when I got home I kept thinking on it. I were thinking how funny he looked at me. Like he'd been talking to himself and then he realised I'd heard him.' Ridgeon shook his head. 'I should've called you.'

Zigic tried to push away the anger he felt threatening to swell up in him. Ridgeon had had this information for two days and was only telling them now because Dick Caxton was dead and beyond their reach.

It was a confession.

No matter how he tried to justify it now or what excuses he made for not taking it seriously at the time. It was a confession he'd been given and kept it to himself.

'Why do you think Dick shot Jordan?' Ferreira asked.

Ridgeon considered it for a moment. 'I dunno. He liked the lad. That's what I don't understand about it. Dick were the last person I'd have had down for doing summat like that.'

'Maybe he was worried because Jordan was investigating Marcus Greenaway's death?' Ferreira suggested.

'That were an accident.'

The denial sounded reflexive, habitual. Bruce Humble had told them how many joking accusations had been thrown his way after Greenaway died and Ridgeon must have had them too. Got used to saying 'it was an accident' to defuse the moment.

'What do you remember about Dick's reaction to Greenaway's death?' Zigic asked.

'I don't remember anything about it.'

Ferreira sighed. 'You can't help him now, Lionel. And you can't hurt him either. But we need to know why Dick killed Jordan because, I'll level with you, it isn't making a hell of a lot of sense.'

Ridgeon scratched his head. 'Dick got the worst of it I reckon. I'd had a rough time but I found my Patti. I'm happier now than I've been my whole life. But it all went wrong for Dick when he lost that job. His old woman barely stuck with him for a month. His kids went off with her. They'd remortgaged the house to get his daughter out of debt so his home went not long after.' Ridgeon's jaw worked away at nothing for a moment. 'He were the one who wanted to go after Greenaway in the first place. Right after the factory closed, I mean. Dick were always going on about direct action and how the rich wouldn't give you what you were due, you'd have to go and take it from them.'

'And he ended up doing a month inside for his trouble,' Zigic commented, thinking of what Weller had said about the men coming out of prison even angrier than they went in.

Usually he wouldn't give much credence to Weller's theories but he could see the logic of it with someone like Caxton. No family to go home to. Nothing to lose.

Marcus Greenaway takes everything from him and gets him locked up for a month to boot. A more severe punishment than a crime like that generally warranted.

How would Caxton have dealt with that?

Slunk meekly home and licked his wounds. Or come out of prison with his beliefs hardened and a desire to inflict the punishment he felt Greenaway deserved?

'Dick could have done it,' Ridgeon said thoughtfully. 'He were a toolmaker. Back when that actually meant summat. He were one of the last lot of them trained up proper before everything started getting imported.'

The kind of man who'd have no trouble converting a replica pistol to a fully serviceable weapon, Zigic thought. And not much cost involved because you could buy a replica for fifty quid.

Fifteen minutes later, Ridgeon released, they stood in front of Marcus Greenaway's board, Ferreira with her arms folded and a serious expression on her face.

'Is this it?' she asked. 'Caxton sabotages Greenaway's helicopter, then, when he finds out Jordan's looking into the crash, he feeds him another story because he's scared that Jordan's smart enough to actually find the evidence the AAIB missed?'

Zigic stuck a photo of Caxton up in the suspects column for Greenaway.

It looked right there.

More so than it looked on Jordan Radley's board. But everything they thought they knew about Dick Caxton had been based on lies, he realised. The men at the Greenaway Club feeding them a line about how close the two had been, all those quiet chats, the alignment of their political beliefs and Caxton's purely innocent interest in Jordan's work.

The men shielding Caxton without knowing he was the person they were covering for. All assuming Marcus Greenaway's death was murder these past four years but nobody prepared to admit that because, ultimately, he'd got what he deserved.

CHAPTER FIFTY-THREE

'Sorry to keep you waiting,' Ferreira said smoothly, as they entered Interview Room 1. 'We'll try to keep this brief. We know it's been an ordeal for you.'

Steve Gurney thanked her in a subdued tone. Where Ridgeon had recovered during the last couple of hours, Gurney seemed to have gone the other way. He looked smaller and inward-turned as he sat at the table in his plastic coverall, elbows on the table, fist tucked into his palm, hiding his mouth.

He'd got through two cups of tea, a Coke and a chocolate bar while he waited. He had told the guard his blood sugar was low but Zigic suspected it was the taste of vomit he couldn't seem to wash from his mouth. It might be with Gurney for days. A faint whiff sneaking up on him when he least expected it.

'What were you doing at Caxton's place?' Ferreira asked, once the tapes were turning.

'We were worried about Dick,' Gurney said, touching his fingertips to the mug in front of him. 'He seemed out of sorts at the Club on Friday.'

'How was he out of sorts?'

'He was quiet. Drinking. He don't usually drink much. Can't handle it.' Gurney's tone made it sound like a personal failing. 'Me and Lionel decided to go and get him out of that crappy bedsit. Take him for a pint and a curry, see if he wanted to come to the match. He ain't been to the POSH since he gave up his season ticket. We thought it might perk him up a bit, you know.'

'Whose idea was that?' Ferreira asked.

'Mine.'

'That was very nice of you,' she told him.

He shrugged. 'What you do for your mates, innit?'

'Even the mates you'd got into a fight with a couple of days before?'

'You don't get it.' He shook his head. 'Men can do that. We have a bit of a barney then we let it go. It don't mean the same thing as when you women fall out.'

Ferreira stiffened slightly in her seat.

'What was this "barney" about?' she asked.

He made a dismissive gesture. 'Dick was drunk, it was nothing.'

'It obviously wasn't nothing,' she said firmly. 'We've spoken to Bruce Humble. He said he had to drag the pair of you apart.'

A quick flash of anger in his eyes. 'We were playing darts. Dick didn't like losing, that's all it was.'

Humble had painted a different picture when they called him. Couldn't tell them what words were said but made it clear they were heated and that Caxton was trying to provoke Gurney.

'The way Bruce Humble tells it you were about ready to batter Dick,' Ferreira said. 'And now Dick's dead.'

'He topped himself,' Gurney snapped. 'What does it matter if we had a bit of verbals? Dick topped himself with a fucking gun!'

Ferreira pulled an innocent face at him. 'So?'

'So he was off his fucking head, wasn't he?' Gurney turned to Zigic. 'Jordan got shot then Dick shot himself. He must have killed Jordan, right? You know what happened, why're you giving me the third degree?'

Zigic said nothing, just stared back at Gurney, letting his anger hang in the air, souring slowly. Letting him hear how wild he sounded.

'Why would Dick want to kill Jordan?' he asked finally.

Gurney threw his hands up, defeated rather than furious. 'How do I know? I'm not a bloody psychic.'

'You were his friend,' Ferreira reminded him. 'How had Dick been lately?'

'He was the same moaning old cunt he always was,' Gurney said, exasperated. 'Going on about his arsehole job and his bellend of a boss. Moaning over never having any money, moaning about that bedsit. His back hurts. His legs hurt. His medication's giving him the shits.' Gurney sighed, shaking his head. 'It was a shock, him doing that. But it weren't much of one, you know what I mean?'

'What did you two fight about?' Zigic asked him.

Gurney slumped in his chair. 'It was nothing.'

'On Friday afternoon, a couple of hours before you two went toe to toe in front of a room full of witnesses, Dick Caxton sat in that very chair and he looked at this photograph.' Zigic brought out the still image from the security footage at Holme Airfield and pushed it across the table. 'We asked Dick if he recognised either of these men.'

Gurney gave the photo a cursory glance and pushed it away. 'What's this supposed to be?'

'Footage from a break-in at the hangar where Marcus Greenaway's helicopter was kept,' Zigic said. 'A fortnight before he died, these two men broke into the hangar.'

'So what?'

'We asked Dick if he recognised either of them,' Ferreira said.

Gurney looked at it again, kept looking. 'I don't know who they are.'

Zigic thought of how Dick Caxton had reacted to the photograph. How Ferreira's escalating questions had driven the man to his feet and across the room and to the door. The urge to run overcoming the pain he'd been in.

Two days ago, he'd read fear into his behaviour. A man covering for someone he was too scared or loyal to name. But that was before he killed himself. Before they found Jordan Radley's things in his room.

The photograph wasn't of the men who sabotaged Marcus Greenaway's helicopter, Zigic realised, and Caxton's sudden urge to flee wasn't provoked by the photo, but by the much simpler fact that they were questioning him about Greenaway's death.

Ferreira sat forward in her seat, pressing ahead.

'Did Dick tell you we'd questioned him about Marcus Greenaway's death?'

'No.' The anger back, a warning flash across Gurney's face.

329

'Or maybe he did tell you and that's what you were arguing about?' Ferreira suggested. 'The man there, on the left, he's about your build, Steve.'

'It's not me.'

It wasn't, Zigic thought, hearing confusion in the denial.

'Jordan Radley was investigating Greenaway's death,' Ferreira went on. 'And he was starting to get somewhere.'

'Before he was murdered,' Zigic added.

'He believed Greenaway's crash wasn't an accident. It was sabotage. The kind of very clever sabotage that could only have been carried out by a skilled engineer.'

Gurney's eyes widened. 'Is that what this is? You've got me in here to accuse me of killing Marcus fucking Greenaway?'

'We've spoken to Lionel about it,' Ferreira explained, calm and even in the face of his rising ire. 'Maybe you'd like to give us your opinion on what happened.'

Gurney drew himself up in his seat. 'I think Dick killed himself. And seeing as he had a fucking gun, I think he shot Jordan too. You say the kid was trying to find out who killed Greenaway, yeah then, maybe Dick did it. He had the know-how. He was fucking livid about how the sale went down and he wasn't exactly a fan of the bloke before that.' Gurney shook his head. 'Look, I don't know what's going on here. I've just seen one of my mates dead with a fucking hole in his skull.'

They were pushing up against the limit of good practice now, Zigic realised. Questioning Steve Gurney without a solicitor present, two hours after he'd walked into the scene of a suicide. Anything damning he said now could be struck off the record as the confused ramblings of a man in a state of shock. Or be taken as evidence of them manipulating someone in an unfit state to be interrogated.

Anything he knew about Marcus Greenaway's death and Dick Caxton's role in it would have to wait.

'I wanna go home.' A pained look crossed Gurney's face. 'Please, I can't do this shit right now.'

Ferreira glanced at Zigic and he nodded for her to stop the tapes.

They released Steve Gurney, sent him home in his plastic cover-all in the back of a patrol car, and returned to the office. Empty on a Sunday afternoon; the two officers officially on duty away answering some call.

'What do we do?' Ferreira asked, dropping into her chair.

'Wait for the post-mortem.' Zigic went over to Jordan Radley's board and started to write up the new information they had, ready for tomorrow's morning briefing. 'Tie up the loose ends.'

'Caxton didn't have an alibi for Jordan's murder,' Ferreira said. 'He claimed he took a bus home but Keri couldn't find any sign of him at the stops near the Club. And he didn't have his mobile on him that night so we couldn't pinpoint his movements from cell tower data.'

'Looks convenient now, doesn't it?'

She sighed heavily, the sound of her chair creaking as she swivelled back and forth. 'If he did kill Greenaway I don't see how we're going to be able to prove it.'

No physical evidence. No witnesses. No suspect to be put in the interview room and questioned as many times as it took to get a straight answer.

'That's if Greenaway even was murdered,' Ferreira said, coming up alongside him, staring at Caxton's mugshot; four years old but he looked a decade younger than he had when he died. The intervening years so much harder on him than the rest of them. 'Other than the independent expert's opinion, we still don't have any really compelling reason to think it was sabotage.'

'Except that Caxton needed a motive to kill Jordan,' Zigic reminded her. 'And if it wasn't because he was trying to stop that crime coming out, then why the hell did he do it?'

'It feels like he's beaten us,' she said.

'I know.'

'He gets to check out fast and leave all this shit behind for us to try and untangle.' She gestured at the board. 'What are we going to tell Jordan's mum?'

Zigic turned away from Caxton's defiant glare.

'That's a problem for tomorrow.'

DAY SEVEN

MONDAY

FRIDAY SEVEN

MONDAY

CHAPTER FIFTY-FOUR

Three boards lined up along the wall now. Three faces looking out across the office at the men and women who were supposed to make sense of their suspicious deaths.

- Jordan Radley
- Marcus Greenaway
- Dick Caxton

Zigic called the team to gather around. Riggott sat at an empty desk at the periphery of the group, puffing away on his vape pen. He'd been drawn down to the morning briefing by the promise of closure on Jordan Radley's murder, but it was Marcus Greenaway's death that really held his interest, Ferreira thought.

'Okay.' Zigic clapped his hands together. 'For anyone who doesn't know already, Richard Caxton died on Saturday night by what appears to be a self-inflicted gunshot.'

'With a converted replica?' Parr asked.

'Yes, Zac.' Zigic gestured at the point on Caxton's board where he'd written those exact words and underlined them. 'Now, preliminary forensics have come back on the gun and there's only one set of fingerprints on it. Belonging to Caxton.' He glanced at the board, where the highlights of Kate Jenkins's report were written up. 'Kate also recovered two different blood types from the grip, one matching Caxton, the other Jordan Radley.'

'Got the murder weapon,' Weller said triumphantly.

Zigic stiffened slightly at his tone, went on. 'Being a conversion we can't say with absolute certainty if this is the same gun but I think it's safe to say we're looking at the murder weapon, yes.

The post-mortem is scheduled for this afternoon and hopefully we'll get a match on the composition of the bullets.'

'Had Caxton already decided to kill himself when he killed Jordan?' Bloom asked. 'Is that why he kept the gun rather than dumping it?'

'Possible,' Zigic said slowly, as if it hadn't occurred to him before.

Ferreira realised she hadn't considered it either. Had wondered about Jordan's bag and his tech stashed in the fireplace and decided Caxton was waiting for a safe opportunity to dispose of it. Assumed the gun was meant to be part of the bundle he eventually dropped into a lake or consigned to the River Nene.

'What were those two doing at his place?' Murray asked, nodding towards Gurney's and Ridgeon's photographs on the board in the witness column.

Zigic went through the men's accounts of Sunday morning, keeping it short because there wasn't much to it. 'There was an argument between Gurney and Caxton a couple of days earlier but that doesn't seem to be a factor.'

Murray rocked back in her chair. 'Did we find a note?'

'No,' Zigic told her.

'Why would he want to kill Jordan?' Bloom asked.

Zigic took a deep breath, moved over to Marcus Greenaway's board. 'One potential motive – our only credible motive, at present – relates to Jordan's investigation into this crash.'

'I thought nobody knew what Jordan was working on,' Weller said, surprised.

'They've been covering for him, right?' Parr asked. 'Maybe the rest of the blokes didn't *know* Caxton killed Jordan, but they knew damn well he'd been poking his nose into what Jordan was working on and they'd have *known* that made Caxton a suspect.' He chucked his chin up. 'We should do them for withholding information.'

Murray shook her head at him. 'We can't prove that.'

'Caxton was a highly skilled toolmaker.' Zigic pressed on, seeming uncomfortable up there this morning and Ferreira couldn't decide if it was Riggott's presence in the room or the constant interruptions putting him on the back foot. 'If anyone had the skill set to sabotage Greenaway's helicopter, it's Caxton. Our problem now is proving that he was responsible.'

'I don't see how we're going to do that,' Murray grumbled.

'Is Caxton a match for either of the fellas who did the break-in at the airfield?' Riggott asked.

'No,' Zigic told him. 'Not even close.'

'Ah, must be that we're looking at two lads on the rob, then.' Another cloud of vapour dispersed slowly across the room.

Riggott could see a straight line from Jordan Radley's death through to Marcus Greenaway's and he obviously liked how it looked. A scalp for the family and the Chief Constable, with the added bonus that it belonged to a dead man so they wouldn't have to undertake a full-scale investigation or a trial. Just write up a report turning the accident into sabotage and say that in the light of Richard Caxton's death they would not be pursuing other suspects.

'We don't have anything to back up the theory that Caxton was responsible,' Zigic said, unwilling to take the easy win that Riggott was setting up for him. 'And at four years' distance I don't see how we can ever confidently say we know who was responsible.'

Ferreira willed him to back down. Not get into this with Riggott in front of the whole office. Riggott might be on the way out, but he wasn't gone yet, and she didn't want Zigic shackled to his desk as well as Billy.

'Before you go running on ahead of yourself, you might want to wait until that CCTV footage has been cleaned up,' Riggott suggested. 'Always pays to keep an open mind about these things, Ziggy.'

He gave Riggott the barest of nods.

'What we can do and what we will be doing today is nailing down Caxton's movements on the night of Jordan's murder,' he said. 'Keri, I need you to do one last pass on the CCTV and see if there's any sign of Caxton around the crime scene. We've got

337

his clothing up with forensics and hopefully we'll get a match for the shoe prints at the scene. Rob, you're on door-to-door at Jordan's place – take Caxton's photograph and see if anyone saw him there. Colleen, I need you out at Caxton's talking to his neighbours.'

'We've got the gun,' Parr protested. 'What else do we need?'

'We need to lock this down,' Zigic said firmly. 'I want to be able to tell Jordan's mum with absolute certainty that we know who killed her son.'

CHAPTER FIFTY-FIVE

Mid-morning, the tech department sent down Jordan Radley's laptop and Ferreira took it to her desk, hoping to find the vital evidence that would link Richard Caxton to Marcus Greenaway's death.

It was a rose gold model, borrowed from his aunt Tanya she now knew, and the sticker on the lid gave the password as 'mrsidriselba'. Ferreira smiled as she typed it into the box under Tanya's avatar.

It was obviously intended as a short-term loan because all of her files were still there in yellow folders on the right-hand side of the desktop, a single purple one on the left with Jordan's name on it. Barely a handful of files inside because he'd only been using it for a week or so before he was murdered and it was stolen by a killer who had no idea this wasn't where the bulk of his writing and research lived.

Alongside the innocuous articles he'd been working on for the *Evening Telegraph* and the essay his lecturer had set on the best methods of procuring interviews, she saw that he'd spent the week before his death pulling together the story about the Stillwater Rise Apartments.

A single file contained all of the evidence he'd managed to gather: the report from Drury Prior and their refusal to respond to his questions; the test results that his friend from the charity near Cambridge had given him; a long interview with Sheila Yule about her husband's death; and there at the bottom a quote from a respiratory specialist from Addenbrooke's Hospital stating that, yes, the levels of heavy metals on the site did pose a serious threat to human health.

Jordan had evidently decided that Derek Yule's doctor wouldn't give him a quote or he'd judged this expert's name carried greater weight.

But this story didn't matter now, she reminded herself.

It wasn't what got Jordan murdered so she was supposed to let it go. No matter how infuriating it felt doing that.

She clicked through to Jordan's emails and found the conversation with the specialist, knowing she was wasting her time but unable to ignore the unfolding story. She found the man was happy to have his name put to the quote, even though Jordan had promised him anonymity.

'Someone has to stand up and tell the truth,' he'd written.

Looking at his senior position in the hospital, Ferreira supposed he was well enough protected to say whatever he wanted to. That perhaps Ms Leung hadn't felt quite so secure in her role.

Ferreira thought of the cease and desist letter Hugo Docherty's solicitor had sent to Jordan, a warning she guessed he wouldn't have heeded. Not with so much work already done.

Across the room, Parr was still grinding through the material they had from the corrupted hard drive of Jordan's proper laptop, an air of feverish concentration around him as he scrolled and clicked, pausing for a quick mouthful of coffee, never taking his eyes off the screen. He'd been right and she'd been wrong and it was an uncomfortable sensation.

It was partly ego, she could silently admit to herself. But it was more because the contamination seemed like a story Jordan might have willingly staked his safety on. Derek Yule dead, Tom Geary walking wounded, hundreds of people blithely occupying flats built on ground steeped in a lethal chemical cocktail.

But Marcus Greenaway's murder, an act of revenge by a man whose life had been ripped apart ... she wasn't so sure Jordan would have knowingly and willingly endangered himself to expose that.

She wasn't even convinced he was still working on it during the weeks leading up to his death.

There was no sign of fresh impetus to the investigation anywhere on this borrowed machine. Jordan seemed to have lost all interest after he'd spoken to the independent air accident expert.

Had he seen a potential sabotage and worked out it might lead back to the men at the Greenaway Club and decided to shelve it? Save them another round of suspicion and visits from the police.

Ferreira rolled a cigarette and went downstairs to smoke it, Billy catching up to her as she lit up.

'You'll be getting your gold star from Riggott anyway.' He took her lighter. 'This is a dream outcome for him. Telling the Chief Constable he's found Greenaway's killer but you don't have to prove it in court.'

'You don't think Caxton did it?' she asked.

'Course he did. Unless you've found another reason for him to kill Jordan Radley.' Billy took his mobile out of his pocket. 'I just got an email. The paper for the bedroom's back in stock.'

'Which one?' she asked, happy for the momentary distraction.

He showed her a photo on his phone. Ink blue, gold geometric print. 'Your call. This or the grey one. I'm easy either way.'

'Okay,' she said. 'Let's go for that one.'

For a few minutes they talked about whether to tackle the bedroom straight off or not, do it while the dust sheets were out and before they tossed the rollers into the cupboard under the stairs where they would inevitably harden and become useless. Billy seemed to be enjoying playing at manual labour. He'd put together a flat-pack shelving unit for the hallway a fortnight ago and she still caught him standing there, admiring it on an almost daily basis. Had even seen him pat it a couple of times, smiling stupidly to himself.

'We could move everything into the spare bedroom and do it at the weekend,' he suggested. 'If we order the paper today, I can pick it up on Friday.'

She murmured agreement, thinking of the apartment at Stillwater Rise she'd viewed, the bedroom there painted the same shade of midnight blue they'd managed to agree on. That was where she'd seen it, she realised now, why she'd liked it immediately when Billy put the colour chart in front of her.

He was talking about buying a paste table, his phone in hand, scrolling through the options.

And she was thinking of how she'd been suckered by the apartment. Someone as professionally sceptical as she was supposed to be had been won over by a bit of boutique hotel styling. If she hadn't been turned down for a mortgage, she'd be living there now. Sitting on her balcony with the odour of tainted earth wafting up from the surrounding landscaping. Being slowly poisoned along with all the other people in the flats around her.

'We need to do something about Docherty Construction,' she said.

Billy was ordering the table. 'I'm not sure there's anything you can do.'

'There are hundreds of people living on that site,' she reminded him. 'And we've got the paperwork now to prove they haven't made it safe. We can prove they're at fault in Derek Yule's death. We should be arresting Rachel Greenaway and Hugo Docherty for manslaughter.'

He frowned. 'You'd never get that past a jury. Can you imagine the kind of legal team they'd bring in?'

'It doesn't need to convince a jury,' she said. 'Even if they walk it opens up the possibility of a civil case. Lawsuits. Everyone who bought a flat there deserves to be able to sue them. Sheila Yule deserves to be able to sue them out of fucking existence for what they did to her bloke.'

'Have you put this to Riggott?' Billy asked, slipping his phone away again.

'He thinks it's a waste of time.'

'But he's having his strings pulled by the Chief Constable.' He took another drag on his cigarette. 'So, you need a way to go around Riggott.'

She heard the needle in his tone, the never fully buried desire to see his old mentor suffer.

'Okay,' she said. 'How do I get around Riggott?'

342

'You don't need me to tell you that.' He smiled wanly. 'You just need to decide if doing the right thing's going to be worth the fallout.'

Ferreira scrubbed out her cigarette and went back into the station, trying to decide whether he was encouraging her or warning her off. It was a conversation for a later date and a private setting.

When she walked into the office she saw Parr on his feet at his computer, Zigic with him, smiling broadly at something on the screen.

'What is it?' she asked, rushing over.

Zigic stepped back. 'See for yourself.'

Holme Airfield. The looming grey bulk of the main hanger in darkness, pools of light and areas of shadow. Two men at the side door. The security camera they knew about had been sprayed out. The one they didn't watching from a safer distance.

The image was sharper now than when they'd first seen it, the contrast turned up, the frame tighter on the faces of the men. Paused on the moment one of them unwisely looked up into the sky, a moment of frustration or a quick prayer for divine intervention as his accomplice worked on the locked door. The thoughtless movement slipping the covering from the lower half of his face.

Every feature clear and sharp and beyond question.

CHAPTER FIFTY-SIX

The tapes were rolling.

Three of them at the table, no solicitor yet, despite the patrol car and the warning that this interview was taking place under caution. They'd made the offer and had it batted away, but Zigic knew that by the time they were finished here one would be requested, the play of innocence so thoroughly shredded that there would be no route left except the one that went through the truth.

Next to him Ferreira sat bolt upright, her hands on top of the tablet she'd brought in with her, underneath it a slim manila file containing a single photograph.

'This,' she said, opening the tablet and placing it in the centre of the table, 'is footage recovered from a break-in at Holme Airfield. You'll see two men forcing their way into the main hangar.' She slid the tablet across the table. 'The man on the left is quite clearly you.'

Bruce Humble cleared his throat. A quick look at the photo and then away again. No denial, not yet, and Zigic could see the cogs turning.

'And this,' Ferreira said, slipping a single eight-by-ten photograph out of the file and placing it next to the tablet. 'Is Dick Caxton's head.'

Bruce Humble recoiled from the image, his hands over his mouth and his eyes widening. Caxton on the mortuary slab, a close-up of the gunshot wound that had killed him.

'Did you know he was dead?'

Humble nodded. 'Lionel called and told me.'

'What Lionel won't have told you, is that the gun he used was the same gun that killed Jordan Radley.'

'No.'

'Yes,' Ferreira said. 'Now, our working theory is that Dick murdered Jordan because he'd started to get close to figuring out Dick killed Marcus Greenaway. But judging by this security camera footage, Dick wasn't working alone.' She opened up her hands. 'So, now we have to ask ourselves if he was working alone on *Jordan*'s murder. Or if you were involved in that crime as well.'

For a few seconds Humble said nothing, stared through her while the tapes turned and the camera mounted high in the corner of the still white room recorded the subtle play of thoughts across his face. Zigic could almost have read his pulse from the pump of blood through the vein at his temple. Was sure he could actually hear the thunder of his heartbeat from across the table.

'I need a minute,' Humble said finally. 'I'll tell you but I just need a minute.'

'You need a solicitor too,' Ferreira warned him.

They wanted one in the room for them as much as Humble. No way they were going to let his confession slip on the grounds of lack of legal counsel.

'Who do you want us to call?' she asked.

'I don't have a bloody solicitor,' he said wearily.

'We'll call the duty solicitor,' Zigic assured him. 'Interview suspended 11:19.'

They returned to the office, leaving Humble to think over his options, take the time he obviously needed.

'Do you think he's going to talk?' Ferreira asked.

'If he's got any sense he won't,' Zigic said grimly. 'All we *really* have on him is a link to a break-in and theft of some tools. They took the tools for some reason and if they were in there to sabotage Greenaway's helicopter, they were obviously thinking ahead.'

'Take the tools so they could admit a lesser charge if they got caught?'

He nodded. 'Humble isn't stupid, Mel.'

'Who do you think the second man is?' she asked, moving to Jordan Radley's board. 'McLeary might be a good fit.'

Zigic looked at Daniel McLeary's mugshot, still up there but long since sidelined by his alibi and his apparent social distance from the rest of the men at the Club. 'They don't seem to be very friendly any more.'

'Killing a man together could destroy any friendship,' she suggested. 'And he's fallen a lot further than the rest of them. I mean, he's been homeless for a few years judging by his record.'

'What about Steve Gurney?' Zigic asked, thinking of the man's quick temper and bad attitude, trying to map his build onto the figure of the second man on the security footage. 'He's desperate to get out of the country suddenly.'

She murmured. 'Ridgeon seems like he's living his dream now. He wouldn't want it coming back on him and wrecking that.'

'He's a bit bulky,' Zigic reminded her. 'The bloke on the footage was slim.'

'Maybe he's put some weight on.'

'The new woman feeding him up?'

Ferreira nodded. 'The thing is, we're concentrating on these four because they were all together the night Jordan was killed and they're obviously a bit of a unit now, but we don't know who else might have been in that gang four years ago.'

She was right, Zigic realised, with a plummeting sensation. They'd spoken to all the men who were present at the Club the night Jordan was shot, thinking that his killer must have been there to make following Jordan a feasible prospect. But now that Caxton was dead and firmly linked to Jordan's murder, it opened up the possibility that his accomplice could be any man he'd worked with. A friend long since moved on or away or just gone.

'The logical answer is Caxton, right?' he said, hearing the hope in his voice. 'Caxton shot Jordan so he has to be our second man.'

'He's too tall,' Ferreira said. 'Our guy's nowhere near six foot and Caxton's well over that even with a bit of a stoop.'

They needed it to be Caxton, Zigic realised. So much easier to tie this all up that way. Rather than face down the challenge of identifying the second suspect among the 150 men who'd lost their jobs when the factory closed down.

They needed Bruce Humble to talk but they had nothing to threaten him with, no compelling leverage to made him pivot around.

Any decent solicitor walking into that room would tell him to keep quiet and would force them to prove the charge. With Dick Caxton dead the case was stalled.

If Humble held his nerve, they were sunk.

CHAPTER FIFTY-SEVEN

'Humble's solicitor's here,' Ferreira called across the office.

Zigic looked up from his computer screen, saw her at Murray's desk, hand in the jar where Murray kept her home-made biscuits, body turned to hide what she was doing in case Colleen returned and caught her in the act.

'They're not yours,' he called back.

'Col doesn't mind.'

'Yes, she does.'

'I'll replace it,' Ferreira said, stuffing one into her mouth.

Murray was going to have to put a lock on that jar, he thought, flipping to his emails as a new message pinged.

The preliminary report on Caxton's post-mortem. He scrolled past the photographs, homing in on the findings that were as expected, Ferreira coming into his office with her phone in her hand, reading the report as she sat down.

'Six one,' she said. 'So Caxton's definitely out of the running for the second man at Holme Airfield.'

Zigic agreed, checking Caxton's medical history. A list of medication he was on to manage his diabetes and hypertension, anxiety pills and something for depression, high dose opioids for the pain. His blood alcohol level four times over the legal limit. Enough to cause serious interactions with his prescribed coping mechanisms, Zigic guessed.

'Cause of death, gunshot wound to the head,' Ferreira said flatly. 'Hold on, what's this polyethylene residue they recovered from the wound?'

Zigic found the section she was looking at, read on.

"Polyethylene is a commonly occurring compound in pipe lagging. In this context it usually suggests the use of an improvised silencer.'

'Fucking hell.' Ferreira's eyes were wide and lit with urgency. 'Caxton didn't commit suicide. Someone killed him.'

'And then took the silencer away with them, so we'd put it down to suicide.' Zigic nodded slowly, imagining Caxton's killer removing the length of grey pipe from the muzzle of the gun, wondered if it felt hot against their hand, if that residual burn had been painful. If it left a mark. 'You know what this means?'

He watched her work through it. 'Humble and some mystery second man broke into the airfield.'

'Right.'

'And *they* were worried about Jordan getting too close the truth – identifying them even – so *they* killed Jordan to stop the story coming out?'

'Yep.'

'And then *they* killed Caxton, making it look like suicide so there're no loose ends. But Caxton is completely uninvolved? He's just a scapegoat?'

'Caxton takes the fall for everything and we close the case,' Zigic said, finding it sounded right. 'Humble and his accomplice get to go back to their lives.'

Ferreira smiled tightly. 'That's what they think.'

Humble had switched chairs since they'd left him almost two hours ago, was sat closer to the wall now, looking bulkier trapped between the table and his solicitor. Jo Tate was former CPS, a smart and capable prosecutor who'd turned defender a couple of years ago. Zigic had worked with her before and trusted her to give Humble the best advice for his situation. Knew her old loyalties didn't run as deep as a lot of detectives would like.

But Zigic didn't need her to do his job for him.

She just had to provide the required support for Humble and stay out of the man's way as he finally told the truth.

Ferreira set the tapes up and Zigic watched Humble as he stated his name, seeing the same unease as when they'd left the room but no signs of a change in the man.

'So,' Ferreira said. 'Let's pick up where we left off, shall we? You were about to explain what exactly you were doing breaking into a hangar at Holme Airfield in the early hours of the morning of January 2nd, 2016.'

'That was me,' Humble said weakly. 'On the camera there.'

'We've already established that, Mr Humble,' Ferreira told him. 'Why were you breaking into the hangar?'

Humble cleared his throat. 'We were short of money. We thought there might be some kit in there we could steal and sell on. We took some tools and some money from the petty cash box in the office.'

Next to him Jo Tate's expression was neutral and Zigic guessed she probably believed Humble's story, that he wouldn't have told her much more than the version he'd decided upon all that time ago.

'You're claiming this was a burglary?' Ferreira asked.

'Yes.'

'How many places had you broken into before this?'

Humble rubbed his hands together. 'We'd never done anything like that before. I didn't want to do it then either but I was getting desperate for money. I'd kept applying for jobs and not getting them. My wife was keeping us afloat but I didn't like her having so much pressure on her. I'm not trying to excuse what I did.'

'Who's the other half of this "we"?'

'Dick,' Humble said, as if it was obvious.

'How did you come to chose that particular place to rob?' Ferreira asked.

'It was out of the way,' Humble said dismissively. 'Dick thought it would have some expensive stuff laying around.'

'Pretty specialised stuff,' Ferreira suggested. 'Surely you'd have been better off stealing things that'd be easy to sell.'

'Mr Humble has explained what happened,' Jo Tate interjected. 'I don't see that you have any further reason to question him. I suggest you charge him with the offence and we can all get on with our day.'

'Did you know Holme Airfield was where Marcus Greenaway stored his helicopter?'

'No,' Humble said quickly. 'I barely knew the place existed before Dick mentioned it.'

'How is that relevant?' Tate asked.

'Didn't your client explain?' Ferreira frowned. 'Mr Humble is suspected of involvement in the sabotage of Marcus Greenaway's helicopter. An act which led to Greenaway's death.'

Jo Tate gave her a thin smile. 'And do you have an evidence to support that?'

'We'll get to it,' Ferreira assured her, knowing they didn't. She opened the file she'd brought in with her, removed the still from Holme Airfield and pushed it over to Humble once again. 'Just for the record, please. Is this man, you?'

'Yes, I already told you.'

She tapped the second man. 'And this is Richard Caxton?'

'Yes.'

'No,' Ferreira said.

'It is.' Humble directing the words to his solicitor more than Ferreira.

'This man is around five eight, going by the fixed dimensions of the door frame,' she explained. 'And Richard Caxton was six one. *This* isn't Dick.'

Humble swallowed hard.

'So, who is it?'

'I just told you.'

'No, you just lied to us,' Ferreira said firmly. 'Which means you tried to put the blame on Dick because he's dead and he can't defend himself. Because you're trying to cover for whoever you were really with and that suggests you were doing something rather more serious than a spot of tool theft.'

Humble turned to Jo Tate. 'Do I have to tell them?'

'It's your decision,' she said.

'I've admitted what I did.' Humble drew himself up straighter in the chair. 'I'm not saying anything more.'

Here was the man Zigic had seen in the interview with DI Sawyer, loyal to his compatriots when they'd been harassing Marcus Greenaway and his family. Refusing to name a ringleader, refusing to give Sawyer what she wanted in return for leniency.

'Fine.' Ferreira shot him a withering look. 'Can you tell us where you were on the night of Saturday, November 30th, between 8 p.m. and 11 p.m.?'

'Saturday gone?' Humble asked and she nodded. He seemed perplexed, glanced at Tate but got no assistance from her. 'That's when Dick killed himself.'

'Dick didn't kill himself,' Ferreira said. 'He was murdered.'

Humble huffed out a big breath, shock all over his face. 'No, that can't be right. Are you sure?'

'We're positive. Somebody shot Dick in the head and tried to make it look like suicide. Not very successfully.' Ferreira opened up her hands. 'So, where were you?'

For a moment he didn't reply. Zigic expected to see fear or the rapid eye movements of somebody scrambling for an alibi but instead he saw only shock. Humble trying and failing to process what he'd been told.

'Usually innocent people can tell us where they were,' Ferreira pressed.

Humble snapped out of it. 'I was in London, with my wife. She bought me tickets to *Jersey Boys* for my birthday last month.'

'You'd have been home before midnight though,' Ferreira said.

'We stayed over.' He gestured, vaguely frustrated. 'Did a bit of window shopping, went round a couple of galleries.'

'Where did you stay?'

'The Premier Inn on Leicester Square.'

Zigic noticed a near imperceptible slump across Ferreira's shoulders. Humble's story too strong not to be true.

'Just because you checked into a hotel it doesn't mean you stayed the whole night,' she said.

Humble glared at her. 'We got talking to a couple in the hotel bar. We were there till gone one.'

'And can they vouch for you?'

'My wife can vouch for me,' Humble said fiercely. 'My credit card can vouch for me. And I'm not a detective but I'd imagine the security cameras in the hotel could vouch for me if you went to the trouble to contact them.'

'We will,' Ferreira told him, irritation coming into her voice now, the pendulum swinging into Humble's favour, the balance of the interrogation shifting in a direction she wasn't happy with or prepared for.

'That clears that up, then,' Jo Tate said pleasantly. 'Now, is there anything else you'd like to speculatively accuse my client of or are we done?'

Ferreira settled back in the chair, looking relaxed but Zigic knew she was buying time, thinking, just like he was, of where they would go next. And the longer she waited the more agitated Humble became, eyes straying to the door, clasped hands knocking gently against the tabletop.

'Dick was murdered,' she said, eyes fixed on Humble. 'You understand what this means, don't you?'

'Mr Humble has an alibi for the time in question,' Jo Tate reminded him.

'Friday night at the Club,' Ferreira went on. 'Dick argued with Steve Gurney, what was that about?'

Humble's brows drew together. 'The usual rubbish.'

'That's not an answer,' Ferreira said sharply. 'Gurney and Dick fought, twenty-four hours later Dick was shot in the head. You need to tell us what was going on with the two of them.'

Humble shrugged, helpless-looking. 'I don't know. They just blew up. Me and McLeary pulled them apart and that was an end to it.'

'You pulled them apart?'

He nodded.

'Then you must have been close enough to know what they were saying to one another.' Ferreira looked reasonable. 'What was it?'

'I don't know,' he insisted, but his tone wavered and he looked away from them.

'Was it about Jordan?' Ferreira asked.

'I didn't hear what they were saying.'

'Or was it about Marcus Greenaway?'

Jo Tate placed her hand on the table. 'Mr Humble has admitted to being responsible for this break-in. And since he has an alibi for the murder you're investigating, I can't see any good reason for you to keep questioning him about some altercation he clearly has no more information about.'

Ferreira scowled at her, then turned sharply back to Humble.

'Don't you care about what happened to Dick?' she asked. 'He's supposed to be your friend and someone murdered him. If it *was* Steve Gurney, don't you want to see him punished for that?'

'Steve wouldn't,' he said falteringly. 'It was just a game of darts. They were arguing about the darts.'

'You think that's why Dick was killed?' Ferreira said, letting her disbelief show. 'No, Bruce. Jordan Radley was investigating the circumstances around Marcus Greenaway's death and he got shot for it. Then someone walked into Dick's room and shot *him* in the head, using a gun fitted with a home-made silencer.' He seemed unable to look away from her now. 'Whoever did that wanted us to think Dick killed himself.'

A queasy expression twisted Humble's face, but he said nothing.

'Now, you were close to Dick, you know he wasn't living a full and complicated life. He went to work and he went to your club. Not much opportunity to pick up enemies anywhere else. So, if he *was* shot by someone from the Club, you owe it to Dick to tell us whatever you know.'

Humble slumped in the chair, swiped one big hand down his face. 'I don't know what was going on with Dick. We were mates, alright, and I *thought* I knew him, but now you're saying he shot Jordan. That isn't the Dick I knew.'

The words came out more regretful than accusatory, had the unmistakable ring of finality about them. Zigic knew that tone. Had heard it countless times over the years, the moment a suspect or a witness reached the end of their knowledge.

He might have believed it if Humble hadn't lied about Dick Caxton being with him during the burglary.

'Let's take a break,' he said.

'Can I go?' Humble asked, already rising from his chair.

'Not yet,' Zigic told him. 'You should take some time to think about whether whoever you're protecting is worth it, though. Because there's a good chance they killed Dick Caxton and if you keep covering for them, we'll be inclined to charge you as an accessory.'

Humble looked to his solicitor and she gave the barest nod.

'Yes, Bruce,' Zigic said. 'That's how it works.'

CHAPTER FIFTY-EIGHT

'Are you having an episode?' Murray asked, not looking up from her computer, fingers skipping over the keyboard. 'Or pulling a go-slow?'

'I'm thinking,' Ferreira said, toying with an elastic band.

'I dunno. Looks more like you're fannying about to me.'

Ferreira's eyes strayed to Dick Caxton's board. Nothing new to report since the post-mortem came in. Murray had been and questioned Caxton's neighbours. None reported seeing or hearing anything unusual the night Dick Caxton was shot. The same story for the night Jordan Radley was shot.

Despite the close proximity the people lived in, or maybe because of it, they seemed uninterested in monitoring their neighbours' movements.

Weller had returned from door-to-door around Jordan Radley's home, similarly lacking in new information.

'What are you thinking then?' Murray asked. 'I can hear the cogs turning.'

'I don't think Humble's a killer.' She'd been saying it in her head for a while and found she sounded even more certain voicing it out loud. 'I know we get caught out now and again but you can just see some people don't have it in them.'

Murray gave her a wry look. 'Your gut's tallying nicely with the evidence there, girl.'

Parr had been in touch with the Premier Inn on Leicester Square and they stumped up the security footage within twenty minutes. Bruce Humble and his wife sitting in the loudly decorated bar with another couple, things very friendly-looking, drinks going down at an impressive rate until well past 1 a.m. Then footage from the camera in the lift: Humble's wife kissing him, laughter, them stepping out of the lift holding hands.

A man without a care in the world.

'I meant with the Greenaway thing,' Ferreira said. 'We've got him breaking into the hangar with person unknown and we're thinking it was done to gain access to Greenaway's helicopter, but I just don't see that on him, you know? Actually killing someone.'

'Not like walking up to someone and stabbing them though, is it?' Murray asked. 'Bit of sabotage and the helicopter falls out the sky. That's impersonal. Cowardly. You get what you want but you can go off feeling like you didn't really do the deed.'

'It can't be a coincidence, right?'

Murray shook her head. 'Humble and some mystery fella breaking in two weeks before Greenaway crashes. No way that's a coincidence.'

Across the office Bloom let out a gasp.

'What is it, Keri?'

'I've found Caxton,' Bloom said, rising from her seat.

Ferreira went over to her desk. 'Where is he?'

'I did another pass on the CCTV but there was no sign of him, so I got in touch with the bus company.' She was talking fast, animated. 'And they sent over the footage from inside the vehicles that were running on the route between the Greenaway Club and Caxton's address and …'

She stepped aside to let Ferreira see the screen.

Dick Caxton, stooped and tired-looking, dropping some coins into the tray and taking a ticket from the driver. The time stamp in the corner of the screen showing 10:09 p.m.

'Six minutes before the people near the scene reported hearing gunshots,' Ferreira said. 'Caxton couldn't have shot Jordan.'

Zigic emerged from his office. 'What's this?'

Ferreira gestured him towards the screen and he stood with his arms folded, frowning deeply.

'Maybe we're wrong about the time,' Murray suggested. 'We've got a silencer used on Caxton. What about if the killer used it on Jordan and those gunshots we've been timing everything off of weren't gunshots at all?'

'But there was no residue recovered from Jordan's wounds,' Bloom pointed out. She glanced at Zigic for approval or agreement and he nodded. 'So, the killer must have been more concerned about a neighbour raising the alarm when he shot Richard Caxton and improvised a silencer to allow him a better chance of getting in and out without being seen by witnesses.'

'Stupid bastard,' Murray muttered. 'If he knew how to make one, he should have used it from the off.'

'I don't think we're dealing with a criminal mastermind here,' Zigic said.

He went over to Jordan Radley's board and removed Dick Caxton's photograph from the suspects column. The space empty again.

'Right,' he said sternly. 'Caxton's no longer a viable suspect, meaning we're in all likelihood looking for the same perpetrator in his murder *and* in Jordan's.'

'They stashed Jordan's stuff at his place to frame him and we bought it,' Murray said. 'You sure we're not looking for a criminal mastermind?'

'We're looking for someone who can think on their feet, but not very fast,' Zigic told her. 'And we're going to start with Lionel Ridgeon and Steve Gurney.'

He shifted their photographs into the suspects column and Ferreira thought immediately how right they looked there. More than Dick Caxton ever had with his bad back and his sad air and the obvious admiration he'd felt for Jordan.

'Gurney and Caxton had a bust-up at the Club,' she said. 'He's got to be prime suspect.'

'His alibi for the night of Jordan's murder was sketchy.' Parr rose from his desk and joined them at the board, everyone focused now. 'I talked to his wife and she said he was home when she got in but she couldn't give me a concrete time.'

'What about Ridgeon?' Murray asked.

'The wife corroborated.'

Ferreira thought of the interview with Ridgeon after he'd walked in on Dick Caxton's 'suicide'. His apparently stunned demeanour and his patience and how reluctantly he'd admitted that Caxton might be in the frame for Greenaway's death. Citing his interest in Jordan's story and his skill set as a toolmaker.

But Gurney was the one with blood on his clothes. Gurney who'd supposedly unthinkingly reached out and checked Caxton for a pulse despite the hole in the side of his head. Putting his DNA on the body. Giving them a solid explanation for why they'd find it there.

Gurney who'd gone toe to toe with Caxton. A physically frail man who only a bully would square up to.

Or someone terrified of what he might be about to say in front of a club full of witnesses.

'Okay,' Zigic said. 'Let's bring them in.'

CHAPTER FIFTY-NINE

'Here we go then,' Parr muttered as Ferreira pulled up behind the patrol car they'd trailed across the city centre and all the way to Lionel Ridgeon's home on Fletton Marina.

She got out of the car, Parr telling PCs Baxter and Hughes to go around the back in case Ridgeon decided to make a run for it, waited to hear the side gate bang before she knocked on the front door.

A moment later Lionel Ridgeon opened up, dressed in cut-off jeans shorts and a Van Halen T-shirt, a tea towel tossed over this shoulder.

'Alright,' he said, wary but polite. 'Is there summat up?'

'We have a few more questions for you,' Ferreira told him.

'Come on in then, I'll stick the kettle on.'

'Best we do this at the station,' she said. 'Shouldn't take long.'

Ridgeon frowned. 'What's this about?'

'We can discuss that at the station.' Ferreira handed him a search warrant. 'And I need you to acknowledge this before you go.'

He opened it but she could see he wasn't reading, just taking the pause. Weighing up his options, thinking about slamming the door in their faces maybe, tearing up the warrant. A common reaction usually stifled.

'I reckon I want to know what's going on before I go.' He crossed his arms.

Ferreira nodded at the navy blue Mini parked on the driveway. 'Is your wife at home?'

'She's nipped out.'

'I'm sure you'd rather spare her the unpleasantness of seeing you being bundled into the back of a police car,' Ferreira said gently. 'We're going to talk about Richard Caxton again and we can either take you in forcefully or you can cooperate, but you *are* coming with us, Mr Ridgeon.'

'Alright.' He sighed. 'Let's get this over and done with.'

Parr called Hughes and Baxter back and had them place him in the car. Ridgeon got in peaceably, a few curtains twitching in neighbouring houses as it became clear what was happening on this nice quiet close.

'Come on,' Ferreira said, leading Parr into the house.

'What are we looking for?'

'Our eyewitness has the suspect at the locus dressed all in black, wearing some kind of scarf or snood, and a woollen hat. That's what we're looking for.'

Parr headed up the stairs, Ferreira went through the kitchen into the small utility room at the back of the house. The washing machine was running, a white wash inside. The tumble dryer above it was empty. She pulled a pair of gloves on and began to rifle through the linen basket. It was mostly women's clothes. On a metal airer set close to the radiator, a dark wash was slowly drying, the items heavy and damp-feeling even through her gloves.

Jeans and jumpers but none of them dark enough to have been worn during the murder.

And how likely was it they'd only just been washed, she thought, when the crime was committed a week ago. Unless Ridgeon had put them through the machine again and again, hoping to comprehensively remove any trace of Jordan Radley's blood.

In the hallway she took a set of keys from the hook above the radiator and went outside. She unlocked the garage door and hauled it open onto Ridgeon's workshop.

Everything laid out just so. Metal shelving units filled with clear plastic boxes stood along the right wall. A hefty workbench along the left. Three different-sized vices were clamped to its thick wooden top. Ridgeon's tools all hanging from hooks in a long strip of white pegboard.

Ferreira went over to the drills. She didn't know exactly what kind you'd use to bore out the barrel of a replica pistol, but felt sure that there would be something suitable among the extensive collection of tools and the bits boxed up underneath them.

She called for a SOCO team.

If there was anything that could link Ridgeon to the gun, they'd find it.

As she was dragging the garage door back into position, swearing as it stuck, she heard the fast click of high heels coming up the path behind her.

'What the bloody hell are you doing in my garage?'

Patti Ridgeon was fierce-looking in white jeans and vertiginous snakeskin boots, swaddled in a teddy-bear fur jacket. Early fifties behind her mirrored aviators, Ferreira guessed, with platinum hair in a shaggy bob and her face perfectly made up for a quick trip to the shop, judging by the bulging tote bag she carried.

She was a hairdresser, Parr had said, and Ferreira could see it. A woman concerned with her appearance and making no concession to low-key good taste or the dictates of age-appropriate style.

'DS Ferreira.' She held up her ID. 'Lionel's helping us with our enquiries. He's on his way to the station now.'

'You've arrested him, you mean?' Patti said, eyes narrowing. 'What for? He's not done anything.'

'Maybe we should talk inside.' Ferreira motioned for her to move, but Patti Ridgeon stayed firmly planted on the pavement. 'Mrs Ridgeon, I'm happy to do this in full sight of your neighbours if that's what you want and I'm happy to take this to the station as well, but all I need from you are some simple answers to some simple questions.'

Grudgingly Patti went inside and Ferreira followed her into the kitchen, where she slung her coat over the back of a chair and dumped the shopping on the worktop.

She stayed standing, arms folded, and Ferreira decided to give the ground, let Patti feel like she was in control in her own home. She pulled out a chair and sat down at the table.

'One of Lionel's friends – Dick Caxton – died at the weekend,' she said. 'How much has he told you about that?'

Patti's face softened slightly, from anger to concern. 'Lionel found him. It's not been easy on him, that. It's, uh, brought up a lot of old trauma.'

Ferreira nodded. 'He told us about his suicide attempt when we were here last.'

'He was doing alright until all that,' Patti said, red nails toying with the sleeve of her houndstooth jumper. 'Dick'd been a really good mate when he was in hospital. Going in and sitting with him, taking him magazines and that. I'd met him a few times there myself.' She shook her head. 'You could see he weren't happy and Lionel knew that but it was still one hell of a shock for him. I mean, you hear about it second-hand, that's one thing, but actually walking in and *finding* him.' Patti opened a drawer and took out a packet of cigarettes, lit one. 'He's not slept right since.'

Fear, Ferreira wondered. Or a guilty conscience?

'It's brought it all back,' Patti said, emotion clogging her voice. 'I can see on his face he's reliving it all. Clear as day. All that with his wife and *everything*. And I say to him, "Babe, just talk to me," but he won't. And I know he's only trying to protect me but I'm worried about him. You look at him and you see this big tough fella, but he's a pussycat. Totally. I've seen him cry at toilet roll adverts for Christ's sake.'

She'd be a good hairdresser to go to, Ferreira thought. Would talk throughout your appointment and save you the trouble of making conversation. If they didn't wind up arresting Lionel, she might switch salons.

'He's not said anything about it?' Ferreira asked.

Patti shook her head, taking a drag on her cigarette. 'He was the same about the young mate of his that was killed. The one that was in the paper, Jordan. I do a lady who worked at the college where he went. She's in the coffee shop. Said he was a lovely young lad. He never had much money so she'd always give him a large for the price of a regular.' Patti pushed away from the worktop with a start. 'He was shot, right?'

'Yeah.'

'And Dick shot himself?' Pointing at her with the cigarette. 'Do you think they're connected?'

'We're not in a position to say just yet,' Ferreira told her, seeing a new intensity in her heavily kohled eyes. Not suspicion, she thought, just the innocent curiosity of a gossip fastening on something juicy she could share in the salon tomorrow. 'How much did Lionel tell you about Jordan?'

She settled back again, gave a slight shrug. 'Only what a nice boy he was. Seems to me that he was a bit lost, though. We thought he was looking for a father figure or something.' She lowered her voice. 'No dad at home, you know.'

A car pulled up outside, a second vehicle following. SOCO arriving.

Ferreira took her notebook out, saw Patti's demeanour shift immediately. Chat over, official business beginning.

'Okay, I just need to ask you a couple of things,' Ferreira said smoothly. 'Standard procedure, nothing to worry about.'

Patti stubbed her cigarette out.

'Where were you on Saturday night?'

'Why does that matter?'

'When somebody dies we have to build a picture of where the person or people who found them were at the time of their death,' Ferreira told her, trying to maintain a casual tone. 'So we need to know where Lionel was.'

'We were at home,' Patti said quickly.

'All night?'

She pursed her lips and Ferreira could see her debating how much to say, knew there was something she wanted to keep back but maybe didn't dare to.

'You do this for suicides?' she asked.

'All gunshot deaths are treated as suspicious,' Ferreira explained. 'The presence of an illegal firearm means we have to be very particular. Did you go out at any point on Saturday night?'

'No,' she said slowly. 'Lionel went over the chippie on the big estate but that was it. We were in all night.'

'Which chippie?'

Patti told her. A busy shop on a dodgy road, one that would have a security camera, Ferreira thought.

'What time was this?'

'About eight,' Patti said. 'I couldn't be faffed cooking.'

The post-mortem had put Dick Caxton's death between 8 p.m. and 11 p.m. but Ferreira struggled to imagine a sequence of events leading up to murder that would involve stopping off at a chip shop.

'What time did Lionel get back?' she asked.

'Before 9,' Patti said. 'There's always a massive queue. It's because they use beef dripping. The chips taste better.'

Ferreira nodded, writing everything down except the dripping.

She stood up, slipping her notebook into her bag, and thanked Patti Ridgeon for her help, getting a nervous look by way of reply.

'This is just procedure, right?' she said, as Ferreira went out through the front door, eyeing up the scientific support van and Kate Jenkins suiting up at the boot of her car.

'Just procedure,' Ferreira reassured her.

As she pulled away from the house, she glanced back in her rear-view mirror and saw Parr out on the front lawn with Patti Ridgeon, explaining that the searching of her house was just procedure too, Ferreira guessed.

CHAPTER SIXTY

'Fucking come off it,' Steve Gurney said, throwing his trowel down into a bucket of mortar. He got to his feet, steadying himself on the low wall in front of his house that he'd been repointing when they pulled up. 'Can't you see I'm in the middle of something.'

'State of that wall, I reckon it can wait a few more hours,' Murray said, nodding at the gaping crack in the brickwork.

Gurney turned to Zigic. 'I've got the estate agents coming round tomorrow.'

'Then they'll have to wait as well,' Murray told him.

'No.' Gurney dropped back into a crouch and retrieved his pointing trowel, started smearing mortar into the crack. 'You want to talk to me, you can do it here.'

Murray leaned down, into his face, and Zigic was shocked to see the anger on her.

'We'll talk to you wherever *we* fucking decide,' she snapped. 'Now, on your feet.'

Gurney's eyes widened, his hand curling tighter around the handle of the trowel. The two PCs moved in on him but Murray didn't step back, just stared down at him, wearing a vaguely contemptuous smile as he gathered himself with some visible effort, carefully placing the trowel in the bucket this time and standing up.

The front door opened and a woman in a dressing gown and fluffy slippers appeared, light brown hair scraped back off her long face and her nose pink as she dabbed at it with a tissue.

'Steve, what's going on?'

'Go back inside, love,' he said too brightly. 'The detectives just need to have a word with me. Nothing for you to worry about. Go on in, now. Don't get yourself cold.'

The woman closed the door.

'Take him in,' Murray said to the PCs.

Zigic watched Gurney being led to the car, wiping his hands on the back of his jeans, looking around to see which of his neighbours might have witnessed the scene.

As the patrol car pulled away Zigic and Murray went to the front door and he knocked, told Murray to take the lead.

'Hazel, is it?' she asked, when the door opened again. 'You mind if we come in for a minute?'

Hazel nodded, let them in and led them through to the living room that looked like it hadn't been decorated since the eighties. Floral wallpaper at the top, striped at the bottom, separated by a dark-stained dado rail. Heavily patterned curtains were drawn at the bay window, the only light coming from a couple of brass-based lamps with fringed shades.

Strange decor for a couple in their early fifties and Zigic supposed it explained Steve Gurney's zealous home improvement activities.

'Sorry about the mess, I'm full of flu.' She hastily folded up the blanket she'd been sitting under on the sofa, gathered up the spent tissues and tucked them into the pocket of her pink waffle dressing gown. 'Have a seat. Can I get you a cup of tea?'

'We're okay, thanks,' Murray told her, taking one of the armchairs, Zigic moving to the other. 'Nasty, this flu that's going around. You getting plenty of fluids?'

'That's about all I can manage at the moment.'

She hadn't asked why they'd taken in her husband and Zigic wondered how long they could talk about other things before she'd finally crack. And if she'd believed Steve when he insisted it was nothing.

'How long have you had it?' Murray asked.

'Five days now,' Hazel said, smoothing her hand back over her unwashed hair. 'I need to get back to work really but they've told me not to come in until I'm ready. I think they're worried I'm going to give the rest of the office the plague. This is the first morning I've been able to get out of bed.'

Meaning she would have been like this on Saturday night, Zigic realised.

'Did Steve tell you what happened to his mate?' Murray asked.

'It's so sad.' Hazel dabbed at her nose again. 'There isn't enough help for people going through mental health crises. It makes me want to weep, thinking of anyone going through that alone. Can you imagine it? Feeling desperate enough to take your own life?'

Murray made the right noises.

Zigic thought of what they'd been told about Hazel Gurney's reaction to the article Jordan had written in the *Big Issue*. Everyone insisting she'd been livid with Steve for baring his soul there, talking about his own depression so publicly, and he struggled to square the image they'd been given of her with this woman in front of him. He knew she could be putting it on, saying what she thought they wanted to hear, but he wasn't convinced.

'Steve had his own struggle with depression,' Zigic said.

'He's always been that way,' she told them. 'Some people turn it inwards and some people turn it out.'

'And he turned it out?' Murray asked.

Hazel looked spooked momentarily.

'We know about his record,' Murray said in a reassuring tone. 'Believe me, Hazel, I know all about being with a fella who channels his depression into dust-ups with other lads. They think they're hiding it acting all macho but we know, don't we? We can see the cry for help.'

'He always started on the tough nuts.' Hazel pressed her knuckles to her mouth. 'It was as if he *wanted* them to get the better of him.'

'Punishing himself.' Murray nodded her understanding. 'Can't have been easy for him after the factory shut down.'

'He's a proud man,' Hazel said regretfully. 'They all were. People see a factory close down and they think, oh, they're only manual workers, they'll find some other crappy job. But they were *engineers*. They had good, highly skilled jobs. Good pay.

Respectable jobs.' Her voice was heating up and Zigic wondered how many times she'd heard this from her husband, how many times she'd said the same thing to other people in defence of him. 'Being an engineer was such a big part of Steve's identity, then ... it went away and he, I mean, lots of them, I suppose, they didn't know who they were any more.' She pursed her lips thoughtfully, the skin cracked and dry. 'Steve said Dick was always saying it. He'd been one of the most skilled men at Greenaway and then suddenly all he's fit for is stacking shelves in a supermarket. That does something to a man.'

'There's nothing wrong with working in a supermarket,' Zigic pointed out. 'Lots of people do it.'

'But it's not *man's* work, is it?' Hazel protested, turning to Murray, expecting her to understand. 'You know how they are. They need to be the breadwinner.'

'My old man was like that,' Murray said. 'He couldn't cope with me earning more than him. Drove him wild, it did.'

Hazel squirmed. 'Steve isn't like that. He just wanted another job as good as the one he had, but there's nothing here for someone with his skills any more. It's all distribution centres and retail. One of the agencies he went to even suggested he try taking some seasonal fruit-picking to tide him over.'

'Is he working now?' Murray asked.

'I can keep us going,' Hazel told her.

'Must be tough running the house on your own.'

'It was my mum and dad's place.' Hazel looked around the room, smiling fondly. 'We lost our home after the factory shut. We were in Werrington before. A lovely cottage in the old village.'

There was pride in her voice and now Gurney's simmering sense of injustice made sense. This was a nice area, quiet and decent, but it wasn't as affluent as where they'd come from, didn't have the cachet of the house they'd lost. Evidently that loss had weighed heavy on Steve Gurney and maybe the fact of being saved by an inheritance from his in-laws didn't help either.

It hadn't driven him back to work though. Hadn't made him swallow his pride and do a job that millions of other people went to every day without it destroying their ego.

For all that Hazel wanted to defend him, Steve Gurney had decided to let her bear their financial burdens alone rather than take a job he thought was beneath him.

'Poor Dick didn't have anyone to help him through it,' she said. 'You know his wife left him within weeks of him losing his job? What kind of woman does that?'

An unhappy one, Zigic thought.

'How's Steve coping?' Murray asked. 'It can't have been easy finding his mate like that.'

'He's holding it together,' Hazel said. 'He's been a bit quiet, I suppose, but I've not really been good company these last few days.'

For a moment nobody spoke, Murray knowing that they'd reached the point where things would become official. No more poking around the edges of the couple's life, probing her for background information they might use in Gurney's interview. The things that would tell them what kind of man he was.

Now they needed hard facts.

'Saturday night,' Zigic said. 'Between eight and eleven. Where was Steve?'

'Here.'

He expected her to ask why it mattered, challenge them or at least show some curiosity but none came.

'All night?'

'Yes.'

'How could you be certain about that?' he asked. 'You've just told us you were in bed.'

'He was here,' she insisted. 'He didn't have any reason to go out.'

It was a thin denial, Zigic thought. And wasn't backed up with some story of him bringing her a hot chocolate at ten or another dose of aspirin at eleven. None of the things a good husband did when his wife was ill in bed. He hadn't kept her company. Apparently hadn't checked in on her during that vital three-hour period.

Ambivalence didn't make him a killer but it gave them a window of opportunity.

370

And it told them Hazel wouldn't lie for her husband.

Zigic stood up, Murray following as he thanked Hazel for speaking to them, seeing the relief soften her face.

'Is that everything?' she asked.

'Not quite,' Murray said, taking the search warrant from her handbag.

CHAPTER SIXTY-ONE

Ferreira was on him the second they walked into the office, Steve Gurney heading down to the cells, a solicitor already called for his interrogation.

'Humble wants to talk to us,' she said eagerly. 'It sounds like he's ready to confess.'

'To what?' Zigic asked.

She smiled. 'Only one way to find out.'

A few minutes later they were seated in Interview Room 2 with the tapes rolling. Humble ashen-skinned and slack-faced, staring into the tabletop, his decision apparently made but maybe now they were actually here, the reality was hitting home. Next to him Jo Tate sat very straight in her chair, hands clasped in her lap. No notepad now, nothing to challenge or question, Zigic guessed. Humble had run this past her already and she'd seen the logic of it, advised him to go ahead.

Zigic felt a stirring of hope in his gut. A small prickle of pre-emptive triumph thinking that their previous interview with Humble had been working away on him as he sat alone in a cell in the basement.

'Mr Humble has opted to make a statement regarding the sabotage of a helicopter belonging to Marcus Greenaway,' Tate said in a neutral voice. 'We trust that his decision to cooperate fully with your investigation will be appreciated as a sincere effort to make amends for the *very* minor part he played in the unfolding of this unfortunate incident.'

Humble's forearms were flat on the white melamine surface, next to an empty water bottle.

'Whenever you're ready, Bruce,' Ferreira prompted.

He bunched his fists in front of his mouth, brows drawn down.

'You have to understand,' Humble said slowly. 'We weren't in our right minds. The factory had been shut six months. We were angry when it happened but we thought we'd be okay. We'd find other jobs, pick ourselves up. But it wasn't happening. There wasn't anything out there for blokes like us. Even me. It was all minimum wage. Zero-hours contracts. Getting treated like shit. How can you rebuild your life with jobs like that?'

Zigic nodded, showing him a sympathetic face because he *did* get it. How that must have felt to them, the sudden upending of their lives. But it wasn't the hardship Humble was making it out to be. It was just life. The one most people lived now, frustrated and insecure, pay cheque to pay cheque. Not good enough to make you happy but not bad enough to justify murder.

'We'd all been fucked over but nobody cared,' Humble said, sadness rather than anger in his voice. 'We'd protested – peacefully – and we'd been punished for that. Knocked about, thrown off the site, threatened with all sorts of legal action we couldn't afford to defend.' His nostrils flared and Zigic could see him fighting the urge to say what he really wanted to, blame them for it because it was people just like them who'd waded in with batons to break up the protest. Under orders but maybe enjoying it too much for anyone's comfort. 'We're on our knees and there's Greenaway all over the news boasting about the redevelopment of *our* factory into "luxury apartments".'

He wiped his mouth on the back of his hand.

'We'd been giving him some stick,' Humble said, shifting his gaze to Ferreira. 'But it didn't feel like enough. Smash his car? He can afford a hundred cars like that. Put in the windows at his solicitor's office? They've got insurance.'

Jo Tate frowned, her displeasure obvious but he had probably tarred her with the same brush as them the minute she walked in.

'Then we got arrested.'

For a moment he said nothing more and Zigic thought about the two weeks he'd spent in a category C out in the Northamptonshire countryside, an open prison for old men and white-collar criminals. Hardly a punishment but it would have felt like one to Humble. He could see it on him now, the remembered sting of it, the shame.

'After I got out my wife told me to put it in the past. Find another job, knuckle down. Forget about that part of my life. She didn't even want me going to the Club. She thought I was "wallowing".' He was bitter-sounding, resentful. 'She didn't get it. That place *was* my life.'

Ferreira wanted to interject, Zigic saw, but she stopped herself, parked the questions for later, knowing that they needed to let him speak for now. Give the version of events he was prepared to commit to the record. They could unpick it later, if necessary.

'Most of the lads were getting the same thing at home. Move on. Man up. Stop moaning. The Club got busier because it was the only place you could talk about it with people who understood how you were feeling.' He shook his head. 'I don't think any of the women understood what it felt like to go to work one morning and find yourself shut out of the place you'd given decades to. It didn't feel like a job, it was more than that. I spent more time there than I did at home.' His eyes tightened, face pained as he searched for the right words. 'It was like coming home and finding all your stuff out on the road and knowing there was nowhere else to go. You were nothing suddenly.'

Humble was justifying himself now, Zigic thought. Maybe to them or maybe to himself. But Zigic heard too much guilt in the explanation to be swayed by it.

He tried to put himself in Humble's place. Imagined coming to work tomorrow morning only to be locked out of the station, the office closed. But he realised he had other options. Another station would take him on. His experience and education would likely find him a decent position somewhere.

Perhaps that feeling of uselessness had fed into Humble's already burning sense of injustice? An additional, fatal prick to his ego, which had made violence seem like the only remedy. But you would have to be primed for it already, he thought. Would have to be someone who believed your own pain deserved pain given in response.

DI Sawyer had seen it, Zigic realised. Remembering how she'd challenged Humble when he'd made the same thin justifications during the original harassment interrogation.

'You spent years building automation systems that robbed *thousands* of people of their jobs,' she'd told Humble. 'They didn't attack their bosses' homes and terrify their families. What makes *you* so special?'

After all these years Humble still didn't have an answer.

'We were all pretty drunk,' he said gravely. 'It was late and we were joking about how we'd kill Greenaway.' A sickened expression twisted his face; guilt for thinking it or guilt for admitting it to them, Zigic wasn't sure. 'We did that a lot. Blowing off steam, you know? How we'd burn his house down or cut his brake lines. Stupid, angry shit, but we were never serious.'

Ferreira's eyebrow lifted a millimetre or so before she lowered it again. Humble hadn't seen though, too focused on the blank white surface of the table he was addressing now.

'Then out of nowhere Dick says, "His helicopter's where he's vulnerable." And it was different all of a sudden. No more joking. I sobered up like *that*.' His gaze stayed fixed on the tabletop. 'Steve said he knew how to sabotage it so it would look like an accident. Which part would need to be weakened. Where we could buy a spare, age it up, introduce a flaw. I realised he wasn't making it up on the fly. He'd been thinking it through. He explained how easily the piece could be replaced. Twenty minutes, he said, maybe half an hour. That was all we'd need.' He pressed his big hands together and Zigic saw that he was trembling. 'Dick asked about security and Lionel said his brother was an alarm technician. All we needed was the spec and he'd be able to get us the installer's override codes. Within ten minutes they had it all worked out.'

'And where did you fit into this?' Ferreira asked.

'Logistics. I got hold of a van,' he said. 'Got rid of it when we were done.'

'You did a bit more than that,' Ferreira reminded him. 'We've got you on camera, remember?'

'I'm not denying involvement. I did my bit. Went along with Steve and broke into the hangar. Acted as lookout while he replaced the part with one Dick and Lionel had tampered with.' He looked to Zigic. 'Like I said, we weren't thinking straight.'

'You put a lot of trust in one another,' Zigic suggested.

Humble shrugged as if it was the most natural thing in the world. 'We were friends.'

'And now you're not.'

'No.' He rubbed his face, palm rasping over a day's worth of stubble. 'Bloody Jordan coming in and stirring it all up again.'

'Is that why he was killed?' Ferreira asked.

'I don't know who killed him,' Humble said quickly. 'Or Dick. But I know for damn sure it must have been Steve or Lionel because nobody else had reason to do it.' His mouth twisted queasily. 'Greenaway was different. He brought it on himself. But Jordan was just a kid. He didn't deserve that.'

'The fight at the Club,' Ferreira prompted. 'Was that about Jordan?'

He hesitated, clearly still anchored in that world, if not as securely as before. So used to lying for his friends and covering for them that it took a clear force of will to get the words out now.

'Dick was in right state. He'd been putting down the drink, giving Steve the hairy eyeball all night. Then they start playing darts and Dick was winding him up, bumping into him. Then it gets serious.' He banged his fists together. 'I tried to break them up but they were about ready to kill one another.'

Still not saying it. Back in the moment, eyes unblinking, shoulders and arms tensing as if he was physically prising them apart again.

'What did Dick say?' Ferreira asked.

'He accused Steve of shooting Jordan.' Humble frowned. 'He said it quiet but I heard it. Steve told him not to be fucking soft. But Dick wasn't backing down. He said he'd had enough of lying for us all.' Humble sighed. 'He threatened to come and tell you everything.'

But he hadn't, Zigic thought. Then again, he'd not been given much chance. He threatened Steve Gurney on Friday night and was killed less than twenty-four hours later. Maybe he'd woken up the next morning with a pounding hangover and no memory of what he'd said while he was drunk. No idea how much danger he'd put himself in.

Humble took a deep breath. 'Steve said if you grass us up …'

'What?' Ferreira asked, leaning forward slightly.

'Just that,' Humble told her. 'He didn't need to say it, did he?'

CHAPTER SIXTY-TWO

'Save yourselves the debrief,' Riggott said, as they went into his office. 'I saw you on the live feed there. Soft aul shite should have kept his mouth shut but we take our wins where they come, aye?'

He looked happier than Ferreira could remember having seen him for months. Years, maybe. She wondered what his reward from the Chief Constable would be for closing this case. So close to retirement there was no more career progression to be dangled like a carrot, no threatening stick to be lifted from his back.

A bottle and three glasses came out of his desk, and he poured stiff measures of whiskey it was too early for and neither of them wanted. Ferreira noticed the thin film of dust on her glass and wondered how long it had been since Riggott last saw fit to bless two of his officers with this little display of approval.

'It's still only Humble's say-so,' she said, wanting to puncture the elation lighting his face. 'We've not got any actual evidence to back his statement up.'

'Sure, haven't you got the CCTV footage?' Riggott said, raising his glass. '*Slainte.*'

She raised her own glass the minimum required distance, saw Zigic do the same. As close to a protest as they could get away with at the moment.

'All the CCTV footage shows is Humble and Gurney breaking into the hangar,' she went on. 'And Gurney's unidentifiable. Even if Gurney admits he was there, he can claim they broke in to steal some tools they flogged off because they were both short of money. I don't see how we can prove he's lying.'

'You won't need to prove it,' Riggott said, giving her a pointed look. 'You've done your piece. Not your place to worry about how the next part of the process develops.'

She threw back her whiskey, hating the taste of it but the burn down her throat felt pleasantly raw. Almost hot enough to scorch away what she wanted to say to him.

'And what about the contamination at the Stillwater Rise site?' she asked. 'The two men who were poisoned. Is it my place to worry about *that*?'

'We've got the soil tests back over the weekend,' Zigic explained, as Riggott's face darkened and he reached for the bottle again to pour himself a second drink. 'The levels of hazardous chemicals are exactly the same as they were before work started on site.'

'And we've got a statement from a senior respiratory infections specialist at Addenbrooke's stating that they pose a serious and ongoing threat to human health,' Ferreira added. 'Not an anonymous source. This guy's prepared to stand up and say his piece in the public arena.'

Riggott stared into his drink, looking like he was willing them out of his office.

'Docherty Construction haven't done *any* remedial work,' Ferreira went on. 'They were given a schedule of work by an environmental engineering firm and they ignored it. Despite the fact that their planning permission requires the site be decontaminated before any above-ground development begins.' She placed her empty glass on his desk. 'They've broken the law and, in this case, we actually *can* prove it. We have to arrest them.'

Riggott filled her glass again.

'I wasn't asking for a top-up,' she said.

'You'll be needing it,' he warned, slipping the bottle away into his drawer, sliding it home with deliberate slowness, his expression clouding over. 'I've spoken to the Chief Constable about this –'

Ferreira swore.

'Aye, he's that alright,' Riggott said. 'But he's still your boss and my boss and he holds a sight more sway over our futures than

379

I think you'd be comfortable accepting.' He pointed at her over the rim of his glass. 'There's none of us could stand him taking against us, Mel.'

The word hung between the two of them unspoken.

Murder.

Riggott doing her the courtesy of not spelling it out in front of Zigic but even that felt threatening in its way. A warning that if it came out she would have to deal with Zigic's reaction as well as everyone else's.

'The Chief Constable's vetoing the charge against Docherty Construction?' Zigic asked.

'Not officially,' Riggott said. 'But he made well fucking sure I appreciated how much of our budget would get sunk into a prosecution he felt was doomed to failure.' He frowned. 'We've lost London Road Station, we can't afford to take another hit.'

'He's blackmailing us,' Ferreira said incredulously.

Riggott gave her a thin, humourless smile. 'Sure, it's not like that now, is it? He's *appraising* us of the financial fitness of our station as we move into a challenging period of privatisation and increasing social instability. He just wants us to *understand* that any budget shortfall caused by undertaking a protracted and complex investigation into an environmental incident will need to be made up in the next fiscal year.'

'With job cuts?' Zigic asked.

'Aye, son. Significant job cuts.'

'If the rest of the station knew we were being pressurised into dropping an investigation into his rich mates, he wouldn't need to worry about cutting jobs to balance the books,' Ferreira said fiercely. 'He'd have a bunch of resignations on his hands.'

'Catch yerself on, Mel. There's not a man or woman in this station can afford to make a stand over something like this.' Riggott swirled the last few millimetres of whiskey around in his glass. 'Not professionally and not financially.'

Zigic sighed and she knew he'd already been here with Riggott. Had argued the toss days ago and run into the sheer, inescapable force of the Greenaways' influence.

It didn't help that they'd colluded with that influence the moment they opened a murder investigation into Marcus Greenaway's then entirely accidental death. Signalled their willingness to play the politics game.

Perversely, finding his killer had only made the situation worse, she thought. Because now the Greenaways would be delighted with the Chief Constable. He'd proven himself useful and he wouldn't want to slip out of their good graces with something as damaging as the case she was proposing.

Everyone's hands were tied now.

All but Rachel Greenaway and Hugo Docherty. Filthy and blooded, their hands were still free to do whatever they wanted.

CHAPTER SIXTY-THREE

'We have to go for Gurney first, right?' Ferreira asked, her voice still sharp from their talk with Riggott, but Zigic saw the fresh energy on her, the anger she was metabolising and turning onto a new target.

'Non-existent alibi and Humble says he threatened Caxton at the Club.' Zigic nodded. 'He's the most likely of the pair.'

The SOCO team at Gurney's house had returned with some clothes and a few tools from his garden shed, hopeful of finding trace evidence on them that would link him to one of the murders. There were drill bits the right size for the barrel of the murder weapon but they would take time to examine.

The same story with Lionel Ridgeon's place.

Parr had written the name of the chip shop Ridgeon had visited on the evening of Caxton's murder under his photo in the suspect's column. No security footage, no hard and fast evidence to give them a time, but the owner said he'd been in, bought his usual: one cod and chips, one battered sausage and chips.

It didn't mean he wasn't guilty.

They had Steve Gurney brought up from the cells and placed in Interview Room 1, gave his solicitor a few minutes with him while they waited in the hallway; Ferreira sitting on the radiator, Zigic leaning against the wall, thinking of how the confines of a cell had worked on Bruce Humble's conscience. Hoping they might pull a similar trick on Gurney.

But when they went inside he was all defiance, sitting ramrod straight in the chair, hands tightly clasped on the table. His head whipped towards them.

'What's with the wait?' he demanded. 'I've stuff to do.'

'This shouldn't take long,' Ferreira assured him, sliding into her own seat. 'Just a few questions.'

She set up the tapes, closely watched by the solicitor, Ms Jellen, as if she suspected some chicanery might be in the offing. When she stated her name it was in a rich, plummy voice that perfectly matched her austere navy-blue suit and the severe chignon her auburn hair was swept into.

'The first matter I think we should put to rest is Marcus Greenaway's death.' Ferreira took out the photograph of Gurney and Bruce Humble breaking into the hangar at Holme Airfield and slid it across the table. 'This is you and Bruce gaining access to the building where the helicopter was stored.'

Gurney swallowed hard, said nothing.

'That's okay, we don't need you to admit it,' Ferreira told him.

'You have a man you claim to be Mr Gurney entering a barn,' Ms Jellen said flatly. 'That is an awful long way from murder. Or is it manslaughter? You didn't clarify.'

Ferreira ignored her and Zigic saw how little she wanted to discuss the details of Greenaway's death, still stinging from their meeting with Riggott. But without this there was no route into Jordan Radley's and Dick Caxton's murders.

'We showed Bruce Humble this photo earlier today,' she said, staring at Gurney.

He lowered his eyes, remained silent.

'Mr Humble laid out for us, in very clear and precise detail, exactly how you and he came to be breaking into the hangar,' Ferreira explained. 'We know about the plan you concocted, along with Richard Caxton and Lionel Ridgeon. We know that you supplied the technical know-how on the Daedalus D55's weakness.' Ferreira slid a photograph of the crashed helicopter across the table. 'We know that Caxton and Ridgeon tampered with the part you identified as a weak spot and which you then replaced in Greenaway's machine during this break-in on the morning of January 2nd, 2016. You introduced a fatal flaw into Greenaway's helicopter,' Ferreira said, voice low and hard. 'Then you waited for it to fall out of the sky.'

Ms Jellen glanced at Gurney, a quick flicker of discomfort on her face. Zigic wasn't sure if it was because he'd kept this from her or if the mention of Marcus Greenaway had done it.

'This is why Jordan Radley was shot.' Ferreira steepled her fingers on the photograph. 'And this is why you framed Caxton for Radley's murder.'

'My understanding is that Mr Caxton committed suicide,' Ms Jellen said smoothly.

'I didn't kill Dick.' Gurney sounded weary and saddened, as if this was just the kind of thing he expected to happen to someone like him. 'Dick killed himself. He was off his head with grief or – I don't know, guilt – over Jordan, and he killed himself cos he couldn't hack it any more.'

Another photo came out of the file.

'This is Dick getting off a bus outside his house a few minutes prior to Jordan Radley's murder,' Ferreira said. 'It's impossible that he could have reached the crime scene within those few vital minutes.' She shoved the photo towards Gurney. 'Dick didn't shoot Jordan.'

'Then why'd he have a gun?' Gurney demanded.

'Exactly.' Ferreira nodded at him. 'How *did* the gun come to be in Caxton's bedsit? And how did a laptop stolen from Jordan Radley's house by his killer come to be hidden in a boarded-over fireplace there too?'

'I rather think it's your job to work that out, Sergeant,' Ms Jellen said, flicking an eyebrow up at her.

Ferreira gave Gurney a pointed look. 'I'd like Steve to tell me.'

'I don't know,' he said, discomfort rippling briefly across his shoulders.

Two more photos came out of the file.

'This is the head of one of the screws in the sheet of plyboard that had been used to cover up the fireplace in Caxton's bedsit,' Ferreira said. 'You'll notice the scratch marks where the paint came off when the screw was loosened.'

Gurney didn't even glance at it.

'And this photo shows a fleck of paint that was recovered from the knee of the jeans you were wearing when you "discovered"

Dick's body,' she told him. 'It's a perfect match for the paint that was chipped off this screw.'

'There are any number of ways Mr Gurney might have come to have paint on his jeans,' Ms Jellen protested. 'You can see that he's been doing DIY.'

Again Ferreira ignored the interjection.

'You unscrewed the panel over the fireplace when you shoved Jordan Radley's messenger bag in there,' she said, bringing out a photograph of the bag. 'You shot Caxton and then you hid the things you'd stolen from Jordan's house in the fireplace in an attempt to make us believe that Caxton was responsible for your crime.'

'No,' Gurney insisted. 'That's not how it happened.'

'Then how did it happen?'

'Presumably Mr Caxton had opened up the fireplace boarding to retrieve the gun he used to kill himself,' Ms Jellen suggested. 'It's quite feasible that when he did that some of the flakes were transferred onto other surfaces in the room where Mr Gurney subsequently came into contact with them.'

Gurney gave her a relieved look. 'Yeah, what she said.'

'We know you threatened to kill Dick,' Zigic told him. 'The night before he was shot dead, you warned Dick, in front of witnesses, not to come and speak to us.'

No denial this time.

'Jordan was getting close to exposing the four of you,' Zigic went on. 'He was going to ruin your life, get you banged up for Marcus Greenaway's murder. And you weren't about to let that happen. So you shot Jordan and then you framed Caxton. Except it wasn't enough just to frame him for Jordan's murder because the first thing Caxton would have done when we pulled him in, would be to tell us what you'd done to Greenaway and you'd still have got arrested.' Zigic lowered his voice, 'So Dick had to die.'

'This is beyond speculative,' Ms Jellen protested.

'You were the brains behind sabotaging Greenaway's helicopter.' Zigic kept going, seeing how Gurney couldn't meet his eye, how tightly his jaw was clenched and the fists his hands made on the table. '*You* are the person most responsible for Greenaway's death and you're the one who was going to sit in prison the longest if it came out.'

'No,' Gurney snapped. 'I never killed anyone.'

'You killed Marcus Greenaway,' Ferreira reminded him. 'That's not even open to question any more.'

'It very much is,' Ms Jellen said.

'I didn't kill Dick and I didn't kill Jordan,' Gurney said, looking sick now, the anger and the fear swirling together and turning toxic in his gut.

'You've all carried on like killing Greenaway was an act of justice for what he did to you but the simple fact is you're a murderer.' Ferreira watched him attempt to summon up some final moment of defiance in the face of the truth. 'You wanted Greenaway dead and it didn't matter to you if anyone else got hurt. Jordan Radley and Dick Caxton were just acceptable sacrifices to keep you out of prison.'

'Alright,' Ms Jellen barked. 'That is *enough*. You don't have any evidence to support these wild accusations against Mr Gurney, and I'm not going to allow you to sit there and barrack a man who discovered his friend's dead body barely twenty-four hours ago.' She gathered the photographs together and shoved them back across the table at Zigic. 'Mr Gurney is in a delicate mental state and you are endangering his health. This interview is over and if you want to question him again, I suggest you find something more substantial than paint flecks and fantastical theories.'

Zigic leaned back in his chair. Gurney still couldn't meet his eye.

'Interview terminated 15:47.'

Chapter Sixty-Four

'You didn't have to drag me out my house like a buckering criminal,' Ridgeon said, as Ferreira took the seat opposite him. 'I done my best to help you and you go and humiliate me like that in front of my neighbours.'

'Is it important to you?' Ferreira asked, fitting two fresh tapes into the recorder bolted to the wall. 'What your neighbours think?'

'It's a nice little road,' he said defensively. 'Patti's lived there nigh on twenty years. She's in the Neighbourhood Watch. She'll be getting all sorts of earache now.'

'Thing is, Lionel, when you're a criminal you're occasionally going to have the police turn up at your door. It's one of the reasons most people don't go off doing whatever the hell they like. They don't want the social stigma. Like how you must have felt after you got out of nick last time.'

'Let's get the tapes rolling if you're planning on opening questioning,' Ridgeon's solicitor suggested.

Paul Kent was one of the ever churning pool of publicly provided defenders. A short, stooped man with curly grey hair and rimless glasses, he carried himself with the perpetually harassed air of a supply teacher trying to move unnoticed between classrooms.

Ferreira turned the tapes on and Zigic watched Ridgeon square himself for the interview, shoulders going back, head going up.

'Right, Lionel,' Ferreira said. 'You should know that earlier today we spoke to Bruce Humble and he's given us a full and detailed confession for his part in Marcus Greenaway's death.'

Ridgeon blinked rapidly at her. 'Aren't I here to talk about Dick?'

'This *is* about Dick,' Ferreira said. 'Because we now know you and he and Steve Gurney and Bruce Humble were all involved in a conspiracy to sabotage Marcus Greenaway's helicopter. An act which led to his death.'

Ridgeon shook his head. 'I don't know what I was doing back then. My wife were on her last legs. I were in a bad old way. I weren't all there.'

'It's okay that you can't remember,' Ferreira told him. 'Because Bruce remembers exactly what you did. Dick knew how to sabotage the part but his hands weren't as steady as they used to be, so he stood over you, giving you instructions while you did the work.'

'No,' he said firmly. 'I give them the code for the alarm. That were it.' He drew his hands off the table into his lap. 'I never knew they was going to do owt with it.'

'Even if that *was* true, you could have come forward and reported them at any stage, but you didn't do that, despite having multiple opportunities to do so, which makes you equally culpable.' Ferreira leaned forward slightly. 'But we all know you did a lot more than handing over an alarm code. *You* were the one who made sure Greenaway's helicopter fell out of the sky. *You* killed him.'

'I'm not going to deny it,' Ridgeon said, lowering his eyes. 'And if some bugger wanted me to do it now, I'd tell them to sod off. I can't believe I was daft enough to get involved back then. Maybe that's what happens when you're not fussed if you live or die. Your moral compass goes all skew-whiff.' He knotted his fingers together. 'I don't even know the man I were back then.'

Zigic had been expecting more. Shock and outrage, denial and justification. But he saw nothing in Ridgeon but a kind of grudging acceptance of the facts.

'That's as may be,' Ferreira said dismissively. 'But your moral compass isn't skew-whiff any more, is it? You're not in that dark place now. In fact, by your own admission, your life's better than it's ever been. It's worth defending. No matter what you have to do.'

Ridgeon glared at her. 'I never killed Dick, if that's what you're aiming at.'

'We've spoken to Steve,' she went on, clasping her hands on the table. 'We've discussed Greenaway's death with him, and Jordan Radley's investigation into the circumstances surrounding it. So, now we'd like to give you the opportunity to set the record straight about what really happened to Dick Caxton on Saturday night.'

'He killed himself,' Ridgeon said firmly.

But there was a slight tremor in his voice and Zigic could see how much it troubled the man to hear it. That he understood exactly how they would interpret it.

'Dick was murdered,' Ferreira said. 'And Dick didn't kill Jordan either. We have proof that he was miles away from the crime scene when Jordan was shot.'

Ridgeon shifted uneasily in his chair.

Ferreira cocked her head at him. 'You don't seem shocked.'

'You're telling me one of my best mates were murdered,' he snapped. 'I'm buckering shocked alright.'

But the words rang hollow, despite his sharp tone.

'Dick called you on Saturday afternoon,' Ferreira said, bringing out a piece of paper with Caxton's phone records on. Barely a sheet for the whole month and the one they wanted was the very last he'd made. 'At 14:35 Dick called you and you talked for over half an hour. What did you discuss?'

'Nothing much,' Ridgeon said too quickly. 'He were pissed up. Rambling on. He always did go on when he'd had a skinful but he were worse than usual. Going on about Jordan and his kids and how he never saw them any more.'

'What did he say about Jordan?' Ferreira asked.

'He were saying what a waste it were.' Ridgeon sucked his bottom lip into his mouth, shook his head. 'Dick and his grandson never saw eye to eye. Boy's not right in the head, so Dick said. They never had anything in common. But I reckon he saw Jordan like family.' Ridgeon's eyes narrowed painfully. 'It sounds sad and I reckon it probably is sad. But Dick was that sort of fella. Bit lost, you'd say.'

Ferreira nodded and Zigic saw Ridgeon relax very slightly, thinking he'd convinced her.

'So, Dick didn't call threatening to expose you for killing Jordan?'

'Don't be daft,' Ridgeon snapped, spine stiffening again. 'Now, you listen to me. I'm telling you I were involved with the Greenaway nonsense. Wouldn't make no sense me coming in here and admitting that if I'd gone and killed two buckering people to keep it quiet, would it?'

'It makes sense because you failed to get away with it,' Ferreira said icily. 'And now you think your best chance of evading justice is to show some contrition for one crime we've already proved, in the hope we'll believe it exonerates you from two more.' She smirked. 'You're not the first person to try that tactic, funnily enough.'

Ridgeon buried his face in his hands. 'What the buckering hell is this?'

Ferreira pressed on, scenting weakness.

'The thing is, Dick *was* guilt-stricken, you're right. He was torn up over Jordan's death because he knew one of you killed him and he felt responsible because he knew you'd done it to try and cover up Marcus Greenaway's death, which he'd played an integral part in.'

'No.' His face emerged from behind his hands, reddened, eyes wide.

'Dick went to see Jordan's mum just before he died. He apologised to her,' Ferreira told him. 'Dick was trying to make amends; he couldn't live with knowing what one of his *friends* had done to Jordan.' She jabbed her finger at Ridgeon across the table. 'He told you he was going to come forward. So you killed him.'

'No, no, *no*.' Ridgeon shoved himself back from the table but stayed in his seat and Zigic saw how quickly the control mechanism kicked in. Lose it but don't stand up, don't tower over them, ranting and raving. Ridgeon knew how that would look and he'd stopped himself doing it.

His solicitor cast a quick, warning look in his direction.

Slowly, Ridgeon drew himself back to the table.

'You almost got away with it,' Ferreira said, voice low. 'If Dick had walked home instead of getting on a bus, we would have chalked Jordan's death up to him, written off the suicide. Closed the book.'

For a few long seconds Ridgeon stared back at her, his face all fury, but still he held onto the sides of his chair, his arms rigid, his muscles flexed. The sharp tang of sweat was rising off his body. Zigic willed him to say it. Break down, confess, turn on Steve Gurney.

Just tell them the truth.

'I want to see Jordan's killer get what's coming to them,' Ridgeon said finally. 'And I'm doing my best here to try and help you find the bastard. But I can't tell you what I don't bloody know.'

A low growl broke out of Ferreira's throat.

'Just because you got away with Greenaway's murder for years, don't think you're going to get away with Jordan's,' she snapped.

Ridgeon recoiled in his chair.

'This isn't right,' he said to Mr Kent, a wobble in his voice. 'I can't tell them summat I don't know, can I?'

Mr Kent slipped his glasses off and pinched the bridge of his nose. 'I think that's enough for now, detectives. You don't appear to have any actual evidence.'

CHAPTER SIXTY-FIVE

'I'm almost wishing Dick Caxton was responsible now.' Ferreira cupped her hand against the wind blowing up London Road, sending her lighter flame jumping. 'It'd make our lives a lot easier.'

'We're getting closer,' Zigic said, returning her coffee and shoving his hand into his pocket. He'd remembered to bring gloves to the scene this time but they weren't quite up to the air temperature. 'Forensics have got a bunch of stuff from Gurney's place and Ridgeon's. There'll be something among it all.'

The pair of them were still at the station, would be spending a night in the cells, thinking over what they'd been told and what they'd said in return. The charges for Greenaway's death enough to keep them locked up but Jordan Radley's and Dick Caxton's murders the real focus now.

Only one of them could be responsible and Zigic suspected the innocent man, whoever that was, might know more than he was letting on.

All they could hope for now was a break tomorrow.

A tired-looking guy in chef whites and a long anorak walked past them. They knew he'd walked by four nights out of the last seven, caught by the team who'd been here on Monday night, who questioned him and found he hadn't seen anything. The same as with most of the people they'd spoken to already this evening, but with so little other evidence Zigic believed it was a job worth sticking at. Although he suspected the rest of the team didn't appreciate losing a precious hour of their downtime to a job nobody seemed to believe would yield a lead. Even with the overtime pay.

He sipped his coffee. 'You like Ridgeon for it?'

'I don't know,' Ferreira admitted. 'They're both up to their eyes in it. But Gurney's got a record of violence and ... weak as it sounds, I keep thinking about that photograph Jordan tweeted of him and Gurney watching football at the Club. He's basically got Jordan in a headlock, right? And you could say that it's all just blokes messing around but there was something more there.'

'Too much aggression?'

'Yeah,' she said. 'Like Gurney knew what he was going to do later in the evening.' She took another deep drag on her cigarette. 'Though, I did wonder why Ridgeon was laying on the country bumpkin act so thick.'

'Sir,' PC Baxter called from across the road.

A runner had stopped to talk to them, still jogging on the spot, trying to keep his heart rate up. Zigic vaguely remembered the feeling from the last time he'd actually managed to get out for a few miles.

'DI Zigic.' He gestured towards Mel. 'DS Ferreira.'

The man stopped jogging finally. 'Alex Wharton. I was just saying, I don't know if it's important but I thought I should stop and tell you just in case.'

'Did you see something here last Monday night?' Ferreira asked.

'Not here exactly.' His gaze drifted away towards the yellow incident board, dirtied by a week of road grease now. 'It was just along the street there.'

'Can you show us?'

'Sure.'

They walked with him away from the scene of the crime, Wharton telling them he only did this circuit on Monday nights, that he liked to change things up a bit. He stopped on the bridge over the railway line.

'It must have been around quarter past eleven,' he said. 'I was heading home and I always leave the house at half ten. It's a forty-five minute circuit and I live down on St Margaret's Road there.'

11:15 was a long way out of their time frame for him to have witnessed Jordan Radley's murder and Zigic was already half disregarding him, wondering if he just wanted to be involved, to have a story to tell.

'I was coming over the bridge,' Wharton said. 'And I saw a man heading down the embankment here.'

There was a steep cut, scrubby and untended, from the pathway down to the car park of Phorpres House. There were no steps to make the journey easier, but it was a shortcut onto St Margaret's Road and clearly too useful to be ignored by the locals who had created their own pathway through the undergrowth.

'Why did you notice him?' Ferreira asked.

'There wasn't anyone else about,' he said, with a slight shrug. 'You know how it is when you run on the road, you have to keep your wits about you. I was going to head down the embankment myself and I thought if he looks dodgy I'll go the long way around.'

'Did he look dodgy?'

'No, not really. He had a shopping bag so I figured he'd probably come back from Hampton. Then when I got a bit closer I noticed that he didn't seem to be moving brilliantly. And I realised he was getting on.' Wharton gave Zigic an apologetic look. 'Shouldn't really say that, should I? Bit ageist.'

'Did you get a good look at him?' Ferreira asked.

Wharton nodded. 'Not right then, but as I was coming up behind him, he started down the embankment and then he fell. I suppose he lost his footing because he yelled pretty loud and I thought I'd better go and check he hadn't damaged himself.'

Zigic nodded for him to continue, trying to not push him or show any encouragement. Let him get it out in his own time, as he really remembered it.

'He was laying in a heap at the bottom of the incline,' Wharton said, pointing over the bridge. 'I went down and helped him up, found his bag for him. Then when I picked it up I realised there wasn't any shopping in it, there was just a leather bag inside it.'

Again Zigic nodded, trying to hold his face steady, not give Wharton any hint of the significance of what he'd seen.

'And then I thought, God, has he wandered off from the nursing home? Is his family wondering where he is right now? So I asked him if he needed help or if there was someone I could call to come and get him.'

'What did he say?' Ferreira asked

'He told me he was fine,' Wharton said. 'But he seemed really shaken and a bit out of it, and I thought how am I going to feel if I find out he's been reported missing and he never makes it home? I told him I only lived around the corner and that I could call him a taxi if he knew where he needed to go,' Wharton explained. 'And that *really* set him off. He told me to mind my own fucking business and charged off across the car park.'

'Did you go after him?' Zigic asked.

Wharton shook his head. 'I figured he was either fine or he was going to be impossible to help so I let him go. I didn't feel good about it, but what else could I do?' He looked between the two of them. 'Is that helpful?'

'You got a good look at him, right?' Ferreira asked.

'Yep.' Wharton gestured towards the car park. 'Most of the street lights are working so I think I could probably identify him if you needed me to.'

Ferreira smiled at him, genuine pleasure on her face. 'That would be very helpful.'

DAY EIGHT

TUESDAY

CHAPTER SIXTY-SIX

'It's going to be a busy day,' Zigic warned them, opening the morning briefing at 8 a.m. He was standing in front of Jordan Radley's board, buzzing with the knowledge that they would have his killer charged by the end of the shift. Only one photograph was in the suspects column now, the rest of them cleared away.

One man to focus on. One man to gather enough evidence against so that there would be no question of him evading them any longer.

Zigic ran down the tasks for the next few hours and Ferreira watched how his certainty pulled the rest of the team up in their seats, all nods and stern 'yes, sir's, felt it herself. The optimism that had sparked the moment Alex Wharton described seeing a man with Jordan Radley's leather messenger stuffed into a Tesco bag for life.

'We have a solid sighting,' Zigic reminded them, pressing his hands together. 'But he's a slippery bastard and I want to put this beyond any shadow of doubt.'

Half an hour later, Ferreira was standing in the car park outside Phorpres House, looking up the steeply rising embankment that linked it to London Road. Two fully suited forensics officers were going over the uneven and tangled ground, searching for anything that might link their killer to the route he'd taken as he returned from Jordan's house. In daylight the path was precarious enough, at night it must have been easy to slip, and she silently thanked the terrain for upending their man. Knew that without it Alex Wharton might have run on past him without getting a clear sighting of his face.

But eyewitnesses were easy to shred in court. All the opposing side had to do was discover Wharton wore contact lenses and that he hadn't updated his prescription in eighteen months, and his testimony would be thrown into doubt.

They needed back-up.

'What are we looking for?' Weller asked.

Ferreira was staring up at the long sash windows in Phorpres House's east-facing wall. Five storeys of flats, curtains and blinds drawn at some but open at others. The backs of photo frames and pot plants were on display as she scanned down. Vases and crystal pendants catching the sunlight and then the glimmer of black glass.

'*That*'s what we're looking for,' she told him. 'Security camera.'

Upstairs to the second floor, where the corner flat's owner was still home at a little after nine but was unwilling to let them in until they'd allowed her to fully examine their identification and call Thorpe Wood Station to check their credentials.

'Have you had trouble with cold callers?' Ferreira asked the young woman, when she finally let them in.

'Not exactly.' She twisted her fingers together and Ferreira noticed the dark smudges under her eyes, more worry than concealer could fully obscure.

She recognised the look and just like that she was back in the parking area under her old flat. Feeling small and vulnerable and certain that if she screamed nobody would come to her aid.

'You've got a stalker,' she said, her voice catching.

'Two years.'

'Have you got a designated liaison officer?' Weller asked her.

She nodded. 'That's why I've got the camera. I'm supposed to keep a record of everything so we can take him to court.'

'Night vision?'

'State of the art,' she said, with faint regret.

They followed her into the kitchen, where her breakfast was laid out on the granite bar under the window. The blinds were drawn, despite the brilliant blue sky and fierce winter sunshine. She didn't want even her silhouette to be visible from outside,

Ferreira thought, as she lifted the blinds just high enough to check the camera's sight line.

Behind her, Weller was discussing how the footage was recorded and backed up, promising they would return everything to her within a couple of hours, saying he understood how important it was, sounding genuinely sympathetic. Doing better here than Ferreira would have guessed.

Back to the station and she left Weller to take the hard drive up to tech.

Murray was gone from her desk, Parr too. Even Bloom had been let out of the office for a while. Only Zigic present. At the board he was filling in the long blank space where they'd tried and failed to add evidence during the last week and she marvelled at how one eyewitness could change everything.

A week of postings at the locus, four officers speaking to everyone who passed on either side of the street, all of those resources and they'd been focusing on the wrong time. Had no idea Jordan's killer had come back that same way after going to his house.

No idea that their frame for potential sightings went so much further into Monday night or down London Road.

'What have we got?' she asked, approaching Zigic.

'Keri's just called in from Hampton,' he said.

'Jordan's neighbours see something?'

He smiled. 'Yep. Two positive sightings a few doors down the road just before eleven. They were coming home from the pub so not the most solid eyewitnesses, but he was the designated driver so nobody's going to be able to accuse him of having beer goggles on.'

They'd put requests for witnesses through the neighbouring letter boxes a week ago and got no joy, sent Weller there yesterday and somehow missed the couple. But this was why you had to keep going back. Catch the people who didn't know what they'd seen until you could talk to them in person.

Bloom was bringing the couple in to make a formal ID and do the paperwork and sign it off before they found something better to do with their Tuesday morning. They'd add it to the statement they'd taken from Alex Wharton last night, bringing him in here so late that even the cleaners were finished for the day. Only a skeleton staff on shift. Reception closed to drop-ins. The place unsettling enough at that time of night that he'd said, 'It's like something out of a zombie film.'

But they got what they needed from him.

Ferreira drank a cup of coffee and went through the phone records again. There was nothing new in them but she felt restless and useless hanging around the office with nothing to do now but wait for whatever fresh information the rest of the team might bring in from the field.

She looked at Murray's empty desk for a moment, then grabbed her keys and left the office again.

Across town she found Murray's Fiat parked out front of the house, behind a scientific support van. All the activity was going on in the back garden, centred on a cream-painted shed tucked into the far corner. The doors had been thrown open and a couple of lawnmowers had been pulled out of the way onto the grass, strimmers and chainsaws tossed down alongside them.

'Don't know what to do with yourself, do you?' Murray asked, as she walked up the stepping-stone path through the grass.

'They found anything yet?'

Murray nodded towards an evidence bag sitting on a cast-iron table. Ferreira shoved her sunglasses back up onto her head to get a better look at it. Some goblet-shaped chunk of metal, dark through the plastic.

'I give up,' she said. 'What is it?'

'A crucible,' Murray told her, smiling slightly.

'For what?'

'You smelt metal in them.'

Ferreira picked it up, felt the heft of the thing. It was lighter than she was expecting but still substantial enough to feel somehow wrong and dangerous in this suburban garden.

'This is how he made the bullets?'

Murray nodded. 'I've just checked it out online. This model's designed to work on a gas stove. You can use the bloody thing in your *kitchen*. Get yourself a handful of scrap metal and one of

402

these for a couple of hundred quid and you're good to go. Start your own armoury in the comfort of your own home.'

'Is there any residue in it?'

Murray shrugged. 'Won't know until Kate's had a look at it but no good reason to have one of these bastards kicking around, is there?'

'Where was it?' Ferreira asked, looking into the shed, seeing Kate's assistant Elliot squatting down under an old pine kitchen table half-covered in packing boxes cockled with damp.

'Well hidden,' Murray told her. 'Wrapped in some old hessian, buried about as far from the door as you can get.'

'He should have dumped it.'

Murray shrugged. 'Arrogant piece of shit never thought we'd catch up with him.'

'We've got filings,' Elliot called from the summer house.

Ferreira went to the door and was told not to come in.

'I'm staying right here,' she assured him. 'Do the filings seem right for the gun we've got?'

Elliot reached for a plastic tube from his kit box. 'Funnily enough I can't tell just by looking at them, but there are marks on the table that suggest someone had a vice screwed onto it.'

She thought of the replica handgun clamped into a vice, under the caged task light she saw hanging from the rafters above the table now, seeing how easily it could have been done there. Bore out the barrel, the flakes falling to the floor and getting lost among the dust and grit and all the accumulated brown matter that gathered in sheds like this one.

'I'm not seeing any more here,' Elliot said, returning his attention to the floor under the table, slowly sweeping an intense torchlight across the space. 'It might just be the two bits of metal.'

'Does it look like he tried to clean the area up?' Ferreira asked.

'Oh, yeah. It's spotless under here compared to the rest of the shed. Same with the tabletop.' Another pass with the torch, back and forth, and then he snapped it off with an irritated grunt. 'The flecks I found had dropped down into a crack in the concrete. *Really* easy to miss if your eyesight isn't great. But it looks like he got most of them.'

'We only need one to match,' Ferreira reminded him.

She left the house, drove back across town with Zigic on speakerphone, filling him in on what Murray and Elliot had found, getting a rare growl of triumph out of him.

It was only when she rang off she began to wonder if they should have put all of this together sooner. The house had been searched once already – two days ago, her and Parr being thorough, she'd thought – and the crucible had been missed. As well hidden as it was, she knew it should have been found. Was it purely because of how unusual the thing was? She wouldn't have known what she was looking at, coming across it in the shed, would have disregarded it as just another weird household thing people bought, then stashed away because they'd never needed it.

These were the margins you worked in, she realised. The difference between Elliot going into the shed and someone slightly less experienced at their job and in the ways of the world. Even Murray had been forced to resort to an internet search to understand how the crucible functioned and, God knows, she'd seen more than enough in her long career.

It was too much a case of luck, she thought, as she pulled into the car park of Thorpe Wood Station.

Find the right witness. Have the right SOCO present during a search.

Justice shouldn't come down to that.

CHAPTER SIXTY-SEVEN

At five o'clock they had Lionel Ridgeon brought up from the cells. He was still dressed in his unseasonable denim shorts and Van Halen T-shirt, but he looked more dishevelled than he had yesterday when they'd interviewed him; the night on a hard bench with an itchy blanket telling on him.

According to the custody sergeant he hadn't eaten the dinner he was taken the evening before or any of the meals he'd been given since, and as he waited to state his name for the tapes, his stomach rumbled loudly.

Next to him his solicitor enquired if he'd been fed, the question brushed away dismissively, all of Ridgeon's attention fixed on the file Ferreira held under her hands, fingers twitching against it as if she couldn't wait to get started.

Zigic felt the same urge to press on. To finally get to the truth after a week of lies and obfuscation and denials.

Now they had it.

'Right,' Ferreira said firmly. 'I think we've been through this enough times to cut the preamble and get right down to business don't you, Mr Ridgeon?'

'There's nothing else I can tell you,' he muttered. 'I don't understand why you've dragged me in here again.'

'Because you've lied to us,' Ferreira told him.

Ridgeon kneaded the muscles across the back of his neck, trying to massage out the uncomfortable night and day in the cells, the tension that must be pressing there. No way he didn't sense what was coming.

405

'Now, I'm going to tell you what we know and then you can decide whether you want to keep lying or if you'd rather do the slightly more honourable thing and make a full confession.'

Mr Kent's eye narrowed behind his rimless glasses, hearing the confidence in her voice. Not the bravado and bluster of yesterday's session. Kent would know the difference, Zigic thought.

'Around 11:15 on the night of Monday, November 25th, you took a tumble down the embankment between London Road and the car park of Phorpres House,' Ferreira said, attention fixed on Ridgeon. 'There's no point denying that because we have a witness.'

'Eyewitnesses are notoriously unreliable,' Mr Kent said quickly. 'Especially in the dark.'

'The car park is very well lit at night.' Ferreira took a photograph out of the file. 'As you can see. But we also have footage from a security camera belonging to a resident of Phorpres House, showing you falling down the slope and being helped up by our witness.'

Mr Kent dragged the photo closer to himself.

'This is very clearly you, Mr Ridgeon.'

Ridgeon swallowed, his Adam's apple bobbing under his stubbled skin. 'Could be anyone, that.'

'You were identified by the man seen here.' Ferreira brought out another image of Alex Wharton helping Ridgeon to his feet. 'You were also identified by two of Jordan Radley's neighbours as you left his house, carrying the distinctive Tesco bag seen in this same photograph. We now know it contained the messenger bag you took from Jordan's house.'

'It weren't me,' Ridgeon said weakly.

'Let me explain something to you.' Ferreira opened her hands up affably. 'We don't need you to admit to being the man in these images because we *know* it's you. I'm not asking for your cooperation right now, I'm simply trying to help you understand how completely pointless it is to continue lying to us.'

Ridgeon looked to Mr Kent but the solicitor had nothing for him.

Zigic saw the numbness beginning to settle on Ridgeon's face. He hadn't expected it from the man. Despite how defensive he'd been throughout their previous interviews, Zigic'd thought there was a nasty temper in there somewhere that would snap to the surface the moment he saw he was caught.

There was still time though, he reminded himself.

'So,' Ferreira said smartly. 'We have you returning from Jordan Radley's house, after you shot him in the back and stole his house keys. And we have you with the laptop and USB drives you took on your person. We also have Jordan Radley's mobile phone, which was recovered from the undergrowth where you took your tumble. Did you know you dropped it?'

Ridgeon just blinked at her. No sign of any thought process at all.

'We also found some rather interesting items this afternoon while we were searching your garden shed.'

Ridgeon's lips parted but nothing came out.

Ferreira smiled. 'Smart work, Lionel, not converting that replica in that nice, tidy workshop in your garage. But you should have cleaned up after yourself better.'

She pulled out a photograph of the metal filings that SOCO had recovered from the floor of the shed, set it alongside a complicated-looking chart Jenkins had sent down in her report.

'This is all a bit sciency now,' Ferreira admitted. 'But what you're looking at here is proof that two metal flecks we found on the floor of your shed are a perfect match for the material you drilled out of the barrel of the converted replica you used to shoot Jordan.'

Ridgeon shifted his weight from one buttock to the other. 'I don't know what's in that buckering shed. I've only been living there a couple of years.'

'Three and half years,' Ferreira corrected him. 'And we know you've been working in the shed because we found your DNA and fingerprints all over it.'

'I never said I never went in there,' Ridgeon protested, a little heat coming into his voice now.

'It's possible those metal flecks have been in the shed for years,' Mr Kent added.

Ferreira gave him a withering look before she returned her attention to Lionel Ridgeon.

'The other interesting thing we found in your shed is this.' She took a photograph of the crucible out of the file. 'Now, as you know, this is used to smelt metal. And it's how people who illegally convert firearms typically make the bullets they need for them.'

A glimmer of surprise on Mr Kent's face.

Ridgeon rubbed his cheek. 'I bought it to melt down some old scrap gold. I were going to make a ring for Patti.'

'That's cute,' Ferreira said. 'Or it would be if you actually did it. But there's no sign of this crucible having been used to smelt anything other than lead.' She pulled out images of the bullets removed from Jordan Radley's and Dick Caxton's bodies: dull, slightly misshapen things. 'This lead.'

Ridgeon's face clouded over.

Reality had hit, Zigic saw.

He hadn't expected to see them again. Fired that gun and it was like the bullets were gone forever.

'Strange, isn't it?' Zigic said. 'Seeing them again like this?'

'I never seen them before.' With visible effort Ridgeon dragged his gaze back to meet Zigic's eye. 'I don't know what were in that crucible before I bought it but I never buckering used it for that.'

'The deposits we've recovered are a perfect match for the bullets.' Ferreira tapped the photographs but he refused to look again. 'I cannot stress this enough, Mr Ridgeon; we are not *asking* you, we are *telling* you. The gun that shot Jordan Radley and Dick Caxton was converted in your garden shed and filled with bullets made in your crucible. Now, unless you'd like to try and blame Patti, I think we can be certain that was your handiwork.'

Ridgeon scowled at her.

'*Did* Patti do it?' Ferreira asked. 'She's the only other person with access to the shed, right?'

He didn't answer.

She gave him an unpleasant look. 'For the benefit of the tape Mr Ridgeon has declined to reply.'

Ridgeon was breathing more heavily now, the numbness wearing off as reality came at him in a rush.

Zigic felt a dark kind of satisfaction, seeing the fear come into Ridgeon's eyes, the scrambling for an excuse, any excuse that would magically stop this. Make it all go away.

'I'd like a few minutes with my client,' Mr Kent said.

'If you want to delay the inevitable, sure.' Ferreira shrugged. 'Interview suspended 17:28.'

They went out into the hallway, Ferreira pressing up against the only working radiator.

'I always think it's going to be warmer in there than it is,' she said.

Zigic leaned against the wall opposite, folded his arms. 'I still want him to confess.'

'Of course you do.' She rolled her eyes. 'You're never satisfied until they admit it to your face. But we don't need him to. We know he's guilty. We know why he did it. And we've got plenty to keep the CPS happy.'

'Still ...'

She rocked away from the radiator. 'If he admits it and apologises and all of that bollocks, he's going to get a lighter sentence. Is that what you want?'

Zigic scratched his beard, knowing how much that would infuriate him. But a confession and a guilty plea would save Moira Radley the hell of a trial. All the attention it would draw down on her, the days sitting in a courtroom under constant scrutiny as she was forced to listen to the self-serving lies of the man who killed her son.

And there was always the risk of things falling apart at the last moment. An unusually strong performance by the defence, any number of potential procedural issues that might arise.

No, they couldn't risk that.

CHAPTER SIXTY-EIGHT

Ferreira hung back as they returned to the interview room, letting Zigic take the chair opposite Lionel Ridgeon this time, filling the space more completely than she could, blocking Ridgeon's field of vision. Immediately she realised how uncomfortable that made him, saw how Ridgeon drew back in his seat slightly, elbows tucking into his sides, chin dropping lower towards his chest. But he stared hard at Zigic as he restarted the tapes and spread out the photographs Mr Kent had tidied into a pile while they were absent from the room.

The solicitor had shifted a little in their absence too, inclined himself away from Ridgeon by a few vital degrees. She guessed Kent had looked at the quantity and quality of the evidence and done what any self-respecting legal adviser would do. Told him to confess, apologise, show remorse and make them believe it.

That was not what Ferreira wanted to hear from him. She wanted him to fight it until the end, go down screaming, receive the harshest punishment the law could lay on him. But Zigic was right, as much as she hated to admit it, they didn't want to trust this to the whims of a jury.

The silence in the room was already becoming uncomfortable. Zigic sifted through the photographs, finally drawing out an image of Dick Caxton's head. Taken under the fierce light in the mortuary, the gunshot wound to his temple was scorched and ragged, the skin blackened around the bullet hole. But it was his face that was the most unsettling part of the image. His head was turned in profile, eye closed, wrinkles in soft folds around it, almost peaceful.

'How long had you known Dick for?' Zigic asked, pushing the photograph into the space in front of Ridgeon. 'Twenty years?'

'I never killed Dick,' Ridgeon insisted. 'I told you. Steve did it.'

'That's not what I asked you, is it?' Zigic replied stiffly. 'How long were you and Dick friends?'

'We weren't friends. We worked together.'

Another lie, Ferreira thought, albeit a small one, but she saw weakness in it. Leverage, maybe.

'How often did Dick come and visit you when you were in hospital?'

Ridgeon frowned, heavy grey brows knitting together. 'What the buckering hell's that got to do with anything?'

'Bruce Humble tells us Dick was a frequent visitor,' Zigic said. 'And when you got out of hospital, back when you were in your dark place, Bruce reckoned Dick spent a lot of time round your house, making sure you were eating, keeping you company.' He gave Ridgeon a questioning look but got no reply. 'Sounds like more than just someone you worked with.'

'He were an old woman,' Ridgeon mumbled. 'Always fussing about.'

'The way Bruce tells it,' Zigic went on, softening his tone, 'Dick was the one who brought you up out of your depression.'

'No,' Ridgeon insisted, 'Patti did that. She saved my life.'

'But Dick got you to a place where you were ready to be saved,' Zigic said. 'If it wasn't for him maybe Patti wouldn't have wanted you.'

'She loves me,' he said fiercely.

'Do you think she'll still love you after she finds out you shot one of your closest friends in the head?'

Ridgeon's nostrils flared. 'I'll tell her it's a lie. She'll believe me. She knows what you bastards are like.'

'We've questioned Patti, you know.'

Ridgeon strained forward in his seat, face flushing. 'You leave her out of this.'

'Oh, she is very much part of this,' Zigic said. 'Because when we questioned her earlier today about your movements on the night of Jordan's murder and what happened to the clothes you were wearing when you killed him and the phone call you had with Dick the afternoon before you murdered him, all we got from Patti was "no comment".'

'That's because she don't know anything about any of it,' Ridgeon said, and for the first time Ferreira heard a tremor of fear in his voice.

'No,' Zigic said. 'If she didn't know anything about it, she would have told us that. Because innocent people, when they come into an interview room, do everything in their power to convince us of their innocence. They give us every scrap of information they possibly can, so they never, *ever*, have to go through being questioned again.'

Ridgeon turned to Mr Kent but the solicitor had nothing for him.

'Even you,' Zigic went on, 'Coming in here guilty as sin, didn't sit there and give us a relentless string of "no comment"s.'

'Patti didn't do anything,' Ridgeon said, the muscles of his face going taut.

'No, she didn't,' Zigic agreed. 'She didn't do anything when you came home from the Club hours later than she was expecting you and she didn't do anything when she saw the state of the clothes you were wearing when you shot Jordan. All covered in blood and dirt and bits of grass where you fell down the embankment.'

Ridgeon stared at him, stunned by the sudden shift.

Zigic pressed on, voice low and deep and relentless.

'Patti didn't do anything while you converted a replica handgun in her garden shed. And she didn't do anything when you were smelting lead for home-made bullets on the gas stove in her very nice kitchen.'

'She never knew anything about it,' Ridgeon said quickly.

Ferreira bit down on a smile. The admission made on tape but Zigic wasn't finished with him.

'Patti has been covering for you this whole time. Legally, she's your accessory. You made her that, Lionel.' Zigic nodded at him. 'And when she goes down for it, you'll be responsible.'

'I swear on my life, she never knew anything.' Ridgeon put his hand over his heart and for a moment Ferreira thought he was in physical pain. 'She's out working in her salon all day, she never knew what I were doing.'

'I find that very hard to believe,' Zigic said, faintly disgusted. 'You know what melted lead smells like, Lionel. Are you seriously telling us she didn't walk into her kitchen and ask what the hell you'd been doing in there?'

'I told her I burned a pan,' he said quickly, looking to Ferreira, wanting any back-up he could get now. 'She believed me because I'm always putting summat on the hob and forgetting about it. I'm always ruining her pans. Ask her yourselves if you don't believe me.'

'What's the point?' Zigic asked. 'She'll only tell us no comment again.'

'No, you explain to her.' Ridgeon pounded the table. 'You tell her she needs to tell you the truth.'

'We gave Patti ample opportunity to do that already,' Zigic said. 'And she chose not to cooperate. She made her decision and she'll be charged accordingly.'

'I'll tell you everything.' His hands spread wide in a pleading gesture.

'We already know everything.' Zigic leaned back in his chair. 'You killed Jordan Radley and Richard Caxton and Patti covered for you before and after the fact.'

'She never,' Ridgeon groaned. 'Honest to God, she never knew a thing about any of it. I killed Jordan, yeah, alright. I did. And Dick. Everything you said. I done it. Jordan were poking his nose into Greenaway's death and I didn't want to go down for it. Dick were going to come clean about Greenaway. He reckoned if he got all what happened out into the open, you'd have a better chance of finding whoever shot Jordan.'

'He didn't suspect you?'

Ridgeon shook his head. 'Stupid old bugger were convinced Steve done it.'

Zigic leaned forward again, perplexed-looking. 'And what did you say to this plan?'

'I tried talking him out of it,' Ridgeon snapped. 'I said, you're going to get the lot of us sent down for Greenaway just because

413

you can't wait for the police to do their bloody job.' He swallowed hard. 'He weren't in his right mind. He didn't care what happened to him no more, and he sure as hell didn't care what happened to any of us. So, I killed him.' Ridgeon folded over in his chair, the admission, coming at last, crumpling him like a blow. 'I never wanted to do it. I never wanted to do any of it but I couldn't go back to prison.' His eyes filled with tears. 'I couldn't lose her.'

Zigic seemed to deflate slightly. Relieved but completely spent.

'Okay, Lionel,' he said gently. 'We understand.'

They returned to the office, paperwork and formalities still to be sorted out but the hard part over and done with. Four faces turned towards them as they walked in.

'Well?' Murray asked.

'He confessed,' Zigic told her.

There was a brief flurry of congratulations and Ferreira watched Zigic take it in his usual awkward fashion, wincing even as he smiled, uncomfortable with the praise and quickly switching it around onto the team.

'This was a tough one but you've done great work,' he told them, standing in front of Jordan Radley's board, with the young man's serious face watching over him. 'You've solved a four-year-old murder that everybody believed was an accident and you've made sure we can tell Moira Radley that the man who killed her son is going to prison. You should all feel very proud of yourselves right now.' He made a show of checking his watch, it was almost seven o'clock but nobody had wanted to leave without knowing the result. 'It's been a long day. Get off home and try to enjoy what's left of your evening.'

The office emptied out quickly. Kitson and her team were already gone, Billy had left too, and Ferreira hoped he was working on dinner, couldn't face the prospect of cooking when she got in.

'Funny, isn't it?' Zigic said, sitting down on the edge of Murray's vacated desk. 'We solve a double murder but Riggott doesn't think *that* deserves a drink in his office and a standing ovation.'

'I should think he's knocked off already,' Ferreira suggested.

'Yeah.' He smiled humourlessly, 'That'll be it.'

She sat down next to him. 'If you want a celebratory drink, we know where he keeps a bottle.'

Zigic rubbed his beard and for a moment she thought he was actually considering breaking into Riggott's office. But then he sighed and hauled himself up again.

'We should probably do the paperwork instead.'

'You know what,' she said. 'I'd actually rather do that than drink any more of Riggott's terrible whiskey.'

EPILOGUE

The *Big Issue* seller outside Peterborough railway station wasn't doing much business, despite the steady stream of commuters passing him by, everyone in a hurry, carrying bags from Waitrose and takeaway coffees. The smokers gathered a few metres from the main doors were also studiously ignoring him and the grey-faced black dog curled up on a blanket by his feet.

You knew it was going to be a slow day when people weren't even stopping for the dog, Ferreira thought, as she crossed the road. Five weeks after Christmas, she supposed most people were too concerned about the state of the credit card bills to worry about anyone else's precarious finances.

She bought a copy of the magazine and took it back to her car, flicked past the interview with a comedian she quite liked and the film reviews, looking for Jordan Radley's byline. Found the article spread across pages 8 and 9.

A large photograph of the Stillwater Rise Apartments taken under a harsh winter sun that exposed every imperfection in the brickwork, every inconsistency in the paint colour of its anthracite panelling, making it look shoddy and precarious even before you started to read the article. A smaller photo at the bottom of the opposite page showed Derek and Sheila Yule and Ferreira recognised it from the cabinet in Sheila's flat in Bretton. A holiday snap from years ago, taken when he was still healthy and they were still happy. She imagined Sheila deciding that this was how she wanted the world to see Derek; young and tanned, a smile on his face that only hinted at whatever he'd said to make her laugh a split second before the shutter snapped.

Seeing Jordan's article now, actually holding the magazine in her hands, Ferreira felt a momentary prickle of unease.

When Riggott found out, there was going to be trouble. Not directly from him but he would be the conduit her bollocking came through. And then she would either deny her part in the publication or stand tall and admit how she'd personally returned Jordan's effects to his mother, sat in her living room with a cup of tea and carefully explained to Moira what was in the file on his laptop marked 'SRA' and what it meant. How she'd given her the contact details for the editor at the *Big Issue* who'd printed Jordan's previous article about the Greenaway Club, and Sheila Yule's number and that of Lily Hargreaves, the friend who'd run the soil tests and found the final, damning, piece of evidence. Handing Moira everything she needed to make sure Jordan's last story gained the attention it deserved.

Nothing explicitly wrong about her actions.

Nothing she could be formally punished over, but she knew the punishment wouldn't come through formal channels.

She'd seen what could happen to a copper who fell foul of a superior officer. Thought of Billy still grinding away at his never-ending money laundering case, stuck in his office, trying to keep up a placid façade while inside he raged.

That was what you got for pissing off a detective chief superintendent.

She dreaded to think what happened when you did the same thing to a chief constable.

She had considered it, she reminded herself, as she looked at Jordan Radley's photograph. Fresh-faced and serious and dead far too young, killed for trying to expose the truth. Not *this* truth, but it was all one and the same. A small and personal example of a wider and more dangerous problem.

Nobody should be able to buy silence. Not with a gun and not with money and definitely not by using the police to do what they feared their legal people might fail to achieve.

She began to read.

'High-end living for high-achieving professionals,' the glossy brochures for Stillwater Rise Apartments promise. They boast of panoramic views and granite worktops, rainforest showers and access to a beautifully landscaped private park.

What they don't tell you about are the lethal levels of cadmium and asbestos in the topsoil of that park. A cocktail of contaminants that the developers, Docherty Construction, claimed to have removed from the site prior to construction.

They don't tell you about Derek Yule ...

ACKNOWLEDGEMENTS

First and foremost thanks to my wonderful editor Alison Hennessey for bringing her customary wisdom and clarity to bear on this book. Thanks as well to Sara Helen Binney for all her help, to Lindeth Vasey for her eagle-eyed copy editing and Ros Ellis for all her support on the PR side, and to Michal Kuzmierkiewicz for his excellent work on the cover. The whole team at Raven have been a delight to work with and I am deeply grateful to them for bringing Zigic and Ferreira back to readers.

Thanks to my agent Phil Patterson for talking sense when needed and the far more entertaining opposite the rest of the time. Thanks as well to all at Marjacq Scripts for their hard work and good advice.

It hasn't been a great year to try and write a book and I wouldn't have managed it without the support of my family, who as usual know just the right moment to put a drink in my hand or a cake in front of me. Thanks you guys.

A NOTE ON THE AUTHOR

EVA DOLAN was shortlisted for the CWA Dagger for unpublished authors when only a teenager. The five previous novels in her Zigic and Ferreira series have been published to widespread critical acclaim: *Tell No Tales* and *After You Die* were shortlisted for the Theakston Crime Novel of the Year Award, *After You Die* was longlisted for the CWA Gold Dagger, and *Between Two Evils* was shortlisted for the CWA Ian Fleming Steel Dagger. In 2018 *Long Way Home* won the *Grand Prix Des Lectrices*. Dolan's first stand-alone thriller, *This is How It Ends*, was longlisted for the 2019 Theakston Old Peculier Crime Novel of the Year. She lives in Cambridge.

@eva_dolan

A NOTE ON THE TYPE

The text of this book is set in Linotype Sabon, a typeface named after the type founder, Jacques Sabon. It was designed by Jan Tschichold and jointly developed by Linotype, Monotype and Stempel in response to a need for a typeface to be available in identical form for mechanical hot metal composition and hand composition using foundry type.

Tschichold based his design for Sabon roman on a font engraved by Garamond, and Sabon italic on a font by Granjon. It was first used in 1966 and has proved an enduring modern classic.